The Navigators

Jackson Peoples-Rosenblatt

ISBN: 0-6156-7166-7
ISBN-13: 9780615671666
Library of Congress Control Number: 2012944880

dedication: For my husband, Larry "L.C." Cline

Sail forth—steer for the deep waters only. . .
For we are bound where Mariners have not yet dared to go
—Walt Whitman, "Passage to India"

San Francisco: 2008

In his wildest dreams, Wulf never expected to see this day. Others like him, a generation or two farther into the future—yes, certainly they would. That certainty has been one of the constants of his life, decade after decade: there will eventually be justice for his people. It has been a reason to go on day by day, year by year. But justice for Dave and him? Probably not. Partial justice, certainly. Or an illusion of justice. But not the real thing. Not complete justice. Not true equality. They were born too soon. They wouldn't live to see the promise fulfilled, no matter how fervently they believed in it. Still, there is no question they have enjoyed a better life than either of them believed they could reasonably expect, and that has been sufficient consolation most of the time. Then, out of the blue, this season of miracles. The last few months seem to have stood the planet on its head. The impossible has become, well, not commonplace exactly, but the two of them have been to a wedding almost every weekend all summer. They have stopped counting. And now, with astonishing suddenness after a lifetime of waiting, it's their turn.

Just a few hours yet. By nightfall the previously unimaginable will have become reality.

He gazes up at the ceiling, shadowy and indistinct in the pre-dawn dimness of the bedroom. Beside him, Dave's snoring is barely audible. One of the dogs twitches in its sleep. Wulf feels the tremor against his left ankle. As he grows more wakeful his mind gropes for some sign of the impending wonder, but nothing manifests itself. It might as well be another ordinary day. In his long experience they almost always start out just like this, regardless of what impends.

He clambers slowly out of the bed. He aches in every bone, just like he has each morning for decades now. In this very concrete way he never escapes his past. He pulls a robe around himself against the chill. Dave snores on. The dogs don't stir. He closes the bedroom door quietly and shuffles down the hall toward the bathroom.

* * *

Morgan hits the master switch and listens as fluorescent fixtures buzz on all over the building. The chain collars of the Labradors jingle as the dogs trot off on their accustomed tour of inspection. After keying in the alarm code he's right behind them on his own quick walkthrough, satisfying himself that the overnight cleaning crew's work is up to his standards. When he renovated the building eighteen months ago he refused to go the obvious route and transform it into something trendy and upscale. Only a fool would do plastic surgery on the Mona Lisa or put arms back onto the Venus de Milo. A fool or someone who works for Disney. Instead, he chose to maintain its original utilitarian/industrial 1930's aesthetic. His architect, Jared Bartok, shared this vision: he's a member here himself and didn't have to be talked into or out of anything. Upgrades were restricted to mechanical systems, materials and fixtures. Seeing the spaces empty like this each morning, he's deeply satisfied with his choice. The place does well precisely because it makes no effort to be fashionable. It is what it is, an old school, hardcore gym.

Morgan unlocks the front doors and swings them open. Regular as sunrise, though most of the year they precede it, Kirk, Tristan, and Nick hoist their gym bags and file past him. Nearly thirty years ago when he bought the business from Manny Horowitz, these three and their buddies were the reigning demigods here. Men came from all over the city to work out alongside them—or just to witness their rituals. Silver haired now, they're still remarkable: Olympian to be sure, but in a more austere, less opulent manner than in their youth.

"Crazy at your house this morning?" Nick suggests, peeling off his sweatshirt.

"No worse than any other morning, really," Morgan shrugs. "Everything seems pretty much under control."

"It would be," Tristan muses, "given your husband's organizational skills. Not to mention the comprehensive resources of Cooper's rolodex."

"Nobody uses those anymore," Kirk objects. "You'd have to go to a museum to see one. Most people have forgotten they ever existed."

"Or weren't born yet when they were still around," Morgan grunts.

"Or wouldn't know what to do with one if they saw it," Nick laughs.

"It's a metaphor," Tristan protests.

"These days nobody seems to be able to say anything without calling attention to their figures of speech," Nick laughs.

"You're right, though," Morgan says, "Buzz and Cooper could stage a successful *coup d'etat* in a small tropical nation. Without either of them breaking a sweat."

"Has anyone ever seen Cooper sweat?" Kirk laughs.

"Griffin has," Morgan says, "presumably."

"He sweats plenty when he's in here," Nick says.

"But his sweat doesn't stink," Tristan laughs.

"The fact remains," Kirk says, "those two could organize a world's fair. Over brunch. While critiquing the décor of the restaurant, the technique of the chef, and the grooming regimens of the wait staff."

"Or a coronation in an obscure European principality," Nick agrees. "A double wedding is mere child's play for the likes of them."

"You'll see," Tristan predicts, "it'll be perfect down to the last detail."

* * *

"Rise and shine, sweetie," Scott says, looking down at Jared half asleep amid rumpled bedding. Here in their oh, so tasteful bedroom the scene is as if some gay advertising whiz kid managed to sign the Farnese Hercules to appear in an ad layout for Bed Bath and Beyond.

"Mmmphm."

"Ready for our big day?"

"What is that?" Jared asks, squinting out of one eye.

"Our breakfast."

"Oh, sweetheart," Jared says, hiking himself up to sit leaning against the headboard, "you shouldn't have gone to so much trouble."

"No trouble," Scott says, setting the tray down on the dresser. "No trouble at all. But it really is time for you to be up and moving."

"Already?"

"Yes."

"I don't see why you're so keyed up about this," Jared yawns. "I mean, talk about an anticlimax. It isn't as if we're really going to be newlyweds. We've been together for thirty years."

"Thirty-one," Scott says. "But it's not every day that two average guys like us get to go out and make history."

* * *

As he steps off the MUNI, Griffin notices Louisa's Cadillac in her reserved space. Even if she wasn't supposed to be on vacation this week, it would be unusual for her to be at work so early, particularly on a Friday during summer school. She is a creature of habit, and her habit is to arrive at school in time for lunch. So he can't help being a little alarmed at her presence. Glancing in at her office door, he sees her peering intently at the computer screen, reading glasses teetering on the extreme tip of her nose. This particular body language means "do not disturb", so he foregoes his customary greeting. As he walks toward the mail room his anxiety ratchets up another notch.

Inside his classroom it's as quiet as a church sanctuary on a weekday afternoon. The incongruous serenity disorients him for a moment. He must be dreaming. Reality soon intrudes. He's the perfect codependent. Louisa behaves uncharacteristically—he stews about it. And while he stews he fidgets, straightening things he straightened before leaving yesterday afternoon, brushing away imaginary dust, picking up a stack of books and moving it six inches down the counter. Satisfied that he is prepared for the coming onslaught, he sits down at his desk, boots up the computer, and signs on to the district system to check his email. Three messages from Louisa in the last half hour. Sure enough, something's really got her spooled up.

I've taken the liberty of calling a substitute for you for Tuesday. We have candidates to interview for two English positions. Love, Me!

I can feel you panicking from here—no, Cam Stewart's wife has not convinced him to take a job at Walden, so you can relax. It's this new grant Fiona's been awarded to coordinate university readiness activities. It pays to release her from classroom duties full time, so we have to hire a replacement. It also pays for an additional English 12 instructor so we can pare down those class sizes. Love, Me!

Hugs and kisses to Cooper. I went to Aggie Rothenburg's housewarming Saturday night. What a fabulous condo he found her! Tell him it almost made me want to put my house on the market and let someone else worry about the roof, the plumbing, the seismic thingie, the...

* * *

The office is quiet this morning. Ned is all but retired these days and rarely comes in—as it should be. He's nearly ninety, after all. Nevertheless, his cubicle is kept in a perfect state of preparedness at all times as if his arrival is imminent. Now that it's legal for gays to get married in California, Elizabeth and her long time boyfriend Yuri, their decade-old vow fulfilled, have tied the knot themselves and are honeymooning in Fiji. And Cooper wouldn't dream of showing up until he's been to the gym. So Buzz has the place to himself. His official title is Office Manager and under normal circumstances he wouldn't be the one reviewing the overnight voicemails, sorting the faxes that have come in and routing them to the appropriate desktops, confirming the ads in Saturday's and Sunday's newspapers for Cooper's scheduled open house in Pacific Heights. But the people who would once have performed those duties no longer work here. The housing downturn has hit the agency hard. Revenues have fallen off a cliff. The partners are proud of the fact that they haven't actually laid anyone off. But it has meant that when people leave they aren't replaced. Those who remain have to pick up the slack. This isn't the problem it might appear, because the volume of work has fallen off so much that Buzz can easily do his own work and that of the two assistants he used to have. It's a relief, in a way, from the frantic pace they got used to during the boom. He doesn't mind the additional chores but he can't seem to get used to the quiet.

Elizabeth and Cooper haven't taken commission draws in several months. Instead, they've put the junior agents on salary. If their earnings in a given quarter don't reach a certain level—and they rarely do, lately—they're still guaranteed a minimum paycheck. Not a lot, of course, just something to help them get by. Buzz isn't being paid these days, either, at his own request. He and Morgan live comfortably on what Morgan brings in from the gym, though things are slow there too. And once the house sells and they move to a smaller place they'll have more money than they know what to do with. At least that's the plan.

Thinking about that particular listing, is, of course, Cooper's cue to arrive. It's as if he is equipped with some sort of sensitive device which alerts him to thoughts of real estate percolating in any brain in his proximity. Buzz hears him on his cell, taking the stairs two at a time. Griffin swears that Cooper only has two settings: "off" and "damn the torpedoes".

"Two o'clock," Cooper barks. "And if you're a minute late showing up, I won't be there. My schedule is full later in the afternoon."

On the day the firm goes bankrupt Cooper will still manage to look like a million dollars. Not a strand of hair is out of place. He smells like the most expensive flavor at the men's fragrances counter at Nordstrom, whatever that is currently. If you went down on your hands and knees, you could check your reflection in his shoes.

"Morning, Buzzy."

"Morning, Coop."

"Everything shipshape?"

"And Bristol fashion," Buzz answers.

Neither of them knows what "Bristol fashion" refers to. It's one of Ned's many evocative but cryptic idioms. They constitute the essential expressions of the corporate argot.

"Listen," Cooper says, "I know it's the worst possible timing, but I've got some clients in from the east coast. Real whales, right? I've told you about them—the guys Griffin and I met in Curacao last winter. And I need to show them your place this morning. After dicking around for half the year, now they want to buy something yesterday. They have cash."

"No problem," Buzz says. "The caterers and florist aren't due until one. Morgan's got the dogs at the gym. You've got the extra garage remote and your set of keys. Just let yourself in."

"If I play this right, I'll have an offer for you guys by sundown. Did I mention they're paying cash?"

                                    * * *

Ash stands in the corridor and scans Trevor Weitzmann's chart. The T-cell count hasn't budged in the last five years: it's still poised precariously at the edge of the abyss. It might be right where it is five years from now, but it could just as easily go into freefall later today. He raps on the examining room door and steps inside.

"Good morning," he smiles.

"Dr. Sainte-Claire." Vladimir rises from his seat in the corner and steps forward, extending his hand.

"Mr. Zitronblatt. Always a pleasure. And Mr. Weitzmann. Good morning to you, too."

"Hey, doc."

Trevor lounges on the examining table like he's between takes and the white gown is just another costume he can't wait to shed in order to get down to business. His lion's mane of hair is finally beginning to show gray. It lends him the aura of an Old Testament prophet. Jeremiah, most likely. Ash's Baptist upbringing left him with various gaps, but he feels certain Jeremiah is the one with just the right tinge of insanity to attract Trevor's notice. He wonders what the directors think of Trevor's recent refusal to continue touching up his hair color.

He suspects that they've already come up with some angle. Any consideration of Trevor's career makes Ash feel like he needs to take a shower.

The examination is totally routine. To all appearances, Trevor is in his mid thirties and in perfect health. Neither of these things is actually the case. The numbers on the chart don't lie. Ash thinks there's a certain evil irony in the disconnect. What you see is never what you get, of course, but in this instance the gulf between appearance and reality is large enough to swallow an aircraft carrier: the chart is Trevor's equivalent to that picture of Dorian up in the attic. Ash asks the requisite questions, the answers to which present no surprises. He makes the appropriate suggestions knowing they'll be disregarded if not completely forgotten. The futility of his efforts to help Trevor makes it hard to see the point of this visit beyond updating the chart. He shakes both Trevor's and Vladimir's hands, tells Trevor he can get dressed, and turns to leave.

"If I could have just a moment, Doctor," Vladimir says, stepping out into the corridor with him.

"What is it, Vlad?"

"I can't do a thing with him."

This is Vladimir's timeless mantra.

"Is he at least compliant with his meds?"

"Only because I watch him like a hawk. I practically have to hold a gun to his head to get him to take them. And yes, I know that's two too many clichés. But that's Trevor. He always makes you think in clichés. I suppose that must be the secret of his success."

"I know it's hard," Ash says. "But your nagging is probably what's keeping him alive. If that's any satisfaction."

"You know I'm a sucker for that kind of talk," Vladimir smiles.

"You're welcome."

"It's just that he thinks he's invincible. He believes that he's come to some sort of rapprochement with the virus."

Ash has heard this one before. Far too many times.

"Whatever you do, don't buy into that."

"Oh, I don't, Ash, believe me, I don't."

* * *

After breakfast at their usual place up the block from the gym, Nick heads downtown to his office and Tristan is off to St. Dunstan's. Their purposeful, businesslike departures leave Kirk momentarily discombobulated. Everyone he knows seems so adult, with their schedules and agendas and briefcases, and here he is still stuck in adolescence. That's not a subject he can afford to dwell on. Superannuated teenagers have places to go, too. He climbs aboard the Land Rover and aims it southward. Ever since he got sober, Kirk has been determined not to spend another day of his life playing the role of spoiled trust fund baby. So when he opened the shelter he kept his name off the project as much as possible. Very few people know that he's the landlord or that he personally funds roughly sixty per-cent of the operating budget year in and year out. The members of the board are conversant with the reality, of course: for the most part they're personal friends and know the story chapter and verse. But as far as the staff and the army of volunteers are concerned he's just Kirk, always there, eager for and equal to any task, exact role undefined, "no dog left behind" his mantra. Some have speculated that he is the assistant to the director, but such a position has never existed on any iteration of the organizational chart.

When he pulls into the courtyard, half a dozen volunteers are there being welcomed by Ariel Montoya-Leon, the shelter director. They look like a group from the gay and lesbian youth center, and Kirk peels his eyes for a likely wing-man. He's off on a sweep of the East Bay kill shelters today to see who can be rescued. With this week's adoptions there's room for a dozen or so new dogs, more if he finds smaller breeds or puppies who can share kennel space. Ordinarily Trevor Weitzmann accompanies him on these missions. Trevor never met a dog he wasn't willing to try and help, is absolutely fearless, and refrains from unnecessary chatter on the trip. In other words, he's ideal for the job. But Trevor isn't available today, which means either a doctor's appointment or a porn shoot—perhaps even both. Kirk has to find a replacement. And that's a tall order.

He picks a likely looking boy out of the crowd, a skinny, anxious type who's nothing special to look at now but will be a beauty at thirty in the unlikely event he can manage to live that long. There's no mistaking those scars on his wrists. They quickly load doggie crates into the Land Rover. A brief conference in Ariel's office, and they're away.

"So," Kirk says, after five minutes of awkward silence in the front seat, "when I attempted suicide it was because the man I loved had been killed in an automobile accident that happened because he was distracted by a fight he had just had with his husband over me. What's your story?"

* * *

Of all the private schools on the west coast, it is perhaps St. Dunstan's which most adheres to the traditional Old English ideal. It certainly looks the part, with its cluster of gothic revival buildings surrounding the greenest, most velvety of quadrangles and its broad, smooth athletic fields sloping gently down to the north shore of the bay. But its ambiance goes far beyond mere architecture and landscape. Every detail of school life, from the uniforms and slang of the boys to the recipes followed by the dining hall to the correction markings used by the teachers as they grade papers, apes the original. Presumably this obsessive faithfulness to tradition was the intent of the founders, though their written testimony, recorded for posterity in the *Founders' Book* on display in an alcove of the school chapel, is strangely nonspecific in its musings on the subject, which tend heavily toward the abstract and metaphysical instead. What is absolutely unambiguous is the conception of the school's long time benefactor and patron, Ned Westerleigh, whose generosity and dedication have made the school what it is and garnered him an amazing reserve of influence among his fellow members of the board of governors, many of whom, indeed, owe their own seats to his clout with earlier generations of that body. For the last several decades it is his vision more than anything else which has defined the school, though he would be the first to tell you that he knows next to nothing about the education of the young. He went to school himself once upon a time, and that experience is about the extent of his expertise. That school was Winchester, as quintessentially Old English a school as has ever existed, so he knows what authenticity is at least. The more faithfully St. Dunstan's emulates his beloved alma mater, the happier Ned is. That authenticity is what the parents pay for. There are many schools in the Bay Area where the sons of the wealthy can get a good education, but there's only one St. Dunstan's. That's a point Ned has made at least once at every board meeting Tristan has ever attended. That and its corollary: keep those wealthy parents paying those exorbitant fees, and the school will continue to be able to take hundreds of scholarship boys. Scholarship boys are a particular passion of Ned's. He fancies himself a sort of wiser, higher class Henry Higgins. And as that fictional gentleman's experiences vividly demonstrate, education is one thing, but good form is paramount. This is as close to a credo as Ned will swear allegiance to, because as a quintessential Englishman of the upper crust, his clear understanding of the world is that it is upon good form that all civilized behavior is based. As long as good form is maintained any challenge can be overcome, any misfortune endured. As long as good form is maintained any matter concerning the running of the school can be resolved easily and without undue conflict, and any and all decisions can be taken in total confidence.

So the replacement of John St. Crispin-Caldwell, the former headmaster, upon his retirement a year ago, which might have occasioned all manner of disruption at another school, was accomplished with a minimum of rumor, jockeying for position, raw displays of ambition on the part of candidates for the position (either real or aspiring), factionalism, and general politicking. Those were all examples of bad form and they had all been avoided. Instead, good form had been maintained from beginning to end of the process, to Ned's obvious satisfaction, and the new headmaster installed with all the ceremony which would have typified similar events at his beloved alma mater.

Tristan knows this first hand. He was a member of the board during the search for the new headmaster. He remembers clearly the stacks of resumes they reviewed, the dozens of calls they made verifying references, the exhaustiveness of the search, the lengthy deliberations, and finally, the exact moment when Ned looked up from the legal pad he had been doodling on and expressed the opinion that they were engaged in a fool's errand because it was obvious the best possible candidate was already on the staff. Knowing Ned the way he did, Tristan had foreseen this move, had been expecting it for weeks. He was frankly surprised that it had taken Ned so long to get to the point. With every eye on him and every ear tuned to catch the subtle frequencies of voice which would tell them the degree of his seriousness, Ned spoke the inevitable name: Rupert FitzMerlin.

At any other school, invoking the name of the most junior member of the faculty at such a juncture might have led to rioting in the board's conference chamber. Traditionally, headmasterships are doled out grudgingly. When a school appoints a headmaster from inside, it is typically a reward for years—decades, actually—of loyal service. Of sober, responsible performance of classroom duties, uncomplaining membership on committees, faithful adherence to rules both carefully delineated and unspoken, and unassailable professionalism. Though he could lay claim to no such lengthy record at the school, Rupert Fitz-Merlin, unlikely a candidate as he was with regard to seniority or institutional service, was, nearly everyone agreed, the perfect choice. If he hadn't existed, Ned would have had to invent him.

In his early forties, Rupert FitzMerlin is tall and powerfully built, handsome in a Nordic manner which reminds Tristan of Nick Romanovsky when they first met over thirty-five years ago. Rupert's family was ennobled by William the Conqueror, the original bearer of the FitzMerlin name having been a Viking mercenary in his service, Olaf the Silent, who first distinguished himself at Hastings and was practically indispensable by the time William came to rule all England. The conquest accomplished, Olaf forsook his marauding forthwith, settling down, marrying a princess from a particularly ferocious Saxon line, and founding one of England's oldest surviving yet most obscure noble houses. Rupert's male forebears have been Wykehamists since the founding of Ned's beloved alma mater and were Oxonians for generations before that. He speaks five languages fluently, graduated from university with triple firsts, served the U.K. faithfully and courageously in some nebulously defined role during the waning years of the Cold War, and is for all practical purposes the platonic ideal of the man every English schoolboy of his class aspires to become. A warrior athlete with an IQ over 160, he is what passes as a renaissance man in the early twenty-first century.

After a long silence while the members of the board digested Ned's remark, the question was put to a vote. The selection was unanimous.

There was the slightest of ripples on the surface of that placid pool, however. The school chaplain, the Rev. Alistair Holland, tendered his resignation a few days after the appointment was announced, subsequent to a private interview with Ned, the details of which were never made public though the generally held hunch was, Tristan knows, correct. The chaplaincy of the school was not a position under the purview of the board of governors. Ned had endowed the position himself, and Ned retained the power of appointment. Providing a chaplain for the school was another service he performed—to satisfy his own requirements and ensure his own satisfaction. He advocated the most rigorous possible adherence to the forms and rituals of High Church Anglicanism while simultaneously insisting on a theological position liberal enough to verge on anarchism on the part of the school chaplain, and up to that point Rev. Holland had met the challenge. But the selection of an openly gay headmaster was a bridge too far for the octogenarian to cross. He was invested later that term as Chaplain Emeritus. Historically, Ned had appointed retired churchmen to the post of chaplain, but broke with precedent this time. Newly graduated from seminary and freshly ordained, Tristan was prevailed upon to accept the position, necessitating, among other things, his resignation from the board of governors. As far as he's concerned, he'll burn in hell for doing Ned's bidding and accepting the position in the place of some more experienced, more orthodox candidate. But contrary to what you might expect given his upbringing and general temperament, over the years Tristan has come to love the school passionately, and despite his earlier reservations he relishes his new position.

Tristan understands that it entails far more than helping to maintain the culture of the school, nurturing the spiritual welfare of the students, and supporting the faculty and staff. More than anything, Ned's intention is for him to be a kind of unofficial assistant headmaster, Rupert's right hand man. An additional set of eyes and ears. And in this regard Tristan's appointment makes a kind of sense, though it is predicated more on his status as a retired police officer than on his ordination. Ned has a lot invested in the school, and though confidence in Rupert is high in all quarters there are all sorts of possible pitfalls. It truly is too big and complex a job to rest on one pair of shoulders, even a pair as magnificent as Rupert's. Tristan's role is far from being a chore as far as he is concerned. He thinks of Rupert as a close personal friend. They see eye to eye on everything of consequence. They even finish each other's sentences on occasion, eliciting raised eyebrows from their respective partners. It's a duty that is truly a pleasure.

This morning, as the organist blasts away at JERUSALEM and light streams in through the stained glass windows, and Rupert, golden haired, ramrod straight Rupert, leads the procession up the aisle of the chapel for the opening of Friday morning service, which will be a resolutely secular conclave once the opening hymn has been sung and he has read from the Gospel of Mark, Tristan thinks what a long, strange journey it's been that brought him to this loveliest of destinations.

* * *

"Good morning. You have reached the law offices of Nikolai Romanovsky and Associates. How may I help you?"

"Good morning, Rita. It's Chad Wilson for Nick."

"Good morning, Mr. Wilson. He just came in. I know he's expecting your call. One moment."

"Thanks."

"Chad. Good morning."

"Morning, Nick. Have you had time to look over the contract?"

"I have. You can tell Trey it's 100% kosher."

"Great. He'll be glad to hear it. The producers want it signed and sent back, like two days ago."

"Incidentally, that's a very nice payday for our boy."

"Yeah, but you know, Nick, I almost think he'd do this project for free."

"Really."

"The other night I saw him at the mantel talking to the Oscar. He told it, 'I know you're lonely. I'm going to try and get you a playmate.'"

"No shit. Is the picture going to be that good?"

"Well, by the time those guys get finished with it it'll probably be an action flick about bionic weasels. But I read the script, and in its current form it's amazing."

"Well, good luck to him then."

"Listen, Nick, thanks again for reviewing the contract."

"Don't worry. My business manager will invoice you. See you at the wedding, I hope."

"We'll be there." Chad hits end and then punches in a second number. Superstitious Trey won't allow him to put it in speed dial until the deal is done.

"Good morning. Arkangelsk Productions. How may I direct your call?"

"Chad Wilson for Alicia Morgenstern."

"One moment."

Thirty-seven seconds of overblown movie score—definitely not Trey's work—shrieks over the line.

"Chad, Alicia here."

"Morning, Alicia."

"Give me some good news, big guy. Barney and Zvi are *schvizting* like goyim, no offense. They say it's Duncan Wakefield or nobody. 'He understands subtlety', they say. 'His music is alive: it breathes nuance'."

"Really? In that case, maybe we should hold out for more cashola."

"Please, Chad, don't bust my balls here."

"Relax. I sent the contract to our counsel, who checked its pulse and took its temperature and made it open its mouth and say ah and ended up giving it a clean bill of health. And Mr. Wakefield elected to find the terms satisfactory."

"So we have a deal?"

"He's signing this morning. I'll fedex it this afternoon."

"Terrif. I owe you."

"My pleasure."

"Now our guys want to take meetings with your guy ASAP. I'll get onto travel department and they'll let you know when we can have a plane into SFO. Plan on Tuesday and Wednesday down here and a return to San Fran on Thursday unless Mr. Wakefield would like to stay through the weekend—on us of course. And I'll have them book his usual suite at the Chateau Marmont, if that's all right."

"I'm sure it'll be fine."

"Thanks, doll. I'll be in touch."

* * *

Sandy is in his office composing a letter that will go out to the freshmen he has recruited for next season's squad when there's a knock on the door.

"Come in."

"Coach York?"

"Yes."

"I'm Ricky Fredericks," the boy stammers. He's brown haired, green eyed, nondescript. Sandy places him after a moment. In street clothes these kids don't look special at all.

"I know who you are," Sandy says. "Nice job at Nationals. I caught your pommel horse routine on cable."

"Thanks," Ricky blushes.

"So?"

"I need to talk to somebody."

"Coach Grymkowski will be back from vacation Monday."

"I don't think I can talk to Coach G. about this."

"Really?" *But you can talk to me?*, Sandy thinks. Here we go again. Every couple of seasons there's one of these. "In that case, have a seat."

"The thing is," the boy says, unable to meet Sandy's gaze, "I think I may be gay."

"You *think* you may be gay," Sandy says, unable to completely master his sarcasm: he's been set up before and still isn't completely sure this boy is on the up and up. "And just what makes you *think* that?"

"I don't know. I guess it's because I like to have sex with guys."

"What about with women?"

"Women? What are those?" The boy loosens up just enough to muster a faint grin.

"That bad, huh?"

"If that's really bad."

"I don't think you may be gay," Sandy says, "I think you are gay. In fact, I don't think it, I know it. See there? Problem solved."

"I guess," the boy says.

"You guess?"

"I guess that's not really the problem."

"Now we're getting somewhere," Sandy says. "O.K., here goes. Do you need your scholarship to stay in school or can your parents pick up the tab?"

"I have to have my scholarship."

"Then not a word to Coach Grymkowski. He's not a real, honest to God homophobe, but he doesn't want to deal with it on the team and the university holds its nose and allows him to make that call, understand?"

"I think so."

"Stop thinking so much. Understand or not?"

"Understand."

"Good. Go to the bars much?"

"Only a couple of times, so far."

"Stop immediately. There's nothing wrong with the bars, but anybody can show up there and you can't guarantee that word won't get back to campus. I'm giving you a number to call. It's a support group that meets off campus where you can get to know some O.K. guys and learn about socializing away from the bars."

"Thanks."

"Now there are some people around the university who'll pressure you to stand up and be open about yourself and all that political stuff, and they're good people and have good intentions, but they don't have to live your life so you don't have to do what they say. All you have to do is look out for your own best interests. What are you anyway? A sophomore?"

"Junior in the fall."

"Right, so you only have to play it cool for four more semesters. Then you can be your own man. And here: here's my cell number and personal email address. Any time you need help, let me know."

"Thanks, Coach York."

"One more thing. Listen to me and listen good. Do not under any circumstances come here to see me ever again."

"I'm sorry, Coach York. I thought it would be O.K."

"It's not what you think. It's just that everybody knows about me. My wrestlers can come and go all the time and nobody thinks a thing about it. But you're not my guy. You're Coach Grymkowski's property, and that makes it too conspicuous for you to be here, see? So if you need to speak to me, call or email and we'll arrange to meet somewhere safe."

"I understand."

"I hope so," Sandy says. "And good luck to you, Ricky."

* * *

Ross checks his hair in the rear view mirror one last time. He clambers out of the Aston-Martin as gracefully as is possible for a man of his height and breadth of shoulder given the proportions of the car. It's a typical Hillsborough palazzo, the kind Cooper is always selling to or on behalf of someone or other, and he strides up the walk like a man who takes for granted he's being watched. The monumental front door swings open almost before he has located the bell, and it's no majordomo there to greet him but a typical Hillsborough matron, a tennis togged, pearl necklaced, spray tanned stick figure of defiantly indeterminate age.

"Oh my God," she brays, "it really is you. I can't believe it."

"At your service, Mrs. Higgins," he smirks, shifting instantaneously into character.

"Ross Boucher, *the* Ross Boucher, in the flesh."

"Too, too sullied, I'm afraid," Ross says.

"You actors and your Chekov." She makes a sound that's obviously meant to be a girlish giggle, but years of neat scotch and unfiltered cigarettes sabotage the effect beyond remedy. "You know, when I saw your name on the website I didn't think it could possibly be you. I told myself there are probably dozens of Ross Boucher's up and down the west coast."

"I'm sorry I'm late," Ross says, though he's actually right on time.

"Nonsense. Traffic down from the city is always a nightmare. Doesn't matter what time of the day or night. I have no idea where they all think they're going. Oh, my, Mr. Boucher, this is *such a pleasure*."

Ross is accustomed to this reaction. Nearly a decade on one of America's most popular soaps made him, if not exactly a household name, at least a vaguely familiar face. Soap fans are nothing if not loyal, and in his experience they're especially attached to their villains. Perhaps it's for the same reason that Ross always had more fun playing the evil twin.

"Well, do please come in. And you must call me Mary Ellen. My God, you looked just like James Bond getting out of that DB-5. It is a DB-5, isn't it?"

"It is, indeed."

"I had one of those," she says. "For a very brief period of time. Rolly put it into a lake, unfortunately. He wouldn't buy me a replacement. Said Astons had always been jinx cars. He was such a drunk. Speaking of which, I've got a pitcher of margaritas in the fridge—can I tempt you?"

"Not quite so soon after breakfast, I think," Ross says, careful not to sound disapproving.

"You're probably right. Let's go into the morning room and take a load off."

The space she leads him into is oppressively baronial. She slumps into a club chair like a private school girl spoiling for a fight with the headmistress.

"You received our informational packet?"

"Yep, sure did," she says.

"And have you had time to look it over?"

"My son and I went through it thoroughly. I'm supposed to ask you if your commission is negotiable."

"I'm sorry," Ross says, "but the figures in the packet are firm."

"That's what I told Steven. A reputable firm like yours doesn't have to discount its services."

"I'm glad you understand."

"Steven is of the opinion that I should put the car on something called ebay motors. It's a specialized auction site, I believe."

"Many people are taking that route these days," Ross says. "What you have to understand is that with the kind of car you're thinking of consigning there are no sight unseen purchases. Depending on the condition of the vehicle, restoration costs on a Gullwing can run as high as half a million dollars. No matter how thoroughly you photograph and document the car for the website, serious buyers are going to want to see for themselves. Or at the very least have it inspected by an expert. You can certainly make arrangements for that through their website, but what it means is people coming here. To your house, Mary Ellen. And then there's the matter of having to monitor your email constantly and field any and all questions that it may occur to people to ask. Some of them are quite bizarre—the questions, I mean. But, really, the people too, I have to say. Many sellers find that it's really more trouble than they prefer to deal with. Sign with us and it's all done for you. Any viewings and inspections take place at our facilities. You go on with your life. And our corporate website gets tens of thousands of hits every week. Your Mercedes will receive plenty of exposure."

"Yes, exactly," she nods. "Thank you for explaining it to me. I knew it was a bad idea, I just couldn't have told you why. I can't imagine dealing with all that. Steven assures me he would take care of everything, but his track record is far from perfect, I'm afraid. He's currently unemployed, you see, and he's always on the lookout for money making opportunities."

"That's certainly commendable."

"As long as those opportunities don't entail actually getting a job."

"Perhaps this would be a good time for me to view the car," Ross suggests.

"Yes, I suppose it would."

* * *

Owen steps into the waiting room and checks the name on the manila folder one last time.

"Paul des Jardins."

"Here."

He's in the far corner of the room. Tall and broad shouldered, gym toned, ginger hair slick with product, wearing excruciatingly tasteful and extremely expensive clothing: another of those stockbroker-banker-corporate attorneys. This *uber* white collar type is a particular fetish of Owen's. Ironic, since Boone is a firefighter. It takes an act of Congress to get him into this sort of getup. How many of these guys does Owen see in an average month? Handsome, successful, affluent; they appear to have the world by the balls, yet they show up here in some sort of desperation or other.

"Good morning. I'm Owen York."

"Good to meet you, Dr. York."

"Just through here," Owen says, holding open the door. "It's a bit of a maze, I'm afraid."

They walk down the corridor in silence. Paul des Jardins is apparently not a man given to small talk. This is no surprise, really. Owen could have predicted it. His first glimpse of that jawline was enough. Inside Owen's office they sit facing each other.

"Now, Mr. des Jardins..."

"Please, call me Paul."

"Now Paul, I see from your file that you've been on medications for depression and panic disorder for the past six months."

"That's right."

"When exactly did your depression start?"

"Far as I can recall, right about at birth."

"Really? Have you ever been in treatment before?"

"Guys generally don't get help, do we?"

"You're one of those, are you? That must have been hard."

"Life's hard for everybody. One way or another."

Yes, Owen thinks. One of those spartan types. But the tougher they are the harder they go down when they finally fall.

"So your primary care physician put you on medication and then a few weeks ago you saw my colleague Dr. O'Toole for two sessions. Now you've asked to be assigned to a different psychologist. Any particular reason for that?"

"I didn't feel I could work with Dr. O'Toole."

"I see. That happens from time to time. His notes from your sessions were forwarded to me, and I've had a look at them. You're apparently not satisfied with the result you're getting from your medication. Could you tell me about that?"

"I'm not sure the medication is having any effect at all," Paul says, "except that it leaves me too apathetic to care about being depressed. I suppose some people might find that an improvement."

"You know, there are other medications you could try. I'm surprised your physician didn't discuss that with you. Or refer you to a psychiatrist."

"He offered to. But I'm not sure that medication is the answer for me. It's not just that it doesn't seem to be working, it's the side effects."

"Did you discuss that with your physician?"

"He offered me a prescription for Viagra. I'm afraid I really don't see the point of taking a pill to counteract the effects of another pill. I went to Dr. O'Toole in the first place to, well, find out about my options."

"Options beyond medication, I take it."

"There are some. At least according to the internet."

"There are plenty. I'd be happy to discuss some with you. Now when you first consulted Dr. O'Toole, did he have you complete a personal profile? It should be in your folder, but I can't seem to find it."

"I don't remember anything like that. Is it important?"

"Well, it would help me to focus on the alternatives most appropriate to you as an individual. All I really know is your name, your medical record number, and a few basics: 'white male, thirty-two years old, excellent health'."

"And the profile would tell you...?"

"Oh, about your profession, your interests and pastimes, your relationship status; all that information can be helpful in any discussions about how to proceed."

"Well, I'm a stockbroker. And I go to the gym—oh, I guess you'd say quite a bit. People say I'm obsessive about it."

"Yes, that's pretty apparent."

"You seem to spend plenty of time there yourself."

"Probably more than I should," Owen grins.

"And what else do you want do know?"

"Are you single? In a relationship?"

"I'm single."

"Have you ever been in a relationship?"

"I've been in lots of them. That's not why I'm depressed."

"No?"

"It's not because I'm gay, either, if that's what you're going to ask next."

"We don't ask about sexual orientation," Owen assures him. "Clients disclose it in their own time. Or not at all."

"What you mean is you don't need to ask."

"I don't follow you."

"Well, obviously, you can tell."

"It's not that easy," Owen insists.

"Of course It Is."

"We don't like to make assumptions," Owen says.

"Oh, come on, Doctor York, do I look straight?"

"Lots of men are particular about their appearance these days. It cuts across orientations."

"Please don't use the word *metrosexual*. It's idiotic. And I hope that your gaydar doesn't go off every time you see a well dressed man with a good haircut and a decent pair of shoes carrying a gym bag down the street."

"We mental health professionals don't generally use the term gaydar. At least not while we're on duty. But I take your point."

"Thanks. I'm here because that homophobe O'Toole wanted to make my sexuality the issue."

Owen has heard this sort of complaint about O'Toole in the past, but there's no way he'd acknowledge that to a client.

"Well, I can assure you that you don't have to be concerned about that with me."

"I know. I checked you out already. You're solid."

* * *

Whenever he can slip away from the showroom, Knut likes to come back to the service bays and watch Daniel Kmetko at work. With his close cropped silver hair, ridiculous shoulders, monumental pecs, and biceps constantly straining against the confines of his rolled up shirt sleeves, Daniel is the walking, talking definition of the term muscle daddy. Knut is a dedicated connoisseur of this type, the proof being that he relentlessly stalked and eventually married one. One night not long after Daniel came to work for them, with Ross ravaging Knut's nipples and fucking the living daylights out of him, he flashed on Daniel for an instant and a moment later experienced one of the most intense orgasms of his intensely orgasmic life. He classified this as a random occurrence until a few nights later when it happened a second time. A third episode led Knut, ordinarily not one to waste time on self-analysis, to give this new phenomenon some consideration. The epiphany wasn't long in coming. The deep set cobalt eyes and craggy, Viking chieftain's face were the tipoff. If Knut's late father hadn't been such a useless, drunken closet case, and if he had ditched his ridiculous Republican golfing buddies and gotten his ass to the gym, Daniel Kmetko is who he might well have turned into. Once Knut recognized Daniel as an avatar of Dad everything went back to normal. Fundamentally monogamous—despite all appearances—Knut found that his focus shifted back to his husband. But this didn't dampen his rampant fantasy life. And so, with Ross off trying to drum up business in deepest, darkest Hillsborough, Knut trips the light fantastic.

"Oh, ho, ho," he guffaws on final approach, "what have we here? It looks remarkably like Tristan Bentley's 1967 Maserati 3500GT."

"He thinks the carburetors are out of synch," Daniel grunts, glowering into the engine compartment like a warrior surveying something he's not sure is sufficiently dead. "I told him I'd bring it in and have a look."

"And are the carburetors the problem?"

"Certainly felt like it as I drove her in," Daniel says. "You know, it's a shame about these old Masers."

"What's that?"

"Well, when they were new they cost just as much as a Ferrari or Aston, but these days the market can't be bothered. Even in near concours condition like this one, they're worth less than ten per cent of what a comparable Ferrari or Aston would bring at auction. They're just as nice to drive. And easier and cheaper to maintain. I've never understood it."

Knut's starting to tingle all over watching Daniel's heavily corded forearms and almost magically dexterous fingers as he adjusts the carbs. Then his cell goes off. Ross's number flashes on the display.

"Hey, sweetie,"

"I'm on my way back."

"How did it go?"

"Mrs. Higgins signed. It's a very early Gullwing. Aluminum body car with full belly pans. Absolutely immaculate and unrestored. Full, uninterrupted service history. Even the original fitted luggage. We'll pick it up on Monday. You wouldn't believe what else she's sitting on."

"Try me."

"A Jag XKSS, a Porsche 904, a DB4GT Zagato, an Alfa GTZ, a Cooper Monaco, and a tipo 61 Maserati."

"Daniel says old Maseratis are hardly worth anything." Out of the corner of his eye, Knut sees Daniel nodding.

"Tell him 'birdcage'."

"Birdcage," Knut repeats. Daniel's eyebrows shoot up.

"Now what about that Benz *Grosser*? Is it back from detail yet?"

"Within the hour, *mon capitain*."

"It better be. We're picking up Wulf and Dave at 4:00, and we have to go home and dress before that."

* * *

These days, any property with the least hint of Mediterranean in its architecture is labeled "Tuscan", but in the case of the Lundquist-Montgomery house the description is right on the money. Ned and Elizabeth always refer to it as "Il Palazzo," but Cooper prefers Griffin's nickname for it: "The Ruritanian Embassy." Once he was on the point of asking Ned where Ruritania is so he could stop feeling less informed than his husband but uncharacteristically held his tongue. When he looked it up later he was glad he'd kept his mouth shut. He hates doing anything that supports the notion he's just a pretty face. Cooper steers the Bentley into the garage stall beside Buzz's vintage Sting Ray. He remembers selling this house to Forrest, giddy at making his first seven figure deal and faintly shocked that a man just a few years older than himself could afford such a purchase—and in cash. When Forrest died, the whole gang had expected Morgan to sell up and move on. But he hung on, at first by himself and later with Buzz, who had been Cooper's office manager by that time. It's a terrible time to be selling a house. Cooper tried to convince Morgan to rent it out and wait for the market to recover. The place will bring less than seventy percent of its peak value, but Morgan wants out.

This is one of the best blocks in Pacific Heights. Directly across the street is the mansion Cooper always thinks of as the wedding cake house because of its elaborately sculpted white stucco exterior. Ned Westerleigh says it reminds him of a house on the Black Sea that his mother's family lost in the Russian Revolution. Thirty years ago, it was the site of some of the most legendary parties in the history of gay San Francisco. Cooper sold it back in the 80's on behalf of the estate of that celebrated host. The man's notoriety and the paranoia of the times had made it a hard sale. It has changed hands several times since then. He has no idea who the current owners are. One thing for certain—nobody gives parties like that these days.

Trust Buzz: the place is immaculate. Cooper hardly needs to look. Not a blade of grass or rose petal out of place in the gardens, and indoors the marble flooring looks smooth and shiny enough to skate on. Everything is in readiness for the arrival of caterers and florists and the wedding planner and her small but relentless army. Why had he thought this was a bad day for a showing? He'll just add a little riff about a double wedding later in the afternoon to his standard spiel and watch the buyers' mouths fall open. "*You can entertain in grand style here*" is the message. "*You can host your own wedding, if you get a move on and schedule it before November.*" He'll have a signed offer to present at the reception.

One nagging detail, however. And when he's showing a property, Cooper hates nasty surprises more than he hates televangelists the rest of the time. Out the french doors and across the garden to the guest house. Cooper lets himself inside. No, not a sign of habitation. As immaculate as the rest of the place. They must have gotten rid of Nelson. Finally.

Bloomington, Indiana: 1966

Scott finishes dressing and heads downstairs, where he starts the percolator and then spends the next forty-five minutes gathering up empty bottles, setting glasses in the kitchen sink to soak, emptying and sponging out ash trays, filling a trash bag with beer cans, and vacuuming crushed pretzels and potato chips out of the carpet. Dad's Tuesday night Advanced German Conversation class, which is supposed to meet at the university but convenes more often than not in the Bailey's living room, degenerated into the usual drunken riot. He hasn't bothered to look into any of the spare bedrooms but knows what he'd find if he did. When he gets home from school he'll have to strip the sheets off every bed in the house except his own and launder them in hot water and bleach. The bathrooms will have to be doused with Lysol, and if no more than one of the toilets is clogged he'll consider it a miracle. No wonder Dr. Patterson Bailey is one of the most popular professors in the entire university, running this tavern/whorehouse/dance hall/opium den. Scott doesn't begrudge all these near-adults their fun, but he certainly wishes Dad would decide they can afford a cleaning lady.

By the time he's finished tidying, it's time to go upstairs. He fixes Dad's usual tray of strong black coffee and scorched toast and carries it, complete with extra cup, upstairs. He doesn't bother to knock. If these girls will insist on sleeping with Dad, they can just get used to Scott's early morning ministrations at his bedside. As many of them as have witnessed this ritual, he can't believe it comes as a surprise to anyone. Girls, Clay has told him, talk about their sexual exploits just like boys do so word must have gotten around by now. And if they take their coffee any way but black or think they'd like something more substantial in the way of breakfast than a dry piece of toast, they can get their lazy asses down to the kitchen and make their own. He sets the tray on the only clear space on top of Dad's dresser and walks over to the bed. He ignores the girl, who he's sure looks like all the rest. He's seen plenty of them come and go over the years; enough, he sometimes thinks, to populate a small town. He grabs Dad's bare, fish belly white shoulder for a good hard shake.

"Rise and shine, oh great paterfamilias," he yells into Dad's left ear. "You have an eight o'clock meeting with Dean Sherwood about Paul Robertson's tenure and it's now exactly six forty-five."

He keeps tugging on Dad's shoulder until he's sure the man is at least awake enough that he won't go back to sleep. On occasion he has to roll Dad out onto the floor to get him up and moving and he once broke Dad's left wrist in the process, but it doesn't look like this is going to be one of those mornings. He knows the girl's awake but pretending not to be so he goes right on ignoring her, which he would in any case.

"Oh. Oh, shit," Dr. Bailey mutters, blinking twice and then farting operatically.

"And by the way, Dad, don't forget your dentist appointment this afternoon. Three o'clock."

"Yuh...wuh," Dr. Bailey grunts, starting to roll over and encountering the girl. "Oh, God, who can this be?"

"Your guess is as good as mine," Scott says. "Have a nice day."

* * *

Next door, Clay's mom, Sally Rexford Horstmann, is presiding over her family's breakfast like the antebellum matriarch she fancies herself, though she's only from southern Illinois, which makes her accent pretentious and her imperiousness blandly unconvincing. Scott feels like sending her to his Grandmother Bailey, who could have taught Scarlett O'Hara a thing or two, for lessons. Mrs. Horstmann is tall and slender, with the perfect posture of a kindergarten teacher and a thick head of snowy white hair that gives a mistaken impression of her age. Scott knows Coach Horstmann wishes she would color it like he does his own. The Horstmann menfolk don't look up from their plates as Scott comes through the kitchen door without knocking. He might as well be Butcher, the Horstmanns' prize Abyssinian, or one of their neurotic Labradors, Daisy and Violet, coming in through the pet door, so routine is his appearance in their kitchen. His place is already set at the table and by the time his butt has made contact with the cushion of the chair, Mrs. Horstmann is already shoveling biscuits and gravy onto his plate and Clay is pouring his orange juice for him.

Mrs. Horstmann is the only person in the world who both remembers Scott's mother and is willing to talk about her. This, more than her cooking and nearly as much as his blood brotherhood with Clay, implicit since the cradle but officially sealed one rainy afternoon on the way home from kindergarten, is what keeps him coming back to her kitchen table. He makes better biscuits and gravy himself, God knows. And the Horstmanns have absolutely no conversation worth hearing or participating in during their meals. Instead, they talk about exactly what you'd expect a high school football coach and his five sons to talk about. Scott can't imagine anything more boring to listen to, but hearing is only one of his senses and there's not one of the Horstmann menfolk, from Coach himself right down to Clay, the youngest, that Scott wouldn't walk barefoot over hot coals and broken glass for the opportunity of staring at.

He bolts down the biscuits and gravy because he knows Clay will leave for school without him if he's not ready and this morning's already been bad enough. Being deserted is the last thing he wants to think about.

* * *

Scott is the envy of the whole eighth grade, just as he was the envy of sixth and seventh. He can swear more fluently and scandalously than any high schooler in town. Dad lets him drink as much as he wants (just enough that it can be detected on his breath), smoke as much as he wants (just enough to impress the guys on the soccer team), stay out as late as he wants as often as he wants (which is midnight or later practically every night), and read as many porno magazines and dirty novels as he can get his hands on. These he finds more baffling than titillating, though he passed one paperback on to Clay once and never got it back. Clay still goes around quoting certain passages of it like a prophet declaiming texts from the Pentateuch. This habit made him a minor celebrity even before he hit puberty, grew six inches, gained fifty pounds, and became a junior high school Adonis virtually over night. Scott, who'd watched each of Clay's brothers undergoing the same metamorphosis, was perhaps the only one in the whole eighth grade not to be surprised by Clay's transformation. Instead, he'd been awaiting it like the devout of old awaited the Messiah.

In addition to all this daring permissiveness on his part, Dr. Bailey has never shown the slightest interest in Scott's schoolwork or classroom deportment. Not even during Scott's earliest kindergarten days. He's never darkened the door of Scott's schools, avoiding open houses, parent-teacher conferences, Christmas programs, spring concerts, and all manner of athletic events with what Scott suspects is calculated neglect. Scott has no particular complaint about this arrangement, because Dad is sufficiently embarrassing safely hidden away at home. But he suspects it has occasioned much comment in faculty rooms and principals' offices over the years. And according to conventional wisdom, Scott should be a holy terror and the bane of the entire school district. But he realized very early in childhood that misbehaving in order to elicit Dr. Bailey's attention would prove to be futile, and that the most spectacularly perverse thing he could possibly hope to accomplish in his life was to confound the expectations of everyone who expected him to turn out rotten because of his upbringing. As it happened, this included just about everyone he and Dad know, especially his Grandma and Grandpa Bailey, with whom he and Dad never communicate except to argue. He's never met any of his German relatives. Dad was all ready to take him to see them one summer, but suddenly the Berlin Wall went up and the whole tribe of his mother's family was on the wrong side of it. All he knows about them is what little he remembers hearing his father say, most of it extremely unflattering unflattering, and the few photographs he's seen, all taken before the war.

So his blond, blue eyed, angelic appearance in no way belies his actual nature, though he's surprisingly adept at keeping his peers, including Clay—or rather, especially Clay—from realizing what his true nature is. Because nothing will ruin a kid's reputation faster than being good, and small, pretty blond boys have to be mean as snakes to keep from being constantly tortured by their peers. Above all, Scott is an expert at survival.

* * *

When he gets home from soccer practice, a strange young woman is in the kitchen within seconds of accidentally killing herself with a butcher knife. Why their mothers don't teach them the most rudimentary of culinary skills is a question Scott finds himself pondering at least once a month, when some Sue Ann or Betty Lou or Donna Jean—because the ones playing the domesticity card always seem to have two first names—shows up with the misguided intention of producing a meal and feeding it to Dad and incidentally him.

"Hi," she says, beaming and missing slicing her left index finger off at the first knuckle by about a micron and a half. "You must be Scott."

"If you say so," Scott says, watching her continue to chop carrots with the blissful oblivion of a retired circus tightrope artist nearly catatonic on barbiturates.

"I'm Mary Elizabeth."

"You certainly seem to be," Scott agrees.

"I thought I'd drop by and fix you and your daddy a nice not meal," she confides, as if under the impression he might not recognize the activity she's engaged in. "I bet you get awfully sick of him feeding you out of boxes and cans, a growing boy like you."

Scott doesn't bother correcting her. It would take too long to explain that he, not Dr. Bailey, prepares every meal consumed in this house; that he not only cooks but does all the shopping, laundry, and cleaning; that the morning after that horrible night three winters ago when there was no light or heat in the house he marched into this father's study and spent two hours figuring out how to use the checkbook so he can make sure the household bills get paid on time and the insurance policies don't lapse; that he hardly ever uses canned goods because he considers it beneath him; and that only an idiot would attempt to chop carrots that way and expect to live to tell about it.

She'd never believe any of it. None of the girls who constantly chase after Dr. Bailey frantically auditioning for the role of housewife and stepmother is the type to listen to such a story without expressing skepticism, must less grasp its underlying pathos. And forget about their eventually accepting its veracity. Such a thing is unimaginable for the simple reason that Dr. Bailey's fatal charms make it impossible. He is so unmistakably a paragon that no evidence to the contrary is admissible. There is an easier, not to mention far more entertaining, way of telling her what a hopeless fool Scott knows her to be.

He pulls a Budweiser out of the refrigerator and a bottle opener out of the drawer and he's in business.

"Scott!" the girl shrieks. "What do you think you're doing?"

"It's O.K." Scott says, taking an ostentatiously loud swig. "Dad lets me have a beer before dinner. He says it's good for the digestion."

"I'll just bet. Now, put that down this instant."

"Sorry, miss," he says, smiling sweetly. Before she can get over the shock of his refusal to do as he's been told—by an adult!—he's out of the room and halfway up the stairs. He hears her following him, stumbling along and babbling hysterically. He slams his bedroom door and locks it. He moves to the window. Frantic knocking rattles the door in its frame. He grins to himself. Getting the better of Dad's girls is such child's play.

"Scott, you come out of there right now and give me that beer. If you don't, I'm going to have to tell your father about this. And I know you don't want to upset him like that."

As if anything short of nuclear war could get Dad's attention. Scott moves to the window, shoves it open, and pours the beer into the lilac bush downstairs. Who does she think she is? How the hell does she presume to think she knows anything about them?

* * *

For dinner, Mrs. Horstmann has fixed all Scott's favorites. There is shepherd's pie with pearl onions and real lamb (not the usual hamburger) in it, a red cabbage slaw in her own vinaigrette dressing, and a lime jello mold containing crushed pineapple and small curd cottage cheese. A heaping platter of fresh cornbread sits steaming like an elaborate centerpiece. And Scott's highly trained nostrils have detected the unmistakable, heartwarming aroma of blackberry cobbler, the one dessert she does really well. Sally Rexford Horstmann is obviously in one of her "that poor little Scott Bailey" moods, which come along every five or six weeks. He wonders what has prompted this episode. Is there new and more than usually scandalous gossip about his father he's not yet aware of? Dr. Bailey is a notorious drunkard, despoiler of virgins, communist sympathizer, and all around corrupter of youth, and the checkout lanes of local supermarkets are constantly abuzz with horrified tales of his depravity. Perhaps Mrs. Horstmann heard something especially alarming at the A&P recently. Or could it be he's looking particularly woebegone today? Not a difficult effect to achieve in this robust company, but he generally prefers to be in more conscious control of his self presentation. Is she menstruating this week? Or is it just on general principle that she's decided to pamper him thus?

He digs in. He's already one helping behind the rest of the wolfpack. After they've stuffed themselves, they'll all go into the family room and sit around belching and watching *Voyage to the Bottom of the Sea* on the color television until time for ice cream sundaes.

* * *

Several evenings later, Dr. Bailey surprises Scott by appearing at the front door right about the time normal families all over the neighborhood are sitting down to dinner. He's lost yet another set of keys, which means the Buick is God only knows where and Scott and Clay will spend all night looking for it. Scott's sixth sense usually warns him in plenty of time that such events are imminent, so he invariably has a culinary masterpiece ready to set on the table within seconds of *Herr Doktor Professor's* arrival. Tonight he's flummoxed, and it's not until his father is on his fourth double scotch that he's managed to rustle up hamburger steaks, pork and beans, corn on the cob, and a tossed salad with Green Goddess dressing.

"God, this looks good," Dr. Bailey says, collapsing into his seat at the table and sloshing half a tumbler of scotch onto the floor. "What a terrific little housekeeper you are, sonny boy."

"Watch out," Scott warns. "You're getting your shirt cuff in the butter."

"Sorry. You know, Suzanne was very disappointed that you didn't join us for dinner the other night."

"I'll just bet she was," Scott grunts. "And I thought her name was Mary Elizabeth."

"Was it?" Dr. Bailey asks, looking bewildered. "Was it really?"

"It was."

"If you say so. Anyway, son, I know you knew she was cooking for us, because she said she'd spoken to you when you came in from...your piano lesson?"

"Soccer practice. I don't take piano lessons. You won't get a piano in here so I can practice."

"I won't?"

"You've refused to discuss it."

"That doesn't sound like me."

"It wasn't the man in the moon."

"Sonny boy, now you've made me feel bad. I promise you I'll reconsider about the piano."

"All right."

"But this thing with, um..."

"Mary Elizabeth."

"Right. I know she spoke with you about dinner."

"We discussed several things," Scott says. "Ontological systems, as I recall. And then we took off on contemporary theories of epistemology. That's always extremely interesting."

"You know, you really should be more considerate of people, little man. You could have let her know you had other plans before she went to all that trouble."

"First of all, *Herr Doktor Professor*, you're the one she was going to all that trouble for."

"Granted, but..."

"But nothing. Second, I don't remember her calling ahead of time to clear the date. She just showed up and assumed I was free for the evening. How considerate is that? You know how dangerous it is to make assumptions about a relative stranger's calendar. I have to say, it seems to speak of a certain social ineptitude on her part."

"That's true," Dr. Bailey admits glassily, accustomed to being on the wrong side of any argument with Scott.

"And while we're on the subject of consideration for others, just who did she think was going to clean up that pigsty she'd made out of our kitchen in the course of her labors? Honestly, Dad, if I hadn't seen her in action with my own eyes, I'd have thought someone had been performing ritual sacrifice on a herd of goats in there. Or do goats come in flocks?"

"Oops, sorry, Scottie. That was my fault. I just kind of got carried away. I don't think we actually finished dinner."

"I think you're right. It was still sitting right where you left it when I got home that night, festering away in the moonlight and attracting no telling what kind of vermin."

"Sorry," Dr. Bailey says. "*Mea culpa, mea culpa.* It won't happen again."

* * *

Scott swings into the saddle of his Peugeot ten speed and sprints down the street after Clay. Ever since Clay got so big all of a sudden, it's hard for Scott to keep up with him. This is very troubling. What if Clay decides some morning that he doesn't want Scott to keep up? What if despite pedaling with all his might Scott arrives at school three minutes behind and suddenly nothing will ever be the same? What happens next fall when they start high school if Clay decides he wants a best friend his own size? One who has to shave like Clay does? One with honest to God hair growing in his armpits, not to mention other places, like Clay has?

Scott has always been the shrimp. And his short, scrawny body is hairless as a boiled egg. As Clay continues to mature, the difference between them grows more and more striking. Scott keeps waiting for the same thing to happen to him that has happened to lots of other boys in the eighth grade this year. But he shows no sign of even starting to catch up. Except for the fact that his voice has changed, he could easily pass for a fourth grader. People who hear him speak, especially adults, seem bewildered at the sound of that big, deep voice emerging from the mouth of such a small, baby faced person. He has no older siblings to look to as examples of what he might expect to be like in maturity. He has first cousins in Arizona, but he hasn't seen any of them since he was three years old. Dad is over six feet tall and unusually broad shouldered, but what if Scott is destined to take after his mother? How many times has he heard Sally Rexford Horstmann describe his mother as small and pretty and delicate? How many times has she stared at him and shaken her head and remarked on his uncanny resemblance to that sad faced young woman whose photographs his father packed away and refuses to take out of their boxes and look at? What if he stays small and pretty and delicate forever? Who's going to want to be his best friend then?

* * *

Except during football season, Friday nights are party nights in the Horstmanns' basement. Clay's brothers and high school friends and their girls dance to the 45's they play on a tinny sounding old RCA. They shoot pool. They play cards. They drink from smuggled in bottles and cans. The girls gossip and the boys brag. They go into the back yard to make out in the bushes or behind trees. Occasionally there is a fight about something, or more often, nothing. Clay and Scott, though technically not invited, manage to sneak in at will. Rumors about Clay's popularity with high school girls have somehow found their way back to the junior high. Daily, Scott finds himself face to face with some eighth grade girl or other, being interrogated exhaustively and compelled to confirm or deny some snippet or other she's glommed onto. He does neither, preferring to confuse the issue as much as possible. He answers their questions with questions. He is mysterious on the subject of Clay and his women. He is inscrutable. He hints at spectacular romantic exploits, lurid scenes of conquest and betrayal. He is Scheherazade incarnate, elaborating, embellishing, exaggerating madly. The girls believe at least half of what he tells them, which of course is far too much. And it doesn't matter which half. It has the effect of making Clay even more desirable in the eyes of their female classmates. Scott bathes in the reflected glory. Tonight he stands with his back to the wall of the room pretending to smoke—a lit cigarette dangles from his left hand—and watching Clay try to put his hand down Nancy Ballard's sweater. Nancy is in the eleventh grade and has her own car, a gleaming new MGB, the envy of half the kids in town. Her breasts are the stuff of legend. That she will have anything to do with an eighth grader is nothing short of miraculous.

"Got any more of those?" a husky voice asks.

He pulls his vacuum cleaner eyes away from Clay and Nancy. Paula McGinty has just come out of the bathroom. She's a tenth grader with a nasty reputation. She towers over Scott in her tie dyed granny dress. Her huge mane of clown red hair glints psychedelically.

"Sure," Scott says, "but you can't smoke in here. Mrs. Horstmann doesn't allow it."

"You're smoking."

"I'm different."

"That's what I hear. Come on, give me a drag."

"No," Scott says, looking away from her one green and one sky blue eye.

"Let's go outside, then."

"Why?"

"Because Ellie Caulfield says you like to go outside," Nancy smirks. "She says you're a nasty little boy and you do amazing things."

"That Ellie," Scott rolls his eyes, squirming inwardly at the memory of Ellie, and Charlotte, who told Ellie about him, and Roberta, who told Charlotte, and Margie, and so on. "You can't believe a word she says."

"Come on."

Paula grabs him by the hand and starts pulling him toward the door. She must outweigh him by forty pounds and she's determined. He tells himself he doesn't have a choice, but he knows that's really just an excuse. The kind Dad would make. The kind Dad probably is making this very minute. He sees Clay watching him be dragged outside. He won't tell Clay what happens out there. He never tells Clay. He likes Clay to have to guess. He likes Clay to hear the same stories he hears fifth or sixth or seventh hand about himself.

"Ellie said you do this thing," Paula says, heading across the back yard toward the garden shed, "where you hit off your smoke and then exhale into her mouth. She said you drove her half crazy doing that. She said you even did it to her with a reefer once. Where'd a junior high pipsqueak like you learn a trick like that?"

"I have many secrets."

"So I hear. Come on, show me."

She's got him backed up against the side of the garden shed now, hidden from the house, deep in shadows. She could strangle him to death and nobody would see a thing.

"You sure?"

"Stop wasting time."

Scott fishes the pack of Camels out of his pocket. He lights one, takes a deep drag off it. Next thing he knows, Paula's lips are stuck to his like the sucker of an octopus and her tongue is forcing his mouth open. He lets the smoke go slowly.

"Hmm," she says a moment later. "Not bad."

"Want to do it again?"

"Maybe," she says. "Ellie also told me there's something different about your thingie. That it's not like the ones the other boys have."

"Like she'd know," he drawls, amused at the curiosity his foreskin has been generating lately.

"She said you let her look at it," Paula says, nibbling on his ear.

"I may have."

"She said she gave you a hand job."

"You just can't believe that girl."

"Oh, yes you can."

"If that's true, then I'm surprised any decent boy will be seen in public with her."

"Let me just see it, O.K?"

Scott closes his eyes and tries to imagine those words coming out of Clay's mouth. Of course Clay has seen it, multiple times. But he's never expressed any interest in it. That's what Scott really dreams of. Impossible, of course. It could never happen in a million years. He carries with him the nagging suspicion that this will prove to be the great tragedy of his life. But closing his eyes and pretending it's Clay he's out here with always gets him in the mood.

"All right."

Her tongue shoots into his mouth again like a hungry snake. Her hand fumbles with his zipper. Then she's reaching inside with terrifying fingers.

"No underwear," Paula grunts, breaking the suction between their mouths. "Just like Ellie told me. You still say she's a liar?"

Scott doesn't answer. He takes another drag on the Camel. He closes his eyes. He stands still as Paula pulls his jeans down.

"Damn," she says. "It's too dark. I can't see a fucking thing. Come over here."

Jeans bunched at his ankles, he stumbles around the corner of the garden shed into the glare from a spotlight mounted on the back end of the garage. Paula gets down on her hands and knees and has a look.

"Jeez, Ellie was right. What is it? Some kind of birth defect?"

"It's called a foreskin. All boys are born with them."

"You're joking."

"Nope."

"Well why don't any of the other guys have them?"

"They're surgically removed when baby boys are born."

"Cut off, you mean?"

"Yes."

"They would do that to a baby boy? Chop off part of his thingie? Why?"

"It says you're supposed to in the Bible."

"So why do you still have yours?"

"My father is a Satan worshipper."

"Really? Neat. What's it for?"

"I have no idea. But watch this."

He pulls it back.

"Oh, wow, underneath it you're just like everyone else."

"Right," Scott says. "It's just an extra flap of skin."

"Can I do it?"

"All you want."

"We'd better get out of the light. Somebody could see us."

"Do you care?" Scott asks.

"Do you?"

Paula gets up off the ground dusting off her hands. Scott takes another pull off the Camel. Paula lowers her face to his. He closes his eyes and pretends that the mouth sucking the smoke out of him is Clay's mouth and the hand greedily stroking him is Clay's hand. He pretends that he and Clay are alone together and Clay has just promised to let him do anything he wants.

* * *

Scott stares disconsolately at his report card. Straight A's again. Where did he go wrong? Why can't he make himself take things more seriously; set some goals and concentrate on achieving them? What does he have to do? Just one B, honestly earned. That's all he asks. Just one would be enough to prove that he's human like everybody else. Still, though it's too late to keep his teachers from knowing the truth, there's no reason to inflict this indignity on Dad. Because Dad, for all his benign neglect, somehow always remembers when report cards come out and insists on seeing Scott's, not that he's ever expressed an opinion about what he reads there. Scott grabs the special eraser he found in the office supply store downtown and rubs a corner of it carefully against the pasteboard. An extremely tricky thing, this, to rub hard enough to obliterate the ink mark without leaving a telltale abrasion on the surface of the card.

But he goes about his business with the concentration and precision of a member of the French Resistance forging identity papers as if someone's life depends on the undisputable authenticity of this document, and forty five minutes later he's got something much more to his liking. Thee C minuses—English, Math, and History; two D's—Science and Health; and the *piece de resistence*, an honest to God F in P.E. It's the worst he's ever done. That's something he'll be proud to place next to Dad's dinner plate this evening. Who knows? He might even get the man's undivided attention. For a moment, at least.

* * *

For Clay's birthday, and also because he's kept his grades above C throughout eighth grade, he's being allowed for the very first time to go camping unaccompanied by his father or brothers. Scott has spent weeks listening with mounting anxiety as Clay plans this expedition. If Clay's going to cut him loose, this could well be the occasion. And as the days pass and Clay says nothing about Scott accompanying him to his chosen site on the banks of a large pond at the southern extreme of his grandparents' farm, Scott grows more and more certain that his worst nightmare is coming true: Clay is finally outgrowing him.

They spend long afternoons in the Horstmanns' garage together inspecting and organizing the equipment Clay will need. Which pup tent should he take? Will one ground cloth be enough, or should he plan on putting down a double thickness on account of the dampness? Which Coleman stove is the easiest to operate? Which lantern the most reliable? And never once during all these hours does Clay allude, even in the most oblique of fashions, to any role Scott may play in the adventure.

Night after night Scott lies awake staring across the yard at Clay's dark window and praying for a miracle. But his neo-Trotskyite father has raised him in the certainty that there is no God, and that means, of course, that no miracle can be expected. Nothing can be done. Disaster has already struck. Clay has become a man, and Scott's not certain he ever will.

* * *

"What do you mean, you're not ready to leave?"

Scott stares at Clay, paralyzed.

"Scott, what the hell is going on? Don't you want to go camping with me?"

"I thought you wanted to go by yourself," he finally manages to stammer.

"Where the hell did you get that idea?"

Scott shrugs.

"Dammit, Scott," Clay snarls, grabbing him by the shoulders and shaking him like a rag doll. "What is wrong with you? We swore a sacred oath, remember? We said we were blood brothers and we'd be together forever. Didn't that mean anything to you? I can't believe you thought I'd go off by myself and leave you behind. Don't you know I wouldn't do that for a single day, much less a whole weekend? I just can't fucking believe this."

"I'm sorry," Scott croaks, staring into the truly terrifying blaze of Clay's cat green eyes. This is exactly the way he's always wanted Clay to talk to him. This is the way he's always wanted to be held, just this tight, just this close. It's like those dreams he's always having. But this is real; the heat of Clay's body enveloping him, Clay's scent filling his nostrils. He could die right this minute because he's already gone to heaven.

"Sorry?" Clay shakes his head, still clutching Scott's shoulders like a drowning man clutching a life preserver. Their heads are so close together that Clay's hair falls across Scott's forehead. "Don't you remember what it was like that afternoon? Sitting in that old hollow tree with the rain pouring down? Remember how I sucked the blood from that cut I made in the palm of your hand? Remember how scared you were when I took the knife out of my pocket, and how I promised you it would only hurt a little bit?"

"Yes." Scott remembers. Like it was yesterday.

"Remember where I cut myself?"

"It wasn't your hand," Scott murmurs.

"I couldn't get you to do it to me. But once I did it to myself, you licked off every drop. It started bleeding again after I got home. Mom wanted to know how I got my shirt bloody like that. 'How did you manage to hurt yourself right there?' 'Course I never told her. But she told Dad about it, and I think he had a pretty good idea what we'd been up to. He told her to forget about it. Boys will be boys, you know?"

Scott nods.

"And remember how I said I'd always protect you and never let anything bad happen? Jesus, it was like being in church or something. It was like saying prayers to each other. Exactly like that. Well look at me. I'm still here, you know? I'm right here just like always. And I never, ever forgot that day or the promises we made. And I always thought you hadn't forgotten, either."

"I didn't forget."

"Then why did you think I would?"

"You're so big now," Scott says, starting to sob. "You're so strong. You're all handsome and grown up. Everybody wants to be friends with you."

"I'm big and strong for you, buddy," Clay says. He lets go of Scott's shoulders. He pulls off his t-shirt and uses it to wipe Scott's face. "Just for you."

* * *

So it's with a feeling of rapturous disbelief that Scott finds himself pounding tent pegs into the rich soil of Clay's grandparents' farm the next afternoon, a Friday afternoon in late May. During that brief eternity in the Horstmanns' garage, with Clay talking to him like it was a scene from some lost Shakespeare play, Scott felt the earth settle back into its accustomed orbit after all that vertiginous wobbling around on its axis. The ground beneath his feet finally stopped its violent shaking. The end of the world had been postponed indefinitely.

While Scott finishes with the tent, Clay fries up catfish he just caught and cleaned. With them he cooks flat yellow hoe cakes made to Scott's recipe, not Mrs. Horstmann's hopelessly soggy hush puppies. The smell of food makes Scott lightheaded. He stares at Clay huddled over the stove, his sturdy looking back turned, the last beams of daylight glinting off his light brown hair, the muscles playing under the marble smooth skin of his shoulders.

* * *

Scott stares at the huge orange moon rising above the line of trees just beyond the far side of the pond. The water caresses his bare skin as he floats on his back on its dark surface. Clay floats silently beside him. They move their arms and legs just enough to stay in one place, and occasionally their fingers brush against each other's as they comb the water. Closer at hand, Scott hears the gentle splashing of water against his body. And those scant feet away, Clay hums a tune Scott should recognize but can't quite.

* * *

"You really should stop smoking, you know," Clay says, reclining on his sleeping bag. "I mean, if I can, you can. It's kid stuff, after all. And we're starting high school next fall."

"I guess you're right," Scott says. He turns his back to Clay, unzips the net flap of the tent and flicks the cigarette into the dewy grass outside. He watches the firefly glow slowly flicker out, then zips the netting back shut and turns to face Clay again. Clay's eyes are closed. Scott wonders if he's dozed off. The warm glow from the lantern washes across Clay's golden skin. Scott drinks in the glorious vision like a thirsty man in the desert who finally reaches an oasis after days of searching in the trackless dunes. Every detail he observes intoxicates him further. The long, curling lashes of Clay's eyes. The lean face that has emerged the last few months from its cocoon of baby fat, with its purposeful cheekbones, square jaw, and dimpled chin. The firm roundness of the chest and shoulder muscles, the strong swell of the arms. The tiny hairs sprouting around the perimeter of the berry dark nipples. The thin fringe running southward from the navel. And the mysterious, intimidating bulge in his perfectly laundered briefs. What Scott wouldn't give to caress these things with more than just his famished eyes.

* * *

Scott sets the tray down on Dad's dresser and moves to the side of the bed.

"*Wachet auf*, oh patriarch and *grand fommage*." He grabs Dad's shoulder for the usual wrestling match. The skin is cold, and his heart starts to race.

"God dammit," he mutters, reaching under the covers for Dad's wrist, which is also quite cold. "Don't you dare."

He searches frantically for a pulse.

"God damn you," he hears himself shout. "Don't you dare do this to me, you bastard."

The girl in the bed stirs.

"What's the matter?" she asks, through a yawn.

"God damn you, you fucker," Scott sobs.

Willcox, Arizona: 1969

By the time Scott gets home from school he's ready to jump out of his skin. All day long he's heard the whispers and muffled snickers trailing him around campus. All day long he's felt people's eyes burning into him. No one spoke to him in the halls. No one sat at his table in the cafeteria at lunch. He's a loner, but he's never been a leper. By midmorning, his teachers were tongue-tied around him, unable to look him in the eye: obviously they knew all about it.

If he could disappear, he would. Just vaporize. Or dig a hole, crawl in, cover himself with dirt and stay there. But if he did, one or the other of his cousins would find him and dig him back up and contrive some new, even worse torture to subject him to. This is just the latest in a long line of humiliations he's suffered at their hands. And he knows they're not through with him yet like he knows the sun rises in the east. Ever since he was sent here to live with Uncle Bob, Dad's younger brother, his cousins have done everything in their power to make him feel like the lowest form of life on this or any other planet. They're relentless. They're ingenious as agents of the Spanish Inquisition, as methodical as the Gestapo, as implacable as the KGB. They afford him no respite. If it's not Andy going after him, it's Ben. If it's not Ben, it's Charlie. Usually it's at least two of them. Sometimes they all team up for something extra special, good Eagle Scouts that they are.

And now this.

* * *

When Dad died, Grandma and Grandpa Bailey insisted that they were too old to take charge of a thirteen year old boy. Dad's older brothers, Wayne and Tyler, had no intention of taking Scott in either. They argued that they'd been embarrassed by Dad's scandalous behavior for long enough and didn't want a living reminder of it under their roofs. That left Uncle Bob, who was a Baptist preacher and couldn't, on general principle, refuse to offer a home to his or-phaned nephew. At least he couldn't by the time Grandpa and Grandma and his older brothers got through with him. That's how Scott ended up in this hellhole.

He realized within a few days of his arrival in Willcox that Uncle Bob is the white sheep of the family. He's the photographic negative of Dad, identical yet opposite. He's responsible and thrifty. His eyes are bright and his skin is clear and taut and he never skips a day, much less a week, shaving. He never partakes of alcohol or tobacco, so he never smells of those substances. He's up at the crack of dawn every day without resort to an alarm clock. He's faithful to Aunt Mollie, a tall, pale woman who gives the impression that the reason she never smiles is not that she's unhappy but simply that she doesn't know how. Uncle Bob is a kindly and affectionate—but strict—father. He's revered all over the county, being regularly called on to pronounce invocations and/or benedictions at city council, board of supervisors, board of education and P.T.A. meetings, at junior and senior high school graduations, at the annual county rodeo, and a myriad of athletic events. He officiates at funerals for unchurched persons of all descriptions. He performs weddings for anyone with a license and fifteen dollars, even when the groom is Mexican and the bride isn't but is pregnant and no other clergyman in town will have anything to do with them. He drives drunks to A.A. meetings, sits with them, buys them coffee afterward, drives them home to their shabby apartments or run down trailers. He helps unwed mothers find suitable adoptive parents for their babies. He visits young men in the county jail and phones reports to their mothers out of state. He has a weekly program on the local radio station which consists of his reading scriptures and then praying for listeners who have mailed in cards and letters describing an amazing variety of afflictions and predicaments. His good works are the subject of constant discussion all over town. In the barber shops and beauty parlors and greasy spoons and hardware stores people call him a saint. Maybe he is, but Scott can't help feeling in his heart of hearts that he's too good to be true.

Scott misses the freedom he had back in the old days with Dad. He misses their bizarre comradeship, the scrapes Dad got into and Scott got him back out of. He misses living with someone fluent in the scatology of every major European language and generous with the knowledge. He misses having someone to speak the language of his long dead mother with. He misses living with someone who can beat him at Scrabble, even dead drunk and without really trying. Above all, he misses the bullet proof security he believes can only come from having someone to take care of.

It makes Scott uneasy somehow to have his clothing laundered for him, never to have to prepare a meal or clean up afterward, never to have to worry about the household bills being paid or how he'll manage to buy next week's groceries. It all goes against his grain. It's like being in prison or an insane asylum. It's like being an animal in a zoo.

* * *

Scott sits in his bedroom listening to the rock and roll station from Oklahoma City and doing his trigonometry homework. He tries to ignore the angry voices coming from Cousin Andy's room down the hall. Raised voices are all but unheard of in this house. Uncle Bob and Aunt Mollie don't argue with each other or anyone else and won't allow other members of the household to do so in their hearing. So the hubbub he hears is extraordinary, the surest possible sign of the gravity of his predicament. He tries to lose himself in the tangle of sine and cosine and tangent and numbers of degrees and squiggly, alien looking symbols the textbook authors have craftily conspired to befuddle him with—to no avail. The problems are discouragingly simple. They engage less than half his brain. They provide no respite.

Ever since the phone call from Principal Harrison came during dinner, Scott has known something's about to happen. Uncle Bob didn't come back to the table after hanging up but left the house without a word to anyone. He was gone for several hours. Scott heard his car pull into the driveway no more than ten minutes ago, listened in spite of himself to the slamming of car and house doors and the thunder of Uncle Bob's footsteps rushing down the hall to Andy's room.

Scott prints out his work neatly on the white, lined paper and hums along as the Mamas and Papas sing about California and he doesn't pay attention as the angry voices down the hall rise to a crescendo and a sudden, brief silence falls and a moment later a door slams and heavy, portentous footsteps advance inexorably in his direction. And when the door to his room swings open and then slams shut again, he doesn't raise his eyes from the textbook, doesn't stop humming.

"Scott," Uncle Bob's voice throbs with more emotion than even during the crucial moments of a Sunday sermon.

"Just a sec," Scott says, finishing up the problem. "There. All done. What's up?"

"I think you know what's up."

"Oh?"

"Scott, turn around and look at me."

Scott turns. Uncle Bob's eyes are blazing. A vein at his right temple is pulsing vigorously. His usually perfectly combed hair is just sufficiently disarrayed for it to be noticeable. He reminds Scott more of Dad in this moment than he ever has before. Scott almost expects to see a vodka bottle swinging from a limp fingered hand at his side.

"How could you do such a filthy, disgusting thing?" Uncle Bob demands.

"How could I...?" Scott gasps, realizing he's been stupid to think that Cousin Andy would tell the truth. Or anyone else would, either. Especially Gary. Of course Gary would have lied. But the hunting knife had been real. Three football players and the smallest of them had outweighed him by at least fifty pounds. And that knife. If that's not rape, what is?

"I've seen the pictures Principal Harrison confiscated from your cousin. I can't believe you'd do such unspeakable things. I can hardly comprehend how any human being could be capable of such...and that poor Gary Hodges. Joey Gillespie was always a thug, but Gary Hodges. How did you ever trap him into such a thing?"

* * *

January nights are cold in the desert. Scott pulls the denim jacket more tightly around him and stares at the house. It's been nearly an hour since the last light went out: the one in Cousin Andy's room. At his feet are heaped the few things he was able to carry out of the house in the five minutes Uncle Bob gave him to gather them up.

He wonders if, were he to show up at the front door first thing tomorrow, Uncle Bob would really make good on his threat to have him taken to juvenile detention. He can't quite believe the man would go that far. It's almost worth risking it. But for what? To eventually resume his residence in that cell of a room? To go back to school and face everyone he's learned to despise so thoroughly? He never wanted to live in that house with those people. He's been counting the days until high school graduation, still three semesters away, when he can leave this town and everyone in it behind. Come to think of it, hasn't Andy done him a favor, springing him from this asylum? Stupid old Andy, who's probably lying awake thinking he's really cooked Scott's goose. Ha.

He exhales noisily, watching the condensation from his breath form a cloud in front of his face. It's probably safe by now. Though Andy doesn't realize it he's about to do Scott one last favor.

Scott sneaks along the fringe of the mesquite thicket until he's behind the garage and out of sight of the house. He covers the fifteen yards of open ground to the side door in seconds. He blesses the pig-headed innocence that keeps people in this town from locking up anything at night and slips into the rickety structure. He finds the flashlight hanging on its hook. He switches it on, careful to keep its glare from reaching the side window. From the jumble of his cousins' scouting paraphernalia he pulls free a backpack, a sleeping bag, two ground cloths, and a pup tent. From behind the loose board he's not supposed to know about he takes the coffee can. His three Eagle Scout cousins are enterprising young men. They've all but cornered the market on marijuana at Willcox High. Scott counts out a little over two hundred dollars in fives, tens, and twenties. He was expecting to find more than that and is bitterly disappointed. He leaves nothing but loose change rattling forlornly in the bottom of the can and slips it back into place.

"*Hasta la vista,* motherfuckers," he mutters as he slips back outside. "*Au revoir. Auf wiedersehen.* Eat shit and die and rot in hell forever."

* * *

Willcox has one all night gas station. Scott locks himself into the men's room and takes stock. One black eye. A badly split and swollen lip. Various other bruises. An inch long gash over his left eyebrow. Pretty nasty. He wets a paper towel under the tap and gingerly sponges himself clean. Once the dried blood is cleaned away he looks better. But not much. He briefly considers spreading out his sleeping bag and camping out on the washroom floor. It's relatively warm. There's a toilet.

But the station attendant could come in at any time and find him. Everybody in town knows who he is. He can imagine the phone call to Uncle Bob, who will, to avoid any more embarrassment, have to come and get him and at least pretend to take him home. In the process, he'll lose the stuff he took from the garage and perhaps get beaten some more. It's not worth it just to have shelter for one night.

He hoists the heavy backpack crammed with what's left of his life, the sleeping back strapped on underneath. He lets himself out of the tiny room. The cold attacks him again but he ignores it as best he can. Twenty minutes later, he's camped out underneath a freeway overpass, ready to hitch a ride west as soon as it's daylight.

Venice, California: 1969

Bone weary, sweat soaked, wreathed in restaurant kitchen fumes, Scott trudges homeward. It is well after midnight. Dozing panhandlers lie oblivious as he passes. Prostitutes look through him as if he's invisible. He's as habituated to these alleyways as the stray cats slinking among the dumpsters. A lone siren screeches distantly, perhaps in response to the clanging of a burglar alarm, perhaps merely a coincidence: in this neighborhood ringing alarms are nearly as ubiquitous as the white noise, almost but never completely subliminal, of the surf hissing onto the sand yards away. It's Venice, not Venus, he reminds himself repeatedly each day: just California, not the alien planet it appears.

The VW van full of hippies who pulled over for him outside Willcox that freezing dawn deposited him here. In his whole life he'd never seen the ocean. Palm trees were on postcards or in the movies. But over the weeks and months since his first glimpse of it, he's begun to feel as if its presence out there is a replacement somehow for another, earlier presence he's lost touch with. The solicitude, perhaps, of his long dead mother; the protective vigilance he'd have enjoyed throughout his abbreviated boyhood if his father hadn't been a philandering drunk; a stand-in for the God he's pretty certain doesn't exist, despite, or perhaps because of, the turbulent, unceasing religious clamor of his relatives.

Now, this minute, the sea reaches out to him as he stumbles home, soaking his thin, grimy t-shirt with its clammy exhalations. The resulting shivers remind him that he's alive.

On that trek across the desert the hippies had shared their food and water. They'd offered more than that, but Scott, with his newly developed terror of intoxication in any form, declined. Their friends, they had assured him, would welcome him if he needed a place to crash. And so it proved. He'd assumed this meant a temporary refuge, but by the time just a few days later when the van roared away northward, it was clear that no one in residence had any idea who the place actually belonged to, or what, if any, arrangements there were about rent. Or utilities. They were all squatters, and if they could squat there seemed to be no reason Scott couldn't squat too.

The first three floors of the building contain a warren of small apartments. The fourth floor is a giant loft, organized according to some anarcho-communal ethos that doesn't recognize even the most basic of property rights. If Scott had any valuables, he'd never dream of leaving them unattended while at work. Not even clothing, ragged as his is, is sacrosanct. Any food must be consumed off the premises unless he's willing to share with any and all comers. He's profoundly uncool about this. His defense is that, a) he's constantly starving, and b) he's the only one in the place who has a job. He's bourgeois, not to mention desperate, enough to believe that those who actually work deserve to fill their bellies first.

Tonight, his bed—a mattress on the floor, more accurately—is occupied. Tanya, a girl from New York. She might be fifteen; she might be twenty-seven. It's impossible to tell, and she gives no clues. The most intimate thing he knows about her is that she doesn't shave her legs or armpits, believing such hygienic efforts to be merely another way of giving in to the male chauvinists—and worse, her mother. He suspects her of having the clap, and this isn't the most objectionable thing about her. He's about to slip away in search of alternate accommodations when someone turns off the stereo, or more likely merely kicks the plug out of the wall by accident, and in the sudden silence he hears her snoring like a chainsaw and he knows he can lie down next to her without having to defend his virtue.

* * *

Tanya's real name is Barbara. She's from New York. She describes her parents as, "like, these, you know, really filthy rich Jews," who want her to go to a good university, marry a doctor or lawyer, and provide them with grandchildren who will repeat the cycle. She would rather live in filth, take any and all drugs she can get her hands on, and fuck anything that moves than submit to such atrocities. Whatever she ingested last night still has her comatose in the morning. But her breathing is steady and her color is good. An expert at evaluating the vital signs of the chemically impaired, Scott judges that she's in no particular danger, except perhaps of an existential variety, and he rolls out of bed and leaves her there unsupervised with a reasonably clear conscience.

As on most mornings, there is no hot water in what passes for a bathroom. He drags a snoring girl who could be Tanya's twin out of the tub and subjects himself to the briefest of showers. There's no one to complain to about the state of the plumbing, but Scott suspects that even if there were his loft mates wouldn't bother. They subscribe to the belief that cleanliness is inexcusably middle class. It's easy to feel this way, he senses, when you have a choice in the matter. Like Tanya and unlike Scott, they all have somewhere else to go whenever they get hungry enough or just tired of the squalor.

He finds an almost clean t-shirt, and yesterday's jeans aren't too disreputable but he really has to do laundry later. Tanya's still snoring—drooling now, too—when he's ready to leave for the day. On his way down the stairs he runs into the boy from the third floor coming up. His heart stops beating and he forgets to breathe. But it's just for a moment.

* * *

On his way to the bus stop he ducks into the kosher bakery and picks up two bagels, a small tub of cream cheese and a pint carton of orange juice. He's a regular, and as always Mrs. Schoenbaum undercharges him. Some days she shorts herself a nickel, sometimes a dime. The first time she did this he corrected her, but the steely look she gave him as she insisted he was confused convinced him she knows exactly what she's doing. She looks old enough to have helped Moses bring the stone tablets down from Sinai, but she's as sharp as a stiletto. He wishes her good day and he's back out the door just in time to see his bus halfway up the block. God knows how the place manages to stay open in a neighborhood like this, but he's never the only customer in there.

It's not that far up to Santa Monica, but traffic always moves at a crawl. It can take well over an hour to get to the ed. center where he's studying for his GED. He ignores the ranting crazy in the seat just behind the driver and eats his bagels and stares out the tinted windows. The streets are teeming with young people just like him engaged in their various endeavors: panhandling, picking pockets, shoplifting, small time house breaking, half assed drug dealing, casual prostitution. "All you need is love" and "give peace a chance" are the mantras, but the ethos on the street is decidedly less than utopian to Scott's thinking. Come the revolution, how will they all survive with no bourgeoisie left to leech off of? And though there's a young girl selling flowers on every steet corner, and "have a nice day" is the perennial greeting out there, it's hardly the summer festival it appears. Every night some unfortunate girl is raped in an alleyway, and last week a kid generally regarded as homosexual was beaten within an inch of his life while several dozen spectators watched. A few of them even cheered. So much for the Age of Aquarius.

* * *

"Scott, let's talk about your *Billy Budd* essay," Mrs. Jankel suggests, pulling a chair up next to his desk.

"Sure," Scott says, mustering a smile. "How did I do?"

"Exceptionally, as always," she says. "The first couple of papers you wrote for me, I had my doubts."

He nods. He remembers. She thought he was getting unauthorized help with his assignments.

"The maturity of thought evidenced by your compositions surprises me now and then, but you've made a believer of me. Now you're going to be finishing your studies here soon, and I want to talk to you about your plans."

"I have no plans."

"I know, I know. We've been through all that. But I have to tell you that I think you're making a mistake not to at least try a couple of community college classes. Right this minute you're sitting on the campus of one of the finest community colleges in the nation, and it just breaks my heart to think that a student of your abilities would pass up an opportunity like that."

"Money makes the world go 'round, Mrs. J."

"I know, Scott, but it's not an insurmountable obstacle. I know your circumstances are difficult, but try to forget that. I'd love to see you in one of my college composition classes here next fall."

"What will be, will be," he says.

"Just as long as you don't sit around waiting for it to fall into your lap, young man."

Mrs. Jankel is the kind of idealistic teacher they make movies about every now and then, as opposed to the kind you almost always encounter in real life. She believes that nothing can stop the truly determined student; that anything is possible with God given intelligence and some perseverance. In the decades she's worked in this place she must have heard literally thousands of hard luck stories, yet her optimism never seems to waver. He wishes he could share her passionate faith. But as he sees it his options are limited. He knows exactly how much Dad's life was insured for and has a pretty good idea how much the house brought in when they sold it. He knows the provisions of Dad's will. And yet from what he can tell not a cent has been spent providing for him. If he were twenty-one, he'd get an attorney and sue. But it's highly unlikely that a sixteen year old could get decent representation for ready money, much less on contingency. And once his relatives have been served with papers, they'll know where he is. There will be nothing to stop them from having him institutional-ized for having Joey Gillespie's cock up his ass and Gary Hodges' cock in his mouth, however involuntarily. He's researched it at the public library: the best he could hope for is that he might be released when he's twenty-one: that magic number again. So the only money he has is what he makes at the restaurant bus-sing tables. And even living rent free, he doesn't see how he can afford college. Even community college part time. Mrs. Jankel has talked to him before about financial aid, but his circumstances make it pretty much impossible to apply. For now, more school after his GED is a pipe dream.

* * *

Scott has decided that the human race spoils everything. On his way back south on the nearly empty bus, he stares out the windows at palm trees, sun washed streets, and an occasional glimpse of the beach, and it's easy to think of the place as paradise. But the run down buildings and garbage clotted gutters ruin the view. What is it about people? They build things only to turn away and let them rot. It is more than just distraction or laziness. It almost seems like fate: a cycle universal, unending, perhaps even inescapable. Take Dad: handsome, intelligent, highly educated. The way he started his career he might have ended up a university dean or even vice president. Then he drank and fucked it away. He never actually got tenure and he was dead before his fiftieth birthday. Or Scott's mother. What he remembers about her and what he's been told: she was a charming, pretty young woman who spoke six languages, painted water col-ors, and played the piano divinely. She had a handsome, successful husband and an adorable toddler son. What inscrutable force compelled her to say no to that? What does that same force, invisible beyond sunsets and tides, have in store for him? Why should he believe that he alone of his family can escape it?

* * *

He sneaks into the laundromat through the back way off the alley, avoid-ing the gang of flower children on the sidewalk who think of the place as a boundless source of "spare change". He sorts his meager wardrobe into three machines: whites in one, colors in a second, jeans in the third. He buys deter-gent from a vending machine, furious at the cost. At the supermarket in the next block he could buy ten times as much for the price, but where could he stash a package that large where it wouldn't be appropriated "for the people"?

He starts the machines and sits down with his reading for Mrs. Jankel next week. *The Rise of Silas Lapham*, by William Dean Howells. He remembers the leather bound copy on the shelf in Dad's study, between *Maggie, a Girl of the Streets*, and *News From Nowhere*. He was never able to decipher Dad's shelving system.

Mrs. Jankel thinks he should major in literature.

The odor of marijuana seeps into the laundromat through the open front door, mingling surrealistically with detergent smells and bleach fumes. Somebody out front is playing "The House of the Rising Sun" on an out of tune guitar—very inexpertly. Two girls are taking turns reading each other's Tarot. The perennial burglar alarm clangs away farther down the street and now and then squealing tires or a honking horn testify to drivers losing their patience. He's aroused from the novel by a barely perceptible increase in the volume of murmuring coming into the steamy room from outside, or maybe it's no more than a heightened sense of expectancy among the crew there: the guitar player ceases his hypnotic repetitions, a couple of the girls smooth their hair, several people rise to their feet.

Scott stares out the window, curious, as the boy from the third floor saunters past, the crowds parting for him and the two girls who flank him like a cross between groupies and bodyguards. He smiles beatifically, acknowledging them all like a priest of some obscure sect. A few snatches of greeting reach Scott inside. Then he's gone, and everything settles back into place and the guitar player resumes—it's "Michael Row Your Boat Ashore" now—and Scott goes back to his book.

* * *

In *The Great Gatsby*, one character observes that there can be advantages to staying sober when you're surrounded by people who indulge: it makes it easier to get away with indiscretions. The only indiscretions Scott concerns himself with these days have to do with hanging on to his stuff rather than surrendering it to "the people", but the principle itself turns out to be sound. His loft mates' paranoia about their stashes notwithstanding, they're hopeless at serious concealment, whereas he's developed a level of expertise that probably qualifies him to join the CIA, as long as the item he's hiding is small enough. He gives one sharp tug, the floorboard shifts, and there, just where he left it, is a small box of saltines. He stuffs it into his book bag alongside the jar of supermarket brand peanut butter he's always packing and replaces the board. In two shakes he's outside, turning his back on the building and heading down the beach. Mid afternoon on a weekday in summer: the beach is crowded. Joggers, skaters, surfers, sun worshippers everywhere you look. Small children build sand castles, doting parents photograph their handiwork. It's Venice Beach at its most photogenic, most iconic, most reminiscent of all those songs, movies, television shows. It's the pot of gold at the end of the rainbow, the American Dream come to life. It's all you ever dreamed of. At least until the sun goes down and it becomes downright dangerous. The local gypsies have their hands full generally making nuisances of themselves and he heads for the fringes of their territory. There are gypsies here, too, but not his gypsies. It's easier to ignore them if you don't live with them, he's found.

His math teacher at the ed. center is Mr. Faust. His first week there, he and Mr. Faust struck a deal—no joke, though Scott loves the irony. Confident in his ability to pass the math section of the GED without help, he finagled Mr. Faust into issuing him a trig text from the community college tutoring center which shares their facility. That's what Mr. Faust is coaching him through: trigonometry. Mr. Faust is all too obviously burnt out with tutoring boneheads on simple arithmetic: he jumped at the offer. Scott's part of the bargain is that he has to pass the GED on his first attempt and give Mr. Faust a glowing evaluation form. There have apparently been problems with Mr. Faust's student evaluations in the past. Scott suspects these have something to do with the man's general creepiness. It's all too easy to imagine him as a child molester or ax murderer. Whatever else he may be, though, he's a savant at math. Scott's always been good at math without particularly enjoying it, but Mr. Faust is obsessed. This, it turns out, makes him the perfect tutor for Scott, who's considering moving on to calculus. Mrs. Jankel will cut him loose the minute he finishes his GED. That's the rule and that's the kind of by the book person she is. But he just bets that Mr. Faust will let him hang around for more instruction, if indeed Mr. Faust actually realizes it when Scott receives his certificate.

He finds a spot on the sand that's relatively quiet and he gets out the trig book and his picnic, and the world starts to look a little less oppressive. There are normal kids here doing normal teenage things. Girls flirt with boys and boys pretend to be too cool to notice. The weightlifters strut and sweat in their enclosure, but Scott doesn't watch them too closely, nor the men sitting in the bleachers observing them. Those guys are as conspicuous as fireworks at midnight. It may be fine for them, but Scott has to live here and he assumes that whenever he's in the open like this someone is watching. His loft mates may go around chanting "all you need is love", but they really only mean their own specific kind of love. He is certain they don't consider any other variety groovy at all.

They probably wouldn't consider trigonometry groovy, either. In the unlikely event that he encounters one of his loft mates out here, he plans to flash the book: he expects it will have the same effect as flashing a crucifix at a vampire.

* * *

"Did you see her?" Sheila the hostess demands, stalking up to the Hobart where Scott's unloading a bus tub. The waiters here at *Chez Sammie* are all college boys with names like Skip and Bart, who race around in their little Triumphs and M.G.'s and fling the hair out of their eyes with artful tosses of their heads. They wait tables dressed in Sammie's interpretation of buccaneer getup. Their name tags proclaim their fake French appellations. Sammie believes this is a crucial detail, obsessed as he is with maintaining a Polynesian atmosphere. Even lowly busboy Scott has a fake French name: his tag reads "Marcel". Only Sheila escapes the indignity of being addressed as Alphonse or Henri. But she pays for this in spades. Her sarong and daringly tailored halter top make her look like a refugee from a Dorothy Lamour movie. The place is a monument to kitsch, and by all rights people should stay away in droves. But for some obscure reason it all works. When Scott's loft mates chant "death to Amerika" it's this place they dream of seeing in flames, whether they realize it or not.

"See who?" he asks, slipping half a slice of prime rib into the baggie he keeps in his apron to receive such treasures. He's astonished that the waiter didn't grab it.

"Hollie Tepper," Sheila says.

"Who?"

"Hollie Tepper. The actress. You know, *Honeymoon for Three*."

Scott shrugs. Celebrity sightings aren't terribly unusual at *Chez Sammie*. The waiters are pretty blasé about famous diners, or at least pretend to be. But not Sheila, who's a connoisseur.

"Don't tell me you didn't see *Honeymoon for Three*. Everybody saw *Honeymoon for Three*."

"Sorry," Scott says. "I must have been out of the country."

"It is just the best film ever. If it ever comes around again, you've got to go."

"Promise you'll remind me."

"I will, Scottie, I will. See, she's just this ordinary girl, you know? And she impersonates a mime so she can marry this mysterious millionaire. But then she accidentally falls in love with his valet. Who's just soooooo cute. Oh, my God, Scottie. Anyway, on the night before her wedding to the millionaire, the valet convinces her to elope with him. And that's when the surprise twist comes in."

"The cute valet turns out to be the actual millionaire, and the guy pretending to be the millionaire all along turns out to be the valet."

"You liar," Sheila pouts. "You did see it."

"No," Scott says. "It's just, if that film was going to have a surprise ending, that's the only possible surprise ending there could be."

"You think?" Sheila considers this.

"Absolutely."

"Damn," she says, "I've gone and spoiled it for you. If you ever do get to see it, I mean."

"Actually, I think the screenwriter and director probably beat you to it."

"Ha, ha. You're such a genius, Scottie. I swear to God. I bet you're only working here to get ideas for your own screenplay. Admit it."

"Then it won't be a surprise."

"I know!" Sheila says, slapping her forehead, "Hollie Tepper can play me."

Sheila has indicated to Scott on more than one occasion that she'd be thrilled if he asked her out. She thinks she's just the girl to help him get over the girl she's sure must have broken his heart. She nurses bizarre images of him sitting on Venice Beach in the moonlight writing poetry inspired by the loss of that unworthy young woman and has often advised him that the only way to mend a broken heart is to "get right back on the bicycle". There is no girl, of course, and Scott does nothing to encourage Sheila's fantasies except deny their veracity, which serves only to strengthen her conviction.

"And you know what," she says, lowering her voice to keep from being overheard, though a rivet gun wouldn't be especially conspicuous in the chaos of this kitchen, "it's not the first time she's dined here."

"Really?"

"No. She remembered me from before. Scottie, she knew my name. Can you believe it?"

"It's on your name tag."

"Exactly. She said to me, 'Sheila, I remember that cute name tag of yours'."

"So which one is she?"

"The pretty blond one in the mini-granny dress."

"Mini-granny dress?" Scott is baffled.

"You know, like a granny dress, only really short."

"Oh."

"At Jean-Pierre's table."

Scott didn't notice the girl or the mini-granny dress. He was preoccupied. Jean-Pierre's real name is Marty. He has luxuriant chestnut curls and a nose that's as perfect as a Beverly Hills plastic surgeon could make it. Sometimes working here, Scott feels like a Jehovah's Witness kid on Halloween.

"She's really pretty," Sheila says, happily repeating herself. "And so nice. You can just tell that about her. The next time she comes in I'm going to give her one of my short stories to read."

"She can read?"

"She's an actress. How else would she learn her lines?"

"I thought you said she played a mime."

"Her character was impersonating a mime."

"Oh, right. Completely different."

* * *

As far as Scott is concerned *Chez Sammie* is a pretty good place to work. The menu prices are fairly steep, and that and the unlikely cachet of the place keeps tips healthy. Sammie himself is adamant that hostesses and bussers share generously in these funds, so Scott has no complaints about his pay. The hostesses are generic California girls, and Scott's completely indifferent to them. What Sammie has an eye for is great looking waiters, and Scott keenly appreciates this. If you have to work for a living, why not work in the company of hot looking guys? But what really clinches it for Scott is the food. Truth to tell, it's no better than average: the place survives on its location and bizarrely picturesque atmosphere and Sammie's eccentric charisma. The attraction for Scott is his access to it. Meat and seafood he has to pay for, except what he can salvage from diners' leavings. But the rest, that bounty he sometimes even dreams about, is all free for the taking. He can have one bowl of soup per shift. But he's permitted unlimited trips to the salad bar, unlimited helpings of the rice pilaf, unlimited baked potatoes dressed as elaborately as can be imagined.

Tonight for his mid shift break he's pulled two whoppers out of the warming drawer next to the waiters' station. He's piled them high with fresh broccoli florets and garlic seasoned croutons, doused them with the house's signature mushroom and burgundy sauce, and garnished them with romaine and grated cheddar. He heads out to the alley exit and perches on an overturned ten gallon plastic bucket. For this few minutes he begrudges no affluent diner inside his chateaubriand or crabmeat stuffed filet of sole. This is as sumptuous a feast as he needs, and there's still that healthy chunk of prime rib in his apron pocket—he's saving that for his walk home. All in all, not a bad night.

The click of a cigarette lighter behind him distracts him from his repast. He turns to see which of the waiters has sneaked out for a quick smoke. He's kind of hoping it's Michel, aka Brandon, his current crush, but it's not a waiter at all. It's the boy who lives on the third floor, big as life. Silhouetted in the doorway he looks to Scott like some heavenly manifestation.

"I'm sorry, sir," Scott mutters. "Restaurant guests aren't allowed out here."

"Really," the boy says, voice soft but strangely harsh. "Well, you don't need to worry about it, because I'm hardly a guest. I'm just a working guy like you."

"Seriously, sir."

"I won't get you in trouble. Promise."

Scott's dubious. But the guy's so gorgeous that being yelled at by Sammie seems a small enough price to pay for a few moments this close to him.

"Say," the boy says, looking at him more closely, "don't I know you?"

"I don't think so."

"Yeah," the boy nods, "yeah. Sure I do. You live upstairs from me. With all the hippies."

"Guilty as charged," Scott croaks.

"I'm Zane," the boy says, offering Scott his hand.

"I'm Scott."

West Hollywood: 1970

Atlas and Tigger are Zane's cats, but they always sleep in Scott's bed. Zane blames this on their natural feline perversity, but Scott doesn't see it as perverse in the least. To his thinking, they're consummate pragmatists, which is as it should be. After all, he's the one who feeds them morning and night, who keeps their litter box immaculate, who gives them saucers of cream at least once a day, who brings them scraps of chateaubriand and poached salmon from the restaurant. He's the one whose regularity of schedule and routine aligns with their disdain for unpredictability. Zane's adventures frequently entail nights away from home. He's regularly gone for entire weekends, and once or twice has even disappeared for a week at a stretch. But Scott is always here. You could set a clock by his arrivals and departures, and his absences never stretch to more than the eight hours of his school day. The cats know they can depend on him. And if anyone living under this roof is perverse, Scott thinks, it can only be Zane.

Atlas is a tortoise shell, the largest domestic cat Scott has ever encountered. He's slow moving, dignified, fastidious. He has an uncanny knack for making himself appear not to be present. He doesn't disappear; rather, he becomes so still that he seems to have transformed himself into an inanimate object. He can remain in this state for hours, then open an eye slowly, stretch with what seems to be infinite patience, get up, move halfway across the room or simply change position, and resume the suspension of his animation. Tigger is a flashy looking golden tabby; a young, rackety cat with apparently no class consciousness at all. He treats Atlas with an inappropriate lack of respect. He is as lithe and agile as a cheetah and as implacable as a tiger. His conviction that the sole purpose of his life is to gain the attention of any and all of his fellow creatures is apparent in everything he does. Atlas and Tigger are the yin to each other's yang, and Scott can't imagine one without the other. Until he and Zane moved in together, Scott had no experience of this species beyond having seen them slink around in bushes and hiss at dogs. Now the depth of his fascination astonishes him. He is quite certain that they consider him their property, rather than vice versa.

This morning, as always, he is awakened by the purring of Atlas, curled on the pillow next to his. He's more reliable by far than an alarm clock. Scott does wish, however, that he could teach Atlas the difference between school days and days when he doesn't actually have to get up this early. Under the bed, Tigger is in the process of killing something which will probably prove to be one of Zane's socks: Scott's are all accounted for. Tigger has made the space under the bed his own special territory. The fact that Atlas can't comfortably follow him there is, Scott understands, its chief attraction. He pulls the covers up over his head and waits. It's just a few seconds until Atlas bats his head twice with a massive forepaw, the signal that he'd better get himself moving.

The door to Zane's bedroom is closed. In the bathroom Scott finds that Zane's towels are damp: he must have come home sometime during the night. Scott has finally trained himself to sleep through Zane's returns home in the wee hours. When he goes into the kitchen to fix the cats' breakfast, and incidentally his own, he'll find an unfamiliar Rolex on the counter. An unusually successful outing, particularly for a Tuesday night. If Zane is home for dinner, Scott will hear all about it.

*　*　*

Zane and Scott live on a narrow street east of Doheny and north of Santa Monica Boulevard. The bungalows sit almost on top of each other, their front yards the size of postage stamps. They share a Moorish Revival place that looks like the Alhambra scaled down for a tribe of Lilliputians. It's furnished in a style Zane describes as "high middle junk shop". Scott's bedroom is so small that the double bed takes up nearly all the available floor space. There's insufficient clearance to open the closet door, so Scott took it off its hinges and stored it in the garage. According to Zane, the house is owned by a friend of his who lives in unimaginable splendor in Palm Springs but is too attached to the place to sell it and too paranoid to rent it out: they're doing him a favor living in it rent free and keeping it occupied. Scott was dubious when Zane first suggested they move in here. He wasn't sure he wanted Zane for a roommate, and the deal sounded too good to be true. He was sure there had to be a catch. Even that early in their friendship he sensed that Zane's relationship with the truth was a love/hate one. Subsequent events have confirmed that suspicion, but not to an extent that Scott can't live with. It's not that Zane actually lies. What he does is explain, and his explanations, while accurate for the most part, often omit some minor detail which eventually turns out to be the crucial one. Most important, Scott hasn't yet had the experience of being misled about anything of material importance to himself. That seems to be an indication of Zane's ethical system.

Then, too, in those very early interactions with him, Scott hadn't yet realized that Zane's definition of the word "friend" was so damned elastic, not to mention all encompassing. To Scott, a friend is someone you have things in common with, or whose company you enjoy, or who you just might one day find yourself falling in love with under the right circumstances. For Zane, a friend might be any of those things but is more likely to be anyone who has ever done him a favor in the past or might conceivably do so at some point in the future. At first, Scott thought that Zane had an amazing collection of friends. What he has, actually, is an amazing collection of kindnesses received and/or anticipated.

* * *

It's a long bus ride all the way out to Santa Monica. Scott uses the time to reread a chapter in his humanities text and review his psychology notes. Well into his second semester, he still thinks of college as a miracle. The few times he mentioned setting up a repayment plan Zane told him not to be stupid, so he hasn't said anything about it in a long time. But he still feels as if he's taking advantage, and he doesn't like it.

He was sitting out on the beach one afternoon a couple of days after meeting Zane when it happened. He was reading the college catalogue Mrs. Jankel had insisted on giving him that morning as he left the ed. center because despite his best intentions he hadn't tossed it into the nearest trash receptacle before catching his bus. Zane sauntered up and sat down next to him in the sand. The two girls stood off to one side, ostentatiously yet unconvincingly pantomiming disinterest.

"What's that you're reading?"

Scott handed the book to him.

"College, huh? When do you start?"

"Won't be any time soon," Scott said. "Don't have the money."

He stared out at a couple of surfers while Zane leafed though the book—randomly, Scott assumed.

"Girls, come here."

They shuffled over.

"What is it, Zane?"

"Scott needs money for college," Zane said. "Who's holding the roll today?"

"Sybil is," the shorter of the girls said.

"We're going to give him tuition for the year. And there will be books, too."

Scott watched fascinated as Sybil reached into a fold of her granny dress, pulled out a roll of bills and began peeling them off.

"And what are those things called?" Zane asked. "Those other things?"

"Incidentals?" the girl who was not Sybil suggested.

"That's right," Zane nodded. "Incidentals. Don't forget the incidentals."

Sybil nodded, peeling off even more bills.

"Hey," Scott protested, thinking that the joke was going on too long, "I can't take her money."

"It's not her money," Not Sybil said.

"Whose is it?" Scott asked.

Not Sybil rolled her eyes. This didn't really seem like an answer.

"It's got to be somebody's," Scott insisted.

"It's the people's money," Zane explained.

"And the will of the people is that you should go to college," Sybil said, stuffing the wad of bills into the collar of Scott's t-shirt.

"But…"

"But nothing," Zane said. "There's more where that came from. Lots and lots more."

"What are you?" Scott asked, "some kind of Robin Hood?"

This question made the girls giggle uncontrollably.

"There's one crucial difference between old Robin and me," Zane said.

"Right," Scott nodded. "He's been dead for five hundred years or so."

The girls giggled harder, though Scott wouldn't have thought that was possible.

"Robin Hood had to steal from the rich," Zane explained. "They fight with each other for the privilege of giving their money to me."

"I don't know what to say."

"Don't say anything," Not Sybil said.

"But if I were you," Sybil said, "I'd go and take care of your enrollment stuff tomorrow. The people expect you to live up to your responsibilities."

"I will," Scott stammered.

And he had. It was like something that would happen in a movie, he had thought, watching the three of them saunter away. Zane was just like someone in a movie.

When he left the restaurant after work a few nights later, Zane was waiting for him. The girls were nowhere in sight. Scott didn't ask about them. He was too dazzled. Zane was the kind of person who was so good looking it was impossible to describe. Any attempt to verbalize the details as to height, breadth of shoulders, smoothness of skin, color of eyes, texture and cut of hair, or lines and planes of face would ultimately fail to adequately account for the overall impression. All you could say about him was that he was a guy who took your breath away, who you couldn't help staring at. Scott knew it wasn't just him: the whole neighborhood's mouth hung open when he passed. Their eyes glazed over. Boys were no more exempt than girls were, though Scott was certain that what they were feeling as they stared couldn't possibly be the same sensations he experienced.

"My work is done around here," Zane had said, moonlight glinting off that indescribable head of hair. "It's time to move on."

"Oh," was all Scott could think of to say.

"You should come along," Zane said. "I have this friend who has a little house up in West Hollywood. He says we can live there rent free. And by the way, I checked. There's bus service to that college you're going to go to."

So here he is on the Santa Monica Boulevard bus heading west, to all intents and purposes just like any other college student in the city.

* * *

Scott likes to get to the lecture hall early so he can have his choice of seats. Left handed Scott likes to be well to the right of center so the room stretches away on his good side. Paranoid Scott prefers close to the back, so there's little going on behind him. He wasn't conscious of these influences on the first day of class. He just instinctively plopped himself down in this spot. It all had to be explained to him, and now he can't walk into a room without analyzing each move he makes. He's pulling his notepad out of his book bag when Arianna Gold slides into his row, her russet mane bouncing, her chains and bracelets jingling, every millimeter of her in some sort of motion.

"Morning, bubbie," she pants. Out of breath is her essential look.

"Hey."

She's an amazon, tall, strong limbed, graceful. She played tennis and volleyball in high school. She sits down on Scott's right and begins pulling things out of her pack. Bags of nuts and dried fruit. Her textbook. Her diary. A miniature tape recorder which she says is for taking notes but Scott has never seen her use. A slide rule, though she has no math class this semester. A copy of *Steppenwolf* in the original German. A cigarette lighter which she uses to light incense. A key chain with a pewter Star of David fob. Multiple colors of highlighters. A swiss army knife. A weird Soviet flashlight which is powered not by a battery but by manually operating a spring loaded scissors-like device that generates the electric charge. Scott once asked her where the kitchen sink was, and she spent five minutes rummaging determinedly before looking at him with wide eyes and answering, "damn, I must have left it at home this morning". He still halfway expects her to pull a lug wrench out of there someday. It was Arianna, a psych major, who explained his choice of seats to him. She's also the one responsible for the seating arrangement. When she arrives, seconds before the bell to start class, Ellie Walters will sit on Scott's left, all four feet eleven and ninety-two pounds of her. Ellie's currently understudying the lead role in a production of *Swan Lake*.

Arianna and Ellie go way back. They didn't attend the same high school; their families don't go to the same synagogue or live in the same neighborhood; nevertheless, they could hardly be more intimately associated. They know each other's family histories going back at least four generations. Arianna's older brother Zeb once very nearly married Ellie's older sister Marcia—the girls swear that this was a lucky escape for both parties, but when Scott asked why, they clammed up. Their Schnauzers are littermates. They have already decided which dormitory they will room together in when they transfer to Santa Barbara next fall. They are as close as sisters, though when this simile looms Arianna goes to great lengths to explain that real sisters tend not to be close at all, citing as proof their relationships with their own sisters. The girls finish each other's sentences, laugh constantly at private jokes, communicate in a slang so larded with idioms of their own invention as to very nearly constitute a new dialect, and, in Ellie's words, can account for every bone of every skeleton in each other's closet. They have adopted Scott, though he's not at all sure which one of them found him first. Or why they bothered. He thinks he surely must be too aryan looking for a couple of self respecting Jewish girls to be seen with in public.

Their threesome is only possible because it's a threesome. Scott senses that operating independently the girls would compete for him, though for the life of him he can't understand the attraction. Nor can he imagine the effort it would take to fend either of them off: their greatest similiarity as far as he can determine is their implacability. The idea that either of them might someday decide to go solo terrifies him. Most things about women do, above all their curiosity. Scott's not interested in satisfying anyone's curiosity about him. He can't imagine any good coming of sharing his life story in even the most cursory manner, so he volunteers no information. To the extent he's permitted, he replies to queries monosyllabically. He hones his skills at evasion daily, with the single mindedness worthy of a devotee of some obscure martial art. Over the last few months these two seem to have developed a grudging respect for his privacy. The upshot of this is that instead of having to invent stories for them, they invent stories about him. Some he's heard, others he senses they're keeping to themselves. In addition, they decide for him what he wants for lunch in the student union, explain his behavior to passing strangers as if he's a toddler, and talk about him as if he's not present. He once referred to them as the big brothers he never had.

Ellie said, "fine, as long as she's Bruce".

* * *

The girls escort him to his next class and head off to the library to study for their abnormal psychology midterm. This is no lecture hall, just a small, nondescript classroom. Second semester calculus isn't a big draw on this campus. Once again, Scott is first to arrive and renews his claim to the seat in the right hand rear corner of the room. He sits pretending to review his notes while his fellow students drift in. He always finds it difficult to control his anxiety until the instructor arrives. Eventually everybody's in place and the instructor is already at the board scribbling away, and just as the bell rings, here's Jared Bartok clumping in on his crutches, and Scott feels like he's about to jump out of his skin.

Jared's amazingly handsome face is marred by the faintest of scars that twists through his upper lip, a relic, Scott is certain, of surgery to repair a cleft. His shaggy mop of clown red hair cries out for a comb: even by current standards it's too wild and unkempt to be considered cool. It just makes him look like he's second cousin to a neanderthal. His milk white skin is flawless. Scott can't remember ever having seen anyone with such amazing muscular development in his shoulders, arms, and chest. It hardly seems possible that a living, breathing human can be that massive. His left leg is extensively bandaged below the knee and has been all semester, hence the crutches. The rumor circulating among their classmates is that he was badly wounded in a firefight outside Da Nang. Scott doesn't know if this is true, but Jared certainly seems to fit the stereotype of the deeply traumatized Viet Nam veteran. In addition to his injured leg, he is afflicted with a stammer so severe that he's all but mute. When roll is called he merely grunts. Scott can't decide if he considers Jared magnificent or grotesque. He must simply constitute a new species, and this assessment seems validated by the fact that as unlikely as it might seem, Jared is the star pupil of the class. He has gotten the highest score on every exam so far this semester.

Scott thinks it would be fascinating to know what it is like being unable to speak so much as your own name when meeting new people. But how could you possibly ask anyone a question like that?

* * *

"Here's lunch, kiddies," Arianna calls from ten paces away, balancing a cafeteria tray on one hand at shoulder level like a waitress in a wartime diner. Scott holds his breath, but so far she's never let a tray fall. "Chef salad for you, Ellie."

"Thanks, darling."

"And a chicken taco combination plate for you, Scott."

"So that's what I want today."

"Something different, I thought. And for me, well rumor has it it's spaghetti with meat balls. And who knows? It might be."

They begin eating. Today's mealtime entertainment is the girls playing yet another round of "who'd make a good girlfriend for Scottie?"

"Susie Fisher," Ellie suggests.

"Too tall," Arianna counters. "Betsy Wright."

"Too dumb. Jess Morgenstern."

"Won't date anybody who isn't Jewish. Rachel Lewis."

"That horrible laugh—it'll give Scott nightmares, I guarantee. Ruth Johnson."

"Cat allergies."

Despite the game's title, its purpose is not to identify a girlfriend for Scott but to demonstrate the futility of the search. As long as the problem can be demonstrated to lack a solution, nothing has to change.

* * *

When Scott gets to the library Ricardo is already there, head bowed over a textbook, mop of glossy curls hanging almost to the table top. He stands still for a moment. He loves to stare at Ricardo but does so infrequently. He can't risk being caught at it. Ricardo mustn't know about him. He knows about Ricardo because Ricardo told him one day last fall as they were leaving Dr. Jankel's literature class. They had discussed *Billy Budd* that period, and a jock type had expressed disgust at the homoerotic subtext of the novella: "*this queer stuff is sick—it makes me want to puke*". Scott supposes that this was what prompted Ricardo's declaration. Scott was unspeakably relieved for a long, blissful moment, imagining the deep friendship they'd now be able to share. He was on the point of saying, "I am, too," when Ricardo finished up his confession with that fatal final independent clause; the last thing, really, Scott had been expecting him to say: "*and I'm in love with you*", which made a forthright response on Scott's part impossible. How could he reveal himself without having to explain that he's in love as well?

Scott knows he's crazy to feel the way he does, but he can't help himself. Zane's generous and considerate, but he really does seem to think of Scott in the same way that he thinks of the cats or the washing machine. Not to mention the fact that he spends his whole waking life cultivating the image of the carefree trust fund baby while actually supporting himself accepting gifts from admirers. Scott can barely endure the abject shame of the situation. He can't imagine discussing it with anyone and he'd rather disappear than deal with the campaign Ricardo would surely wage to rescue him from the mess he's in.

It's much better for him to passively maintain the fiction that he's a sensitive, understanding straight guy who's cool with having a gay friend. Who loves hearing all about the adventures, the petty intrigues and minor scandals of Ricardo's life day by day. Who's a safe shoulder to cry on when the latest infatuation turns out to be a disappointment or the older brother disrupts Sunday dinner voicing suspicions that are too close to the truth or some asshole in one of their classes makes an insensitive remark. Despite his appearance, Ricardo is as fragile as antique porcelain. God knows, Scott's good at picking people up and dusting them off and sending them back out onto the playground. Yes, it's better in every way for Scott to keep his life to himself. This way is uncomplicated. This way nobody gets hurt. Scott's guilt doesn't show up on any ledger of misdeeds but his own.

Staring at this beautiful, sweet boy, even for a moment, he can almost convince himself to go with the flow and let things happen the way Ricardo would like. But the minute Zane walks into any room he is already present in, Scott will know that's just not possible.

Ricardo looks up. It's as if he felt Scott's silent, ambivalent adoration as a physical force. Scott reads the desperate question in those dark eyes, but it's gone again almost as soon as it's there, replaced by that smile that never fails to dazzle him.

"I was afraid you weren't coming."

It's Ricardo's perennial greeting.

* * *

When Scott gets home the alien Rolex is gone, replaced on the kitchen counter by an envelope. He looks inside: twelve hundred dollars in fifties. He has no idea what the going rate for a used Rolex is locally. The last one brought in fifteen hundred. He had been suspicious of the steady stream of "gifts" Zane was coming home with: a pair of platinum cufflinks one week, a ruby ring the next, early the next month a tie tack with what looked like a rhinestone in it that turned out to be a three carat diamond, a few days after that a bracelet of heavy gold links. His brain insisted to him that such a regular supply of these luxurious trinkets had to indicate some sort of nefarious activity, if only that Zane was acting as a fence. To demonstrate his innocence Zane took him along to the pawnshop. Scott stood breathless while Zane presented the required identification and signed the statement verifying that he was the legal owner of the item in question. The manager treated Zane like a regular and highly valued customer, and Scott's misgivings were at least partially allayed. That afternoon, Zane had taken three hundred for himself—walking around money, he called it—and handed the rest to Scott.

That's Zane's typical cut: twenty per cent. The rest Scott is in charge of. This is the money he uses to pay their utilities, to buy groceries, to take the cats to the vet. Zane makes only a few stipulations: that it doesn't go into a bank account, and that Scott doesn't tell him where it's kept unless he asks, which he never has. Additionally, Scott's expected to hold onto it all in cash. "In case we have to make a quick getaway?" he once asked, only half joking. Zane frowned at that and didn't say anything. In all these months Zane has never asked for an accounting. When Scott inadvertently complains about anything—the cost of the cats' favorite brand of food, a slow week at the restaurant, the threadbare condition of some article of his clothing—Zane asks him why he lets himself worry about things. Why hasn't dipped into the kitty already?

Scott doesn't like to think about Zane's admirers. He sees one or another of them on occasion when Zane shows up at *Hexagone* on a date. They're invariably the kind of guys who can easily afford to do without whatever it is that Zane will end up bringing home; older, prosperous, defiantly respectable in appearance, which only serves to make Scott more nervous. The one thing they seem to have in common is the general lack of any propensity for displays of sentiment. Perhaps such people give extravagant gifts because they find affection too difficult to express—or even feel. Perhaps the extravagance is calculated to impress, but Scott prides himself—or perhaps only deludes himself, he can't decide which—on knowing Zane better than anyone, and he can't imagine Zane being impressed by a gesture that transparent.

Even more discomforting than the admirers themselves is the thought of what they get from Zane in return. Scott can only imagine this part, because Zane has never talked about it.

* * *

"Your friend is here," Hostess Kaitlin says. "I put him and his date at your corner table."

"Thanks."

"Wait until you see the guy. Gorgeous. And probably worth about thirty million. Where does he find them? They never look like the type to be interested in boys."

"I think that's the whole point," Scott says. "Besides, how do you know they're interested in boys?"

"Scott, please," she rolls her eyes, "they can't all be his uncles. Or old college friends of his dad."

"One was," Scott says, just to be argumentative. "For all you know, this is just some guy who's bored with his life and decided to try something different."

"Different," she snorts. "That's an interesting way to describe it. It's just so unfair. He hardly seems to lift a finger to get these guys, and here I am this close to entering a convent."

"Hey," Scott says, "it's not like he keeps all of them. Most of the time he carefully removes the hook and tosses them back into the lake."

"Well, nobody ever accused me of being too proud for leftovers," she says.

"That's the spirit. And remember, we've never seen Zane in here before."

"Zane who?"

* * *

The guy is in his late thirties. He's got that slicked back, captain of industry hair and he's wearing a suit that probably cost about as much as a clean, late model Buick. He's very handsome, but, Scott thinks, mean looking. It's something about the eyes. Across the table from him, Zane looks as prim as an English schoolboy taking tea with the Archbishop of Canterbury. So this guy is a new friend. Zane's not like this with old friends. He's always beautifully mannered, but with people he's dated before he's never this stiff.

"Good evening," he says. "My name is Scott. I'll be your waiter this evening. Can I bring you anything from the bar?"

"You have Glenfiddich?" the man asks. He glares at Zane. "You promised me they have Glenfiddich here."

"We have Glenfiddich."

"Neat," the man says. "Rocks. And if it's not honest to God Glenfiddich, you'll be very sorry."

"Yes sir," Scott smiles. "And for you, sir?"

"Rum and coke, thanks," Zane gives him a bland smile. Zane means plain coke. He never drinks on a first date.

"I'll have those right out for you. Now did Kaitlin describe this evening's specials for you?"

"No specials," the man says. "I don't believe in chef's specials."

"Very good. Can I start either of you off with an appetizer?"

"Shrimp cocktail," the man says. "Extra sauce."

"And you?"

"How are your scallops prepared?" Zane asks. Not even a prosecuting attorney would suspect he's had them at least a dozen times.

"They're poached in white wine and *buerre blanc*, with shallots and julienne bell pepper."

"Sounds delicious," Zane says.

"Are they fresh?" the man asks. "A lot of these places try to give you frozen seafood and tell you it's fresh."

"Fresh, sir," Scott says.

"I'll have the scallops," Zane says.

Lucky Atlas and Tigger, Scott thinks.

* * *

Scott wakes from a recurring dream in which he's tied up and subjected to terrifying yet inexplicably exquisite sexual tortures by his calculus classmate, Jared Bartok. He's wet and sticky inside his underwear, but this physical discomfort is nothing compared to the dream's icky emotional aftermath. Usually he doesn't wake up from the dream until Jared has actually untied him. It takes him a moment to realize that tonight's interruption must be due to the yowling of the cats. He tries to shush them, but they ignore him. His bedside clock says it's a little after two. There's no reason for them to be carrying on this way. Except there has to be. Atlas is practically bouncing him out of the bed.

They've never had a break in, but this neighborhood is far from immune to them. He's tempted to pull the covers over his head and hope the robbers will figure out there's nothing worth taking and go back away, but the cats' racket is bound to attract their attention. He considers going out the window and trying to find help. But if the robbers don't catch him, that'll leave Zane alone with them. There's no way he'll leave Zane to face the intruders by himself. He rolls out of bed, pulls on a clean pair of shorts and tries and fails to think of something he might use to defend himself. He tiptoes over to the door and opens it slowly.

It's not a robber. It's just Zane. The cats don't ordinarily react when Zane gets in in the middle of the night. But as far as Scott knows Zane doesn't ordinarily sit on the living room couch sobbing.

"What's wrong?"

"Nothing. Go back to bed."

"It's not nothing," Scott insists, rounding the end of the couch and getting a look at Zane's face. It's covered with blood, which is oozing from a gash over his left eye and a smaller one on his right cheekbone. His hair is a mess. His clothing is ripped. "What happened? Did you get mugged on your way home?"

"No," Zane says. "It was that guy I was with tonight."

"He did this to you?"

"After dinner we went to his place. He had two bodybuilders waiting there. He wanted to watch while they roughed me up and took turns fucking me."

"Jesus."

"Afterwards he wouldn't give me anything. He said I didn't look like I suffered enough."

"Shit. You should call the police."

"Are you crazy?"

"What do you mean? You were assaulted."

"My livelihood depends on discretion. I start talking to the police, I won't have a friend in this town. And what happens then? I end up peddling my ass on street corners. Bad idea, Scottie."

"I guess that means no trip to the emergency room, either."

"You guess right."

"Jesus, Zane, I feel like killing those guys."

"No you don't, Scottie. You're not the killer type. But thanks for saying it."

"There's got to be something I can do."

"As long as you're up, put on the kettle and make me some tea. And while we're waiting for the water to boil, help me out of these clothes and into the shower."

* * *

With the blood washed off and his cuts cleaned and bandaged, Zane looks better, but not much. Bruises are starting to darken alarmingly, and his right eye is swollen shut.

"I wish you'd let me get you to a doctor," Scott complains.

"I'll be fine."

"God, I hope so."

"Say, Scottie," Zane says, squinting out of his good eye, "when did you get to be so big all of a sudden? I don't remember you being so tall. And where did those shoulders come from?"

"I had a growth spurt."

"While I wasn't looking."

Scott shrugs.

"We've got to get you to a gym. You could really look like something. Take some money out of the kitty tomorrow and get yourself a membership somewhere."

"Right."

"Seriously," Zane says. "Now I need you to do me one more favor."

"Anything."

"I don't feel like sleeping by myself tonight. Can I come in with you?"

Beverly Hills: 1973

Scott steers the Mercedes into the parking space and turns off the engine. "You're sure about this?"

"Sure I'm sure," Zane says, climbing out of the car.

"It's a big decision," Scott says, following him up the walk.

"You worry too much."

"That's why you keep me around."

"Is that what you think?"

"Well, isn't it?"

"I hadn't thought of it that way," Zane says, pulling open the door, "but you're probably right. God knows you almost always are."

Inside the building air conditioning is blasting and muzak is playing. Zane saunters up to the reception desk. His ripped, faded jeans look like they belong on a homeless derelict. They cost two hundred dollars. Scott remembers when he used to feed the two of them for a month on half that.

"Good morning."

"Oh my god," the receptionist shrieks, "you're Zane Stark."

"'Fraid so, miss," Zane says. It's his catchphrase from *Check and Mate*. Scott can't remember the last time he saw Zane out of character in public. It's as if the cameras never stop rolling.

"Oh my God."

"We have an appointment with, um…" he looks back over his shoulder at Scott.

"Wayne Robbins," Scott says.

"Wayne Robbins," Zane relays the name to the girl.

"One moment," she says. "I'll just let him know you're here."

* * *

Wayne Robbins' office has floor to ceiling windows offering panoramic views of Wilshire Boulevard. It's furnished in what Scott thinks of as High Victorian Bordello. The tastelessness is breathtaking. It must have cost the earth. He can't imagine visitors being impressed, but they must be. He made careful inquiries: this is the office of one of the most successful realtors in the city.

"Mr. Zane Stark and, um, friend," the girl announces them.

"Zane Stark," Robbins says, rising from his seat behind a desk the size of a Volkswagen. He's a portly middle aged man dressed and coiffed like a twenty-four year old. Regardless of what his friends must tell him, it makes him look older than he probably is. And ridiculous. "This is a pleasure, sir."

"I bet you say that to all your new clients," Zane grins.

"I hope that means that you are a new client," Robbins smiles back, revealing what seems like an abnormally large number of teeth.

"Let's just say you come highly recommended," Zane says. "This is my personal assistant, Scott Bailey."

"Good to meet you Scott," Robbins says, obviously relieved to have Scott's presence satisfactorily explained. "Can I have the girl bring you gentlemen anything?"

"We just came from brunch," Zane says.

"Well, then, let's get down to business," Robbins suggests. "I've gone over the notes my assistant made when you spoke to her. And I have several properties I think might be suitable. I'd like to show them to you."

"Great," Zane says. "When can we see them?"

"Right now, if you have a couple of hours."

                                        * * *

What Zane does is not really acting. He'd be the first to admit it. He describes himself as half puppet and half model. He does exactly what the director tells him—that's the puppet part—and he does his best to look fantastic doing it, though his success in this regard has more to do with genetics than actual effort. The writers give him as little as possible to say in order to keep his lack of training and experience from being too painfully obvious. And what few lines he does speak are ridiculously predictable. He could just about make his dialogue up as he goes along. A few times he actually has, and if anybody noticed—or cared—they didn't mention it.

Check and Mate is not his series. The headliner is an Honest to God Hollywood Legend, an old time warhorse who either wanted to stage a comeback to feed his aging ego or had to generate some income to keep his ex-wives' alimony payments from bankrupting him, depending on whose version of the story you listen to. Westerns having gone out of fashion and the warhorse not being noted for his comedic abilities, a detective drama seemed the most obvious vehicle. But at seventy something years old, there was no question of his being up to even the minimal physical demands of television style crime fighting. The producers scratched their heads and came up with the solution: give him a sidekick. Someone young and athletic enough for the chases and fight scenes and photogenic enough to broaden the program's appeal to take in a generation (two, really) of viewers not familiar with the warhorse's earlier career.

The warhorse had agreed to the plan with one stipulation. The actor cast as sidekick had to be a complete unknown. To this the producers added their own unspoken preference for someone unskilled enough as a thespian not to up-stage their lead, who was no Olivier to put it kindly. This was in fact an unusually low standard even for network television. But it was Zane exactly, except that at the time he'd hardly begun to entertain notions of a change of career. If he hadn't already existed, he would have had to be invented from scratch. It was his friends and admirers who made the thing happen. This admirer was a friend of an associate of one of the producers, who happened to be overheard speaking to someone else about the requirements of the role and that eavesdropper re-layed the information to a friend of a friend of another admirer...and so on. The most difficult part of the whole thing had been getting Zane a SAG card with no previous acting experience. That required the good offices of yet another set of friends and admirers. Scott strongly suspects that sums of money changed hands at some point.

The miracle of it from Scott's perspective had been the willingness of all concerned to promote Zane to a position where they could hardly expect the accustomed quid pro quo to be maintained. He's still shaking his head over that, and here they are on hiatus from season two. Ratings have been far better than anyone involved with the project would have dared to hope for, and pretty much everybody but the warhorse himself knows that has to be chalked up to Zane, who's as gorgeous and charismatic on camera as he ever was in person. To date he's been on several dozen magazine covers, and his poster is a best seller.

* * *

Scott climbs off the BMW and hurries inside slipping the helmet off his head and smoothing his hair. He follows the sound of Zane's voice through the empty rooms. He finds them in the room Zane has chosen for his home gym. Its floor to ceiling windows look out across the pool to the cityscape far down the hillside.

"Sorry I'm late," he says. "Traffic was a bitch."

"There you are," Zane smiles. "Pick up that script?"

"Got it," Scott says, indicating his backpack.

There is no script. Scott wasn't running errands; he was at UCLA attending classes. Zane likes to make people think he keeps Scott busy dealing with dozens of pressing matters. He also likes to give the impression that he's fielding lots of offers. He's sure that the more people talk about how complicated his affairs are, the more seriously he'll be taken. He also believes that the more gossip there is about the offers he's considering, the more offers are likely actually to materialize.

"Gentlemen," Zane says, "this is my personal assistant, Scott Bailey. He's the one you have to thank for this appointment."

"Nice to finally meet you in person," a tall, distinguished looking man says in a posh sounding English accent. "Toby MacPherson. And this is my associate, Kyle Milliken."

"Sorry I wasn't here when you arrived," Scott says. "How's it going so far?"

"Great," Zane says, in that indecipherable tone of his which can denote anything from catastrophic to sublime.

"We're just discussing Zane's plan for this room," Kyle says. He's younger than MacPherson, and his accent sounds vaguely Texan. Otherwise, the men's appearances are similar enough that they could be father and son, preppies who've wandered out of an exclusive gentlemen's club and into Zane's newly acquired house in the Hollywood Hills.

"Uh oh," Scott laughs.

"Tell us, Scott," MacPherson says, "don't you think that this space really deserves better than to be used as a home gym?"

"Hold on, Tobe," Milliken says. "Look who you're talking to. Scott's like an advertisement for gym equipment. You might not get the answer you want."

"Just because he's got shoulders like that doesn't mean he can't have good taste," MacPherson says. "So, Scott?"

"You heard Zane," Scott says. "I'm his personal assistant. Having opinions isn't in my job description."

"But just for the sake of argument," MacPherson persists, "don't you think that the pool house would be a much better place for a home gymnasium?"

"It's impossible," Zane laughs. "The pool house isn't nearly large enough."

"How large does a home gymnasium need to be?" MacPherson asks.

"Larger than the pool house, apparently," Milliken chuckles.

"And anyway," Zane says, "I have other plans for the pool house."

"Which are?" MacPherson asks.

"I plan to have lots of guests, don't I Scott?"

* * *

"As you see, we've already had commercial grade rubber matting installed, so the room is ready to have gym equipment brought in," Zane says. "And since you're going to be my trainer—at least I hope you are—I thought, why not have Chuck pick it all out? You can take Scott with you when you're ready to order. He signs all the checks."

"Sounds great," Chuck says. He's Scott's height but must outweigh him by a good forty pounds—all solid. His inky black flattop is cut with surgical precision and held gleaming and vertical with butch wax. Just being in the same room with him makes Scott a little woozy. "But exactly what am I buying? I mean, how serious are you?"

"I want to look like Scott."

"That's a pretty tall order," Chuck says. "He's got really great genetics. I could have him competing nationally in a couple of years. I don't know if you've actually got that kind of potential."

"You're the expert. I mean, you are a former Mr. America."

"Mr. USA," Chuck corrects him. "And I was runner up."

Scott has seen Chuck's pictures in the bodybuilding magazines. He selected Chuck as Zane's trainer because of his competition record. When he first started going to his new gym in West Hollywood he was astonished to see Chuck there in real life, working as a trainer. Until then, he'd had some crazy idea that the guys in those magazines were like mythical creatures who had no existence in the real world. But it turns out that Chuck is all too real.

"Right," Zane says. "Mr. USA. But just in case I do have that kind of potential, I want a gym facility in my home good enough to take me all the way."

"It'll cost you."

"As long as you keep it under six figures, you won't hear a word of complaint from me."

"We can do it for that. But I'm still not making any promises. I've worked with lots of actors. You guys start out all hot to go, but with the kind of shooting schedules you have, it's tough."

"Fair enough," Zane says. "I promise to do my best with the time I have. And the equipment will never go to waste because at least Scott can use it."

* * *

"You have a very beautiful home," Mrs. Quackenbush says, sipping her sherry. "And you seem to be a lovely person, Mr. Stark. I sense that you are a true dog lover, and I fully understand the possible advantage to my business of seeing a photo of a Hollywood celebrity on the cover of some magazine or other accompanied by a pair of my dogs. But I must tell you I have serious reservations about placing my puppies in your household."

Scott snaps to immediate attention. Zane is not accustomed to having people say no to him. These days it happens so rarely that when it does Scott halfway expects the skies to fall and the seas to part.

"I hope you feel comfortable enough with me to say why," Zane smiles.

"No one has ever accused me of a lack of frankness," she laughs.

Scott decides maybe it's safe to start breathing again.

"First of all, you have a swimming pool."

"I thought Labradors were great swimmers."

"Oh, they adore the water," Mrs. Quackenbush agrees. "And it's wonderful for them to live in a home with a pool. But you see, the pool will be here twenty-four hours a day—and you won't."

"I'm not sure I understand."

"Labradors are great swimmers, as you mentioned. But just say the dogs are here alone and one or the other of them goes into the pool. No matter how well they've been trained, I've known dogs to become confused and unable to find the steps. When that happens, unless help arrives in time a dog can exhaust himself trying to climb out and may eventually drown. Anything can cause an accident like this: an earth tremor for instance, or a siren. In this part of the city brush fires are far from unknown and that can certainly panic a dog."

"There must be something that can be done to prevent it from happening."

"Oh, the solution isn't complicated at all," Mrs. Quackenbush says. "You simply fence off the pool area. It doesn't have to ruin the appearance of your property: there are all kinds of decorative fencing materials on the market these days. But I find you people up here in the hills are extremely reluctant to do anything that obstructs your views."

"If I were to promise you that Mr. Bailey here will make arrangements to have fencing installed and that you'd be free to inspect the property before letting me bring the puppies here, would that take care of your concerns?"

"That concern, certainly. But you see, it's not my only objection."

"Please go on," Zane says.

Scott can tell that his patience is wearing thin. There are other dog breeders, of course, but Mrs. Quackenbush and her Labrador Retrievers are legendary. She's won every important Best in Show on the planet. Zane has his heart set on a matched pair of her dogs. Scott doesn't have a plan B, but it looks like he'd better get started on one.

"You're an actor, Mr. Stark. Actors, especially those working in television, have extremely difficult schedules. I don't have to tell you this; it's your life, after all. But you may not realize the difficulty this presents for dogs. You're away from home far too much. Your dogs will suffer. I can't condone it. I know of some people in your industry who take their dogs with them to the studios. That can sometimes work with the smaller breeds, though I believe a film studio is never a safe place for a dog. Labradors are not small dogs, of course. They only thrive when they enjoy ample physical activity. You surely wouldn't consider it fair to shut them up in that little trailer the producers give you."

"No," Zane says. "I see your point. But it's not the problem you think it is. You see, Mr. Bailey lives here on the property. He almost never accompanies me to the studio. And he's never gone for more than a few hours at a time. He'll take full charge of their initial training, and he'll see to it that they get all the exercise they need."

* * *

The woman at the front door looks confused.

"I'm sorry," she tells Scott, "I think I must have the wrong house."

"No, Madame Tetzlaff," Scott says, "you're here to meet Zane Stark."

"How in the world did you know that?"

"Please come in. I'm Scott Bailey, his personal assistant."

"Astonishing," Madame Tetzlaff declares, striding past him into the entry hall. "Astonishing. And this house. I feel vibrations. Strong ones. There are fascinating things going on in this place."

Madame herself is giving Scott vibrations. Six feet tall and steely haired, she's in an outfit that Isadora Duncan might have willed to her lady's maid. Her makeup is reminiscent of a pierrot. Scott had been warned that this "psychic to the stars" was eccentric in the extreme, and so far she's living up to her billing.

"Mr. Stark was delayed returning from the studio," he explains, ushering her into the living room. "I'm expecting him shortly."

"He'll be here in exactly three minutes and forty-seven seconds," Madame informs him.

"Can I get you anything?" Scott asks. "Coffee? Tea?"

"Tea," she says. "Yes, tea would be exquisite. Herbal."

In the event it's a full fifteen minutes before Zane arrives and Scott introduces him to Madame Tetzlaff, who by now is on her second cup.

"You see," she says to Scott as he and Zane enter the room, tapping her wristwatch with a bejeweled fingernail. "Exactly as I told you."

"Madame, this is Zane Stark."

"I know who Mr. Stark is."

"What a pleasure this is, Madame Tetzlaff," Zane smiles.

"No, no," she insists, "the pleasure is all mine, Mr. Stark."

"I hope my assistant has made you welcome."

"Most welcome indeed," Madame croons. "A very interesting young person, I have to say."

"Yes," Zane grins, throwing Scott a wink. "He certainly is."

"Just between us," she continues, as if Scott isn't in the room, "I think he may have some psychic abilities. Latent, of course..."

* * *

"It's not a large property," Zane says, "but the landscaping is lush, and I like to have it looking just right."

"Of course, Mr. Stark," Israel Gonzales says. "It is a beautiful property. I'm sure my crew will take care of it and make you happy."

"Our last gardener turned out to be unreliable," Zane says. "He would send two men when it really takes three or four to keep things up to snuff. Several times they left in the middle of the job. A couple of weeks they didn't come at all. I understand about personal emergencies and I tried to be sympathetic. But it happened too many times, and I wasn't happy with the way the place was starting to look. I don't like firing people, Mr. Gonzales. I'm a working man myself and I know what it means to depend on your employers."

"Yes, Mr. Stark. I understand."

"And you'll take all your directions from Mr. Bailey here. He is my personal assistant. Any questions you have he'll be able to answer."

* * *

"Thanks for coming in today, Mr. Grant," Zane says.

"No problem, Mr. Stark," Grant says. He's sweating bullets. He's apparently heard the rumor that Zane's bite is worse than his bark. The rumor originated with Zane himself, who cultivates it assiduously. His reasoning is that this is better than actually having to confront people.

"And thanks for bringing Robbie with you."

"He's lucky I didn't kill him already," Grant mutters.

"Now, Robbie," Zane says, looking the kid dead in the eye, "I want you to understand that I don't have a problem at all with the way you've been taking care of the pool. You've always done an A number one job. In fact, that's the only reason we're having this meeting. Otherwise I'd just cancel our account with Marty here and get a new pool service."

"Yes, sir," Robbie says.

"And I want you to know that it wasn't Mr. Bailey who complained about you. He didn't mention the incident at all. When I told him what I'd heard about it, he laughed it off. But you were overheard. It was the next door neighbors who told me. They were at home and they heard you yelling at Mr. Bailey. They say you called him a 'fucking faggot'. Now Mr. Bailey is my personal assistant. Mine: Zane Stark. And when you call my personal assistant a 'fucking faggot' you might as well call me that. Me: Zane Stark. A 'fucking faggot'. Get it?"

"Yes, sir."

"It's no business of yours whether he's a Martian, a giraffe, or a Satan worshipper. He's my personal assistant. He has my authority to supervise everything to do with this property, and that includes making sure everyone who comes here to do work does the job properly and behaves appropriately while they're here. You don't have to like him. But you do have to respect his position as my employee and do your job and keep your opinions to yourself."

"Yes, sir. I understand," Robbie says. He looks like he's about to pee in his pants. "It won't happen again, Mr. Stark."

"You're damned right, it won't happen again," Grant growls. "Because you're fired, you hear?"

"A moment, Mr. Grant," Zane says. "Please don't fire him on account of this incident. I think it would be much better to give him an opportunity to show that he's really learned a lesson from it."

"You sure about that, Mr. Stark?" Grant asks.

"I hope we'll see you here next week at your regular time, Robbie. I'm sure you understand what Mr. Grant and I expect of you."

* * *

"God, Scottie, you're the best," Zane says, pulling on his jeans.

"I can't believe you're not going to shower," Scott says, stifling a yawn.

"No time. The car will be here to take me to the studio in less than five minutes. I hate the look that driver gives me when I make him wait. It's so stupid. He drives like a maniac to get me there so I can sit around for several hours waiting for shooting to start for the day."

"The glamorous life of network television."

"Damned right." Zane zips up, steps to the side of the bed, leans down, pecks Scott on the mouth, and he's gone. Scott watches him trot around the side of the pool and into the main house. A second later lights go on all over the ground floor. Zane likes the studio driver to think he's been up for hours.

Scott gets out of bed. In the bathroom he sponges himself off. He pulls on a pair of gym shorts and some sweat pants over that. He puts on a tank top, runs his hands through his hair, glances into the mirror, slaps on a baseball cap. Back in the bedroom he steps into a pair of sneakers and grabs the leashes. Going into the back yard, he calls the dogs. Zane let them out before he and Scott started to play. Zane is afraid that being in the room when sex is going on might traumatize them. They streak out of the darkness whimpering with excitement, squirming and wriggling as he harnesses them. They're still at that awkward puppy stage: Romulus pees at the sight of the leash. The minute Remus is in his harness he grabs the leash in his mouth and trots off toward the gate. Romulus and Scott follow him and a moment later they're on the street. Dawn is just breaking.

Scott wonders how many other personal assistants in this city have "fuck buddy" included in their job descriptions. It started back before the advent of Zane's current career but was only sporadic until he was cast in the series and all his habits changed. Since then he sneaks into Scott's bed at least a couple of times a week. It's always the same: practically no foreplay, and Scott's cock in Zane's ass. It's apparently impossible to fuck him too long or too violently. God knows Scott has tried. It would be stupefyingly boring by now if Scott wasn't so emotionally invested. On a good day Zane can come without touching himself. He's proud of this trick, though he claims he's only ever been able to do it with Scott. He swears all his other sex these days is with women. Scott assumes this is true, though he's pretty sure it's a career move rather than a genuine reflection of his orientation. He hasn't asked because it's not something it would occur to Zane to discuss.

That's not because Zane is too squeamish to talk about sex. The truth is that Zane doesn't talk about anything of substance. He's always been that way. At first Scott assumed he must be shallow. Over time Zane has surprised him on occasion by demonstrating surprising depth. He just doesn't display this quality in his everyday life. At least no more often than once every six months, and always without warning. Out of the blue Scott will realize that they're in the middle of a conversation about something profound. He will sense something very much like intimacy hovering around them. The next moment the feeling will be gone like a pebble disappearing beneath the surface of a pond. It might never have happened. More importantly, there's always the possibility that it never will again.

Scott knows that in one sense he has very little to complain about. Who gets to go on the kind of adventure they're having? And in every way imaginable Zane is the perfect boss. Patient, considerate, charming, friendly, and generous to a fault. It's just that after all this time it's impossible for Scott to think of him as just a boss. But as a friend Zane is infuriating, because despite the patience, consideration, charm, apparent friendliness, and generosity, there's a part of him he's never shared with Scott. His emotional unavailability is so profound that Scott's never sure they actually ever have been friends.

Which would be bad enough, except friendship isn't really what Scott's always been in it for. And it isn't even a good old fashioned case of unrequitedness he's suffering from, because they're fuck buddies, after all. And what could be more totally fucked up than regularly getting to fuck the guy you're in love with while knowing that feelings will never be part of the equation?

* * *

Friday night in Scott's regular bar. It's crowded and loud and smoky, and he's bored. But where would he be if he wasn't here? It's too early to leave, and besides, he's too frustrated to leave alone. He'd step out front for some fresh air, but the cops in this neighborhood have been hassling gay guys out on the street, an experience he intends to avoid. So he heads into the men's room and hides out in a stall, where he occupies himself planning revisions to the term paper he has due in another week and waiting for a sufficient interval to pass that when he goes back out enough new faces will have shown up to pique his interest.

He's just about to decide he's ready to face it again when he hears two men step into the restroom. Avoiding strangers in this confined space is one of his neuroses. He stays put. They'll go back away soon.

"Nice place," one says. "Do you come here often?"

"Almost every weekend," the second one says. "I like the energy here."

"I can definitely see that. The music's great. And the guys are hot. That big blond...Jesus, Mary, and Joseph."

"He's O.K. if you like the storm trooper type."

"Like you don't. God, those shoulders. And those pecs. I mean, he's built like a fucking god."

Scott squirms in the stall. Listening to them talk about him is excruciating. He'd rather be anywhere else, but there's no escape. He can't possibly show himself. He's stuck until they finish and leave.

"Don't forget his cheekbones," the second man says.

"I wonder what he's like."

"Nine and a half inches. Uncut. And a total top."

"You've had him?"

"No, I told you. He's really not my type. But Benny Watson went home with him once."

"Really."

"He said it was transcendent."

"High praise, coming from Benny. He's quite the connoisseur. I bet blondie never goes home alone."

"Practically never. But not for the obvious reason."

"Oh?"

"Blondie is Zane Stark's personal assistant."

"No. Could you die?"

"It gets better. He lives in Zane Stark's guesthouse. Guys line up to go home with him in case old Zane happens to go skinny dipping."

Beverly Hills: 1974

When they get back from their walk, Scott turns the dogs loose in the back yard. In the pool house Zane is still snoring. In all their years together Scott has never known Zane to sleep so soundly or so late. Perhaps it's not really such a surprise: he's never known Zane to get as drunk as he did last night. Or drunk at all, really. He practically had to perform the fireman's carry to get Zane out of the private room at Club Jiu Jitsu, and he was up half the night worrying that he'd aspirate in his sleep. That's what kind of party it was.

Zane said he wanted a bachelor party that people would be talking about at the turn of the next century. Scott tried his best. There was enough booze to float an aircraft carrier, the strippers were busty and obliging, the decorations as elaborate and cheesy as money could buy. That much had been easily enough arranged. The most difficult challenge had been the guest list. Zane had no friends to speak of, and when Scott had asked about his family all he got in the way of a response was a dirty look and a stony silence. The prospect of a bachelor party attended only by the groom and the best man gave Scott nightmares. Even the addition of Angelica's three brothers and eight cousins who would be acting as groomsmen didn't swell the throng to the historic proportions which seemed called for. Then Zane's agent came to the rescue. He slipped Scott the phone numbers of a couple of agent friends of his who represented male models, and presto, a bachelor party that looked like a casting call for a layout in *Esquire*. The young men had been as raucous as they were photogenic. And friendly. Scott left with enough phone numbers to keep him busy for a month at least.

Now it's all history. Today's the wedding day.

He puts the dogs' leashes away, grabs his gym bag and keys, and leaves Zane snoring.

* * *

It's a 1920's building north of Sunset in the shadows of the Chateau Marmont, beautifully maintained and dripping with period charm. Scott's forgotten the names of the minor celebrities the rental agent told them had lived here over the years. He had never heard of any of them, but Zane seemed impressed. The lobby could have been lifted from a vintage hotel in a European capital. The elevator looks like a relic of *fin de siecle* Paris. The apartment is on the top floor. Scott turns the key in the stubborn lock and steps inside. The smells of fresh paint and newly laid carpeting assault him. He does a quick walk through. The bathroom has been completely renovated: new tile work, new marble floor, new fixtures. It's clean and shiny; pristine as an operating theater. The kitchen is equally exquisite, with perfectly restored period appliances. New drapes frame the windows in every room. New, period reproduction light fixtures have been installed. The chimney has been repaired so that the fireplace is now more than ornamental. It's just as they were promised the day they signed the lease. Zane paid in advance for a year.

"I know it seems like an extravagance," he had said as they drove back toward Beverly Hills. "You'll never be there. But you have to have an address of your own. And it has to be a good one. Zane Stark's P.A. can't live just anywhere."

Zane paid for the furniture, too. It's being delivered on Monday. Scott will move his things in on Tuesday.

* * *

Ordinarily, Scott avoids the gym on Saturdays. Saturday mornings bring out all kinds of posers, gossips, and assorted casual types who clog the aisles and don't rack their weights after finishing sets and spend their time generally making nuisances of themselves. They're there to see and be seen, and exercise is incidental. The crowd usually includes at least one loudmouth who believes Scott behaved badly to him, either by refusing to go home with him or to do so more than once, and shares disparaging commentary with whomever will listen just loud enough that Scott can't believably pretend not to hear. Scott has never figured out how to tell the difference between guys who are O.K. with a one night stand and guys who pretend they're cool but really want boyfriends. There is apparently some trick to it that he can't master. He's sympathetic, God knows: he would like a boyfriend himself. Someday his circumstances may even permit it. Meantime, yes, despite the best of intentions he's left a trail of steaming debris in his wake. He has no illusions about that. He's undoubtedly at least as bad as he's being painted. But these passive aggressive confrontations aren't good either for his workouts—they interfere with his concentration—or his peace of mind, something which is in increasingly short supply. So he knows perhaps it isn't the best idea but he feels like if he doesn't get in a good hard workout he'll jump out of his skin. And today of all days he can't risk that.

Sure enough, he has to park his bike a block and a half away and he gets the last available locker. He changes into his workout gear as quickly as possible. Heads turn as he enters the workout area, but he ignores all the stares. As the neighborhood goes more and more gay and more and more gay men take up working out, this scene becomes almost reflexive: everyone in the room checks out each new arrival as instinctively as they continue breathing. He long since grew accustomed to it. But Scott's aware of an extra undercurrent this morning. The gossip columns have been more than usually breathless this week in the run up to Angelica Viborg and Zane Stark's wedding, and here's Zane's personal assistant, big as life, coming in for a last minute pump. In a town as status conscious and celebrity obsessed as this, he knows he's not just walking in, he's making an entrance. For better or worse, he's not his own person, even here.

It's not a total waste, thank God. He manages a pretty good workout in spite of his distraction. He runs into a couple of gym buddies, Rex, who spots him on his bench presses, and Ted, who's always ready with a relevant critique of his form. They're as studiedly blasé as he is, and the few moments he spends with each of them goes a long way toward preserving his sanity.

* * *

Angelica Viborg, Zane's intended, is Honest to God Hollywood Royalty. Her grandfather owned his own studio in the early days of the industry, and her father is a multiple Oscar nominated director. Her mother, herself the daughter and granddaughter of producers, enjoyed a brief vogue as a forties era blond bombshell before retiring to Malibu, where she breeds Russian Wolfhounds, collects vintage jewelry, and maintains her tan. Angelica's whole life has been spent in front of the camera. From home movies to blockbusters, it's clear she's always had star quality. With that pedigree and her tall, golden haired, overblown beauty, it doesn't matter whether she has any talent or not. She has a career and will for as long as she wants it and her looks don't fade too noticeably. She's just wrapped shooting a romantic comedy on the Cote d'Azur, and the minute she and Zane return from their honeymoon she's off to Tahiti for location shooting on a project being described in the trades as a "South Seas espionage thriller". Scott hasn't yet been able to get his brain around this concept but he's sure the box office will be healthy if for no other reason than the way Angelica looks in a bikini. She's already booked for three features after that, and her agent mentioned to Scott recently that he's in talks with an Italian director who wants her for his science fiction inspired production of *A Midsummer Night's*

Dream. Scott has no difficulty imagining her as a 21st Century Titania. If he tried to explain to anyone that what attracted Zane most about Angelica is that she's almost never in town, he'd be considered a pathological liar or a full blown lunatic. But that, as they say, is show business.

Twenty-two years old, she's already been romantically linked—not to say actually involved—with literally dozens of Hollywood's most eligible bachelors. Somehow Zane made the cut. This was anything but a sure thing. Competition was fierce, as were the aspirational machinations of more than one Hollywood dynasty looking to forge an alliance with the Viborgs. Zane certainly had nothing to offer along those lines. And spectacular looking as Zane is, male beauty is ridiculously common in these parts. He's charming, of course, and well mannered. He can make intelligent conversation, or at least what passes for it in the film community. He's extremely successful, but in television, which anyone can tell you hardly counts. And that's just the start of his deficiencies. He has no education to speak of, no family background, precious little track record. The lack of any compelling personal qualities on his part other than loads of charisma compounds the unlikelihood of the match, and Hollywood, at a loss for a logical explanation, has decided that it must be true love.

* * *

Hexagone hasn't changed in the three years since Scott last worked here. Stepping into the small foyer he could almost be reporting for a shift after a few days off. Except that he's dressed for a casual Saturday brunch, while the waiters he spies are resplendent in crisp white shirts, black trousers, and skinny black ties. He's wondered several times since being summoned to this event who he might see here that he knows from the old days. No one, as it turns out. Not surprising, really. Almost all the other guys back then were actor/models, a species noted for its migratory patterns. If they're still waiting tables, it's not here.

"I'm with the Viborg party," he tells the hostess and notices the tiny flicker in her expression: she's impressed in spite of herself. Celebrities are a dime a dozen here; the staff pride themselves on their impregnable blasérie. But the Viborgs aren't run of the mill celebrities, God knows. And of course, she knows what day it is.

"Right this way, sir," she smiles. "The others are already here."

* * *

Scott would love to know whose idea this was. The suggestion had to have occurred to someone originally, but for the life of him he can't imagine who it might have been. Still, a free meal is a free meal, and there are worse ways to pass the time before he has to drive Zane to the church. When he first received the invitation he assumed that Angelica's cousins would be present. But it's to be just her three brothers and Scott. Except that when he arrives at the table, there are already four men present. Derek Viborg, the oldest brother, is one of those perfectly groomed, sleekly handsome men completely lacking in personality or sex appeal. He's an attorney specializing in entertainment law. According to Zane, he's worth at least twenty million that he earned himself, and his clothing, wristwatch and jewelry support that claim. His wife's family is a tribe of minor central European aristocrats with a pedigree stretching into the previous millennium and a history of bad debts more or less equally venerable. His mistress is a former *Playboy* cover model. She's on this afternoon's guest list, officially as Zane's cousin. There are several other "cousins of convenience" attending the wedding. Dieter, the middle brother, is shaggy haired and scraggly bearded as befits an "independent filmmaker". His bohemianism doesn't prevent him from sporting two hundred dollar loafers and a gold Rolex with diamond decorated hour markers. Shaven, barbered, and polished up, he'd look like Derek's twin. His live-in girlfriend is an Italian fashion model related somehow to the people who make Fiats. Their twin daughters will march down the aisle scattering rose petals in Angelica's path. This required intricate negotiations with the Bishop of the Episcopal Diocese of Los Angeles, which were finalized just in time for the rehearsal and entailed a six-figure donation to the bishop's discretionary fund. Scott has met both of these brothers before but can't claim more than a nodding acquaintance with them. The other two men at the table he doesn't recognize. They look equally likely to be Angelica's baby brother Dylan, and he assumes that the one who isn't must be one of the cousins. Turns out, however, that the odd man is Dylan's roommate, Stewart. They've just finished junior year at UCLA and share an apartment in Westwood. They're ridiculously cute. They look like the kind of young actors who always get cast as fraternity boys, rather than the real thing: Scott's been in this town long enough to know the difference.

"How's your boy this morning?" Derek asks once their orders have been taken and curious ears have retreated to a safe distance.

"Snoring, last time I checked."

"Not surprising," Dieter snorts. "He was blasted comatose last night. I'm surprised you didn't have to have his stomach pumped."

"You know," Scott says, "I'd never seen him like that. Ordinarily, he hardly drinks at all. Of course I know that's exactly what you'd expect his personal assistant to say to his future in laws."

"Angelica tells the same story," Derek shrugs, settling the matter once and for all, and what Scott feared was about to turn into a cross examination peters out just like that.

He hasn't been looking forward to brunching with this crew, certain that his chronic self consciousness will spike unbearably under their scrutiny. In that condition there's no telling what indiscretion he might commit. He's haunted by the possibility that even at this late date he might do something to blow the whole thing sky high. But as their orders are served and drinks refilled, he quickly realizes he needn't have worried. They're cordial enough, certainly. They make him feel completely welcome. But they show no interest in him at all. They grew up rich and attended private schools. They ski in Aspen or Gstaad. If they get tired of the family compound in Malibu, there's the private island in the Caribbean or the villa outside Nice. They know instinctively that Scott's not one of them. He may be the best man in their sister's wedding, but once the reception is over they'll never see him again. There's no reason for curiosity. And their desultory remarks about Zane indicate no curiosity about him either. In Scott's book, this is no cause for offense. Indeed, it's almost too good to be true.

* * *

When Zane first mentioned marrying Angelica, he said, "I've never believed in marrying for money, but I would consider it wrong to allow my scruples to get in the way of Angelica's happiness." Scott recognized the paraphrase of Lady Bracknell and grinned to himself, figuring the discussion was purely hypothetical. Although he understood that Zane had never stopped at anything, it had never occurred to him that marriage was even a remote possibility. At the time they had only been on a couple of dates, and until that pronouncement Zane had said nothing to indicate that the situation was different in any way than it had been with well over a dozen other girls during the previous months.

Not that it didn't make sense. Zane needed something to distinguish himself from those dozens and hundreds of charming, handsome, ambitious young men infesting Hollywood like a parody of an Old Testament plague. Something to forestall the statistical near inevitability that regardless of his current success all too soon he'd be forgotten. Today's sensation turns into tomorrow's nonentity almost as predictably as summer turns into fall. Avoiding that fate couldn't be left up to luck. No good could come from going with the flow.

Patronage had gotten him where he was, and patronage seemed the most logical force to propel him still farther. The Viborgs were demonstrably as nepotistic a tribe as currently existed in the industry. As Angelica's lawfully wedded spouse there was every reason to think that he'd find himself, sooner rather than later, cast in one of Dalton Viborg's spectaculars, particularly if he refused to campaign for it. Failing that, even a role in one of Dieter's intimate little opuses would establish him as more than a mere TV star. With their seal of approval, Hollywood would be forced to regard him differently than it did at present: photogenic in the extreme but ultimately a nonentity. He would be, indisputably, someone.

So yes, the proposed marriage was a career move. Scott could understand that well enough. The riddle was in how all this calculation squared with the little interest Scott knew Zane actually had in his career as such. The motivation must lie far deeper than any stereotypical lust for fame and fortune. It seemed, rather, that Zane was on a quest for some sort of comprehensive validation of his own ideal of himself as the kind of young man who deserved the notoriety and adulation through some grand, karmic imperative. A little too Jay Gatsby for Scott's comfort, but he doubted that Zane had ever read the book.

What made it possible was Zane's most essential quality. Far more than his charisma and his looks, it was his ability to please, to give people exactly what they wanted before it had occurred to them to ask for it and perhaps even before they could have mentally registered their desire, that had been rewarded at every step. All those gifts from his admirers, not to mention their eventual aid in getting him the series, sprang from it. It surely must be the explanation for Angelica's devotion and her family's acquiescence in her choice. To Scott it seemed a horrifyingly tenuous thing on which to hang one's fate.

* * *

Scott lifts the last piece of luggage into the trunk and shuts the lid. He'll drive Angelica and Zane to the airport from the reception. The honeymoon destination is a closely guarded secret. When Scott expressed surprise that the Viborgs' private jet could make transatlantic flights, Zane outlined a route that included refueling stops in Chicago, Gander, Rejkjavik, and Glasgow prior to their arrival in Nice. Zane is already in the passenger seat. The garment bags with their clothes for the wedding lie across the back seat. Scott climbs in beside him. He turns the key and the big V-8 engine throbs to life. He stares down the long, long hood at the three pointed star. They're off.

"Here we go," Zane yawns.

"Nervous?"

"No. Why?"

"I would be."

Zane doesn't answer. Behind his sunglasses he's more inscrutable than ever. Before they've gone two blocks Scott notices that his mouth has gone slack. These days Zane can't ride in a car for more than a few minutes without nodding off. He should have known better than to think the drive out to Malibu would be a chance for them to have a last few moments together. It's just one more in a long line of lost opportunities. He presses a button and Mahler's First swells out of the speakers.

Zane naps. Scott fights the Saturday mid afternoon traffic. It could easily be just another outing, the kind they went on all the time before Zane got famous. There's no indication anything out of the ordinary is going on. It's all surreally normal. Just two guys in jeans and t-shirts heading toward the beach. Even if the car they're in is the size of a battleship, Scott still only half believes what's happening. He never thought Zane would let it go this far. He never let himself believe Zane would want to. He can't begin to imagine how profoundly he's going to regret his miscalculation, or for how long.

There Zane is, in arm's reach but still as distant as ever. He pays Scott a ridiculous amount of money to do a job that's more or less totally undefined and leaves Scott on a sort of permanent vacation. His generosity is ridiculous; he recently tried to buy Scott a Maserati. He's given Scott responsibility over his household, including a large proportion of his money. He's given Scott free run of his body for all these years. Until the last six months, there's been nobody as close to him as Scott has been. Scott's still not sure that has actually changed, but maybe this is just wishful thinking. Still, he has to admit it: Zane has never truly let him inside. He knows him no better than he did back in Venice, before he even had a name. He's no more, really, than a glorious collection of surfaces and gestures.

So how is it that he's never stopped being Scott's obsession?

Everything he does for Zane and everything he has ever done for Zane he'd gladly do for free just to be near him. Zane can't not know it and what it means. It's as if all Zane's generosity is his way of fending off the reality of Scott's feelings. Of making an even trade, as if tangible commodities were being exchanged. Of wriggling free of anything else Scott might think his faithful, uncomplaining servitude entitles him to. Yes, Zane is calculating enough for that.

* * *

"Lock that door."

Scott turns the bolt. Of course Zane doesn't want to be barged in on while he's dressing. Then he feels Zane's eyes on him and looks back.

"You're kidding. In church?"

"What's that got to do with it?"

"You're getting married in less than an hour."

"Get out of those clothes," Zane growls. "There's no time to lose."

There they are: those eyes. That smile. The supernatural silkiness of that skin. The unearthly luster of that hair.

* * *

Scott's touching up his hair at the mirror when there's a knock on the door.

"Mr. Stark?" Scott recognizes the voice of the wedding coordinator.

"Yes," Zane says, grinning at Scott.

"We need you in the sanctuary in five minutes, Mr. Stark."

"Thank you," he says. He turns to Scott. "So this is it."

"As they say."

"Come here," Zane says. With infinite tenderness, he kisses Scott on the lips. It's all Scott can do not to start sobbing. "Listen to me, O.K? This doesn't change anything."

* * *

The sanctuary blazes with candlelight, which on this sunny Southern California afternoon is superfluous, and light from the enormous chandeliers. More light streams in through the stained glass windows. Even the huge floral arrangements seem to glow with some internal illumination. Zane's side of the aisle is filled by fellow cast members, technical and production people, and overflow from the the bride's party. Zane's director is dire in morning coat and tails. Scott can't believe he doesn't know better, and more to the point, no one attempted to dissuade him. Zane's co-star looks every bit of his hard drinking seventy-nine years. He's practically falling down. With him is his brand new fourth wife, a girl who looks young enough to be his granddaughter. Her breasts are said to be the biggest money could buy. Zane gives Scott a quick wink as if to say, "see what I have to deal with?" In all the ballyhoo leading up to the event no one has had the bad taste to inquire as to the absence of Zane's family. It's as if he's an orphan and people are too well mannered to mention it. For all Scott knows, Zane actually is an orphan. As famous as he's become, you'd expect long lost brothers, cousins, parents, etc., to be crawling out of the woodwork, yet there hasn't been any sign. He wonders what Zane has told his prospective inlaws.

The Viborg guests are a mighty throng. Were the building to suddenly implode, Hollywood would have to shut down for months if not years. Present are several Oscar winners. A gaggle of studio executives and their wives. Producers, associate producers and assistant producers almost too many to count. Not to mention the relatives from four continents. And the list goes on. A world renowned symphony orchestra conductor and the slender young Eurasian man who was introduced to Scott earlier as his secretary. A famous biographer who's researching the second volume of his "definitive" work on Angelica's grandfather, *Dermott Viborg, Hollywood Pioneer: a Visionary's Quest*. Two congressmen and a lieutenant governor, all from out of state. Several fashion designers and a Pulitzer Prize winning novelist said to be in negotiations with Dieter regarding a film version of one of his early books. Despite their eminence, these luminaries all wait with the same anticipation as the more proletarian guests across the aisle.

A lithe, floppy haired young beauty who may be yet another cousin escorts Madeleine Viborg up the aisle to her seat. She's a serene vision, thanks to valium, Dior, Tiffany, and the ministrations of a small army of hair and makeup people. The usher returns the way he came, the organist plays a slow cadence in diminuendo, modulates upward by a major third, segues into a voluntary by Purcell, and the parade of bridesmaids begins. They're goddesses all: several of Angelica's cousins, friends from her finishing school in Switzerland including a genuine princess, and bringing up the rear, Hollie Tepper, Angelica's best friend since they co-starred in *What's a Girl To Do?* as sixteen year olds. Though the rumor mongers insist that their relationship is not as close as it once was due to the current doldrums Hollie's career seems lost in while Angelica's just goes from strength to strength, there's no sign of this purported rift. This is Hollie's first public appearance since filing for divorce from her British husband, rock and roll bad boy Cameron Makepeace, who is said to be licking his wounds in an undisclosed location. Her newly titian hair is not the best choice, considering her skin tone.

* * *

With his regal bearing and thick mane of silver hair, Dalton Viborg looks like an Old Testament prophet blessed with a good tailor and an even better hairdresser. Angelica is every inch his daughter. She looks like a prima ballerina portraying the queen of the amazons in the big coronation scene. All that's missing is the *corps de ballet* trailing in her wake. Angelica and her father move up the aisle of the church like they're under sail. It's a director's wet dream of a shot and thank God it won't be lost to posterity. You can hear the cameras whirring even over the blasting pipe organ.

This can't be a real wedding. It's too perfect, too theatrical. It's a scene. This is Zane's directorial debut, and Scott is an extra. Any moment now Zane will yell "cut". He'll give a note or two and order everyone back to their marks for another take.

* * *

"With this ring I thee wed," Bishop Hampshire intones.

"With this ring I thee wed," Zane repeats.

"And with all my worldly goods I thee endow."

"And with all my worldly goods I thee endow."

Scott stares, transfixed. Once again disbelief has him reeling. How many sudden moments of lightheadedness have there been already today? Too many to count, that's for certain. These phrases of the marriage ceremony, so familiar they're practically clichés, have all but done him in. Out of the corner of his eye he sees more than one bridesmaid mouthing the words. But coming from the lips of Zane and Angelica, they're like the cryptic utterances of two gorgeous aliens that just stepped off a flying saucer bringing wisdom that will save the world. The suspense of the moment seems deadly, though everyone present knows exactly how it ends.

"Now if you'll all indulge me," the bishop says, "I'd just like to take a moment to reminisce. It seems like only yesterday that Madeleine and Dalton brought Angelica here to be baptized. And as I look out at those gathered I see among you her godmother and godfather here sharing this most joyous day.

Angelica, my dear, you are truly blessed, not just by the adoration of this fine young man, but in the way you are surrounded and upheld by so many of those who have loved and cared for you all your life.

"And now, by the power vested in me…"

Scott watches the kiss, hears the applause, stares after them as they go arm in arm down the aisle.

* * *

Second only to Scott's dismay at the idea of Zane's marriage was his terror at the idea of making the best man's speech at the reception. He couldn't imagine standing in front of all those people pretending not to feel what he knew he'd be feeling once the time came, much less saying anything appropriate to the occasion. He couldn't possibly be less like the stalwart, heterosexual best friend of the groom the occasion so insistently calls for.

Zane to the rescue yet again: two of the series' writers have done their magic. They're good; very, very good. It doesn't read like a script at all, yet it's the perfect best man's speech: just the right combination of innuendo, sentimentality, and self deprecation, coupled with awkward gallantry directed toward the bride. Best of all it's not too slick. It says everything he would say if he were the kind of best man Zane apparently needs him to appear to be. He'll even try his best to sound sincere. It won't be hard: he just has to pretend he's someone else. He can manage that. He gets enough practice, God knows.

And he has rehearsed. God, how he has rehearsed these last few weeks. If he trusted his emotional state he'd do it verbatim. He rises from his seat, takes the microphone offered to him, unfolds the sheets, takes a breath, and begins.

"Good evening, everyone. My name is Scott…"

* * *

"There he is now! After him!" The cry echoes across the three story tall foyer of the mansion.

"Good spot, Stewie Boy."

"Scott…"

"We've been looking…"

"…everywhere for you."

Dylan and his roommate Stewie collide with him in a chaos of floppy hair, disheveled formal wear, unnaturally bright eyes, and tipsy grins. They each grab an arm and start dragging him away.

"Where have you…"

"…been hiding out"

"…all evening?"

"We've been…"

"…looking everywhere."

"You should…"

"…come with us."

"Where? Where are you taking me?" Scott asks.

They're heading for the grand staircase.

"Upstairs."

"We've got balloons in Dylan's room."

"We're going to…"

"…fill them up"

"…with water and"

"…throw them off the"

"…third floor terrace at"

"…people on the dance floor."

It's exactly the kind of hijinks they look like they would specialize in, and exactly the kind of thing Scott wants no part of. He can't imagine the bride's parents being amused. Their own son can probably get away with it, but Scott doesn't dare contemplate Dalton Viborg's wrath at such a violation of his hospitality being committed by a mere retainer. But there are two of them; strong young guys. And they've got momentum on their side as well as a kind of drunken determination. Not to mention the element of surprise. He simply doesn't have the energy to fight them. He allows himself to be propelled up the broad stairs and down a thickly carpeted hallway that wouldn't be out of place in a luxury hotel. One of the boys—he still has trouble telling them apart—shoves open a door. Next thing he knows they're in a bedroom, and the door has been slammed shut, and hands are fumbling with his clothing and a tongue is invading his mouth.

* * *

When he leaves them an hour or so later, they're snorting cocaine and giggling over another successful escapade. This is apparently their preferred and frequent modus operandi: find an unsuspecting top guy, drag him off somewhere, and take turns getting themselves ravished. They're such experts it's obviously far from the first time they've done it. So despite Scott's best intentions, here he is another notch on someone's bedpost.

He can only hope they know how to keep their mouths shut. He can't imagine the repercussions if Zane's in-laws find out.

* * *

"Scott, there you are," Angelica calls. "I've been hoping all day we'd find time for a chat."

She moves toward him a little unsteadily. Sprawled across the bottom three steps of the grand staircase, he's surprised by her clumsiness at first because she's a very light drinker, but then he notices the slippers hanging by straps from her left hand. She's not tipsy, she's trying not to step on the hem of her dress. Without the lift provided by those three inch heels it's not easy, even for an actress who studied ballet.

"Let's go in here," she says, motioning to a doorway off to his left, "Daddy's study."

It's a study all right. Or at least the set for one. There is the requisite desk with chair and appropriate paraphernalia, the requisite shelving full of books, even the requisite antique globe on a floor stand. The dark paneled room could have been lifted right out of some stately home in Gloucestershire. But somehow nothing about it indicates it's ever been used for its titular purpose. Angelica sinks into one of the diamond pleated leather club chairs facing each other at right angles to the desk and motions him into the other.

"I'm exhausted," she giggles.

He remembers that line and exactly that giggle from *Chelsea Morning*. Since she and Zane became engaged, Scott thinks he must have seen every film she ever appeared in. He has tried so very hard to hate her, but you might as well hate the sunrise. He has to admit it: those millions of fans aren't wrong. She's something very special indeed, even if most of her films have been mediocre at best. He's gradually come to the realization that she doesn't deserve his enmity. She hasn't done anything to him. She's no more to blame for the situation he's in than the man on the moon. And she's certainly always been friendly enough in her funny, distracted way.

"You've had a big day."

"Yes," she says, "I'd say I have."

"It was a beautiful wedding."

"Yes, indeed," she agrees. "The finest money could pay for and Hollywood know how could produce. And you, dear boy, looked incredible. I'd tell you some of the things the bridesmaids have been saying about you but I'm afraid it would give you a big head."

"We can't have that."

"It would never do."

The art deco clock on the credenza strikes the half hour.

"Oh, Scott," she says, suddenly dramatic. "I know you're more than just Zane's P.A."

His heart skips a beat. Is this the confrontation he's been dreading since day one?

"He's told me all about it, you know. How the two of you ran away from home together because his parents mistreated him so badly and you refused to let him go alone. All those times you protected him. And that time he was so sick he nearly died and you stole food for him and got him to that doctor who saved his life with barely a second to spare. You have no idea how much you mean to him. You're not just his best friend, Scott, you're his hero. I used to be so jealous of you, you know? I thought I could never mean as much to him as you do."

"That's silly," Scott mutters, astonished that Zane would bother to make up such elaborate stories about their past.

"I see that now," she nods. "I finally figured out that I should be thankful that he has someone like you in his life. Someone so loyal and trustworthy. I want to thank you for being so patient with me."

"I don't…"

"I know, I know, I come off like just another spoiled rich girl. But I try to be better than that. Honestly, I do try."

"Of course you do."

"So anyway, darling Scott, thanks a million for everything you do for us. *Merci mille fois.*"

"Think nothing of it."

"And I'm so very glad you'll be joining us on the Cote d'Azur. When are you arriving? Wednesday?"

"Very late," he says. "Because of the time change."

"Have you been to France?"

"Never."

"You're in for a treat. And I am too, come to think of it. Zane is always so much happier when you're around. We'll have a lovely time. I can't wait to show both of you all my favorite places. And the house, Scott, the house is gorgeous. You won't want to leave."

"I'm looking forward to it."

"Why, Scott?" she asks, tossing her head just the way she did in that restaurant scene in *Heads You Lose*. "Why do we go on living in L.A. when there's France?"

He doesn't have an answer for that.

"Angelica, darling, here you are. I've been looking everywhere."

"Hello, Mummy."

"The Schoendorffs are leaving, dear. Won't you come and say goodnight to them?"

"Of course, Mummy. I'll see you anon, darling Scott."

* * *

There must have been a moment. Hand on the flimsy railing of the aircraft's folding stairs, Scott takes the metal steps down to the tarmac. A moment ago he received their benedictions: kisses on each cheek from Angelica, the manliest of handshakes and a slap on the shoulder from Zane. They were just like any other honeymoon couple, and he supposes he was just like any other best man. Zane's matter of factness about the whole thing makes him feel more insignificant than he ever thought it was possible to feel. He left them there in the cabin, settling themselves for the first leg of the flight.

There must have been a moment when he could have said no. He crosses the fifty feet of tarmac to where the Mercedes sits, headlights glowing. He climbs into the driver's seat and settles down to wait. Not "no" to today, this cinematic wedding, this unfathomable marriage. Putting a stop to all that would have accomplished nothing. If not Angelica, there's some other woman out there. There's some other prize to be contended for. Some other world to conquer. Wherever Zane looks, he sees things, situations, people ripe for exploitation. This stage in his rake's progress was inevitable. No one knows that better than Scott.

Lights on the aircraft begin strobing. The engines spool into whining and then screeching animation. It has never been a question of saying no to Zane, because you might as well say no to gravity or the tides. But there must have been a moment, back in those gray, gloomy, squalid days in Venice when there was still time to make himself stop.

Eventually, as if with infinite deliberation, the aircraft begins to move. Scott thinks he sees faces peering out of the cabin windows but maybe that's just his imagination. When could it have been? That night when Zane said he was leaving Venice and suggested in that totally offhand way of his that Scott come along? No, Scott remembers clearly the electricity of that moment: even by then it had already been too late. But there must have been a moment when his fate was not yet determined and he could have changed it with a word or even a thought.

The aircraft taxis past, heading now for the runway. They always look ungainly to Scott, lumbering along so slowly and noisily, completely belying their true athleticism, the speed and agility they will display once they have left the ground behind. The flashing lights recede, the fuselage and wings gradually disappear into the dimness along the runway.

The craft accelerates, but from Scott's angle it's hard to discern it. It's only noticeable due to the ever more deafening roar of the engines. Finally, almost imperceptibly at first but then with surprising speed, the lights rise into the blackness and fade all too quickly into invisibility above the city. Scott sits alone behind the wheel, trying vainly to remember that last instant when something other than this desolation had still been possible.

Bloomington, Indiana: 1975

If he were back in West Hollywood, Scott would know exactly why the bodybuilder with the light brown hair is staring at him. It's exactly the kind of stare he'd expect to attract there, exactly the kind of stare he did attract there. Pretty much every time he left home, as a matter of fact. And of course he knew exactly what to do about it when it happened—whatever he was in the mood for at the time. Except for the Mormon missionary haircut this hunk is sporting—not at all unattractive on him, just not a style any halfway fashion conscious West Hollywood gay would be caught dead wearing, at least not this season—he's exactly the kind of guy Scott would expect to find staring at him like that. But this is the produce department at the A&P, and California is two thousand miles away, and men here in Indiana don't cruise as blatantly as this. Men here apparently don't cruise each other at all. At any rate that's the strong impression Scott has formed in the last two months since he arrived "back home again in Indiana" after his nearly decade long exile. Which means all bets are off and makes the guy not somebody Scott would definitely consider fucking if he hadn't sworn off anonymous sex before he left California but more than likely some kind of weirdo.

But a really hot weirdo. Extraordinarily hot, in fact. Scott is intrigued in spite of himself. His stealthy glances have revealed that the man is about his own age and a couple of inches shorter but probably a good thirty pounds heavier than Scott. Staring back is not by any stretch of the imagination a good idea. But oh, those deltoids, plumped up like cantaloupes, and oh, those pecs. The comic book superhero arms are enough to make a grown faggot cry, but worst of all are the eyes. Set in that square jawed, firm chinned, football hero face, they're smoldering like the dying coals of a campfire under a harvest moon. You could melt an iceberg with eyes like those. The guy is as hot as anybody you'd see parading down Santa Monica Boulevard on a Saturday night. So even though he's probably a psychopath and Scott is risking having his throat ripped out and his mutilated carcass stuffed into a dumpster, he eventually can't help himself and returns the attention. But subtly: a glance here, then he turns to examine the eggplants. Another glance, and then a shift of the eyes in the direction of the okra bin. One more glance and yes, the guy is definitely moving closer. It's a dance as carefully choreographed as any *pas de deux* at the Bolshoi. Scott suddenly feels as if he never left California.

"Say," Mr. Universe growls, picking up the oversized zucchini Scott has just placed back in the pile and aiming at him like an accusation, "haven't I seen you working out at the Y?"

"Don't believe so," Scott says. Technically this is not a lie. Though he has in fact been working out there daily he certainly wouldn't have failed to notice this extraordinary phenomenon.

"I'm sure I have," the man grins. "Just yesterday afternoon."

Scott shrugs. He was there yesterday afternoon. Where the hell was this creature?

"Knew it," the man says, grinning still more incandescently. "Never forget a face. Name's Clay."

"Oh my God," Scott gasps. "This is too weird."

"What?"

"Clay Horstmann, right?"

"Yeah," Clay nods. "How'd you know?"

"Scott Bailey," Scott says, poking himself in the chest with his index finger. "Remember me?"

And now it's Clay's turn to be astonished.

* * *

So he wasn't being cruised after all, Scott thinks as he crawls into bed. Clay must have recognized him unconsciously somehow; must have been drawn to him not for the obvious reason, at least the one Scott with his gay ghetto social conditioning thinks of as obvious, but because of some bizarre combination of subliminal forces that reached out across the last nine years and neatly made the unlikeliest of connections. So much for those West Hollywood boys and their highly vaunted gaydar. Scott's was one hundred eighty degrees off the beam, as the events of the evening unmistakably demonstrated. The house, complete, incredibly enough, with the white picket fence, the station wagon in the driveway, the sheepdog in the yard; the pretty, Betty Crocker type wife in the kitchen; the two cute, obedient sons and a third baby on the way; the job teaching high school civics and coaching football and wrestling: Clay's life couldn't be more white bread normal.

Things really are different here. And that's the whole point.

* * *

"Here, let me spot you on your bench presses," Clay's baritone rumble crashes into Scott's consciousness just as he's getting into position to begin his set.

"Hey there," Scott smiles. "Didn't see you come in."

"Just got here. Say, that's some pretty serious weight you've got on the bar."

"My usual."

"Yeah, well it shows. Never would have thought you'd end up looking like that," Clay says. "You were such a scrawny little runt."

"It surprised me more than anybody," Scott says. "Believe me. One minute I was five feet five and weighed one hundred ten, and the next thing I knew I'd grown six inches and gained seventy pounds. I mean literally in about six months. You should have seen me eat. It was like one nonstop meal. That's when I started working out. When I realized I could actually look like something."

"So what are you now? About two hundred?"

"Uh huh."

"Well, we can do better than that. You ready?"

"Sure."

They move around the weight room like they've been workout partners for years. When it's Scott's turn to lift Clay growls out brutal encouragement like a drill instructor. When Clay lifts Scott tries to return the favor, but the patter sounds faintly ridiculous coming out of his mouth. As they move from station to station, Scott finds himself showing off for Clay, slapping more weight than he's used to onto the bar and pounding out more reps. It's as if he has something to prove, but he can't for the life of him imagine why he should feel that way.

When they're finished they hit the showers together, and Scott resolutely refuses to look. That way lies an insanity he's determined to evade at all costs. They wash, towel off, fix their hair, and dress accompanied by Clay's nonstop narration of the events of his day. What will he have left to talk about with Annie when he gets home, Scott wonders? Or will Clay repeat himself to her like a tape recording?

"So how often are you here?" Clay asks as they leave the building.

"Every day. I alternate body parts."

"Good man," Clay nods. "See you tomorrow, then."

* * *

Three months now since Scott returned to Bloomington and his resolve still holds. He hasn't sought out the local gay places. He steers well clear of those few notorious men's washrooms on campus. With Clay as his chaperone the showers and steam room at the Y hold no temptations. Maybe he truly has left all that behind him in California. He gets up in the morning and goes to his classes. He goes to the gym to work out. He goes to his job waiting tables at *La Maison*. On weekends he catches up on his studies, cleans his tiny apartment, does his laundry, and works extra shifts at the restaurant. When men give him that certain look he pretends not to notice. And now that he's tuned in to the signs he realizes that things are far more active around town than he thought when he first arrived. He missed it all at first because it's so damned subtle, as it would have to be here hundreds of miles from anything that could conceivably be described as a center of gay culture. It's a hostile environment, no doubt about it. And so the boys are always tentative. They look but they never actively pursue. They smile, but they never persist. It's all over before it's even begun, fleeting as a heartbeat. And their glances and smiles are so calculatedly friendly and innocent, so completely free of innuendo, there's little if any possibility that some straight boy might be offended by their attentions. Or even notice them.

Occasionally one of his customers at *La Maison* will send out unmistakable signals. It's as upscale a place as there is in Bloomington, and the clientele aren't students but grown men, married or on dates with women. They're never there alone, never in the company of other men. They are far more blatant than the boys on campus. Scott wonders what they can be thinking of: it's hardly any less dangerous for them. Perhaps their affluence makes them feel less threatened. Perhaps their age makes them desperate, and their desperation fuels their risky behavior. He tries not to dwell on it. They're not a species he feels he can afford to concern himself with. He forgets them as soon as they've left the restaurant. He banishes them from his mind even as he pockets their sometimes outrageous tips: transparent, faintly ridiculous pleas that he notice and remember them. Even with their charge cards and expensive clothes and haircuts they're in far less of a position than the boys on campus to intrude on his life. This doesn't seem like much of a life, he knows, but it's what he wanted. Or at least what he thought he wanted. It's what he came for, seeking a sanctuary where he could escape the insistence of the beauties on Santa Monica Boulevard, whom he was finding it easier and easier to say yes to, presumably as some sort of consolation prize. Not to mention the blandishments of the sugar daddies and pornographers, whom he was finding more and more insistent.

It's not being gay he's determined to escape. He knows better. He doesn't feel trapped by it any more than being left handed or blue eyed make him feel trapped. There's nothing about the condition itself that he finds the least bit objectionable, though people's prejudices about it are enough to drive anyone crazy. It's the way his brothers in arms out there all go about it that he's fleeing. The way he was increasingly going about it himself. That's what he came here to get away from. He's fine with being gay if he can be gay on his own terms. While he's trying to figure out exactly what those terms are, he's convinced it's best to keep to himself. And as an added benefit he's taking this opportunity to try and learn the kind of foresight that will help him to avoid becoming involved in horrendous domestic complications. Those who do not learn from history are doomed to repeat it, after all.

And so here he is living in an apartment almost exactly midway between campus and the restaurant with a minimum of furniture and without so much as a television. There's not a single picture on the walls. These days blank spaces are Scott's favorite décor. And though none of the people he knew on the coast would believe it if he tried to tell them so, he's content. When he's tired he sleeps. When he's hungry he eats. When he's horny he heads for the gym, and when a good hard workout doesn't banish that desire there's always the stack of magazines in his closet. When he's lonely he tries his very best to ignore it. Really, he tries not to have feelings at all.

* * *

"Say, bud," Clay grunts, soaping his cock in a way Scott would consider outrageously provocative if anyone else were doing it, "you seem kind of bummed."

"Just tired."

"Not surprised. You go to graduate school full time. You wait tables in that ritzy restaurant I couldn't afford to take Annie to unless I sold my left ball. You work out six days a week. When do you have any fun?"

Scott shrugs.

"Well, listen," Clay says, "your good buddy Clay's gonna take care of that. Soon as we're cleaned up I'm taking you out for beer and pizza. How's that sound?"

"Great, I guess. What about Annie?"

"Told her it was boys' night out before I left the house this morning. She won't be expecting me until late. So move your ass."

* * *

"What'd I tell you?" Clay grins. "Is this the best pizza you ever ate?"

Scott nods.

"More beer?"

"I'm already over my limit," Scott says, regretting the two he's already had.

"Well then," Clay says, "ready to get out of here?"

"Sure. Where are we going?"

"Your place. Must be something good on the tube."

"Um, Clay?"

"What?"

"I don't have a T.V."

"S'all right. I'm sure we'll find something to do."

* * *

"Nice place," Clay says, looking around the spartan living room.

"No it's not," Scott says. "It's squalid. It's a dump."

"It's not a dump," Clay insists. "It's clean and uncluttered. A blank slate. Exactly like you."

"Whatever that means," Scott grins.

"Want another beer?"

"Don't you have to get home?"

"Boys' night out, I told you," Clay says, "but I should at least check in. Where's your phone?"

While Clay makes his call, Scott goes into the bathroom. He's not sure bringing Clay here was a good idea. He's been so careful around Clay, but on his own territory he doesn't know how he'll be able to maintain the illusion. He's not even sure what makes him think he needs to. If they're such good friends, shouldn't their friendship be able to stand the truth? The answer is obvious enough, but Scott's not strong enough to face the risk. He'll just have to tough it out. He flushes the toilet to legitimize his time behind the closed door and steps back out.

"Listen, there's something I need to talk about," Clay says, sounding serious and sending Scott's heart into his throat.

"Is something wrong?" he asks, determined to keep his voice steady. Here it is, though. Clay suspects something. He has to.

"Wrong?" Clay asks, looking surprised. "Why would anything be wrong?"

"I don't know, you just seem so, well, somber all of a sudden."

"Somber," Clay laughs. "There's a good graduate school word."

"That's right," Scott says, glad for the distraction. "Make fun."

"I'm not making fun," Clays says. "What I was getting ready to do is ask you to be my new little boy's godfather."

"What?"

"You're not deaf, are you?"

"Don't I have to be a Catholic to do that?"

"Don't sweat it," Clay grins. "You won't have to convert. I'll fix it with Father Shaughnessy."

"Is that even something that can be fixed?"

"Who are you talking to here?" Clay asks.

* * *

Scott wakes from a dream about a ringing telephone to find the phone ringing. He glances at the clock. Three a.m. He hopes against hope it's a wrong number this time.

"Hello?"

There's nothing but that hated long distance hiss, and Scott hangs up. Immediately the phone begins to ring again. He briefly considers unplugging it but decides to give it one more chance first.

"Hello."

"Scottie? Scottie, is that you?"

Zane. For the third time this week.

"Scottie, please don't hang up."

"Do you have any idea what time it is?"

"Just after midnight."

"Where you are, maybe. Here it's three. I have to be up in three hours, so this better be good."

"Oh, God, Scottie, I miss you so much."

"Zane, don't do this."

"What am I doing?" Zane protests. "I'm not doing anything. I just want to talk to you."

"What do we have to talk about?"

"Anything you want, Scottie. I just want to hear your voice."

"I'm sorry, Zane. I have a midterm exam in the morning and I can't do this right now."

* * *

"Fierce, man," Clay says, lathering up his chest. "I mean, the way you're attacking those weights lately. Where did you get to be such a savage?"

Scott shrugs. Clay's attention always makes him self conscious and here in the showers at the gym it's at its worst. It's like, seeing him naked Clay will surely be able to tell. Scott knows this is absurd but he can't master his paranoia.

"Hey, you never said, but did you get drafted? Is that where you became such an animal? Because I know a couple of guys who went to 'Nam and you're kind of like them that way."

"No, I wasn't in the service."

"Well then…"

"Isn't just living enough?"

"Not for most people," Clay says.

"Well it is for me."

"Yow," Clay growls, giving himself a resounding slap across his soapy pectorals.

* * *

"*You'll never be able to buy something off the rack*," Clay had said when Scott mentioned needing a suit for the christening, "*not if you actually want it to fit you. If it's big enough in the shoulders and chest it'll hang like a parachute everywhere else. And if the waist size is correct you won't be able to pull the pants on over your thighs. You'd better let me take you to Teitelbaum's. They make a lot of my clothes.*"

So instead of meeting at the gym this afternoon, here they are downtown parking their near identical BMW's next to each other in front of the ornate old shop front.

"You remember Jerry and Nathan," Clay says, smoothing his helmet crunched hair. "We were in school with them. Jerry's in med school now, and Nathan starts law school next fall."

"They were always pretty nice to me," Scott recalls.

"I hope so," Clay says. "I'd have killed them if they hadn't been. Anyway, the oldest brother, Solly, runs the business these days. But Pa Teitelbaum still does all the tailoring."

Inside the shop it's as if time has been standing still since the late nineteen-forties. A bell rings somewhere in back as the front door closes behind them. Sample suits adorn tailor's dummies, and the walls are lined with photographs of Hollywood leading men of generations past wearing formal attire.

"Good afternoon, gentlemen," a soft spoken old man shuffles in through a curtained doorway behind the counter.

"Hey, Mr. Teitelbaum," Clay greets him. "Clay Horstmann, remember me?"

"Oh, Clay, of course," Mr. Teitelbaum's face lights up. "It's good to see you. How's things?"

"Things are great," Clay says. "And you and yours?"

"It is what it is," Mr Teitelbaum says.

"This is my friend, Scott Bailey," Clay says.

"Pleased to meet you, Mr. Teitelbaum," Scott smiles.

"The pleasure is mine, I assure you," Mr. Teitelbaum says. "What can I do for you young gentlemen this afternoon?"

"Scott needs a suit," Clay explains. "He's going to stand up as godfather when we christen my new baby."

"My congratulations to you both."

"Thanks," Clay says. "With Scott's coloring, I'm thinking something in the darkest blue you can find in a medium weight wool."

"Perfect," Mr. Teitelbaum says, writing notes on a pad that looks like it should be on display in the Smithsonian.

"Now, about his measurements," Clay continues. "We're still probably eight to ten weeks out from the ceremony and Scott's on an intense weight training regimen, so you'll need to allow a little extra room in the shoulders, chest, and thighs. He'll be bigger by then."

"I remember the last suit we made for you, Clay," Mr. Teitelbaum assures him. "And for that matter, I just did a new one for Solly. You know, I see him every day, but when I put the tape on him I couldn't believe my eyes."

"Great," Clay smiles.

"Now, Scott," Mr. Teitelbaum says, "if you'd just step into the back with me. This won't take long at all."

* * *

"*Hollywood Tragedy*," the front page of the tabloid screams. The shot of Angelica isn't flattering. Her hair is covered by a scarf and she's wearing some shapeless raincoat thing, but there's no question it's her. In spite of himself Scott pulls the paper out of the rack and reads about Angelica's miscarriage while the line at the checkout inches forward. The article oozes sympathy. Angelica and Zane are said to be devastated. A commentator is quoted on the subject of the difficulty of maintaining a dynasty given the rigors of life in the film industry. He cites several examples which Scott fails to see the relevance of.

* * *

"Hello."

The male voice on the line is not Zane.

"Zane Stark, please."

"I'm sorry, but Mr. Stark isn't available right now. Can I take a message?"

"Who am I speaking to?" Scott asks.

"Rick Rutherford. Mr. Stark's personal assistant."

"I see. Well, please tell him that Scott called."

"Scott who?"

"Just Scott. He'll know. Please ask him to call back. He has the number."

* * *

"Scottie, it's Zane. What's up?"

"Oh God, Zane, I just heard about Angelica's miscarriage and I wanted to call and tell you how sorry I am."

"Thanks, Scott. That's very sweet."

"You must be devastated," Scott says. "I can't imagine."

"Hey, buddy, it's no big deal."

"What do you mean no big deal?"

"Wasn't my kid," Zane says. "Ergo, no big deal"

"What?"

"Angelica was in Switzerland for twelve weeks shooting the new Paulo Encarnacion film. She came back pregnant. Some assistant of Paolo's. An Algerian guy."

"Jesus, Zane, doesn't that just make it worse?"

"Take it easy. You know Angelica and I had an agreement about sleeping with other people."

"No, Zane, I never heard about any agreement. I know you kept sleeping with other people after the wedding."

"Person, Scott. Only one."

"All right. But I had no idea that Angelica agreed to it."

"It was her idea. As much time as we spend apart, she thought it only made sense."

"Are you saying she knew about us?"

"No. I'm not saying that at all. I'm saying that in principle she doesn't have a problem with what I do while she's away and vice versa."

"But surely now…"

"Why now?"

"Well, I mean, losing the baby like that."

"Poor Scottie," Zane laughs. "Poor dear Scottie."

"What's that supposed to mean?"

"After all this time you still don't know not to believe what they print in those rags."

"I don't understand."

"The story was a plant. There was no miscarriage. She terminated the pregnancy. We talked about it and we agreed that it was the best thing to do. But a thing like that would hardly do her career any good if it went public. So she and her mom made a few calls, and presto; problem solved."

* * *

The Horstmanns' house has hardly changed. The beech trees in the yard are taller, perhaps, but with their bare branches it's hard to tell. Before the neighborhood grew up around it this was a farm, and the house hasn't lost any of its honest simplicity—two stories, white frame, porch all the way around. The shutters and front door are the same forest green he remembers. The gravel driveway curves around to the rear, where the barn used to stand. Scott remembers the night when what may have been a twister—the weather service never confirmed it—lifted it off its foundation and set it back down a few feet away, still in one piece but very much the worse for wear. He cowered in the Horstmanns' cellar, terrified that Dad would be killed. He was off somewhere getting drunk, and Scott found him safe in bed the next morning, oblivious to what had happened. After the storm, the barn had been demolished and replaced by a single story manufactured structure big enough to house six cars and the family's assorted paraphernalia. It's ugly, but the house mostly screens it from the road. Next door is the house Scott lived in as a boy. It, too, looks the same. But he gives it no more than a glance. There's nothing over there that he wants to remember.

Today there's a light dusting of snow on the ground, and Scott can see a Christmas wreath hung on the front door. Sally Horstmann always liked to have the Christmas decorations up in time for the Thanksgiving feast. So at least that much hasn't changed. There should be a couple of Labradors capering around as he climbs off the B.M.W., but he walks up to the front door unaccosted. The very same chimes sound inside. The door opens, and he's enveloped in the smell of cooking and the clamor that only a large family gathering can generate.

* * *

"I can't believe it's you, Scottie," Sally Horstmann exclaims. "Clay told me you were all grown up, but I never expected you to be so big. You look just like the photo of one of your uncles your mama used to keep on her bedside table. You probably don't remember it, but I certainly do."

"I'm afraid I don't," Scott says. When his mother died, his father put away every scrap. After that, Scott doesn't remember ever seeing any evidence that she'd once been there with them.

"Well, you're just the spit and image, you are," she insists. "Now make that useless boy of mine get you something to drink."

* * *

The house, ample as it is, seems crammed to the rafters with Horstmanns. Clay is the youngest of five boys. They're all there with their wives and children. The women are in the kitchen preparing the feast, the men are in the basement rumpus room watching football, the children are everywhere, and the three Labradors—not the ones Scott remembers but their descendents—are wherever they won't be stepped on or scolded. What Scott missed, being the only child of a widowed father.

* * *

In her kitchen Sally Horstmann is undisputed queen. Whatever her five daughters-in-law may think of her, when she gives an instruction somebody or other hops to it. Thanksgiving dinner is one of the high holy observances of the domestic year: all must be perfect lest the order of the universe be disturbed, leading to unimaginable consequences. The daughters-in-law either share her fervor or at least agree to pretend they do, and the result is a marvel of efficient collaboration. Kind of like if the Bolshoi Ballet put on one of those Saturday morning cooking shows. Scott finds it amazing.

The meal is perfectly timed: it is ready and on the table at the instant of least disruption to the viewing of football games downstairs. The grandchildren's plates are served by the mothers, and the children who are old enough file off to their own table in the kitchen while the younger ones are installed in their high chairs in easy reach of the grownup table. The adults sit down in the dining room, which is opulent with blazing tapers in antique candlesticks and the crystal, china, and sterling silver from Sally's wedding. The tablecloth was crocheted by her grandmother Boone, the cloth napkins were embroidered by her grandmother Cannon. Woe be to the diner who desecrates any of these household treasures. The menfolk, of course, are more or less oblivious to this splendor, but the daughters-in-law are appropriately reverent.

The meal itself is the stuff of dreams. The dark gold of the turkey, the vivid hue of the ham. There's a whole roast pork loin: Scott remembers the Horstmann menfolk's profound appreciation for all the products of the noble pig. The daughters-in-law have been permitted to provide side dishes, but it's apparent from the conversations in the kitchen and around the table that Sally herself retains recipe approval for any dish served at her holiday table. She is the only model Scott has for a matriarch. He wonders how she compares with the other matriarchs represented by the daughers-in-law. It's some trick, he thinks, managing to command the attention of this entire tribe, because much as been made today of the fact that no one is missing.

* * *

Though of course someone is. While football was being watched in the basement and the feast was in preparation in the kitchen, he wandered the familiar rooms of the house, eyes peeled. But there was no sign of the man, that missing patriarch. He's been totally obliterated. It's as if he never existed and Sally Horstmann gave life to those five sons of hers through some divine dispensation under which no father was required. If anybody but Scott is aware of his absence today, there's not a hint of it: not a word about him passes any lips, not a single wistful look flickers momentarily on any face present.

Scott has the story complete because the good people of Bloomington are devoted to their local gossip. He's heard it from enough different sources to have developed considerable confidence in the basics, though nuances and details of the story he remains prepared to adjust his understanding of. One day about four years previous Coach Horstmann just up and left town. He didn't go alone. He was accompanied by a young woman who had been a student of his. Several years after her high school graduation they had run into each other at the supermarket and a scant few weeks later they took off for a new life in Florida with her two small children in the back seat.

Her husband, a police officer, followed on their trail, catching up to them at a motel in Daytona Beach. In the ensuing confrontation, Coach Horstmann suffered a massive coronary and died before help could be summoned. The police officer brought his wife and children back to Bloomington. The young woman is now born again and a model wife and mother. And no one ever mentions the coach's name under this roof.

* * *

Scott watches football downstairs but before long is bored. Scott takes the Labradors outside to stretch their legs. Scott plays Parcheesi with some of the older grandchildren, but before long they are bored. Eventually he finds himself in the kitchen, where the womenfolk are doing a post mortem on the meal and chewing desultorily over the local gossip.

"So Scott," Marcus's wife Anita drawls during a brief lull, "you seeing anybody? Some gal at the university, say?"

"Not really," Scott mutters.

"Thought maybe you were at loose ends today 'cause your gal didn't invite you home to meet her folks."

"No," Scott says, feeling hideously conspicuous.

"You don't mean to say you're available?" Jamie's wife Lydia shrieks.

"I can't believe that good for nothing brother-in-law of mine hasn't fixed you up with somebody," Mary Louise grunts.

"Hey now," Rob stops her. He's upstairs just long enough to pile a plate with cookies to take downstairs. "Does he look like a guy who needs help getting women? Get a grip, girl."

"Well listen to Mr. Grumpypants. Somebody's team must be losing this afternoon."

"Mind your business," Rob growls.

"Mind your manners," his mother warns.

"Speaking of Clay," Pauline says, "where's that Annie gone off to?"

"She went up to my room to lie down," Sally says. "I think I'll go check on her."

"I'll come too, Mom Horstmann," Mary Louise says. She's a nurse, and all the tribe's medical conditions are referred to her.

"I'm sure she's fine, dear," Sally says. "She was just a little tired after lunch."

* * *

"You don't seem nervous," Scott says.

"I'm not," Clay says, sprawling on the waiting room sofa and staring up at the television, where silent football is being played. "Annie's a good strong girl. She didn't have any trouble with the first two. She'll do just fine."

"Still."

"It's a fact of life, Scott," Clay says. "My great grandmother Boone was out plowing behind a team of mules when she went into labor with Poppy Landon. She went back out and finished plowing that field the very next day. Now sit down and stop pacing, will you?"

"Sorry."

"We'll be home in time for turkey sandwiches."

* * *

Scott peers through the glass at the infants. Boone Horstmann is the lone baby awake this morning, and Scott can't help feeling that he's the biggest, handsomest—hell, probably the smartest, too—of them all.

"Which one is yours?"

Scott turns his eyes away from the baby. The man looks to be in his late thirties. He's taller than Scott and broader in the shoulders. His luxuriant chestnut hair is worn in the current style. He's handsome in the manner of a cast member from a daytime soap, an impression that's actually reinforced by the clerical collar he's wearing.

"Oh, I'm not the dad," Scott stammers. "It's my buddy's kid. He's second from the left. Annie and Clay Horstmann's new one."

"You must be Scott," the man smiles. "Michael Shaughnessy. The Horstmann clan are my parishioners."

"Nice to meet you, Father."

"Not 'Father'," Shaughnessy shakes his photogenic head, "Michael. I was just upstairs with Annie. She looks remarkable for a woman who gave birth less than twenty-four hours ago. It's that good farm stock."

Scott can't think of a thing to say. The whole business is so alien to his experience this might be a scene from the science fiction feature Zane is said to be up for next.

"Let's go have coffee and get to know each other," Shaughnessy suggests.

"I should really go say hi to Annie."

"When I left her she said she was going to take a nap. You can always drop by later."

* * *

It's a diner just a few blocks from the hospital. Scott's heard Clay speak of it, but they've never come here. On the Friday morning after Thanksgiving it's pretty quiet. Obviously a regular, Shaughnessy grabs two menus on their way in and heads for a booth in the far corner of the room.

"I don't know about you," he says, "but I'm starving. I didn't eat anything before my workout this morning. Big mistake."

He looks more like a NFL veteran than a priest.

"What gym do you go to?"

"Same one you and Clay use. I find I do best if I go early in the day, before I receive any summons. The omelets here are terrific. You should try one."

"I already ate."

"Oh, come on. A young man like you can always choke something down. I remember what I was like at your age. I practically had to have hourly feedings. Now I know you're in graduate school, but I don't know what you're studying. Our boy Clay is hopeless with details."

"I'm in a master's degree program in German Literature."

"He said you're a brainiac," Shaughnessy nods. "Want to teach, do you? That's a noble profession."

"Actually, I'm thinking translation is more in my line."

"Awfully solitary occupation, seems to me."

"I can probably stand it."

"Yes," Shaughnessy says. "You look like you could stand just about anything."

* * *

The bell jangles as Scott steps into the shop.

"Good morning," the giant behind the counter greets him. He has tightly curled black hair and eyes like chips of obsidian. He seems to fill up all the room in the shop, as if he put it on like an article of clothing when he came to work.

"Good morning," Scott says. "I'm here to pick up a suit. The name is Bailey."

"Oh, I know who you are," the giant grins, flashing perfect teeth. "You don't remember me. I'm Solly Teitelbaum."

"I'm sorry," Scott says. "It's been a long time. I was just a little kid when you were in high school. I remember watching you play football."

"Ancient history," Solly guffaws. He turns and pokes his head through the doorway into the rear of the shop. "Dad, Scott Bailey's here for his suit."

"Can I write you a check?" Scott asks, "or do I need to go to the bank for cash?"

"Your money's no good here," Solly grins. "It's already taken care of."

* * *

Monday afternoon he meets Clay at the gym. Annie went home from the hospital on Saturday afternoon and everything's back to normal. At least that's what he's been told. The Horstmann womenfolk are apparently on four hour shifts helping out.

"Mike Shaughnessy said he met you," Clay says, slipping plates onto a bar.

"Is he really a priest?"

"As real as can be."

"I'm afraid I had rather a 'what's wrong with this picture?' moment when he introduced himself. He doesn't seem the type somehow."

"I get that," Clay says. "He's not your typical priest, that's for sure. After college he played three seasons in the NFL. He was a running back. And he had a recurring role on some soap opera for a couple of years. Seminary came later. But Mom swears he's a great priest, and you know what a critic she is."

* * *

It's a bright day, but the sunshine is deceptive. It bounces off the thin layer of snow on the ground but does nothing to warm the frosty air. Scott strides up the walk toward the church, resplendent in his suit but horribly ill at ease. Surely God doesn't approve of anything about him. Surely this charade won't end well. He hasn't shared his misgivings with anyone, of course. The explanation it would require is too daunting.

He has no real experience of Catholicism. Dad avoided all religion like the plague. Scott's Baptist relatives made Catholics sound like a cross between demon worshippers and aliens from outer space. He knows they got this wrong like they did everything else, but he has no concept of his own to replace their paranoia with. As a student of literature in both English and German, Scott knows the Bible better than most lay people. It fascinates and horrifies him how little organized religion holds itself to what's actually in the book it professes to revere. Christians seem wildly inconsistent in what teachings they choose to be bound by and what they disregard. His own forebears went to war to preserve the institution of slavery, which they believed was scripturally sanctioned and God ordained. A later generation of Christians fought tooth and nail against votes for women—based again on their reading of the Bible. It's apparent that whatever the label, Methodist, Presbyterian, Lutheran, whatever, Christians use scripture more than anything as validation for their own prejudices. Beyond that observation Scott doesn't think about religion any more than he has to. But today, of course, he can't help it.

Inside the building it's almost stiflingly warm, and there's a heavy smell of incense, women's perfume, men's personal care products, and, for all he knows, angels' breath. Two weeks before Christmas the sanctuary is packed for mass, festooned with holiday decorations at least as much secular as they are sacred. He scans the pews, locates the Horstmann tribe. Clay promised to save him a seat.

* * *

Scott had thought that perhaps seeing Michael Shaughnessy in this setting he might find him more comprehensible. There, standing in front of the congregation in his Advent vestments, the athlete and the actor are as much in evidence as ever but there's still no sign of the man. Perhaps he doesn't buy Shaughnessy as a priest because he didn't grow up Catholic and has no frame of reference for apparently healthy, normal men who adopt, or pretend to adopt, celibacy. But even giving Shaughnessy the benefit of the doubt, Scott finds the man shockingly lacking in authenticity. There's no question that Scott's in the minority, however. The good father's popularity is unmistakable. The women of the parish are apparently crazy about him. Scott notices the altar boys gazing at him with unmistakable hero worship.

* * *

Scott holds baby Boone, who squirms energetically but remains silent during the baptism. He can't escape the uncanny feeling he's had since seeing Boone for the first time Thanksgiving afternoon: the idea that this tiny being is inextricably linked with Clay in the most elemental, biological sense is terrifyingly profound. All other realities pale in comparison. It's as if Scott's own life has been further trivialized. How can a man like him have any relevance at all, lacking some similar legacy? How can his increasingly deep feelings for Clay have any validity in the face of this living, breathing testament to love between men and women? It's a mindfuck as total as what he went through with Zane, even though it's completely different. He couldn't say for certain which of the two was more thoroughly negating.

* * *

"Oh, Scott, it was such a beautiful ceremony," Sally Horstmann gushes, dabbing at her eyes with a handkerchief. "Thank you so much for agreeing to be little Boone's godfather. It means so much to all of us. Especially Clay. It's been so difficult for him since we lost his father. But being a father himself has helped him a lot. You'll understand what I'm talking about when you have children of your own. And now you're back, and that's been good for him, too. You really have no idea. What luck that Father Shaughnessy was able to locate your baptismal record in the parish files. I can't believe that I forgot about your parents having you christened here. That seems like the kind of thing I would have remembered."

Scott is astonished at the lie, not to mention her blind acceptance of it, but it's none of his business.

* * *

The next afternoon in the supermarket, the tabloids catch his eye again. "*Hollywood Double Murder Tragedy!*" the headline screams. "*Just weeks after losing her baby, the beloved Hollywood star faces another nightmare*". There's a head shot of a stricken Angelica. Two smaller pictures sit in the lower corner of the cover. They look like high school yearbook photos. Heart racing, Scott grabs the rag and slaps it down on the conveyor belt with his groceries.

* * *

The university library subscribes to the *Los Angeles Times*. There, with end of the semester bustle all around, he reads about the murders. Dylan and Stewie were found dead in the apartment in Westwood that they shared. They'd both been tied up and strangled. They'd both been sexually assaulted prior to death. He feels like his heart will never resume its normal rhythm.

* * *

"I'm so sorry," Scott says into the hissing of the long distance line.

"Sure, Scott," Zane grunts. "Just remember. If you hadn't left, those boys wouldn't have had to go out picking up strangers. They wouldn't have ended up taking home some psychopath, and they'd still be alive. Those two beautiful, sweet boys who'd have done anything to make you happy. You know they would. So in this case, I'm afraid sorry doesn't cut it."

* * *

Scott lets the Labradors out to caper in the snowy back yard. He puts a kettle on to brew tea. He lights the fire in the living room fireplace. By that time the dogs have finished their business and they curl up in front of it. The entire Horstmann tribe has migrated to Florida for Christmas week, leaving Sally's house and dogs in Scott's custody. But her meticulously organized absence over Christmas week doesn't mean she didn't go all out decorating the house where she won't be present on the day. Everywhere Scott looks there are garlands, wreaths, candles, miniature manger scenes, displays of cards collected for decades. Despite the family's absence, the pantry, refrigerator, and freezer bulge with holiday goodies both sweet and savory which are supposed to constitute Scott's provisions. If he were to eat even a fraction of it all, he'd never see his abs again. But this morning, in honor of the day, he breakfasts on an assortment of holiday pastries, savoring the memories they evoke.

* * *

The house next door is decorated for the season like it's an amusement park. This morning, a tall, broad shouldered man and a small, blond boy build a snowman. Scott watches them out the window. From a distance, they look as he imagines Dad and he might have looked to the Horstmanns if it had ever occurred to Dad to attempt such an arduous endeavor.

* * *

With the dogs fed and watered, the fire secured, and the hatches all battened, Scott heads off to the restaurant. He signed up for a shift today. Most of his co-workers dread holiday work, but he's happy for the diversion. The kitschy muzak on the sound system, the elaborate, tasteless decorations, the forced cheeriness of the hostess, the sullen mood of the cooks, these all spell Christmas to him.

* * *

On his way back from break, the hostess motions wildly to him.
"What's up?"
"You should see the guys I just seated on your station. They asked for you. I bet they're good for a hundred dollar tip."

* * *

It's Michael Shaughnessy and a couple of friends. He introduces them as Race and Tiger, former teammates who are visiting from New York for the holidays. They're huge, rugged looking guys. Scott guesses they're in their late thirties. The way they stare at him leaves no doubt about their intentions. They couldn't be more blatant. New Yorkers are apparently as brazen as anyone he ever encountered in West Hollywood. But that's not really what Scott finds himself focusing on. He has wondered about Shaughnessy from time to time, but now he knows for certain. He wonders what the Horstmann clan would think if they knew their beloved priest wasn't everything they believed. He feels their horror himself, as he recalls handing baby Boone to this man for christening. It's not the gay thing he's reacting to, it's the dishonesty. The last person in the world who should be that kind of hypocrite is a clergyman. The secret is safe with him, though: blowing the whistle would be tantamount to making his own confession, which is worse than unthinkable. The look in Shaughnessy's bright, slightly bloodshot eyes tells Scott the priest has already carefully calculated all this Knowing he's being silently manipulated in this way makes Scott feel sick to his stomach.

He is businesslike and correct taking their orders and serving their meal, oblivious to their flirting, deaf to their innuendos. This just seems to encourage them to more and more strenuous efforts. And to linger over coffee and dessert. When they finally leave, not long before closing, it's clear they don't consider their business with him over. The hostess was right. They leave a tip equal to their check. Scott feels dirty picking the bills up off the table. Merry Christmas!

* * *

Last Christmas he was on the Cote d'Azur with Angelica and Zane. Dylan and Stewie joined them in time to celebrate New Year's. As he stares out Sally Horstmann's bay window at the moonlit snowscape, Scott remembers the palm trees and velvety sands of that Christmas night. There had been a gold Rolex from Zane and an extremely fine copy of the 1787 edition of *Die Leiden des jungen Werthers* from Angelica. The sumptuousness of these gifts had only exacerbated his remorse. It was on that very night he had resolved that his life must change.

Now, a full year and thousands of miles away, despite his best intentions he can't honestly say that anything about his life has changed for the better. Once again he's spending Christmas night under a roof not his own and living his life under more or less false pretenses. Once again he's deeply in love with a man who is fundamentally unavailable. The cruelty of this twist of fate is only compounded by the bizarre contrast in landscapes and personalities. Is there no escaping this? Is this really what his life is destined to be about? Zane would say yes, and tell him to get his ass back to California.

And if Zane is right about Scott's life, then going back is exactly what he should do. Staying here in Bloomington is an idiot's daydream, a vain enterprise doomed not just to failure but some catastrophe on a scale with what he's left behind him. He thinks of those boys of Clay's and their cute, sweet mother, Annie. Could it be that by staying here he's putting them all at some hideous risk like the one that snuffed out the lives of Dylan and Stewie? That possibility is more than he can face. But just as surely, so is a return to Zane and Angelica's surreal ménage—a return to the scene of the crime if there ever were one. It would mean, at the very least, an acceptance of his responsibility for what happened to Dylan and Stewie. He's not sure if, once he's done that, recovery of his self respect would ever be possible again.

* * *

"Scottie," Clay barks, sauntering up to the Nautilus machine where Scott's performing lat pulldowns. "Happy New Year."

"Clay. Look at that tan."

"Like it?"

"I want one of my own."

* * *

The minute Scott hangs up his coat Clay grabs his tank top and rips it off him.

"What the fuck?"

"It's what you've been wanting, isn't it?"

"Who says?"

"Come on," Clay says, tossing the ruined shirt on the floor and tweaking Scott's nipples like there's no tomorrow. "You think I don't know about you? You think I didn't figure you out that very first afternoon in the A&P?"

It's like looking into the face of a stranger.

"The way I remember it," Scott says, "you were the one staring at me."

"Yeah? So I like looking at hot guys. It's no crime. I like fucking them, too, so get ready. One look and I knew I could have you."

"That was months ago."

"I made you wait for it, didn't I? Now you're good and hot. You're so hot for me, you'll do anything I want. And that's the way I like it best."

"What about Annie and the boys?"

"What the fuck does this have to do with them?" Clay asks, still working on Scott's nipples, which has him absolutely writhing and completely unable to think straight, not that he cares at this point. "Yeah, you like that, don't you?"

All Scott can manage is a soft whimper.

"Knew it. Nipples this big and fleshy, hell it's always the same. Guy like you turns to jelly when somebody plays with them," Clay growls. "Now here's how it works, see? Just because I've got a wife and kids doesn't mean shit. I do what I like. And what I'm going to do right now is ream that ass of yours like I should have done when we were kids."

"Huh?"

"That camping trip. Just the two of us out there in the boonies. Should have done it back then. Should have given it to you so hard you couldn't sit down for a week. I could have, you know. Thought about it the whole time we were there. That smooth little ass of yours. So perfect and white. Just waiting for some hot stud to blast it to smithereens. I watched you every minute. Never took my eyes off of you. Nearly made my move a thousand times. But I finally decided you didn't want it bad enough. Figured I'd wait another couple of weeks. What with school getting out and all. I was going to make damned sure we hung out together all summer. Down at the city pool, you know? Had my new swim trunks all picked out especially for you. I was going to get you good and worked up. Make you go down on your knees and beg for it. Make you think the whole thing was your idea, you know? And then give it to you 'til you screamed for mercy. But then your old man died. Don't guess I'll ever know why I let them send you away just when I was starting to figure out what the hell you were good for. Anyhow, we've got lots of lost time to make up for. How many times do you think I'd have fucked your ass by now if you'd never gone away like that? Huh? Several thousand probably. So here's what I'm gonna do. We're going in the bedroom now and I'm going to slam your ass clear to kingdom come. I'm going to make you shoot bucketloads of cream and then you're going to lick every last drop of it off my fingers. And you know what else? That's just for starters."

* * *

He lies awake listening to Clay's snoring. This is exactly what he left California to get away from. This is the danger he's been on guard against ever since he came to Bloomington, the very thing he promised himself wouldn't happen because he wouldn't let it. He was going to be strong enough to say no and stick to it this time. He was going to be smart for once in his life and steer clear of potential disasters. But it's Clay. Of all the guys in the world, why did it have to be Clay he ran headlong into on his mad dash to safety? It's Clay, so resistance is out of the question. It's Clay, and that can mean only one thing: God help him, this must just be Scott's fate.

* * *

"Go ahead," Clay grunts, "answer it. I dare you."

"Hello."

"Scott."

"Yo."

"Scott, it's Zane."

"Uh huh," Scott says, squirming as Clay continues chewing on his left nipple. Three weeks of this treatment and he can hardly stand to wear a shirt. Clay's fanatical attention keeps him sore and raw, right and left. Clay asked him last night if he'd let him pierce the right one. Even had a kit with him. God knows where he got it or who taught him how to use it. Clay also wants his name tattooed on Scott's ass and has offered to pay for the procedure as long as he gets to watch. Scott's not sure how long he's going to be able to keep making excuses.

"Listen," that gruff voice comes over the line, "I was thinking maybe I'd come see you as soon as I go on hiatus. Won't that be great? I can't wait to see you again."

"You know, Zane," Scott says, trying hard to keep his voice steady, "that sounds like a really bad idea to me."

"No, it doesn't."

"Yes, it does."

"But I really need to see you."

"What for?"

"To convince you to come back. I know you want to finish your degree, but after that there's no reason you can't come back to California."

"Zane, I can't talk about this right now," Scott gasps.

"No, Scottie, please don't hang up."

"Oh, God," Scott yelps, slamming down the phone. "God, stop."

"Think you've had enough?"

"Jesus, God."

"Well you haven't. So just lie still and take it." Clay gives Scott's right pectoral a slap so hard he'll probably still have a red mark there tomorrow morning.

"Hey now, fuck boy," Clay growls, grinning like the devil himself, "when you're out with other guys, do they have to say they're in love with you before they get to pound your ass?"

* * *

"Scottie," Clay says, shoveling scrambled eggs into his stubbly face, "who was that on the phone last night?"

"Zane?" Scott says, pouring coffee and thanking his lucky stars he still remembers Sally Horstmann's recipe for buttermilk orange pancakes. "Just a guy I knew back in California."

"Guy you fucked back in California. Some big old bottom, I bet."

"More hash browns?"

"Fill 'er up," Clay nods. "Funny name for a guy, Zane."

"Maybe he changed it. Who knows?"

"That what all those California faggots do? Change their names?"

"He's an actor."

"You're shitting me. Zane Stark?"

"Yes."

"Zane Stark is a faggot? You fucked him?"

"Yes."

"Hot damn. Boys got that poster of him in their bedroom. You know the one: no shirt on and those cartridge belts slung across his chest x-ways. Annie bought it for them. 'Course she really bought it for herself. Catch her in there every now and then just staring at it. Can you believe it? With me around? She never misses his show, either. Sits there looking at the TV with her tongue hanging out. With me right there next to her. On the phone last night sounded like you two had some history."

"I lived with him for several years."

"Fuck, Scottie. You lived with him? In Beverly Hills and everything?"

"If you call that living."

"I sure as hell do. Bet you had a great big pool, didn't you? Bet you had a fancy sports car and drove around wearing two hundred dollar sunglasses."

Scott shrugs.

"Fucking unbelieveable. So what happened?"

"I left him."

"Why? With him making all that money?"

"Listen, Clay, he was an asshole. The worst ever. And believe it or not, there's not enough money in the world to make you put up with some people. Now can we talk about something else?"

* * *

"Do it," Clay snarls.

Scott pushes the bar with all his might.

"I said, do it," Clay shouts, spittle flying. "Push, God damn your pansy faggot ass."

The bar rises slowly, slowly.

"Yeah, that's it. Keep it coming. Yeah! Yeah! Almost there. Damn you, push! Be a real man for once in your faggot life."

Sweat stings Scott's eyes. He feels like his head is about to explode.

"All right!" Clay barks, taking the bar from him and lowering it onto the stands, "I told you you could do it. Maybe you'll believe me next time."

Scott lies panting frantically, pecs spasming from the effort of finishing his set. Clay has him handling far heavier weights than he ever thought possible. He's getting bigger and stronger by the week even though he's doing shorter sets and fewer of them. Clay plans his workouts like a general at the Pentagon planning an invasion and then orders him through his paces like he's a veteran storm trooper and Scott's a raw recruit. Clay plans his diet and supervises his shopping. Clay swears that there are no limits. Yes, Clay swears...

* * *

"Did you get your present?" Zane purrs from across the continent.

"I shipped it all back to you yesterday," Scott says.

"All of it?"

"Yes."

"Even the Rolex?"

"Yes, dammit, even the Rolex."

"Oh, Scottie," Zane murmurs. "You shouldn't have done that."

"Why the hell not?" Scott explodes. "Didn't I tell you I don't want anything from you? Do you really think I'll come back if you give me enough stuff?"

"Scott, listen to me. When I send you things, you have to keep them."

"Zane, stop."

* * *

"Do it!" Clay snarls. "Come on!"

"God," Scott wails.

"Shoot, you God damned cocksucker!"

Scott groans. He feels like his head is going to explode.

"I said, shoot, you filthy piece of shit."

Scott gives one last yelp and nearly passes out.

"Yeah," Clay growls. "There it is. Keep it coming. Yeah, that's it. Good boy!"

Scott's sobbing now, tears stinging his eyes.

"I told you I could make you come without either of us touching your cock," Clay sneers. "Maybe you'll listen to me next time."

* * *

"This is Hank," Clay says when he shows up at Scott's door a few evenings later. "I told him all about you. He's been wanting to see for himself."

Hank is gigantic. Six feet five at least. Three hundred pounds or more, and every inch of him looks hard as granite. His black hair is cropped close to his skull. His mustache is trimmed with military precision. His eyes are twin icebergs.

* * *

It's sundown the next day when Scott finally crawls out of bed. His ass feels like he's been fucked for hours with the blunt end of a Louisville Slugger. His scrotum is fiery with razor burn. It aches from the weights they suspended from it. His wrists are covered with abrasions from the manacles. His sore, stiff joints and muscles protest as he reaches up and runs a trembling hand over his head, where his hair has been cropped to one quarter inch. His body is covered with red burns from candle drippings. There are tiny spots of dried blood where Hank made injections directly into his nipples, which are scraped raw and badly swollen. There's a dark purple bruise on the side of his cock where Hank made an injection directly into a vein. And protruding from the mouth of his urethra is some sort of curved bolt, stainless steel from the look of it. Its other end is anchored through a piercing on the underside of the shaft that wasn't there twenty-four hours ago.

His skin is caked with dried semen. How many times did they make him come? How many times did each of them shoot onto him? He lost count just as he was losing consciousness. He roused just enough to hear them leaving. It was turning dawn outside, and they were laughing as they slammed the door behind them. He remembers crawling naked and freezing into the bedroom. It took all the strength he had left to climb into the bed.

The apartment is frigid. He limps unsteadily into the bathroom. He leaves the lights off. He refuses to risk even the slightest glance at the mirror. He knows he'd hate what he'd see there. He adjusts the shower to a gentle stream of lukewarm water, afraid that anything warmer or more vigorous will make him scream.

* * *

Three weeks pass. Then four. He hears nothing from Clay. He doesn't see Clay at the gym though he goes every day and works out like a maniac. A dozen times a day or more he reaches for the phone to call Clay. But what he's already done is bad enough. He can't bring himself to invade the fragile peace surrounding Annie and the boys. He imagines them in that small, neat house with a stranger outside in the darkness splashing gasoline around the foundations and getting ready to strike a match. That's exactly what it's like, sitting staring at his phone.

It's better this way. It's over, and he tells himself he's glad. He tells himself he never wants to see Clay again. But he knows he lies, and when he lies alone in bed at night his body screams out its famished truth.

* * *

He opens the door and there's Clay, innocent as a choirboy, smiling as if that nightmare never happened. As if they saw each other at the gym every day. As if six days have passed instead of six weeks. Most important, as if nothing has changed. Then he sees Hank looming in the darkness and his blood runs cold. He's paralyzed as they push past him into the apartment. He hears the dead bolt click as Clay locks them inside. He begins to sob as Hank's huge hands slowly close around his throat.

"Please don't hurt me."

Hank's coarse laughter echoes in the tiny room and Clay's grin never wavers.

* * *

Four weeks pass, and then five. Clay shows up again on a freezing night in late March. His face is expressionless. His eyes are cold flame.

"Get your coat."

"Where are we going?"

"I'm taking you to a party."

* * *

When Clay shows up at his door the next night, Scott almost doesn't open it. But he knows Clay knows he's home. He knows Clay will find a way inside no matter what he does. There's nowhere he can hide. And God damn him, he knows he doesn't really want to. After everything. He can't believe it. He doesn't know who he is any more.

"Hey," Clay smiles. Incomprehensibly, that smile hasn't changed since junior high school. Nor has the effect it has on Scott. "That was some show we put on for them last night. God, did you see those guys licking it off the wall when you shot all the way across the room? Drove them fucking wild, seeing you blast like that. I have never felt your ass as tight as it was. I bet that's the best fuck you've ever given up for anybody in your life. I'd bet anything on it. God, they were howling."

"Who were they?"

"Just some guys. Friends of Hank's and mine."

Friends. Scott recognized Solly Teitelbaum, of course. And Michael Shaughnessy and his two friends from Christmas night at *La Maison*. But there had been well over a dozen others there.

"They all get together every few weeks to let off steam, and Hank and I provide the entertainment."

"Entertainment. Is that what you call it?"

"All right," Clay says. "All right. Calm down. They're not a bunch of weirdos and perverts, if that's what you're worried about. They've all got wives and children at home like Hank and me. Except Michael, of course. But seriously: no faggots allowed. We don't want to get mixed up with any of that type."

"I'm that type."

"No, you're not. Don't ever say that. Do you hear me? Never. Hank'll kill you if he hears you talking like that. The whole point is we don't have anything to do with queers. The guys don't lay down good money to see us doing our thing with a bunch of fags who actually like that kind of shit. Who'd stand in line for it. It's got to be straight boys. Big, strong butch types. Really hot, manly guys that wouldn't stand for being treated that way if we didn't know how to break them in just right, you know? Who'll fight like hell until they're overpowered and shown by a couple of mongo studs what they really want. Then it's O.K. for them to beg. But not until. That's what those guys will pay good old American dollars to watch. They've got money; they've got clout. They want what they want. And they're willing to pay for it, so we give it to them. There's a couple of doctors. Mike's not the only priest. There's a state senator, but we all pretend we don't know who he is. Several of the guys own successful businesses."

"Why?"

"Because everybody likes something different every now and then, right? Just makes sense. And boy did we drive them crazy last night. You're exactly the kind of guy they like to see having that shit done to him. God, did you put up a fight. I almost thought you meant it."

"I did."

"Sure," Clay guffaws. "Hank and I took in nearly four thousand. Best we've ever done."

"How much?"

"Don't worry. You'll get a cut."

"I don't want money."

"Suit yourself. I'd think you could use a couple hundred, at least."

"Is that why? Just for money?"

"Scottie, I've got a wife and three kids I have to take care of. I've got a girlfriend who likes nice things. Very nice, very expensive things. And boy, is she worth every cent of it. Hottest piece of tail in the whole fucking state. Nobody does me like she can. And I do mean nobody. Now how the hell am I supposed to pay that kind of freight on a high school coach's salary? Moonlight at the A&P? No fucking thank you. Anyway, there aren't enough hours in the week."

This is the first Scott has heard of a girlfriend, but somehow he doesn't doubt her existence for a second. He thinks he's going to throw up. It's bad enough being second choice after Annie, but does this make him third? Or fourth after Hank? Does he actually rank at all? That's one question he'll never dare to ask.

"Did you ever, um, I mean, you and Hank?"

"Hell no. He's never so much as touched me that way. What kind of guy do you think I am?"

Scott can't even begin to answer that one.

"I'm the lure, see? I locate the new meat. I reel them in."

"Like you did with me." Stupid of him not to have realized he wasn't the first guy Clay had done all those things with. Even stupider, apparently, to think he was anything special. How many were there before him?

"You know, you could help out that way. Hank might even go twenty per cent if you were to bring in some hot looking boys. I know you could do it. Must be lots of them following you around campus."

"I don't think so."

"You got no confidence, is all. That's your problem."

"What's that stuff he shoots me with?"

"Crazy, huh? Makes you go off like a rocket. The guys love to see that kind of shit. Especially no hands, like you did last night. Hank's a doctor, you know. It's perfectly safe."

"He's what?"

"Sure as shit. He delivered my three boys. That's how I met him in the first place."

"My God."

"Oh, hey. He said to tell you he'll get you some steroids if you want. He says he can put another twenty pounds on you in no time."

"Does he give them to you?"

"I sure as hell didn't get this way on sweat and good intentions. And you've seen what a monster he is. How whataya say?"

"No thanks."

"You should at least think about it. You'd look great if you got real big like that. Say two-sixty or so. Listen, have I got some things planned for next time. We're going to blow the roof off the place. I mean, like to finish off, Hank's going to pierce one of your nipples while I'm fucking you. We'd do both of them, but he wants to save one for another time. It'll be fucking incredible."

"Next time?"

"Don't worry. It won't be for a while. When Hank and me locate a very special commodity like you we have to make the most of it. So we can't let them have you again too soon. We have to make them beg for it. That way we can charge more. It's all free enterprise, you know?"

"Clay, what makes you think there's going to be a next time?"

"Kind of stupid question is that?"

"I won't do it again."

"Sure you will."

"No."

"Babe, you're hooked. And I don't mean the stuff Hank shoots you up with. It's way stronger than anything Hank could ever give you. Your body wants us doing that shit to it. Now that it knows what all that feels like it won't let you say no to us. Even if you wanted to. And you don't want to say no to me. You never wanted to say no to me and you never will."

Scott shakes his head.

"I know you, Scottie," Clay croons. It sounds just like when he talks to one of his sons. Hearing it, Scott thinks he's about to cry.

"I know you better than you know yourself. Just wait. You'll be begging for it again about the same time those guys won't take no for an answer when they ask us to bring you back for an encore. Now come here and be nice to me."

"Don't touch me."

"Hey, it's O.K.," Clay says. "I know it's a lot to take in all at once. We can just cuddle tonight if you want."

But of course it goes way farther than that.

* * *

Clay doesn't stay the night. Scott doesn't sleep.

* * *

It's another three weeks before he sees Clay again. And every waking hour he knows that Clay is right. He's hooked. He'll never be able to say no. It doesn't matter what anybody wants to see done to him. It doesn't matter how humiliating it is or how much it will hurt as long as Clay's the one doing it. There's nothing he won't do if there's even the remotest chance it will make Clay love him. There's nothing he won't suffer to have Clay touching him again. He almost starts to cry that afternoon when he walks into the gym and sees Clay there.

The boy with Clay is so beautiful it hurts just to look at him, and Clay is barking instructions as the boy grinds out bench presses. Scott can hear the husky growl clear across the room. He walks quickly back out into the corridor, tears running down his cheeks. He wishes he could warn the boy, but even that brief glimpse of him basking in Clay's attention, his young face glowing, his huge eyes full of trust, is enough to tell Scott that it's too late.

* * *

Every time there's a knock on the door, Scott's sure it's Clay. But it's always the girl next door come to borrow laundry detergent or the UPS man with a delivery he needs to leave with Scott for one of the neighbors or the landlord on rent day or more often than not the cute boy from across the court-yard asking if Scott's seen his cat. This is as transparent a ploy as Scott has ever encountered, but hell, the kid can't be more than nineteen and obviously has no idea how it's really done. And if it's not one of these, it's some door to door salesman, or the Jehovah's Witnesses or the American Cancer Society.

It's never Clay. No matter how fervently he wills it to be in the instant before he opens the door. Just like it's never Clay when the phone rings. But that doesn't keep his heart from beating faster every single time. And when he hears the rap of knuckles on hardwood this time, just after midnight on a Thursday in May, he's sure of it. Who else could it be at this time of night? He sprints to the door like a man exiting a burning building.

Who else it is, is Annie. There's no need to try and guess her mood. He knows a furious woman when he sees one.

"I'd like to speak to my husband, please."

"He's not here."

"If you don't mind," she says, pushing in past him, "I'd like to see for myself."

Neither of them speaks as she moves through the small apartment opening doors and peeking into corners. It doesn't take long.

"I don't suppose he ducked out the back way when he heard the knock."

"There is no back way."

"Right," she says. "Damn. I never should have believed him when he told me he was coming over here tonight. That bastard."

"Honestly, Annie, I haven't seen him in weeks."

"How many would that be? Exactly?"

Scott could tell her to the exact minute, but what's the point?

"Six," he says, not counting that afternoon in the gym. "Six weeks."

"Really."

"Really." He watches her deciding whether to believe him or not.

"So you're telling me he hasn't been over here every night until all hours helping you fight the good fight against your alcoholism?"

The cruelty of the lie makes him wince.

"I'm sorry," Annie says, softening slightly. "It's what he told me."

"I've done a lot of rotten things in my life," Scott says slowly. "I'm every bit as despicable as you must think I am. Hell, I'm probably worse than you could imagine. But I'm not a drunk."

"Of course not," she says. "Not with skin like that. It's always the first thing to go."

"I am so very sorry," Scott chokes.

"So am I," she says. "Sorry I met that bastard in the first place. Sorry I married him. Sorry I didn't leave him the minute I realized what all he was up to. Sorry I had those babies. Oh, no, don't get me wrong. I love them. God, how I love them. I love him, too. Even after all the shit he's pulled."

"I know."

"Listen," she says, shrinking by the second. "Do you think? I mean, could I sit down? Just for a minute? I'm no good at that madwoman from hell routine. It's really not me. I just need to park my broom in the corner for a bit while I catch my breath. I'll go soon, I promise."

"Of course. Can I get you anything? Something to drink? An aspirin?"

"No thanks," she says, sinking into the sofa. "So you're not a drunk. I didn't really think you were. So?"

Scott shrugs.

"So," she nods. "Clay likes boys."

"Hey now…"

"Don't worry," she says. "I don't give a damn about that. And if he ever asks me, you never said a word about his guilty secret."

"How?"

"Mary Ellen O'Connell went to her gynecologist a couple of weeks ago with what she was sure was just another yeast infection. Imagine her surprise when Reed Dalton—who's in practice with her husband Hank, no less—told her she had clap. Imagine how awkward that was."

"My God."

"So she walked right out of his office and found herself a private investigator. And damn if he didn't find Big Hank shacked up in a motel room with a couple of nineteen year olds. Boys. Well, that got me to thinking, you see. 'Cause he and Clay have been thick as thieves for years now, and if a guy like Hank could secretly be into guys…and Clay's done everything else, God knows. I mean, I know all about that whore Misty Danielson. I've known since the very first time he screwed her. Day after we got back from our honeymoon, that was. How he thought he'd get away with it is beyond me. Bloomington's not that big a place. People gossip and people who think they're too good to start rumors aren't too good to pass them on. Some people make a whole career out of making sure the poor wife knows every last damn detail. So I know about Misty, all right. And I know all about the women Clay fucks for money."

"What?"

"He's got a whole string of them. Twelve, fifteen, maybe more. All middle aged and married. Their husbands go out of town, they call Clay. Or they tell their husbands they're off to see mother or going out with the girls and they check into a motel room instead."

"How long as this been going on?"

"Since we were in college. And me? What do you think I did when he'd hand me a wad of bills right out of the blue like that? Three, four hundred dollars at a time? Did I ask where he got it? Did I go tell the police I thought my husband might be selling drugs? Did I tell him I wouldn't take a cent of it unless he told me where it came from? Hell, I just kept my mouth shut and took it. We needed it. Couple of stupid kids who got married right out of high school and immediately started making babies. Not to mention the rent and the tuition payments. I never spent a cent of that money on myself, but my boys deserved whatever I could give them no matter where it came from."

Which explains all those nights Scott went to sleep in Clay's arms and woke up alone. All that time he imagined Clay sneaking back home to his wife and boys. After Zane, he thought he knew everything there was to know about bad boys. Stupid, stupid Scott.

"Well then, guess what? Those boys they found Hank with turned out to be a couple of Clay's star football players. First string quarterback and all-state tight end. Graduated last year, both of them. Which was just a little too much of a coincidence, you know? Well, that clinched it. I mean, where else is a high society gynecologist going to meet boys like that? But that bastard Hank wouldn't tell me a thing. And then, well, he talks about you all the time. Clay does, I mean. I thought you must be his steady boyfriend."

"I thought so, too."

"Right," she nods. "So I came over tonight even though he said he'd be here. I thought for once in his life he just might be telling me the truth. Stupid, huh?"

"Not stupid," Scott says, shaking his head. "Not stupid at all. You just keep hoping that the next time will be different. You know that sooner or later there's going to be some miracle and he'll change. He'll figure out how much he loves you and needs you. He'll realize he can't live without you. You plan your whole life around the day that's going to happen. Because that's all you have. And you wait."

"My God," Annie gasps. "You do understand."

Scott nods, mortified to be crying in front of this woman.

"Well, I've made up my mind. That's what I came here to tell him. I'm getting a divorce. Talked to a lawyer this afternoon. And he'd better not even think about fighting me for custody of the boys."

"I'm sorry."

"I know," she says. "So what about you? What are you going to do?"

And for the first time since that afternoon in the produce department at the A&P, he realizes he has a choice. He can go on waiting for the knock on the door that means Clay and Hank are throwing another of their parties and Scott's on the menu again. Or he can grab what's left of his life and run like hell.

"I'm finishing my master's in a few more weeks," he says, making it up as he goes along. "Then I'm out of here. Probably back to California. I'm not sure yet. I'm sorry it's too late to make any difference to you and the boys."

"Hell, Scott," she says. "You and me, we got burned by the same fire. You're not responsible."

"It's not that easy," he says.

"No, I guess not."

"What do you want me to say to him if I see him?" Scott says.

"Whatever it is you need to tell him," Annie says. "Which I expect is plenty. But don't worry about me. I can deliver my own messages."

San Francisco: 2008

On Fridays summer classes get out at noon. At precisely four minutes after, Ned picks Griffin up in front of the school and they go to lunch. Ned still drives the Bentley he had when Griffin first met him. Though it must be nearly fifty years old now it's in showroom condition, thanks chiefly to the TLC provided by Daniel Kmetko. Ned pilots it through the narrow, traffic clogged streets with alertness and skill that belie his age. Griffin always finds Ned's panache and accuracy behind the wheel astonishing, not to mention encouraging. Apparently, getting old doesn't have to be a long, slow nightmare punctuated by dented fenders, cracked taillight lenses, and admonitions from friendly but skeptical traffic cops.

Today it's their favorite little North Beach hole in the wall. They've shared a plate of prosciutto and melon and now they're slurping their way through steaming bowls of stracciatella.

"I first met Dave in London," Ned says. "It must have been the summer of 1943. The buildup toward D-Day was already beginning. The city was full of young Americans. More of them every week. They were so robust and clean looking. Not like us weedy, grimy Brits. It was like seeing a kangaroo in church—that's how out of place they seemed.

"Anyway, there was a kind of twenty-four hour a day party going on at my chum Adam's flat in Bloomsbury. All our gang would scour the streets for likely looking Yanks and take them over there for drinks and a bit of a chat-up. Just to see who, if any of them, might make the running. We were desperate in those days: there was no such thing as a gay club. Often we had to make do in the public conveniences."

"Isn't that called cottaging?"

"Indeed. Adam once got caught in one during an air raid. It was even dangerous trying to seduce a boy in the safety of one's own flat. Oh, the dire scenes that ensued. Adam's flat was like a combination of dance hall, pub, and community center. The local men we took there generally figured out what was up pretty quickly. Either they'd been to school and knew how it worked, or they'd at least heard things about it. Anyway, once they twigged they either cleared out or played along. But the Yanks mostly appeared not to know such a thing existed. Such innocents they were. And so offended when it finally dawned on them what they'd been invited around for. See this scar over my eyebrow? That's where I had stitches on one particularly dramatic occasion. Such a beauty the lad was, too. From Iowa, I believe it was. Might just as well have been Timbuktu for all I knew of American geography at the time. Didn't go to casualty, no sir. Adam's chum Nigel stitched me up in the loo.

"But darling Dave wasn't like that. He'd been around the block."

"They don't call it the Princeton Rub for nothing," Griffin points out.

"The Princeton Rub?" Ned says, looking baffled. "I'm sure I've never heard of it."

"But Dave apparently had."

"If you say so," Ned sniffs. "I don't believe I want to know what a thing called that entails."

"It's extremely vanilla, actually," Griffin assures him. "Not nearly as depraved as what you English schoolboys got up to after lights out."

"Indeed. Perhaps I should read about it online."

"You do that."

"Anyway, Dave. Well, he was an absolute dreamboat. And as I say, he knew how many scones it takes to make six. And your old Ned was thinking he was home and dry that afternoon. But unfortunately..."

"You reminded him of his maiden auntie?" Griffin grins.

"He was keeping himself pure for some boy he'd been in college with. They'd been separated by the war."

"I know you, Ned," Griffin laughs. "When he told you that story, you probably didn't believe a word of it and came on like the Real Inspector Hound or such, cross examining the living daylights out of him."

"You know, I suppose I did, rather."

"But I know what you mean about him being a dreamboat. Wulf has shown me pictures. Yum."

"Dear Wulf. You know, when they first came west from New York I sold them their house on Telegraph Hill."

"Right," Griffin says. He's been married to the business for nearly thirty years and knows that any conversation with a realtor will eventually veer off in this direction. "And of course the place they're in now."

* * *

Matt's goal in physical therapy this summer has been to keep dancing. To start with, he wanted to be able to dance at his wedding. Not because he had any thought of enjoying it, but because he knew it would make Ash happy. Ash has always loved to dance, but as far back as Matt can remember it's one of those things—mercifully few—he's never been any good at. At his first wedding he remembers being horribly self conscious about it. Eleanor, tall, cool, elegant in her ten thousand dollar wedding dress and the fifty thousand dollar pearls her parents had given her, had looked every inch the princess on the dance floor, while there he was, a great lumbering oaf with two left feet. His clumsiness had turned out to be a metaphor for the entire marriage.

He danced at all of his sons' weddings as well. Not with Ash, though Ash was present at every one of them. Matt danced with Eleanor briefly those times before handing her off to Ash, while he and Stormy, Eleanor's third husband who couldn't dance for shit either, got each other good and drunk. He and Ash hadn't been invited to Nate's second wedding. No surprise there. Not after the first one. He has no idea who Eleanor danced with that day. She refuses to say anything about the occasion. His six younger sons are terrific dancers. Eleanor made sure they took lessons. Nate had lessons, too. But he might as well have been Matt's clone. He was never any better on the dance floor than his father. Matt supposes this is one more thing Nate held against him all those years.

For his own wedding last month, Matt had to get it right. Ash deserved it. And by then it was much more complicated than just mastering a basic box step. Neither his doctor nor his physical therapist had held out much hope. But he'd done it, and contrary to all expectations he'd enjoyed it. And now, for as long as this miraculous season lasts, he doesn't propose to stop. He's ready for this afternoon's festivities. He'll bring the cane along just in case but he'll leave it in the car. And when the time comes, he'll take Ash in his arms on the dance floor for those few transcendent moments that are the closest he comes to flying nowadays.

His reward this afternoon is, as always, a short detour on the way home. The Porsche practically steers itself to his regular spot. He has a clear view of the end of the runway. The security people know him by now and don't bother to stop and check. They're just lucky he doesn't have a trunk full of heat seeking missiles. He watches the planes come in and remembers what it feels like to land one of them. He started out in the early Boeing jets. He made it all the way up to 747's before his back trouble forced him to quit.

* * *

It's a warm, sunny early afternoon. A perfect summer day—all too rare in San Francisco. Around Union Square the tourists window shop, gawk at the cable cars, laugh and converse in a dozen languages. Nelson is ready for them. Neatly dressed and perfectly groomed, he looks like a businessman on his lunch break, not someone out to ruin their vacations. Not that he thinks of it that way. In his mind they all have insurance. And they're all affluent or they wouldn't be here in the first place. They can afford it, and what he's about to do won't spoil their visit to the city at all. It won't be more than a minor inconvenience. No worse than a long wait for their luggage at the airport or a surly taxi driver's attempt to overcharge them. Hell, it's one more adventure to tell their friends about.

He spots his first victim of the day. The fat ones, he finds, are the easiest marks. They move slowly, for one thing. And their nervous systems seem somehow less sensitively calibrated than those of skinnies. This one's got her bag slung low on her bovine hip. He'll have the billfold out of it and into his Trader Joe's bag in the blink of an eye. She'll never feel a thing.

* * *

San Francisco is the cruelest lover in the world. Sean knows a thing or two about the cruelty of lovers and he's sure of it. The city's constant seductions keep you there long after you've realized that your dreams will never come true until you leave. This is not an original thought on his part. Appropriating such concepts is what comes of marrying a naval officer with the soul of a poet. He doesn't know if there's such a thing in the United States Navy, but Dmitri swears that it's obligatory in the Royal Canadian. Dmitri's first article of faith is that everything Canadian is superior to everything American. Sean agrees with him but suspects he's just suffering an extreme case of sour grapes.

The plane banks and the flight attendants belt themselves into their jump seats. They're on final approach. It's a short flight from Vancouver. Fairly inexpensive as well. He could easily have come for all their weddings this summer. They all came north for his two years ago. He hopes they understood his absence and that this trip will make up for all those others he didn't make. This one, Griffin assured him, was the most historically significant wedding of all. He didn't have to be begged. Even if he had, Dmitri practically ordered him to come.

He did have to be promised, however, that he wouldn't run into Nelson. All these years later he still won't face that. Not even safely married to Dmitri. It's hard enough being around Morgan. That's the risk you take, getting involved with someone's identical twin. What rotten luck it was to have chosen the evil one. Sean has always had a gift for making bad choices. That's why when Dmitri proposed he did exactly the opposite of what his instincts told him to do and said yes.

* * *

When Kirk calls from somewhere out in the east bay, Ariel has his pad and pencil ready. If he'd been a girl instead of a boy and if his parents hadn't left Cuba, he'd probably be a stenographer today. The Stenographer of Havana. That's it. *The Stenographer of Havana.* He's been after Trey for years to compose an opera. Here it is—the inspiration they've been missing. As soon as he gets off the phone with Kirk he'll grab a clean pad and start writing a libretto. There may be computers everywhere else in the world, but in Cuba, he is certain, people still use pencils and steno pads. By the time Kirk arrives with the dogs, Ariel will have the volunteers organized to give baths, accommodations assigned and ready, veterinary and grooming appointments arranged, and prospective adoptive parents contacted. And Act I drafted, all ready for the addition of Trey's tunes. His title may be shelter director, but Ariel is really a Jill of all trades around here.

When Dominic passed away and left him ridiculously wealthy, Ariel's first thought was that he'd die of boredom. Being a fitness model/housewife had kept him comfortably occupied, but being a fitness model/widow didn't seem to offer enough in the way of diversions. Without a charming slob of an attorney to pamper and pick up after, he suspected the time would hang pretty heavy. And while it was possible to look like you lived at the gym, you couldn't literally move in there. Then Chad left Trey, and Trey decided he had to get out of Hollywood, and holding his hand through the move to San Francisco kept Ariel good and busy.

But domestic tragedy doesn't last forever, and before he knew it Ariel was bored again in a new place where he didn't know very many people. He'd been down that road before and knew the pitfalls, so though he'd been sober for years he threw himself back into the twelve steps, attending multiple meetings each day. He ended up sponsoring Kirk DeHavilland, whose addictions were almost as bad as his own, whose trust funds were even larger, and whose boredom was even more likely to promote abuse. One night, stumbling back to Will Crawford's place drunk as a boatload of sailors, Kirk had been followed home by a stray Yorkie. In the course of rehabilitating the little dog, Kirk found his life's calling. Before Ariel knew it, they were partners in this place. It's been the salvation of them both. Ironic, since the idea was to save unwanted dogs.

"So that's about it," Kirk says, after giving him the rundown on who all he's bringing with him. "Eleven in all. Not a bad day."

"I'll have everything ready when you get here," Ariel assures him.

"Great. By the way, Will said to tell you he's looking forward to seeing you this evening."

"Oh."

"He will be seeing you at the wedding, won't he?"

"I was really thinking about a quiet night at home."

"Ariel, you promised. You really need to get out more, you know?"

"So you tell me. At least six times a day."

"If you don't promise me right now that you'll be there, I'm calling Chad. He and Trey will fix your wagon."

"I'm quaking at the thought."

"Good."

* * *

Yoel holds his hands away from the stick as Nancine puts the Pilatus into a shallow bank and then lines up with the center of the runway. She's a wizard, no doubt about it. She's one of the best students he's ever worked with. Her goal of being an out lesbian commercial pilot is closer than she thinks. He'd certainly fly with her any day, and he doesn't say that about just anyone.

The water of the bay spreads out beneath them like molten silver under the cloudless sky of mid afternoon. Fifty feet, then forty, then thirty, then they're above the tarmac steady as a rock. Barring an act of God, nothing will go wrong now. This is his last lesson of the week. Yoel has no wheels today because Boone is in the middle of replacing the head gaskets on his Harley. Boone is the brain surgeon of motorcycle repair, not to mention having the biggest pecs of their generation. Yoel will catch a ride with Nancine in to the BART station and take the train home. He has to beat Rupert there at all costs. Rupert was in one of his moods this morning: sometimes he's unable to turn off his headmaster switch when he leaves school. Sometimes it's funny, but sometimes it's not.

Well, fair enough. Yoel has switches of his own. Perhaps it's time to turn one of them on, time for another round of one of their favorite domestic games, "Moscow Rules." How can a wedding reception help but be a perfect venue for simulated espionage? He'll enlist Cousin Cooper and funny little Griffin to help him. Yes. Griffin is the perfect straight man for the escapade he has in mind. Griffin has the soul of an innocent, and this invariably shows on his face. No one can imagine that he's capable of deception. And Cooper's always up for anything.

The wheels touch down. Nancine is a wizard, all right. Hardly a chirp from the tires. Smooth as skating on a freshly zambonied rink. He hardly felt a thing. He yanks on the release and the canopy slides back, letting delicious, salt perfumed air into the tandem cockpit. The air is one of the things he likes best about the Bay Area. None of that hot, sultry Mediterranean fug here, just gorgeous crispness. Air like champagne. He actually wrote that once in a letter to his mother—the world famous Israeli poetess. He thought he'd never hear the end of it. But he likes the phrase and repeats it to himself: air like champagne.

* * *

For a long time, Jared wished he had died in Viet Nam. He had lost his hearing in one ear. The doctors had wanted to amputate his left leg below the knee—that war had gone on longer than his actual tour of duty. Multiple operations had been required to save it, and even then, though it eventually functioned as it should and rarely gave him pain, it was a mass of truly horrible scars. Meanwhile, it had taken years of therapy before he was able to speak intelligibly again, and the stammer still came back at moments of stress. And by the time he was halfway back together, his hair had turned gray. At age twenty-two, he was certain no one would ever love him. His parents believed that, too, though they wouldn't say it. He read it in their eyes—those pitying glances he wasn't supposed to notice. And in the fierce protectiveness with which they and his brothers and sisters blanketed him. He was damaged goods. He'd never be capable of anything much. He'd always be alone. Better just resign himself to living in his parents' basement and being an uncle to his siblings' kids. He should be thankful. At least he was alive. But he couldn't force himself to see it that way. Why couldn't he have just given up when that land mine went off? Why go through all of it, if the best he could hope for was to be alone?

When he left he didn't tell them he was coming to San Francisco. He called them every night to assure them he was O.K. but it was months before he told them where he was. By then he had a good job and a nice apartment and he'd met Big Steve and Tristan, who were Viet Nam veterans themselves and got him completely so he could rightly claim that he had terrific friends who were taking good care of him. And by then he'd lost his virginity to Nick Romanovsky, who was transcendent in bed but not husband material. Still, Nick was a hell of a good guy to have for a buddy. He didn't tell his parents the part about Nick. Every time he called they insisted that back under their roof was where he belonged. He suspected they had figured out about him and wanted to shove him safely back into the closet, but he no longer secretly feared that they were right that he belonged there. That was progress. They were only slightly mollified when his Cousin Maya graduated from law school and took a job with a firm here and promised to keep an eye on him. Here in San Francisco things were better than he'd hoped for. But he was still alone. In the bars he couldn't talk to anyone. In the gym it was nearly as bad. He always went home by himself. And he still wasn't sure he wanted to be alive.

When he was discovered by a gang of hyper-fashionable young guys, he thought his dream had come true. They were the hottest guys in the city: everybody wanted to run with that pack. They had the latest haircuts, the chicest clothes, the nicest apartments. They got into the most exclusive clubs without even making an effort. And they seemed to like him. He'd never imagined having that much sex with that many people. It took him a while to realize that though they'd let him do absolutely anything to them in bed they weren't crazy about being seen with him in public. Behind closed doors he was a sex god, but anywhere else they treated him like a troll. They'd fuck him but they wouldn't date him. It was the cruelest of ironies, because all he'd ever wanted was to settle down with someone. By the time he had figured out that he was on a dead end street it was too late. He was in love with one of them. And when romance reared its head the whole thing came crashing down. If the gang had just left them alone, it might have eventually worked out. But those guys didn't work that way. They had a very strict code and they enforced it ruthlessly. Nick had warned him, which made it worse. Before he knew it he was nearly suicidal again.

And then Scott showed up. At first, Jared had little hope. Scott seemed exactly like the guys who had just given him the heave-ho. But he couldn't help himself. And this time nobody tried to stop him. Scott gave him a reason to fall back in love with life. Scott was everything he wasn't: beautiful, socially adroit, physically intact. He'd known from the night they met that Scott was the love of his life. Scott hadn't made it easy. It had taken months just to get to the second date. But Big Steve had insisted they were made for each other and that Jared couldn't give up. So like he had fought to keep his leg and to speak again and to build one of the most impressive physiques in the city, he fought to win the man of his dreams. And keep him.

This afternoon, when Will Crawford reads the lines about "for better or worse, in sickness and health" Jared will know exactly what it all means.

* * *

The Mercedes fires at the first turn of the key. Daniel listens to its idle with expert ears. Yes, just a slight adjustment to the fuel injection system is probably in order. Daniel has always been an Italian car guy. His very first car back in high school was a tiny Fiat, and he has driven Italian makes exclusively since then—with this one exception. When he got out of the military he went to Italy and got factory certification as a service technician from Ferrari and Maserati both. His daily driver is an Alfa-Romeo that was new when he was a tenth grader. He's spent his whole adult life eating, drinking, and sleeping Italian cars. Sandy always says Daniel has olive oil running through his veins instead of blood, and Nick Romanovsky once joked that he was the offspring of a dalliance between Big Steve Fabiani and an Isotta-Fraschini.

But for some perverse reason, he had lusted for this magnificent Benz, a 280SL, since the very first time Wulf brought it into the shop where Daniel works for service. It is silver and has a lipstick red leather interior. It has the extremely rare five speed transmission and the even rarer factory alloy wheels. It even has the European style headlights. There weren't more than a handful of cars equipped like it during model year 1970. Every time Wulf brought it into the shop Daniel found himself more intrigued by it. It was as different from anything he had ever driven before as Wagner is from Puccini, or spaetzele are from rigatoni. Staring at it, he felt like a man staring at his next mistress.

So when Wulf decided a few years back that he wasn't up to shifting gears any more on the steep San Francisco hills and that the Benz needed to go to a new home, Daniel raided his savings account. Wulf couldn't have been happier—the car was staying in the family. Daniel and Sandy have arranged for Wulf and Dave to be photographed with the car this afternoon—an ususual wedding gift, but truly one from the heart.

Yes, he thinks, the idle is just the tiniest bit rough. He'll see to that fuel injection system tomorrow. He backs out of the garage. Timing perfect as usual, Sandy is just coming down the front steps.

* * *

Boone slaps an ample amount of product into his hair. A few deft swipes with a comb and presto: it's gleaming, fashionably tousled, and immune to anything short of a force eight gale or the 10 g's of a shuttle launch. Next comes the dress shirt—custom tailored on account of his shoulders and pecs, spotless, the whitest of whites. Then the tie. Striped, but nothing flashy. It's something a banker would wear. He slips on the bracelet of heavy gold links he bought on his most recent trip to the Caribbean with Owen. Then the rose gold Invicta that's indistinguishable from a Rolex at five paces. Finally the jacket.

He stares at himself in the mirror. He looks like a bouncer at an exclusive club. Probably someplace on the French Riviera, though he doesn't look French. Austrian, perhaps, but more likely somebody with an eastern European accent and a last name with no vowels in it.

"Hey, looka Boonie, gettin' all dolled up." Espinoza's sneer breaks his concentration.

"What? Fixin' to sneak around behind Owen's back, I bet. I'd better give that boy a call, see what he's up for tonight," Morelli guffaws.

This is what passes for humor at Engine Company Fourteen, where legend asserts that the station number represents the penis size of the firefighters. Sometimes Boone feels like he never left the marines.

"Wedding," he says in his butchest growl.

"Another one?" Espinoza asks, looming behind him and staring with him into the mirror. "I figured every last gay in San Francisco must be married by now."

"Just wait," Morelli says, "won't be long before you gays figure out what a raw deal it is bein' hitched."

Berlin: 1938

General Wilhelm von Riedel's midnight blue Maybach Zeppelin V-12 limousine whispers down *Unter den Linden* through the April twilight. In the back seat with his mother and his sister, Amalie, Wulf gazes out at the great buildings, the shining automobiles, the crowded sidewalks. He watches the people lingering in two's and three's at the glowing shop windows, imagines them exclaiming at the glittering goods on display. He watches them sitting in the cafes laughing over their drinks and food as the traffic flows by. He watches them standing at the curbs waiting to cross the broad avenue and imagines a thousand different conversations they might be having. Wulf lives for those all too rare occasions when his mother and father allow him to accompany his friends on an evening jaunt to the very spots the huge car is gliding past. On any other evening he would be begging them even now to stop the car and let him out to wander among the throngs of strangers, to lose himself in the sights and sounds and aromas of Berlin on a warm spring evening.

Wulf loves this street more than any other in Berlin.

Wulf loves a great many things. He loves this time of year, when spring is well under way and summer is unmistakably approaching, when everything is in bloom and the city has once again thrown off the gloom and lethargy of winter. Wulf loves this time of evening, when the setting sun tinges the sky with constantly changing colors, one hue fading almost imperceptibly into another, when the darkness drifts down like a soothing blanket over the city, which, paradoxically, seems to awaken as the shadows deepen rather than prepare itself for sleep.

Wulf loves his glamorous mother and sweet, pretty little sister. Wulf adores his older brothers, Willi, Jurgen, Heinrich, and Georg. Wulf worships his distinguished looking father, a decorated hero of the Great War. Wulf spends blissful hours in the carriage house with Franz, the chauffeur, tinkering with the Maybach, his mother's Horch cabriolet, Willi and Jurgen's twin B.M.W. roadsters, Heinrich's streamlined Adler coupe, and Georg's exotic Alfa-Romeo. He helps Franz perform valve adjustments, tune ups, oil changes, chassis lubrications, suspension alignments, and tire rotations. They sing old army songs together as they wax glossy paintwork, polish gleaming chromium trim, saddle soap the opulent leather upholstery, brush out the carpets, and buff away the smears on the windows of the family vehicles. Franz served in the Great War, too. He is a former infantry sergeant with many decorations.

Wulf loves the other servants as well, though perhaps not as much as he loves Franz. Wulf idolizes his teachers and coaches at the *gymnasium* he attends, a very special one where the classes he takes will prepare him to enter the military academy generations of his male relatives have graduated from. He would willingly face death to please the leaders of his Hitler Youth brigade. Then there are his best friends, Johann and Artur: just thinking of them fills him with happiness and warmth. And he mustn't forget the Dobermans, Fritzi and Elsa and Wotan, who trail along intently at his heels every moment he is at home. He even loves Amalie's new kitten, Schwarzi, though he'll never admit that to her.

Indeed, Wulf muses as the traffic crawls along, he loves just about everyone he knows and everything about his life. Things could hardly be more perfect. He must surely be the happiest, luckiest eighteen-year-old in the entire Reich. And that can only mean that he's the most fortunate young man in the whole world.

But of all the stars in the constellation spangling Wulf's charmed existence, the brightest is a man he has never met but hopes to later tonight, Rudi Wagner, two time Olympic medalist in the decathlon and cinema heartthrob, who sells more movie tickets these days than any other German film star. He's an inspiration to the whole nation: a handsome, blue eyed, golden haired embodiment of the Aryan ideal. Wulf knows Rudi's statistics by heart. Weight, eighty-six kilos. Height, one hundred seventy-seven centimeters. Waist measurement, seventy-four centimeters; chest, one hundred twenty-four centimeters; biceps, forty-one centimeters. Wulf knows Rudi's biography by heart as well. At least the official one, which Wulf doesn't think to question in the tiniest detail. His proudest possession is an autographed photograph of Rudi which he received with the compliments of the Director General of UFA Studios, who is his mother's second cousin. He gazes at it hanging in its place of honor over his pillow every night just before he turns out the light.

The premiere of a Rudi Wagner film is always front page news. His new release, *Der Silberadler—The Silver Eagle*—is no exception. The papers have been full of articles about it all week, some with photos of Rudi Wulf has meticulously clipped and mounted in the special scrapbook he keeps to memorialize all Rudi's accomplishments. There was even an interview of Rudi on the radio, which Wulf listened to breathless, tingling at the sound of his hero's voice coming over the airwaves.

All Berlin wanted invitations to this glorious event. Goebbels will be there. Himmler will be there. Goering will be there. And lucky, deliriously happy Wulf will be there in the company of his father, mother and little sister. At least he will be if Franz can get them there through this hopeless tangle of traffic. Wulf fidgets inside his brand new dinner jacket. Where did all these cars come from? Mercedes-Benzes, Horchs, Maybachs; even an occasional Hispano-Suiza, Daimler, Isotta-Fraschini, or Bentley. Ordinarily he would be salivating over such a remarkable array of machinery as he can see inching along all around them toward the theatre up ahead, toward the huge searchlights which are already ripping the evening sky to tatters. But tonight those gleaming automobiles are just so many obstacles in his path. It's all he can do not to throw open the door and spring out of the Maybach. Surely walking the rest of the way, even through the throngs on the sidewalk, would be quicker than this snail's pace.

* * *

Der Silberadler is the best film Wulf has ever seen. No question about it. And he never misses a Rudi Wagner picture. Indeed, he has seen all of them repeatedly. He is on the edge of his seat during most of it. No one in the huge audience laughs longer and harder than he at the jokes the heroic fighter pilots tell, the hysterical stunts they perform in the mess hall between missions, and the elaborate practical jokes they continually play on one another. No one can possibly be more spellbound by the flying sequences, particularly the dogfights, when Rudi's character, the young Baron von Cmuda, leads his squadron of Fokker triplanes against the Sopwiths, S.P.A.D.'s, and Nieuports of the British and French forces, fighting spectacular duels high above the trenches of the Western Front. No one is more moved by the Baron's speech to his fellow pilots when one of their number fails to return safely to base from a mission. No one is more inspired by the Baron's patriotism and bravery. Indeed, watching Rudi Wagner on the screen Wulf realizes he has finally found his calling. Unlike his brothers, he will not follow General von Riedel into the *Wehrmacht*. It must certainly be the *Luftwaffe* for him. He imagines himself at the controls of a shiny new Messerschmitt or Focke-Wulf, soaring above the green fields and white clouds, flying for the Fatherland.

The general won't be pleased by this resolve. His father only cares about the tanks under his command. For weeks he has been lecturing them all at mealtimes about the long meetings he's been having with Dr. Porsche regarding the newest improvements to his tank designs and the crucial role these enormous, terrifying machines will play should the Reich be forced to defend itself against the ruthless enemies encircling it.

But sitting in the dark theatre and gazing at Rudi Wagner's golden haired glory on the giant screen, Wulf dedicates himself to this new dream and swears that neither family tradition nor his father's intentions will deflect him from his destiny. How could anyone not want to be just like the heroic character Rudi Wagner is portraying up there? And how heroic must the actor be himself? Olympic medalist that he is and idol of millions of Germans? Can it be anything other than his own personal courage and goodness that they are all enthralled by on the giant screen in the most expensive, most spectacular UFA production ever? Wulf stares at the handsome, smiling face, the shining eyes. His stomach flutters like the wings of a thousand butterflies. He almost wishes he could reach up and smooth Rudi Wagner's tousled locks into place. But what he really wishes is that by some miracle he could be Rudi Wagner's best friend.

* * *

Franz drops Wulf and his mother off in front of the Hotel Adlon. For some reason Wulf doesn't understand, General von Riedel never shows any interest in socializing with the top party leaders, though Wulf's mother meets Magda Goebbels for lunch several times a month and the Goebbels children sometimes visit Amalie at home. So the general and Amalie—it is past her bedtime and she's too young to enjoy this sort of party anyway—stay in the car. Franz will return to the hotel after he has driven them home. Wulf listens to the V-12's rich purr as the car pulls away from the curb.

"Happy, my darling Wulfi?" his mother smiles up at him, smoothing a lock of hair off his forehead as they wait for the doorman to admit them into the ornate lobby.

"Happy, Mutti," Wulf grins back, feeling like he's about to burst.

The doorman motions them inside with an efficient nod of his head. They sweep past him, Wulf's mother grasping his arm lightly just as she would the general's were he escorting her. This action makes Wulf feel dizzyingly grown up. He loves it when people mistake him for one of his older brothers or overestimate his age by three or four years, as often happens. He can't wait to be a man just like them, though despite his size and physical maturity his face is discouragingly hairless. He's sometimes terrified that he'll never have to start shaving.

The ballroom is kaleidoscopic with music, gorgeously dressed people, and waiters in spotless white jackets bearing silver trays of champagne glasses. Wulf takes two, presents one to his mother, and holds his out to her. They clink the crystal together lightly and she winks at him as if they're a couple of conspirators.

"To us, dearest Wulfi."

"To us, darling Mutti."

Soon they're in the receiving line, and despite the two glasses of champagne Wulf has downed his heart is in his mouth. In a matter of minutes he'll be shaking hands with his idol. He feels a trickle of sweat inside his clothing, and his bladder seems suddenly full to bursting. All around he hears laughter and snatches of witty conversation. He smells the sweet, exotic perfumes of the women and the deeper, masculine scents of the men—cigar smoke, leather, hair oil. He imagines how Cinderella must have felt finding herself suddenly and unexpectedly face to face with the prince, and nearly laughs out loud. The receiving line inches forward, and his lightheadedness increases alarmingly.

"Marthe, my darling," Frau General von Riedel's second cousin purrs, kissing her hand. As Director General of UFA, he's the host for the evening. "You look simply ravishing. You should leave boring old Wilhelm and come away with me. How does the French Riviera sound?"

"Konrad," Wulf's mother laughs. "Why is it that we can never meet without you making some outrageous proposal or other?"

"I don't understand it myself," Konrad laughs. "The only possible explanation for it is that I'm intoxicated by you, my dear."

"Flatterer," she murmurs, pretending to frown at him.

"No, darling Marthe," Konrad protests. "It's not flattery at all, I assure you."

"Ah, the worst sort of flattery," she accuses him. "The kind that trumpets its sincerity. You're truly shameless."

"I certainly hope so. But how inexcusable of me to ignore our Wulfchen," he smiles, turning to Wulf and offering his hand.

"Hello, Cousin Konrad."

"My boy, you must have grown six centimeters since I last saw you."

Wulf shrugs. It's what Cousin Konrad says every time they meet.

"And that suit. What a magnificent looking young man, Marthe. Those sons of yours. Every last one a head turner. For the life of me I don't understand why you're not already a grandmother a dozen times over. But you, Wulfchen, you're going to break more hearts than the rest of your brothers put together. I'd bet money on it. And you know the von Valkensteins: we only bet on sure things."

Wulf feels himself blushing. But his discomfort is fleeting, for his mother has moved on down the line. He watches breathless as Rudi Wagner takes her hand, kisses it with a gallantry that completely eclipses that of Cousin Konrad, and smiles his incandescent smile. Then, practically before he knows it and long before he's truly prepared, though the wait has been excruciating, Wulf is face to face with the man himself. They're almost exactly the same height. Wulf had known this before, of course, but it's still a surprise to find that Rudi Wagner is not actually a giant. Rudi Wagner smells of the same cologne Wulf's brother Willi wears, and his golden hair glistens dazzlingly with brilliantine. Wulf nearly swoons as the ice blue eyes meet his own.

"Wulf von Riedel," Rudi Wagner murmurs softly, almost as if they're alone together in a quiet room somewhere, "what an honor to meet you at last. I've seen your photograph in Konrad's office, but it hardly does you justice."

"I loved your film enormously," Wulf stammers. "Really, more than I can say."

"Did you?" Rudi grins, resting a hand lightly on Wulf's shoulder, which inexplicably seems to burn under the pressure of that touch. "How wonderful. Hearing that makes all the work worthwhile."

There's so much Wulf would like to say, but he's suddenly tongue tied. Meanwhile, his mother has moved still farther down the line, and he knows he must follow. Still, he can hardly force himself away from this man who's now even more than a hero to him.

"Until we meet again, then," Rudi says, as if they're old friends bound to run into each other in a day or two just as a matter of course.

All Wulf can do is gulp quickly and nod.

* * *

Wulf collapses into the leather cushioned back seat of the Maybach. He has had far more champagne than his father would approve of. His head is spinning and he can hardly keep his eyes open. He feels rather than sees his mother climb into the car. Ordinarily he would have waited on the curb to help her in,

but the last he knew she was still in the lobby talking to Frau Goebbels, and he'd
suddenly realized that if he didn't want to fall flat on his face in front of all those
people he'd better get Franz to help him. Good old Franz.

"Are you all right, darling?"

"Ja, Mutti. Only a little sleepy."

"That's fine then. We'll be home soon."

He listens as Franz shifts the Maybach into gear and they begin to pull
away.

"Stop, Franz," he hears his mother cry, breathless with excitement.

He tries to open his eyes but he can't.

"I wonder what he wants," his mother says, voice trembling slightly. He
listens as she lets down the window. Noise washes into the back seat from outside.

"My dear Frau General von Riedel, please allow me to detain you for just
a moment."

It's a man's voice, familiar and unfamiliar at the same time. How embarrassing to be all but passed out here for the gentleman to see. If Wulf could just
sit up and force his eyes open he might recognize the person at the open window. Most likely not, though. His mother and father know so frightfully many
people, most of them too boring for words. Wulf doesn't know how Mutti
stands them. In any case, he's far too drowsy to feel more than the mildest
curiosity.

"But certainly, Herr Wagner."

Herr Wagner? Has Rudi Wagner himself come out after them? It hardly
seems possible. There must have been a dozen or more "Herr Wagners" at the
reception. They're almost as numerous, after all, as Schmidts.

"Oh, my, Frau General. Is Wulf all right?"

"He seems to have had a little more champagne than was good for him,"
his mother explains, laughing her special, silvery laugh. "I'm sure he'll be quite
all right in the morning. You know boys his age, Herr Wagner. I can assure you
that this one in particular has the constitution of a hippopotamus. It's that good
Prussian stock, you know."

"I'm glad to hear it. But if he's not feeling well at the moment, I wouldn't
think of keeping you. I was hoping, however…that is, if you and General von
Riedel wouldn't object…"

"Object to what, Herr Wagner?"

"It would give me the greatest pleasure if you would allow Wulf to visit me on the set at the studio tomorrow. I thought he might enjoy watching us shoot a scene or two of my new film."

"Oh, Herr Wagner, how enormously kind of you. But I'm sure we couldn't possibly allow it. Wouldn't it present a terrible distraction for you in your work?"

"Not in the least. I thought perhaps my driver might pick him up at your home tomorrow afternoon and bring him out to Potsdam for the last hour or so of our work. Then if he liked, and with your kind permission, I might take him out for an early dinner."

"Dear Herr Wagner. This is so tremendously considerate of you. I know if Wulfi were awake he'd be jumping up and down at the idea of it. I don't see that his father or I can have the least objection to your plan. But do make him behave himself when he is with you. He can be so very high spirited. So noisy. Leaping about like a baboon in the Tiergarten. And whatever you do, don't bring him home in this condition tomorrow evening. Heaven knows how I'll be able to explain this state of his to General von Riedel."

"You have my word, dear Frau General. I shall look forward to seeing Wulf tomorrow and your charming self very soon."

"*Auf Wiedersehen,* then, Herr Wagner."

"'*Wiedersehen* to you both. Do you suppose Wulf can hear us?"

"I'm afraid I couldn't say."

"It's worth a try: *schlaf gut,* dear Wulfi."

Wulf faintly hears the window close. Then the car pulls away from the curb. In the morning when he wakes he will think he has dreamed the whole thing.

* * *

Wulf climbs out of the bath and towels himself off vigorously. He powders himself even more thoroughly than usual, terrified that some unpleasant odor might escape from inside his clothing when he is with Rudi Wagner later. Just to make extra certain, he uses some of Willi's cologne. Then, throwing caution to the winds, he slicks his heavy thatch of straw colored hair determinedly into place with some of Jurgen's brilliantine. It's tricky stuff to work with and he's about to abandon the experiment and climb back into the bath to wash his hair again when he finally gets it to look exactly like Rudi Wagner's hair looked last night. Is this what he wants to look like? *Aber naturlich*, now that he thinks about it.

He must start buying things of his own. It's stupid of him not to have done so already. Johann and Artur are after him all the time about his casual grooming habits. They claim, only half joking he suspects, that he's a disgrace to the whole *gymnasium*. But until last night his appearance didn't seem to matter. Let his older brothers fuss endlessly over their clothes, their shoes, their hair, their scent. It has always seemed like such an enormous waste of time. He rarely goes so far as to run a comb through his hair in the morning, just shakes out the excess water and lets it dry however it will, only getting it cut when his father insists. Cleanliness is another matter. He's always clean, sometimes bathing as many as three times in a day. His teeth are gleaming white and his nails are always perfectly kept.

After cleaning his teeth rather more ruthlessly than usual, he cinches the towel tighter around his waist and runs down the hall to his bedroom. He is still ransacking his cupboard for just the right things to wear when he hears the unfamiliar car engine outside. A few moments later, as he's straightening his tie, there's a knock on his door and Schmidt calls in to him that Rudi Wagner's driver is waiting. He makes a face at himself in the mirror. Then he's out of the room in a flash, galloping down the hall, taking the stairs two at a time.

"Tell Mutti I've gone, Schmidt," he calls. "Tell her I promise to be good."

He knows Schmidt won't relay this latter part of the message. He knows Schmidt suspects he's intent on some mischief. He knows butlers are supposed to be stuffy, but really, Schmidt goes out of his way to disapprove of him. It doesn't seem fair considering that he has nothing but respect for the old man, who has been with the von Riedels since Wulf's father was a boy. Wulf dashes through the foyer, bursts out the front door into the warm afternoon. In the drive, a tall, athletic looking, black haired man in a chauffeur's uniform stands beside a rakish, electric blue Bugatti coupe. The car's futuristic lines take Wulf's breath away. It is as if a grand prix racer and a rocket ship had mated and produced this bizarre but exquisite offspring. His admiration for Rudi Wagner rises even farther into the stratosphere.

"Good afternoon," he says to the driver.

"Good afternoon, Herr von Riedel."

"Please call me Wulf."

"*Also gut*, Herr Wulf. I am Horst, Herr Wagner's driver and bodyguard."

"Bodyguard?" Wulf can't imagine anyone wanting to hurt Rudi. Nor any situation in which Rudi couldn't take care of himself. But of course the Reich has many enemies, ruthless and unprincipled persons who will stop at nothing in the campaign against the Fatherland. No one is safe.

"That's right," Horst nods.

"Are we in a great hurry, Horst?"

"Not really. Why?"

"It's just that I know Franz, our chauffeur, would love to examine Herr Wagner's automobile. I have heard him speak of Bugatti many times, but I don't know if he's ever actually seen one."

"We may certainly take a few minutes to show it to him then," Horst smiles.

"*Wunderbar!* I'll just go call him." He runs inside and practically shouts into the house telephone. He's out the door again almost before the receiver has settled back into its cradle. Horst has raised the Bugatti's hood. Wulf gazes reverently at the gleaming engine, with its eight cylinders in line topped by twin camshaft covers.

"Is that a supercharger?" he asks, pointing.

"*Ja*, Herr Wulf."

"*Gott in Himmel*," Wulf sighs, "she must be a fast machine."

"Herr Wagner reached two hundred and twenty-five kilometers on the Dessau autobahn several weeks ago."

"*Wirklich?* Two hundred and twenty-five?"

Horst nods. Wulf tries to imagine what it must have felt like to go that fast. Willi once drove his B.M.W. at one hundred sixty with Wulf aboard. And that was enough to take his breath away. Of course this is a coupe, not a roadster, and the sensation is probably quite different. He's just about to ask Horst about this when he hears Franz approaching.

"Look here, Franz," he calls. "Have you ever seen anything so magnificent?"

* * *

Horst escorts him to Cousin Konrad's office suite and silently disappears. Helga smiles at him.

"Good afternoon, Wulf. Herr Director General von Valkenstein is on the telephone, but he said you should go right in. He'll only be a few moments longer."

"Thank you, Helga. How are the twins?"

"Growing like weeds. They still talk about that pony they rode at Amalie's birthday party. It was so kind of your mother to invite them."

"You know how Mutti loves throwing parties," he smiles, recalling the boys' delighted squeals as they sat one in front of the other on the fat gray pony's back and waved at Helga. "And the bigger the party, the better."

"And are your brothers well?"

Wulf knows she is really asking only about Georg. She's too old for Georg, but he supposes a still young widow can't be too particular about things like that. Unfortunately, Georg seems not at all inclined to settle down with a woman of any description: old or young, fat or thin, tall or short, blond or dark, he pays none of them any heed. All he cares about are his Alfa-Romeo and the tank squadron he commands.

"Fine, thank you," Wulf says. "Very busy these days. Georg just received a promotion, you know."

"Your parents must be so proud of him."

"Very proud," Wulf agrees. "Perhaps I'll go on in."

"Yes, do. I know he's anxious to see you."

Cousin Konrad is just putting down the telephone as Wulf enters the large office. There are a few new articles of furniture, he sees, all very futuristic looking like the rest of Cousin Konrad's things. He wishes Mutti would furnish at least some of the rooms at home like this office, but she turns up her nose at "all that chromium and glass".

"Ah, Wulf, here you are at last," Cousin Konrad says, rising and moving around the desk toward him. "Rudi's been quite impatient about your arrival."

"I'm afraid I made us late," Wulf explains. "Please don't let Horst get in trouble over it. I just had to show Franz the Bugatti."

"I thought as much," Cousin Konrad laughs, slapping him on the back. "Now would you like some refreshment, or should we head on over to the soundstage?"

Wulf is always hungry these days and wouldn't mind some of the lemonade and cakes he sees on a tray sitting on the credenza, but he doesn't want to delay seeing Rudi any longer. He so wants to make a good impression.

"I think we'll go," he says. "Don't want to keep the star waiting."

* * *

Though Wulf has visited Cousin Konrad at UFA many times, he's never set foot inside one of the enormous soundstages before and he's not quite sure what to expect. Really, they're as large as Zeppelin hangars: he can't imagine why they need to be such a size. There are signs beside the door forbidding entry to unauthorized persons and commanding silence of those who do go inside. He follows Cousin Konrad through the door. It's surprisingly hot inside and it takes Wulf a moment to figure out that this must be caused by the huge lights shining down from scaffolding over the set. The set itself looks familiar somehow—could it be a courtroom? And the huge space teems with frantic activity. People are rushing here and there, hanging from catwalks at dizzying heights like so many circus performers, carrying unidentifiable pieces of equipment back and forth, shouting instructions. He follows Cousin Konrad through a maze of electrical cables and derricks toward the front of the set, where he can see Rudi in conversation with a tall, impossibly skinny looking man wearing a pith helmet and a white linen suit.

"That's Eugen Dichter, the famous director," Cousin Konrad shouts over his shoulder. "He's ridiculously eccentric as you can see, but a genius. This is the first film he's ever done with Rudi."

Wulf stumbles over one last unfamiliar coil of rope or rubber hose or whatever and there he is.

"Wulfi!" Rudi exclaims, pleasure flashing in his eyes and a huge grin on his face. "I was afraid you must have become ill last night and couldn't come after all."

"I wouldn't have missed this for anything," Wulf stammers as Rudi puts an arm around his shoulder for all the world like one of his friends from *gymnasium*.

"It's wonderful to see you again so soon," Rudi says. "Now allow me please to present our director, Herr Eugen Dichter. Eugen, this is my great friend, Wulf von Riedel. He is a relation of Konrad's."

"On his mother's side," Konrad smiles.

"Extremely pleased to meet you, Herr Dichter," Wulf says to the unsmiling, glassy eyed, craggy faced man who towers over him.

"There, Eugen," Rudi says. "Didn't I tell you he'd be perfect?"

"Indeed. I see what you mean," Dichter says. "Much more convincing than Peter Becker."

"We can buy Peter out of the contract," Konrad says. "Don't worry about that. You can take it out of my pay, if necessary."

"I'm not worried about that," Dichter snaps. "That's the producer's problem. But this one: has he ever acted before?"

"Have you, Wulfi?" Rudi asks.

"What are you talking about?" Wulf asks.

"Never mind, Wulfchen," Rudi winks, "just answer the question."

"We do Shakespeare every term at *gymnasium*," Wulf says, blushing. "Last month I was Laertes."

"I wish I had seen it," Rudi says.

"It was capital," Konrad assures them. He never misses the theatricals at Wulf's school. He graduated there himself. "The boy has real flair."

"So what do you think, Eugen?" Rudi asks.

"He's a student. What about his schedule?"

"He graduates in two weeks," Cousin Konrad says.

"Two weeks only, Eugen. Surely the shooting schedule can be adjusted." Rudi is almost pleading now, and Wulf can't believe what he's hearing.

"Well, as you say, he does look enough like you to be your younger brother. And that would be very, very effective dramatically. It might just be worth it. But look here, he's a little too large, I'm afraid. Almost as big as you are."

"But Eugen, he's supposed to be an athlete," Rudi protests.

Herr Dichter shrugs, then stands staring at him. His eyes seem to bore holes into Wulf's head. It's embarrassing. He's even starting to feel slightly ill.

"What do you suppose his parents will say?" Herr Dichter asks.

"His mother will approve," Cousin Konrad says. "We'll probably have to keep it a secret from the general until the film is released. But he's a very busy man these days, so that won't be too difficult."

"As you wish," Herr Dichter says, nodding slowly in a way that reminds Wulf somehow of a giant sea turtle pulling its head into its shell. "You'd better have someone take him over to the wardrobe department for measurements."

"Can't that wait until tomorrow?" Rudi asks. "I want him to watch us shoot this last scene."

"Very well," Dichter says. "And leave all that slickum out of your hair from now on, son. In this film, you're not supposed to be a Chicago gangster but a Berlin schoolboy."

"But Eugen," Rudi roars with laughter, "that's exactly what he is."

Wulf stands there stunned. Unless he's dreamed the last few moments, he's apparently been given a part in Rudi's new film. He feels like pinching himself to make sure he's awake. If this is really happening, his mother will be beside herself when he tells her.

"*Nun kom*', Wulf," Rudi says, still smiling and taking him by the arm. "Sit over here by me. We'll be ready to start in just a moment."

* * *

In the Bugatti on their way back into the city, Rudi fills Wulf in on the plot of the film he's now a cast member of. In *Die Schwimmbad-Spionage*, Rudi plays the wrestling and swimming coach at a fashionable Berlin *gymnasium*. He and his younger brother—Wulf's character, who is the captain of the swim team—work together to foil the plans of the headmaster, a secret Marxist sympathizer, to recruit students as spies for the Soviets.

"You do swim, don't you?" Rudi asks. "Many of your scenes will take place at the pool."

"Of course," Wulf says, leaving it at that. He's afraid he'll sound like he's boasting if he speaks of the medals he has won in swimming competitions. He's also a little apprehensive about how he'll look onscreen in so little clothing, particularly beside the godlike Rudi.

"Good," Rudi says.

"I'm just afraid I won't do a very good job in the film."

"Nonsense," Rudi barks. "You're a natural. If I'm not careful, you'll steal all the limelight from me."

"*Aber nein,* Rudi. That could never happen," Wulf gasps, horrified. "I mean, even if I could, I would never do such a thing. Truly."

"You know, Wulfi," Rudi says after a long silence, "I believe you mean that. I knew when I first met you that you could be trusted."

"I certainly hope you can trust me," Wulf says, not at all certain what they're talking about or why it should particularly matter whether Rudi can trust him or not.

"Oh, I do," Rudi says, still sounding thoughtful. "Now tell me. What do you plan to do with all the money you're to be paid?"

It's the first Wulf has heard mention of this. It hadn't occurred to him in all the excitement of this afternoon, but of course film actors do not work for free. Rudi is obviously quite rich. Still, Wulf is just a beginner. He won't earn very much. And Mutti will undoubtedly make him save it.

"I don't suppose it will be enough to buy a car like this," he sighs.

"You like it, don't you?" Rudi observes, obviously pleased.

"She's the most beautiful auto I've ever seen. And Horst told me how fast you've driven her."

"She is magnificent, isn't she? I know one isn't supposed to express such admiration for things French these days, but I can't help myself. I fell in love with one just like her at the Paris Salon two years ago and ordered her from the works. But I'm afraid you're right. You won't be making quite that much money. Not on this film, at least. Still, no matter. Horst will teach you how to drive her."

"Really?" Wulf yelps, heart racing.

"Of course. Whenever you like."

"I can't believe you would share her with me."

"Ah, Wulfchen," Rudi says, smiling that smile that makes Wulf tingle all over. "There are many things I hope to share with you. You'll see. We're going to be great friends, you and I."

Wulf would like to say something beautiful in response to this, but he's speechless. Less than twenty-four hours ago he was sitting in his father's May-bach on the way to the theatre wishing he could be Rudi Wagner's friend. It's like a dream come true.

* * *

Rudi steers the Bugatti through the gates and parks in the drive. He switches off the engine and the lights.

"Here you are, Wulfi. Home safe and sound. I hope your parents won't mind me bringing you home so late."

"Thank you for dinner," Wulf says, sorry that the evening is over. "And for everything else."

"Are you excited about all this?"

"Of course."

"You don't sound like it. What's wrong? Don't you want to be in our film?"

"Oh, yes. Very much. I'm just not sure what Mutti will say when I tell her."

"I wouldn't worry about that," Rudi says. "I expect Konrad has already telephoned her with the news. Between the two of them they'll make certain everything's all right with General von Riedel. I'm sure of it."

"When you explain it like that," Wulf says, "I feel silly for worrying about it."

"You must never feel silly, Wulf. You're not a silly young man. And you must never worry again, because your friend Rudi is looking out for you, *versteh'*?"

Wulf feels a lump rising in his throat. This wonderful hero of his, saying such a thing.

"*Ja, Rudi. Ich versteh'.*"

"*Also gut.* And you enjoyed our afternoon?"

In spite of Rudi's kind words, Wulf would feel silly telling him this has been the most wonderful day of his life.

"Oh, yes, Rudi. So very much."

"Get some rest, then. Horst will come for you at the *gymnasium* tomorrow afternoon."

France: 1943

A stiff breeze whips the Atlantic into whitecaps off the beaches of Brittany. It's October, but high summer blithely lingers, belying the grimness of great nations engaged in life and death struggles and showing no signs of giving way to autumn. The war has recently entered its fifth year. At age twenty-two, Wulf von Riedel is a hardened veteran. These days twenty-two isn't particularly young for a *Staffelkapitan*; twenty-five year olds seem positively superannuated. Shockingly few German combat pilots have survived to that age, and thirty year olds are practically unheard of. Nineteen year olds under Wulf's command call him "the old man", then turn around and poke fun at the eighteen year old "wolf pups" joining the *staffel* fresh out of flight school each month. Both groups trust him to bring them back from each mission alive, the veterans out of long experience and the new boys out of childlike faith in his near-legendary good luck. He almost always does, though the days when going after the Allied bombers was like shooting fish in a barrel are gone forever. New, long range Allied fighter planes are now escorting the huge fleets of bombers deep into the airspace over the Continent. And their pilots are better trained than earlier in the war, more skillful every time he engages one. His job grows more difficult and perilous with every passing week. When will his luck run out? Wulf doesn't believe in luck. Wulf makes his own luck. All good pilots do.

Today's missions have been successful. After scrambling four times in all, everyone is back on the ground safe and accounted for. None of the pilots have reported damaged aircraft. Wulf is relieved beyond words that he won't have to write one of those letters he hates so much to anyone's mother tonight before he goes to bed. Things will be jolly rather than funereal in the pilots' mess this evening. But that's all merely a personal reaction to their return in such good order, one hardly worthy of a *Luftwaffe* officer. As *Staffelkapitan* there are other considerations: it means an easy night for the chronically overworked maintenance crews. It also means that when the *staffel* scrambles tomorrow—and they will scramble tomorrow, at least twice and perhaps three times: the weather will almost certainly continue fine over the Continent for several more days and the Allied daylight bombing campaign is picking up steam, though he doubts the Allies can send the same four waves they did today after the losses he knows they must have suffered—they will be at full strength, and the men's morale will be high.

It's been a good day. Lots of B-17's and B-24's have been shot down or damaged too badly to continue toward their targets in Germany. Another three kills, if today's two B-24's are confirmed, and Wulf will be an ace seven times over. That means an almost certain promotion to major and a possible posting as *Gruppenkommandeur*. It might come as early as his father's birthday in a few weeks' time. What a fine gift that would be. Two of his older brothers are generals already; the other two, colonels. And his father has recently been promoted to field marshal. They're all on the Eastern Front except Wulf, who sometimes feels guilty about his relative safety. At any rate, no one can say the von Riedels aren't doing their share for the Reich. The German people have been able to depend on the von Riedels for centuries.

The drably painted aircraft of the *staffel* land into the wind. Wulf circles overhead while his pilots take their Messerschmitts down onto the deep green turf two by two. He and his wingman, Ralf Zimmermann, are always the last ones in unless one or the other of them is low on fuel or has suffered damage to his aircraft. Wulf feels it's his responsibility to stay in the air until all his men, or at least all those with any chance of returning to base, are safe on the ground. Every *Staffelkapitan* he ever served under did the same. When Ralf gets his own command, which Wulf knows is only a matter of time, he'll do it too. The *Luft-waffe* has always taken pride in looking out for its own.

He glances rightward out of the canopy and sees Ralf's thumbs up signal, which he returns with a grin. It's finally their turn. In unison they make a last ninety degree turn which lines them up with the field and gives them a magnificent but fleeting view of the choppy Atlantic just a few miles west of base. They go into a shallow dive. Wulf throttles back, mentally giving thanks to the Daimler-Benz technicians at the Marienfelde works for the incredible robustness of this engine, which never gives cause for alarm. Its bass growl falls to an even deeper pitch, and he senses the aircraft slowing. They clear the line of trees a kilometer or so past the end of the field. The deep green of the smooth turf rises gradually to meet them.

And then they're down. After the frantic takeoffs earlier and the noisy chaos of the dogfights, finding himself back on the ground with so little drama or effort is almost anti-climactic. But he knows he can't ever let himself become complacent about his landings. Magnificent as these Messerschmitts are in the air, they're absolute pigs to land. He's seen more than one excellent pilot kill himself simply by allowing his concentration to lapse for an instant, by failing to fly his craft right down onto the field. A split second of inattention, even at an altitude of as little as twenty feet, can be fatal. There are seldom second chances after such errors.

They taxi up to where their ground crews are giving them signals for parking the aircraft. He manipulates the wheel brakes skillfully, turning the aircraft one hundred eighty degrees in little more than its own length. He pulls to a halt right on the spot indicated by his crew chief and cuts the ignition switches to the big Daimler-Benz engine. The propeller windmills to a halt. By the time he's got the canopy open and has unbelted himself, the men have the ladder in place against the fuselage. He climbs awkwardly out of the cockpit and down to the ground. Even this has to be done with care. You can break an ankle or leg with a clumsy, inattentive dismount. It is good to feel the French earth beneath his feet one more time. Gruber slaps him on the back.

"Welcome home, *Herr Hauptmann*."

"*Danke zwei millionen,* Gruber. She flew like a dream thanks to you and the men. I always know I can depend on you to keep her shipshape. Without you, the Allies would have a free ride all the way to Germany and back. You are the real heroes of this war."

"*Vielen Dank, Herr Hauptmann,*" Gruber blushes with pleasure. Wulf is always surprised at how far a little praise goes with his men. And any pilot with half a brain knows he'd best keep his ground crew rooting for him, though surprisingly few seem to learn this most elementary of lessons. "We are always happy to see you return safely. *Also dann*, nothing to report? *Nichts?*"

"*Gar nichts*, Gruber."

"*Also gut.* We'll have her ready to go up again at first light."

* * *

In the officer's mess it's pandemonium. The phonograph is turned up loud enough to wake the dead and a darts tournament is in full swing. The men are eating sandwiches, guzzling beer, joking and carrying on like they've just returned from a Hitler Youth outing. It's always like this at the end of a successful day of flying against the enemy bombers. Victory in its own way is as stressful as defeat. The men have to blow off steam. Wulf understands this as well as anyone in the *Luftwaffe*. Still, he's always watchful. Sometimes one of his pilots will get a little out of control. That's a warning sign a *Staffelkapitan* can't afford to miss. Send a man who's too keyed up on a mission, no matter how routine, and there's a good chance he won't come home. So he only sips at his pilsner and keeps his eyes and ears open.

Almost everyone seems fine, but he's not absolutely comfortable about young *Leutnant* Reinhardt. A popular, stunningly handsome boy, Markus is one of Wulf's best pilots. He's flown more missions in succession than anyone in the *staffel* except Ralf Zimmermann and Wulf himself. He's got potential *Staffelkapitan* written all over him. He's too good to risk losing for no better reason than to protect his ego. Better ground him for forty-eight hours. Which, since they don't fly at night, will give him until Saturday morning to rest up. He won't like it but he's a good boy. He'll keep his complaints to himself, Wulf knows. And someday, when he has his own command, he'll look back on this experience and understand. The *staffel* celebrated his birthday last week. Wulf would dearly love to see him celebrate his next one in such perfect strength and health, so he'll take this precaution.

No sooner than he's had this thought but his orderly is standing at his elbow.

"Telegram for you, *Herr Hauptmann*."

"*Danke sehr*, Hesse. Would you please ask *Leutnant* Reinhardt to see me in my office in twenty minutes?"

"*Jawohl, Herr Hauptmann*. Anything else?"

"Just a moment, while I read this."

He rips open the envelope and scans the wire. It's too good to be true. His request for leave has been granted. Seven days in Berlin.

"Good news, *Herr Hauptmann*?"

"The very best, Hesse. My leave has come through. Starting at 1800 tomorrow. Better tell *Hauptmann* Zimmermann to see me in my office in thirty minutes. I won't have time to brief him tomorrow. And see if you can arrange for me to ride on the mail plane tomorrow evening."

"Already done, *Herr Hauptmann*. I took care of it the moment the telegram arrived. I guessed what it might be about."

"Hesse, you're one in a million."

* * *

Wulf is scanning the latest weather forecasts when Reinhardt's knock sounds on his office door.

"*Herein.*"

Reinhardt enters, closes the door behind him, stands at attention. His coal black hair is damp and gleaming, perfectly combed. He smells faintly of the brand of cologne Rudi wears. Wulf appreciates the respect he's shown in showering and shaving before coming in. Reinhardt's light gray eyes are bright but slightly bloodshot. No question about it—Wulf has made the right decision.

"You wished to see me, *Herr Hauptmann?*"

"At ease, Reinhardt. Please sit. Can I offer you a cigarette?"

"No thank you, *Herr Hauptmann*. I don't smoke."

"Good man," Wulf smiles. "I don't either. Noxious habit. Still, it seems to relax some people."

Reinhardt nods slightly, obviously wary of appearing to take the liberty of too much familiarity with his superior officer.

"Look here, Reinhardt." Knowing he's doing the right thing doesn't make this any less awkward. He recalls how deeply he resented it the few times he was grounded. Each time it almost certainly saved his life, but he'll never forget the sting the words carried. "Wonderful flying today. Absolutely magnificent."

And he's not exaggerating. He's constantly amazed by this young man's uncanny talent in the air.

"*Vielen dank, Herr Hauptmann.*"

"I can't tell you what an honor it is to command men such as yourself. But even the best pilots can give just so much, I'm afraid."

He cringes inwardly as he sees the flicker of disbelief in Reinhardt's eyes.

"Now listen, old man, it's only for forty-eight hours. And I can guarantee you no one around here is going to think any less of you for it. I'm sure you realize the youngsters idolize you. I'm afraid I can't answer for the consequences to their morale if something should happen to you. I have to protect them as much as possible from a loss like that because it might mean losing one of them as well. So you see, I really have no choice. You're simply too valuable to us to take unnecessary risks. Please, take this as a sign of your enormous importance to the *staffel* and my own deep regard for you. And rest up."

"*Jawohl, Herr Hauptmann,*" Reinhardt says. "Is there anything else?"

He can hear the young man struggling to keep his fury from sounding in his voice. And suddenly Wulf sees his way out.

"As a matter of fact, yes," he says, noting with dismay the expression of alarm that Reinhardt immediately suppresses. He's obviously expecting things to get even worse. "I've been granted seven days leave. I'm flying to Berlin to-morrow evening. In my absence, beginning on Sunday morning, you will fly as *Hauptmann* Zimmermann's wingman on all missions."

There. That's done it. Reinhardt's practically beaming now, letting loose of his obsessive dignity just enough to let Wulf know he's instantly gotten over his disappointment at being grounded.

"*Danke, Herr Hauptmann.*"

"No, Reinhardt, thank you. I'll be able to enjoy my leave that much more, knowing that you'll be at *Hauptmann* Zimmerman's side. Such peace of mind is priceless, as you'll understand when you receive your own command someday. You see how much I depend on you? Now go and start relaxing. If I were you, I'd requisition a motor and go to the beach. You could really use some sun. And while you're at it, have the mess hall pack you some beer and sandwiches."

"*Jawohl, Herr Hauptmann,*" Reinhardt says, rising quickly and giving Wulf an exemplary salute.

* * *

He looks in at the main mess hall later that evening on his way back to his quarters. An awkward hush falls as he enters, and he immediately sees the reason: tonight's film, *Die Schwimmbad-Spionage*, was the first he ever appeared in with Rudi Wagner. As Rudi's co-star in five features, he became somewhat famous in his own right. Everyone in the *staffel* knows of his career in films. There's obviously more than a little amusement abroad at the sight of his ado-lescent self onscreen. In the scene presently showing, he and Rudi are standing together at the side of a large swimming pool. They wear matching swimsuits. The skin of their bare chests and arms glints wetly, as if they've just come out of the water. He recalls how embarrassed he was filming this scene, his first in that skimpy swim suit, and how gently Rudi put him at ease in spite of his near nudity. He moves quickly to the rear of the room and stands drinking in Rudi's almost supernatural beauty for a brief moment before heading off to bed. In less than twenty-four hours, with any luck at all, he'll be in Rudi's arms.

* * *

There are no smiles from his ground crew the next afternoon as Wulf clambers out of his Messerschmitt after the *staffel's* third sortie. It's been a di-sastrous day: three pilots lost: Eitzen, Kleinfelter, and Tiemmersma. Not one of them a day over twenty. Wulf is heartsick that these laughing, exuberant boys will never again be seen clowning in the pilot's mess, will never return to their homes and loved ones, will never witness the glorious day of Germany's victory. But even this isn't enough to make him forget his manners.

"*Vielen dank,* Gruber," he says, sorry that he's unable to muster even the ghost of a smile. "Take good care of the old girl for me while I'm in Berlin."

"*Jawohl, Herr Hauptmann.*"

He heads straight for his office. The longer he waits to begin writing these horrible letters, the harder the chore will be. Already he's composing in his mind the phrases he will use, mortified at their inadequacy to ease the terrible pain he knows these messages will cause. He thinks for a moment of Reinhardt off lounging at the beach and blesses the instinct that made him ground the young pilot. The *staffel* couldn't have stood to lose four men in one day, and given the fierceness of the aerial battles he knows Reinhardt couldn't have survived in his current state.

He storms through the door of his office, shaking with fury at the Allied pilots and gunners but most of all at himself for not training those boys better, not teaching them how to protect themselves, letting them die so horribly. Is he even fit to command them? Hesse is standing beside his desk awaiting orders. He has already arranged Wulf's stationery, ink, and pens on the desk top.

"Thank you, Hesse," he says. "I'll need you to organize their personal effects for shipping home."

"*Jawohl, Herr Hauptmann.*"

"And you'd better check the railway timetables. I won't be able to make the mail plane."

This realization causes his spirits to plummet even further. With rail service so disorganized these days it could easily take half his leave just to reach Berlin. He thinks of his darling Rudi back in their apartment and the lost leave time and shakes his head sadly.

But he mustn't allow himself this self pity. How undignified. How unworthy of a German soldier, whatever the circumstances. He is an officer and *Staffelkapitan.* He is the son, grandson and great-grandson of military men. Duty, he has been taught since earliest childhood, must always come before personal concerns. And this duty, sacred above every other, cannot be rushed or neglected. He must take however long it requires to do this job with the appropriate dignity. Those boys and their poor families deserve nothing less than his very best as an officer of the Reich. Three or four days in Berlin will be better than none at all.

"Very good, *Herr Hauptmann*," Hesse says. "Will there be anything else?"

"I could really use some sandwiches," Wulf says. "See what you can get the mess to send over."

He sits down, takes a deep breath, dips a pen in the inkwell, and begins to write.

* * *

It's over two hours before he finishes. He's sealing the last envelope as Hesse appears, almost as if called telepathically to his side.

"See that these get onto Monday's mail plane, if you please, Hesse."

"Unless I'm very much mistaken, *Herr Hauptmann*, they can still make this evening's flight," Hesse says, smiling enigmatically. "It seems their departure has been delayed. And incidentally, sir, your bag is already on board the aircraft."

"What in blazes are you talking about, Hesse?" Wulf demands.

"Your crew chief, sir, *Feldwebel* Gruber," Hesse begins, hugging himself with obvious amusement.

"Yes, what about him?"

"He grounded the mail plane, sir. He had an uneasy feeling about something and insisted on a thorough inspection of the craft. They're just now refueling."

"Is this some kind of joke, Hesse?"

"Look out the window, *Herr Hauptmann*. You see the airplane, don't you?"

Wulf does indeed see the plane.

"If that Gruber isn't careful he'll find himself being court martialed."

"Enjoy your leave, *Herr Hauptmann*."

* * *

The Junkers trimotor lumbers into the air like a lethargic hippopotamus. It is almost inconceivable that this ungainly, corrugated metal contraption is an actual aircraft, so unlike Wulf's trusty Messerschmitt it seems. Still, he knows these beasts are as rugged as the rhinos in the Tiergarten. If anything will get him safely to Berlin it's this machine. Particularly since Gruber has just spent three hours going over the craft with a fine toothed comb. He thanks his lucky stars that he's not stuck on a slow train chugging across France. It's not just a question of the lost leave time. He could be strafed out of existence by those *verdammte* long range Allied fighters and never see Berlin at all. He sits back in the jump seat, and uncomfortable as it is he's out like a light before he knows it.

* * *

Berlin is under blackout, and for the life of him he doesn't see how the pilots find Tempelhof much less manage the smooth as glass landing there hours later just as he's waking up. He reminds himself once again that fighter pilots aren't the only highly skilled fliers in the *Luftwaffe*. These boys are top notch, too. And their life expectancy flying these slow, unarmed planes on the Eastern Front is far shorter than that of his own pilots back in France, so no underestimating their courage either. He slips them a few marks for drinks before he leaves the plane and wishes them a good flight back to France. They're scheduled for a forty minute turnaround. Any longer on the gound and they'll risk getting caught in tonight's raid. Because, as they tell him, weather permitting—and tonight is moonlit and clear—the raids come every night. His good luck continues in the form of a taxi waiting to take him into the city. Before the first sirens sound, he has stripped off his uniform, pulled his silk dressing gown out of the cupboard, drawn a hot bath, dumped an obscene amount of bath salts into the steaming water, and, a bottle of cognac and a snifter sitting beside the tub, climbed in.

* * *

He's still in the tub when Rudi arrives from the theatre. He wouldn't have bothered to call from France even if the phone lines could be relied on and it wasn't against regulations to report on his movements to a civilian. He has always believed it would be tempting fate to let Rudi know he's on his way home. Rudi is accustomed by now to his unannounced arrivals.

"*Liebchen*!" he yelps. "It really is you. I could smell this bath water clear from the landing."

He kneels beside the tub and they kiss.

"I had a feeling," Rudi says. "It came to me during the third act. I almost missed a very important cue. And with Goering in the audience, if you please. Suddenly I just knew that I'd find you here when I came in. I almost walked off the stage and let them finish without me."

"Silly old goose," Wulf smiles. "You'd never have done such a thing, Goering or no Goering."

"No, *liebchen*, you're right. I couldn't have. The show must go on. But I certainly thought about it. And I'm afraid I was very short with all those autograph hounds waiting at the stage door."

"You're always too patient with them," Wulf points out.

"But they're my public. I owe it to them."

"I don't know how much you actually owe them," Wulf says, "but you know it's one of the reasons I love you so much. The way you're always so considerate to others. Even perfect strangers."

"Listen to you," Rudi says. "Sweet talking me like that. Now why don't you get out of that water before you look like a prune. I'll give you a back rub."

"Sounds heavenly."

"Speaking of heaven," Rudi murmurs, kissing him on the forehead and sending electric shocks racing up and down his spine, "how long do we have?"

"Seven days," Wulf says. "Of course, I should really spend Sunday with Mutti and Amalie. But for the rest of the time I'm all yours. Any chance of a ticket to your play one night?"

"Any night you say, darling one."

"Maybe I'll come every night."

"No, no, *liebchen*. You don't want to do that. It's not a very good play."

"With you in it?" Wulf laughs. "How can it be anything but brilliant?"

"Let me count the ways. Propaganda never makes great art, you know. But the brass loves it. And believe me, that's all that matters these days. Now come out of there, do."

He gets a towel from the cupboard and Wulf steps into his waiting arms.

* * *

By daylight the condition of the city is shocking. Wulf knows how many hundreds of bombers he's seen on their way to and from Berlin in the months since his last visit. His *staffel* alone has destroyed over two hundred since he assumed its command. And they're just one *staffel* of many stationed along the air corridors crossing northern France and the Low Countries. But it's obvious that plenty more Allied aircraft have gotten through with their deadly payloads. They drive slowly along cratered streets in the Mercedes roadster Rudi has bought since Wulf last saw him, and Rudi points out familiar buildings and landmarks that have been damaged or in some cases transformed to piles of rubble. Rudi tells him conditions in the industrial districts are even worse.

Wulf misses the Bugatti. Rudi has it stored somewhere outside the city. Driving a French car has finally gotten to be too risky even for a hero of the Reich like Rudi. True patriots can't be seen doing such things at a time like this, with the *Wehrmacht* furiously battling the Soviet hordes in the east and the Allied bombers coming over in huge waves day and night. It seems silly to Wulf. Aren't the French part of the Reich now? Why should the car Rudi chooses to drive matter? He knows his men will laugh when he tells them about it back at base where they take these things far less seriously and often compete with each other to see which of them can be the most fervent connoisseur of the wine, food, and women of the country they've occupied. But seeing what has happened to his beloved Berlin in recent months, Wulf can almost understand what he would have thought of as the wildest paranoia twenty-four hours ago.

They finally reach the countryside. Out among the fields and woodlands it's just like peacetime. Farmers are tending crops, cattle are grazing, children play in lazy, flowing streams under a cloudless sky. The Allies apparently don't conceive of any strategic advantage to be gained by bombing livestock, orchards, croplands. And every bit as much as his beloved Berlin, this is the Germany Wulf is fighting for, the Germany Rudi is working to preserve and protect with his acting talents. The thought of the Americans and British here among these sleepy villages and farms, or even worse, the Russians, those barbarian Bolshevik hordes, sickens him beyond words. That can never be allowed to happen.

* * *

The innkeeper greets Rudi like a long lost friend and Wulf with the deference due to minor royalty. He is obviously not at all surprised to see Rudi in the company of an attractive young man, and Wulf fights off the brief pang of jealously this observation causes. What can possibly be the harm in Rudi having lunch with a friend every now and then? Wulf has his own friends back at the base. Perhaps not the same kind of friends Rudi brings here, but he mustn't let his suspicions spoil their time together. In no time they're seated at a small table and the innkeeper is setting steins of rich dark beer before them. There is no menu to peruse. They request nothing. Dishes merely appear: plump sausages running with juices, pungent sauerkraut speckled with caraway seeds, crusty loaves of dark bread, potatoes seasoned with onion and bacon and fried golden crisp.

"How long does your play run?" Wulf asks through a savory mouthful.

"Until it closes," Rudi shrugs. "It's a big hit. But Martin Kemper takes over my role in three more weeks."

"Really? Why?"

"Because Eugen Dichter's new film begins shooting then."

"Good old Eugen," Wulf grins in recollection.

"There's a part in it that you would be perfect for."

"Rudi, please."

"I've already spoken to him about it. He's been having the devil of a time casting it. He was beside himself at the possibility of getting you for it. Between Eugen's and your Cousin Konrad's influence with Goering, there should be no difficulty having you released from your duties for a few months. Just a few telephone calls and it will all be fixed. What do you say?"

"No," Wulf says.

"Do you have any idea how much I miss you?" Rudi asks, his eyes gleaming. "How much I worry about you off there so far away, flying your airplanes? It would be so wonderful to have some time for ourselves. And to be acting together again. We made such a fine team. People still ask about you wherever I go. They always want to know when we will make another film together."

"Darling Rudi," Wulf sighs. "You make it so hard to say no."

"Then don't say it."

"But I must. We must all do our very best for the Reich these days. And flying is what I do best, just as acting is what you do best. I could never give less than that to our country. You know me better."

"Yes," Rudi admits. "But your flying is so dangerous. You have been such a hero already. All those medals. And surely another promotion soon. Let someone else do all those brave, wonderful things. It's just for a little while."

"*Ach*, Rudi," Wulf says. "My pilots need me. The boys they're sending us these days are so young. Just like school children. If I don't go back, some will be killed who just might have survived if I'd been there to teach them. I wouldn't be the man you love if I turned my back on them."

"You're right, my darling," Rudi concedes. "I knew you would refuse like this. And it does make me love you even more. But luck like yours doesn't last forever. And if anything happens to you, I don't know how I can go on."

"You mustn't think about it," Wulf insists. "Besides, after that guided tour you gave me this morning, I'm quite sure that you're in more danger in Berlin than I am in France. Couldn't you move out of the city? Find someplace where the bombers don't go? An actor can live anywhere, *nicht wahr?*"

"I tried once," Rudi nods. "I borrowed a small house from a friend. Well outside the danger zone. But I felt like such a traitor to you, deserting our home like that. I went back to the city after three nights."

"Please, Rudi," Wulf insists, "you must try again to find a safer place. Promise me you will."

"I'll make some calls tomorrow," Rudi agrees. "Now how about you? Is your answer still no?"

"You know it has to be."

Rudi nods. His lips quiver, but just for a moment. Then he's smiling again, acting his bravest.

* * *

Rudi steers the Mercedes to the side of the road and shuts off the engine.

"Why are we stopping?" Wulf asks.

"There's a river over behind that line of trees," Rudi explains. "How about a swim?"

"But we have no bathing suits with us."

"Still so modest after all these years," Rudi laughs, already climbing out of the car and unbuttoning his shirt. "Come, my darling. There's no one to see you but a few cows and a fox or two."

"If you say so."

"My brave warrior," Rudi taunts him, "completely fearless. Hurry. Get out of those clothes."

* * *

The sound of bombers far overhead wakes them. They are far enough from the city that the falling bombs sound like nothing more menacing than distant thunder. But the mood is broken. And since they know they must return in any case, they waste little time lingering. They brush the grass off each other and pull on their clothes and walk back to the car in silence. It will soon be time for Rudi to go to the theatre. He has already reserved a seat for Wulf at tonight's performance.

* * *

Rudi's new play is about a German spy operating behind Soviet lines just outside Moscow. He is fearless and intrepid, unearthing enemy military secrets and planning and executing daring acts of sabotage. The information he provides is invaluable in speeding up the already lightning fast German advance on the Soviet capital, the knockout blow that must surely end the war in the east. But his luck eventually runs out. He is betrayed by a contact. He is captured and tortured by Soviet agents, but he refuses to divulge any information that would be harmful to the Reich. In the closing moments of the play, he is left to die by his captors as they flee the approaching *Wehrmacht*. Rescuers arrive just time for him to gasp out important details of the Soviet withdrawal. He dies in his comrades' arms, and with his last breath he praises the Fuhrer and predicts Germany's ultimate victory over the subhuman Bolshevik hordes.

It's the most inspiring play Wulf has ever seen. And Rudi's acting has never been more compelling. Wulf finds himself close to tears as the gallant German soldiers gather around Rudi's body and swear that his death will not have been in vain. It all seems so real to Wulf. After the curtain falls he rushes backstage to Rudi's dressing room, half afraid that what he finds there will be a bloody, bruised corpse.

It's not the intrepid spy but his own dear Rudi, alive and well, climbing out of his costume and laughing at some joke his dresser has just finished telling. Wulf's relief alarms him. His disguises his reaction to the play's ending with a joke.

"Do you open your dressing room door to just anyone who knocks?"

"*Liebchen*," Rudi laughs, embracing him, "no one else in the world knocks on a door in that dramatic fashion. Who else could it have been but you?"

"It was wonderful," Wulf chokes.

"Well, look at that," Rudi marvels. "Did it actually make you cry?"

"I'm sorry, my darling," Wulf says. "I couldn't help myself. For a moment it seemed like it was really you up there on that stage, dying."

"It was really me, you silly thing, you."

"You know what I mean."

"Yes. I do know what you mean," Rudi says, finally serious. "What a beautiful compliment to be paid by a member of my audience."

"Your biggest fan, don't forget."

"You know I never do. You're always with me up there on that stage. I don't know why you couldn't have gone on acting instead of running off to fly those planes of yours. You were so wonderful in those films of ours."

"Show business didn't need me when it already had you," Wulf points out. "And no, I won't change my mind."

"You can't blame me for trying," Rudi wrinkles his nose.

"I suppose not."

"I can't wait to turn the role over to Martin," Rudi rolls his eyes. "Though Eugen's film won't be much better. What I wouldn't give to be cast in a comedy for a change. Or play a villain. It's really quite exhausting, having to be such a larger than life hero every time I act."

"You're always my hero."

"Just as you are mine. Now what do you say to some supper? I've a table reserved for us at the Adlon. From there I thought we might look in at *Im Blauen Licht* for drinks. Though it's not much fun these days. Too many plainclothes police officers. Sometimes I think they actually outnumber the real customers. You have to watch every word you say, you can't stare at any pretty boys, and you don't dare hold hands with your date."

* * *

When the noise begins, Wulf thinks it must be an air raid. He sits up and begins shaking Rudi awake. They must head for the basement of the building. Quickly, because the noise seems to be coming closer. And why are there no sirens? There should be sirens if there are bombers overhead. He doesn't worry at the prospect of dying for the Reich while on a mission, but the idea of being exploded in the dead of night by an anonymous bomb terrifies him; or rather, having it happen to Rudi does, whether Wulf's with him at the time or not.

Then he hears heavy, running footsteps making a sound like an artillery barrage. The sound finally rouses him enough from his grogginess to realize that this is no air raid at all. The bedroom door flies open and torches flash into his eyes. The room is suddenly full to overflowing with men in Gestapo uniforms.

"*Raus!*" someone shouts. "Out of the bed, you perverts."

Someone turns on a lamp and Wulf can see them more clearly now. There are three men in civilian clothes and a full dozen others in uniform, their guns aimed at Rudi and him.

"What's going on?" Rudi demands.

"Herr Rudi Wagner and *Hauptmann* Wulf von Riedel," one of the plain-clothes agents shouts, "we are here to arrest you for violations of the Reich Penal Code, Article 175. You will come with us."

"What's happening, Rudi?" Wulf asks. "What do they think we've done?"

"Shut your mouth, you disgusting swine," another of the plainclothes agents yells. "You're worse than animals. Worse even than filthy Jews. Even they know who they're supposed to fuck."

"At least let us dress," Rudi says, standing naked in front of the agents.

"Quickly," the first agent directs. "There's no time for primping, girlies."

Wulf pulls on his clothing and shoes in a daze. There must be some horrible mistake. He has heard of Article 175, but he has always been under the impression that it applies only to men interfering with young boys. Or men committing sexual acts in public places. Disgusting, horrible things like those. How can it possibly have anything to do with Rudi and him?

"Don't worry, Wulf," Rudi tells him softly, "there's obviously been some kind of mixup. We'll cooperate with them and it'll be cleared up almost immediately. We'll be back here in time for breakfast, I promise you."

"No more talking, you two cocksuckers," someone barks. "*Macht schnell!*"

"Handcuff them," one of the agents orders.

"Really now," Rudi protests, "that's not at all necessary."

"That's where you're wrong, you pig," the man shouts, slapping Rudi with a gloved hand. It's all Wulf can do not to lunge at the man in spite of the gleaming gun barrels leveled at them. "You'd better come quietly or there might be an accident on the stairs."

Wulf's blood runs cold. This may be a mixup, but these men are obviously prepared—no, not merely prepared, anxious—to hurt them. What if they should decide to do something horrible before the whole appalling misunderstanding can be cleared up? He feels the handcuffs click into place around his wrists. The man putting them on him gives him a sharp punch to the kidneys. He bites back a yelp of surprise and pain. He won't let them see he's afraid. He can't let Rudi down like that.

"Right," the first agent says. "Let's go."

The Gestapo men rush them out of the apartment and down the stairs. They force them to move so fast that twice Wulf nearly falls. The street outside is dark and silent. A light drizzle is falling and the damp pavement glints in the dim light.

"Into the truck," someone hisses.

It's a difficult climb with his hands behind his back. He moves as quickly as he can. He doesn't want the stinging blow of a rifle butt against his head. By now he can tell they're looking for any excuse to hurt him. He settles on a wooden bench in the back of the truck. Gestapo men flank him. He stares across at Rudi, who can barely be seen in the deep shadows.

"Head down," the Gestapo man on his left grunts and jabs him a hard one in the ribs.

The truck engine roars to life in the still street. Wulf hears the gears grind. The truck lurches into motion.

* * *

The screams die away in the corridor and Wulf gradually stops shaking. The guards have told him that he and Rudi are the only prisoners in this wing of the building. They have repeatedly assured him that the screams he hears are indeed Rudi's. He has no way of knowing for certain that they are telling him the truth, but he can't help fearing that they are. The mere possibility of it curdles his blood. Every scream he hears is a dagger to his heart.

He looks around the tiny cell. It is completely unfurnished. The only place to sit or sleep is on the floor. There is no mat or blanket, just bare concrete. There is no slop pail. Every time he sees a guard Wulf begs to be taken somewhere he can relieve himself, but they only laugh at him. The stench in the cell is horrific.

He has had no food since his arrest. He's not sure he could swallow anything anyway. The guards come with a few teaspoons of water for him three or four times a day and he even gags on this, the smell is so bad.

His body is a truly terrifying mass of bruises. Every inch of him hurts. He can't recall for certain how many beatings he's endured. He prays constantly to wake up from this nightmare, but no one seems to hear.

* * *

"*Hauptmann* Wulf Robert Friederich Andreas von Riedel," the balding, cadaverous man behind the *Wehrmacht* issue desk says tonelessly, not looking up from the file he's reading, "you are under arrest for violating Article 175 of the Penal Code of the German Reich. You are familiar with the provisions of Article 175?"

"Yes."

"You are aware of the seriousness of the charges against you?"

"Yes."

His hands are cuffed and he is naked, as he has been constantly since his arrival at the prison. He feels dizzy, like he's about to faint at any moment. But he knows he'll be beaten if he doesn't stand up straight.

"It would be best for you," the man says, not looking up from the sheaf of papers on his desk, "if you cooperate with us."

"But I'm innocent. I've done nothing wrong."

The next thing he knows he's screaming in pain. He's not sure where he's been hurt, or by which of the guards, but it's excruciating. He can't even think of trying to stifle his cries. The beating continues for what seems like forever.

* * *

Later, he lies on the floor of his cell listening to the screams echoing down the corridor. He closes his eyes and prays for unconsciousness. Listening to Rudi's screams is worse by far than being beaten himself.

* * *

"*Hauptmann* Wulf Robert Friederich Andreas von Riedel," his other interrogator, a hawk faced young man with beady, bloodshot eyes, snarls as he shuffles a stack of papers on the top of the desk, "you are under arrest for multiple violations of Article 175 of the Penal Code of the German Reich. I must ask you; do you understand the seriousness of the charges against you?"

"Yes."

"It would be best for you," the hawk faced man says, riveting him with those eyes, "if you would cooperate with us."

"But please, I beg you to listen," Wulf slurs like a drunk through pulverized lips and loosened teeth. "There must be some mistake. I've done nothing wrong."

"You filthy pervert. How can you stand there and say such a thing? Just who do you think you're dealing with? Regardless of what you *Luftwaffe* types may believe, the Gestapo is not stupid. We cannot be fooled by the likes of you. We have witnesses, you fool."

"What witnesses?"

"True German patriots who have given sworn testimony as to the depraved actions of yourself and your associate in perversity, the actor Rudi Wagner."

"But who are they?"

"So you see, my dear *Hauptmann* von Riedel," the man continues, ignoring his question, "you only waste your time and add greatly to your own sufferings by refusing to cooperate. There is no question of your guilt. There is not a court in the whole Reich that would acquit you in the face of the evidence we have amassed. Your stubbornness only ensures more interrogations. By now you know what we mean when we use that term, I'm sure."

"Yes."

"I didn't hear your answer."

"Yes," Wulf says, louder.

"And when I mention the importance of your cooperation, I'm not thinking of your own welfare. Do you understand what I am saying to you?"

"But there must be someone…"

"Who can vindicate you? You had best put such thoughts out of your mind. The sooner the better, I might add. As I have explained to you, we have witnesses. The evidence they have provided is incontrovertible. All you can do now is cooperate with us and hope for leniency in your sentence. I wouldn't think that's very likely, as much trouble as you're putting us to, but you never know."

"What is it that you want of me?"

"Surely you don't mean to imply that you have to have that explained to you," the man explodes, springing to his feet as if he's ready to leap over the desk and strangle Wulf with his own hands.

"I'm sorry. I don't mean to cause trouble. I'm just so very confused. Surely you must see that."

"Confused? Confused are you? What kind of defense is that? Stop wasting my time. Guard, return him to his cell. Bring in the other prisoner."

"No, please," Wulf begs. "Just tell me what it is that you want me to do."

"You truly don't know?"

"Honestly, sir."

"But you're ready to cooperate?"

"Just tell me what you want."

"I almost think you mean that," the man muses. "What do you think, guards?"

There's no answer from either of them.

"Very well then," the hawk faced man eventually says, "you're aware of course that your associate Herr Rudi Wagner is a famous and important figure, well known and beloved throughout the Reich."

"Of course."

"You know that his films and plays have made an important contribution to the morale of the German people and have thus strengthened the war effort."

"Yes."

"And it would be a shame, would it not, if that brilliant career that has meant so much to so many were to end in scandal and disgrace?"

"Certainly."

"Now if it could be clearly demonstrated that he is no more than an innocent victim of some despicable plot to discredit him and thus disrupt the war effort, such an outcome just might be prevented. There would have to be indisputable proof, you understand, not just some vague innuendos, nothing ambiguous. Of course, we would have to retain him in custody for his own protection until the matter is truly settled. But if we had proof of such a plot, he could return to his crucially important work in a matter of weeks. Do you see?"

"I believe so."

"What do you mean, you believe so?"

"I believe you would like me to confess to being part of this plot against Rudi."

"Now you're catching on. You've almost got it. You see, von Riedel, you've been associated with Herr Wagner for such a long time, after all, that it's inconceivable such a plot could have been put into motion without your collusion. In fact, it seems all too likely that you masterminded the whole affair yourself."

"Do you have such a confession already prepared?" Wulf asks, thinking maybe all he has to do is sign a document and get this over quickly.

"Of course not," the man explodes once again in a spectacle of indignation. "Who do you think we are? Bolsheviks? Trotskyites? We utilize no Bolshevik Trotskyite tactics here. We are no Stalinist vermin. This plot has just this moment been uncovered. Until you have described it to us completely and in detail, we can't even begin to prepare the necessary documents. Do you understand me?"

"Yes," Wulf says. Obviously he is lost. But if there's a chance he can get Rudi out of this mess, he'll take it. There's nothing he won't do to deliver Rudi from the clutches of these barbarians. He understands for the first time his father's thinly disguised antipathy to these people and their leaders.

"And you are not just wasting our time and trying to avoid more interrogations? You are ready at last to cooperate with us?"

"Yes."

"Very good. You will be taken to your cell now."

"Please…"

"Please what?"

"Please may I have a drink of water? And might I be allowed to clean myself?"

"But certainly." The man smiles a vicious, nauseating smile. "You will be given food, drink, and clean clothing immediately. You will be allowed to bathe if you wish. Now you will see that we in the German Reich are merciful even to scum such as you. We mean you no harm. We simply seek to prevent you from harming others. We can't allow men such as you to continue sapping the vital strength of the German *Volk*. But now that you understand your duty in this matter and are willing to perform it, your needs will be attended to and I will see you here again in precisely one hour. I will arrange for a stenographer to be present at that time in order that you may begin dictating your confession."

* * *

The interrogations continue for many days. The questions Wulf is asked are repeated over and over again, sometimes exactly, sometimes with slight variations he suspects may be an attempt to trip him up in some way. He is forced to explain some minor points dozens of times, though not even a child could have misunderstood in the first place. The interrogators may make him recount some occurrence or other through six, seven, once even twenty repetitions before they seem satisfied, and then suddenly they will start asking about the same incident all over again the next day or the next week. And always the stenographer sits in the corner, betraying no emotion as she takes down every word. What must she think of the questions they ask and the answers he gives? How can he bring himself to discuss such things in front of her, a woman his mother's age? The sheer monotony of the sessions is exhausting, even now that he is eating two meals a day and being allowed to sleep uninterrupted all night long. Often the faces of the interrogators appear in his dreams, and often he awakens with the answers to their questions on his lips. Always there is the unspoken expectation on the part of his interrogators that he will make the things he and Rudi did together seem unspeakably vile, that he will twist the most innocuous incidents into lurid new forms which can't help but disgust anyone who hears the accounts. And though he obliges only with the deepest reluctance, he finds himself less and less resistant with each passing day, as if each retelling, each repeated answer to a repeated question, somehow chips away at his fundamental belief in his innocence, threatening to convince him that the Gestapo officers are right to regard him as a repulsive animal. It is a bitter, lonely struggle to continue believing in the purity of the love Rudi revealed to him all those years ago, but it is a war he knows he must win. Because though he must betray with words everything he and Rudi were to each other in order to deliver Rudi from the hands of these devils incarnate, he knows he must never betray those same miracles with his heart.

At least there are no more beatings. There are no more screams echoing down the corridor outside his cell. There is only occasional verbal abuse from the guards. And the Gestapo men become exasperated only rarely, behaving with amazing civility the rest of the time. Every moment of the endless hours he spends with them he thinks of how, as soon as he signs the odious document they're preparing with such glacial speed, Rudi will be out of danger. And because the only hope left to him is that through his efforts Rudi will be spared, he admits to all sorts of things that never happened and others that did but he thought of at the time—still does, for that matter—as perfectly innocent. He even admits to things he would never in a million years have considered doing with anyone, much less the man he loves. He tells his captors everything they seem to want to hear, though often the words he speaks threaten to choke him.

Yet in spite of everything he has endured, in spite of all their efforts to shake his faith, as the days slowly pass he realizes that deep in his heart he still doesn't believe that Article 175 really applies to Rudi and him. He understands that young boys need to be protected from unscrupulous older men intent on corrupting and exploiting them. He understands and shares the widespread disapproval of sex acts committed in public places. He even understands why some people find prostitution, male or female, so offensive, though he doesn't see the evil in it himself. It's merely sad. But he and Rudi have never been involved in anything remotely like those activities. And how can it be against the law to love someone with all your heart? How can their love for each other really pose a threat to the security of the Reich? The truth simply isn't enough to damn them. Which is why the stories of their life together must be embellished with sickening details. Because someone somewhere has decreed that his conviction is required.

These are not true Germans doing this, he tells himself over and over again. They can't be. Beethoven, Goethe, Leibnitz: those are real Germans, and he can't imagine them having anything to do with the persecution he's being subjected to. He recalls his father's lack of enthusiasm for the Nazi party and now understands it. The men in charge of him are not people he would ever voluntarily have anything to do with. He doesn't see how any decent person could.

* * *

In the tiny cell he returns to after each session with the interrogators there is a bed, a tiny wash basin and mirror—a polished sheet of steel, really, not glass that a prisoner could smash and use as a weapon or injure himself with—and a slop pail in the corner, which a grumbling fellow prisoner empties twice a day. There's even a small window through which he can look out at the rooftops of some unfamiliar quarter of his beloved Berlin. He can stand there for hours, if he wishes. He can even watch the Allied bombing raids. The prisoners never leave their cells, even during the worst attacks. If there is a shelter near it must be for the prison staff only. What he can't do is talk to anyone. This is solitary confinement. Nor is he allowed to receive visitors or to hear news from outside. He can sit on his bed, he can pace his cell, he can stare out the window, he can sleep, he can wait for his meals to arrive. It's not enough to occupy a young man accustomed to activity. In some ways the boredom is worse than any beatings he received. Every time he looks out his small window at the sky he dreams of being back up there in the clear blue, operating the controls of a fast and graceful flying machine, feeling the thrill of a powerful engine propelling him through space, seeing the green fields and forests spread out below him.

Still, it could be worse. It was worse very recently. He no longer has to sit or lie in his own filth and stench for days on end. In this wing of the prison he is not forced to listen to the screams of other prisoners being tortured all day and all night and can almost convince himself that all beatings, not just his own, have ceased. He receives a clean pair of prisoner's overalls every other day. He eats simple food. It is not particularly appetizing, but after his ordeal his palate isn't very discriminating. He is allowed to shave and shower once a week. The guards may whisper and snicker behind his back whenever he is escorted out of his cell, but for the most part he is treated like a human being, albeit an inferior one. It is still hell, but by comparison to his first days in captivity it's a quieter, cleaner hell. And if what he's going through is the price of Rudi's freedom and safety, it's a small enough one to pay.

* * *

In the shower one afternoon he counts up the weeks since he signed his confession and wonders why his trial is being delayed for so long. Surely the authorities don't need any more evidence against him. He can't see any reason for them not to get it over with. When he reaches his eventual destination, a fellow prisoner will explain to him the prosecutors' fanatical insistence that in cases such as his all signs of physical mistreatment of prisoners must fade completely before any public appearances like trials or sentencing can be allowed to take place. The members of the public who attend these events must have no inkling of what the defendants have been subjected to. The Reich and its officials must maintain their benign dignity at all costs. After all, he comes from a prominent and influential family; he is himself a decorated war hero. There can be no question of his having been abused in any way or of his confession having been coerced. When he hears this, he'll gaze for a moment at his new surroundings before beginning to laugh.

* * *

The day of his trial finally comes. The first sign of this is that he is taken to the showers several days ahead of schedule. When he finishes there, instead of being returned to his cell he's taken to a small room where he finds his dress uniform laid out for him, complete with newly applied major's regalia. This is the first he has heard of his promotion. He winces at the irony. And he recognizes the new insignia as a sign of the deep antipathy between the regular military and Hitler's goons. If only Germany's men of honor could find a way to rid their nation of this horrible blight. His hands tremble as he puts on the familiar clothing. He finds himself on the point of weeping for the first time since his arrest. Looking in the mirror, he feels almost like himself again. Enough so that for a moment he nearly convinces himself that the whole thing has been a nightmare that he has finally awakened from. This sensation passes quickly, as his guard fidgets restlessly and the sound brings him back to reality.

He wonders who will be in the courtroom watching as his sentence is handed down. Not his father, of course. Field Marshal von Riedel wouldn't leave the front for such a reason. But surely his mother will attend, and perhaps Cousin Konrad. He feels a sharp pang as he imagines how ashamed of him they'll be when the charges are read and the prosecutors inform the court that he has confessed to them. He knows not to expect to see Rudi there. Rudi won't dare be seen anywhere near him after this. Rudi will understand this as the price of his own freedom. Wulf would give anything to see Rudi's face again, even for just a moment, even from a distance. But he knows this is too much to hope for. Until he knows that Rudi can't be further harmed by any contact with him, he'll have to live with his memories of that handsome face and those bright, love filled eyes.

Two guards escort him downstairs where a car is waiting. They climb into the back seat on either side of him. They ride through the cratered streets for a long time until they reach the center of Berlin. The black Mercedes is anonymous in the midday traffic. The city shows even more signs of its ordeal than he remembers from the tour Rudi gave him the day before his arrest. He can only hope that London and Moscow look as bad. And those *verdammte* Americans, with their cities far out of range of any aircraft the Reich possesses or is likely to produce for a long time. How he wishes those Americans could be made to suffer like his people are suffering.

* * *

Inside the courtroom he meets his attorney for the first time. His mother and Cousin Konrad are present, but he only has a fleeting glimpse of them. Neither looks well. Neither familiar face shows any emotion. Everyone rises as the judge enters. Wulf remains standing as the charges are read and the court is informed of his confession. He has experienced great anxiety over the possibility that it might be read aloud in court, but his attorney simply asks that the document be entered into the court record and the prosecutors don't object. It is apparently sufficient that the judge has read it in preparation for the trial.

He remains standing as the prosecutor delivers a deafening, rabid oration demanding that the judge pass the longest possible sentence. It is not enough simply that he be punished for his crimes against the Reich. He must be made an example of in order that others similarly inclined may be deterred from committing their own acts of depravity. Only in this way can the nation be protected from him and hosts of others like him. Only in this way can the purity of German blood be ensured. Only in this way can the triumph of the German *Volk* be guaranteed. Wulf feels sick at his stomach as he listens to the man spew out this venom but he stands straight and tall, determined not to disgrace his uniform any further by appearing weak or cowardly. He owes his fellow officers and comrades in the *Luftwaffe* this much.

Next, his attorney makes a short statement acknowledging his guilt and the heinousness of his crimes but reminding the court of his impeccable military record and recent promotion and his cooperation with the authorities in the preparation of his case. The nervous little man does not go so far as to plead for clemency, but it's clearly the implication of his remarks.

Finally, the judge addresses him directly.

"Major Wulf Robert Friederich Andreas von Riedel, you stand here convicted of multiple violations of Article 175 of the Penal Code of the German Reich. You have confessed to this court your guilt. The crimes you have committed include acts of the most nauseating depravity known to humanity. Not only have you engaged in behavior no decent man could even conceive of, you have seduced others into committing them as well. You have turned your personal charm, physical attractiveness, social position, wealth, and military rank to the task of corrupting other individuals. You have betrayed your unfortu-

nate family, your deluded friends, your comrades in arms, your superior officers, your entire service, the German people, the Reich itself, and our beloved
Fuhrer.

"Major von Riedel, there are not words in our language sufficient to adequately condemn your treachery and depravity. Nor are there words sufficient
to express the disgust of this court and the revulsion all decent, right thinking
people feel when contemplating you and your actions. It is our deepest regret
that the law does not provide for even more stringent punishments for criminals
such as you.

"Therefore this court sentences you to ten years at hard labor."

                                    * * *

Back at the prison, Wulf removes his beloved uniform for what he knows
is the last time. Even should he live long enough to serve his entire sentence,
he knows that never again will he be allowed to serve his country. Never again
will he know the comradeship of the bravest, finest young men in the world.
Never again will decent people have anything to do with him. Upon his eventual
release—a day so remote he can hardly imagine it—he will be doomed to live
in disgrace and solitude, allowed to support himself by only the most menial of
labor, suffered to live in only the most squalid of circumstances. He is certain
that he will never see his beloved Rudi again. All that has been good and beautiful, all that has made his life worth living, is behind him now. In another week
he will be twenty-three years old, and his life, for all practical purposes, is over.

He puts on clean prisoner's overalls. He eats a last lunch of coarse black
bread and watery soup with cabbage leaves and gristle floating in colorless broth.
Then the guards take him from his cell for the last time. He's to be transported
immediately to Bergen-Belsen

He knows he will never forget that slow walk through the long, damp,
dimly lit corridors of the prison to the yard downstairs where the truck is waiting to take him away. Every step of that interminable journey, he thinks of Rudi.
Surely now, with his trial over and his sentence passed, with him convicted and
on his way to the labor camp, Rudi must be safe. And with Rudi alive and well
and free, he will at least have that satisfaction to give meaning to his life.

                                    * * *

The guards shove him into the back of the truck. Other prisoners are
already inside. Apparently he is the last to join this transport. He stumbles to
a seat on one of the benches that stretch the length of the truck bed. Once the

guards tie down the flaps of the canvas canopy, it is as dark as night inside. But not so dark that Wulf cannot recognize the prisoner sitting directly opposite him.

"*Lieber Gott,*" he cries. "Rudi! *Was machst du hier?* What are you doing here?"

"Wulfchen? Is that you? But this is impossible!" Rudi sobs. "They promised me you would be released. They told me all I had to do was confess. They said they had no wish to prosecute you because of the distress it would cause to the Field Marshal, the harm it might do to our war effort in the east. Oh, *liebling*, I would have killed myself rather than see you here like this. What can have gone wrong?"

"They told me the same things," Wulf says slowly, realizing for the first time the absolute immorality of the men whose captives they are and the complete hopelessness of their situation. "They promised me you would go free."

Bergen-Belsen: 1944

Wulf stretches himself to his full height and raises a hand to shade his eyes from the sun. He peers into the cloudless sky at the huge formation of American bombers droning overhead like a giant horde of locusts. On the way east. Hundreds of them, just like every day when the sky is clear enough to see them, and probably on some of the days when it isn't. Less than a year ago at least one of the planes missing from its formation at this point in the journey would have exploded from his gunfire and broken up in midair leaving a trail of flaming wreckage and perhaps a few parachutes blossoming against the blue sky. And not long after that Wulf would have been back at his base in France celebrating its destruction with a pilsner, chalking up another kill for himself on the tally board in the pilots' mess. Congratulating his fellow pilots on their successes—other planes missing from other formations, other plummeting infernos, other fluffy parachutes drifting earthward—anticipating his next promotion, dreaming of Rudi and his next leave. Less than a year ago, seeing the rubble strewn sidewalks of his home city Wulf remembers cursing bitterly those ungainly craft painting their wispy contrails across the heavens and lumbering along under the weight of their payloads of destruction. He can hardly believe those recollections have anything to do with him. It's as if all those things had been experienced by someone else, a stranger he once met briefly, who in the course of one long ago evening told him such vivid stories he clearly envisions them still. Or they could just as well be scenes from a favorite film of his. But they're not memories of his own life: that's simply not possible. His life is here. It has always been here. It began here and it will almost certainly end here, in the camp.

"You there," a guard barks. "Back to work. *Schneller arbeit.*"

Wulf doesn't bother looking around. It doesn't matter which guard it is or where he's standing or if it's even Wulf he's shouting at. He raises his pickaxe and brings it down into the German soil he used to love. The trench they're excavating grows one stroke longer. God knows why anyone thinks there needs to be a trench here anyway. Tomorrow his work detail or one like it will come out here and fill it back in. Tomorrow his work detail or another one like it will dig another useless trench somewhere else. Some days instead of digging trenches they move huge piles of stones from one location to another. Some days they stack or unstack bricks. Some days they build up and some days they tear down. Always there is work. But there is never any rhyme or reason to it. All Wulf knows is that none of the work he has performed since being sent here has done anything to make him free. So much for their slogan—*"Arbeit macht frei."*

He raises the pickaxe again, brings it down, gets back into the rhythm. Up and down the trench everyone else is doing the same thing. He doesn't have to look. He doesn't even have to listen, though it's impossible not to hear the sound of it. Most of all he doesn't have to think. But he knows that not to is a mistake, so he does.

Another few seconds pass. Slowly, agonizingly, they accumulate into minutes. Each stroke of the pickaxe brings Wulf's work detail that much closer to finishing this job and going on to the next one. The one that the commandant or some other camp official is sitting at a desk dreaming up for them. Each sixty seconds that tally up to a minute bring them all that much closer to quitting time, to evening roll call on the parade ground, to lining up for the skimpy, disgusting rations their captors call their dinner, to the almost comforting boredom of sitting around with nothing to do but wait for lights out, to the moment when he finally lies down on the bare boards of the bunk he shares with a dozen or so other men in their flea and roach and lice infested barracks. It brings them all, Wulf included, that much closer to the end of their lives and the end of their sufferings.

Wulf's own afflictions, to be honest, are not as grievous as those of many of the other prisoners. He knows this. He'll be the first to admit it. He refuses to take part in the long, wearying disputes that erupt in the barracks each evening about who's got things the worst. He is younger than many of his barracks mates. He has managed so far to stay healthy. He's lost a lot of weight on the miserable food but what's left of him is hard and strong as an athlete due to the long hours of physical labor he puts in every day. Around here, health and the ability to work are what keep you at Bergen-Belsen, keep you from being crammed into a boxcar with a hundred other miserable unfortunates bound for the extermination camps in the east. And though Rudi is assigned to a barracks clear across the camp and they only see each other fleetingly at roll calls and inspections, they manage to pass verbal messages back and forth—never anything in writing, it's too risky even when materials can be had—several times a week. So Wulf thanks a God he's not sure any more exists that Rudi still stays strong and healthy and off those trains too. Their one hope in the transport to Bergen-Belsen that terrible afternoon of Wulf's sentencing, after their realization they'd both been duped and cruelly betrayed by the authorities, was that they might be together in the camp. It didn't last past sundown of that day. But they're still alive. They're still in love. This will not last forever.

And that is the reason Wulf takes every opportunity to stare up at the Allied planes that seem to fill the skies these days on their way to and from raids on targets all over Germany. It is the reason Wulf never curses the planes and their pilots any more. This will not last forever, and if it doesn't it will be in large part because of those planes and men. He no longer harbors any illusion that the Reich can win this war. He hears the same news broadcasts and speeches as everyone else over the camp loudspeakers. The ones praising the wisdom, vision, and ingenuity of the Fuhrer. The ones extolling the many virtues of the German people: their strength, thrift, obedience, and tenacity, their abiding, steadfast faith in the Fuhrer, their willingness to sacrifice for the Fatherland. The ones reporting on great victories on the battlefield and insisting hysterically that ultimate triumph is just around the corner. But he is not fooled. Nor are any of his barracks mates. Just enough real news creeps into the camp and circulates among the prisoners to tell them that things are going very badly indeed. They hear of defeat after stunning defeat on the eastern front, starting with Stalingrad a year and a half ago, which everyone Wulf knew insisted at the time was a fluke that would never be repeated. He wonders about his father and his brothers. Are they still fighting the Russians? Are they well, or are they in hospitals or rehabilitation homes somewhere? Are they now prisoners in some Siberian camp even worse than this infernal place?

And now the Allies have invaded France and the *Wehrmacht* has failed to hurl them back into the sea as promised. Wulf thinks of his old *staffel*. Were they surprised by the invasion? Were their planes destroyed on the ground or did they escape in them to fight again? What has become of all his old comrades? And what would they think if they could see him now in his prisoner's uniform decorated with its infamous pink triangle?

Wulf is superstitious enough by now to believe that Hitler and his gangsters may still pull off a miracle. If they can and if they do, there's no reason to keep hanging on to what little hope still lurks in the deepest recesses of his being. Better by far, he thinks, to lay down his pickaxe, sit down beside it on the damp earth, and wait for a guard to come and blow his brains out. He'd probably have done so already except for Rudi's messages and Rudi's dependence on his replies. But each passing day, each sunset he witnesses beyond the guard towers and barbed wire, erodes that superstition a fraction more. And as it withers and the possibility of an Allied victory looms larger in his mind, so does the possibility of their liberation: all of them, Rudi and Wulf and all their barracks mates. The whole camp. Everyone in Germany, in fact. They're all prisoners of the madness, whatever their circumstances.

That faint but growing hope of freedom is why he obeys the guards no matter what. It's why he does everything he can think of to stay strong, to stay healthy, to keep his sanity. It's precious little, he knows, but the margins are incalculably slim; the difference between life and death is far narrower than the edge of a razor. It's why he refuses any longer to feel sorry for himself. It's the ones around here who spend the most time feeling sorry for themselves who go downhill the fastest. Wulf insists on surviving. He insists on Rudi's survival also. He prays with practically every second breath he takes to that God who just may exist after all, and who contrary to all the evidence currently available to Wulf just may care about what happens to individual human beings, to keep Rudi safe and well, not to let their good fortune up to this point run out. Just in case what the Jews and Christians in the camp say is true.

For he knows their luck can turn at any time. A sudden illness, no more than a minor inconvenience anywhere else, can end up being fatal here or at least debilitate its victim so thoroughly that he's on a train for the east before he knows what's happening to him. There are injuries among the work crews almost daily that have the same outcome. There's the sudden, implacable rancor of a guard. There's the irreversible mental breakdown. Each day abounds with myriad instances of these and other dangers. No matter how it's cut, the deck is all too certainly stacked against them. But he's still alive and kicking. Rudi is, too. And more and more Allied planes come over every day and the news seeps continually into the camp like an invisible gas that the end is surely coming. If they can just hold out that long. And if they can survive today they've got a shot at surviving tomorrow as well. Enough tomorrows strung together become a week, then a month. There may be hope for them yet, and if there's any chance at all of their resuming their life together he can't let anything in the universe prevent it, even if praying to that perhaps (probably?) non-existent deity is all he can do about it.

* * *

After dinner, during the few moments before curfew when everyone must go inside, Wulf sits with Yakov Rubenstein on the steps of their barracks. Yakov is a rabbinical student from Paris. He claims to speak no German, but Wulf remembers his amusement that first evening in camp when he realized that Yakov's strangely accented Yiddish was nevertheless at least eighty per cent comprehensible to him, and that Yakov, despite his professed ignorance, understood amost everything he heard the guards and officers say. Yakov has brilliant blue eyes and the only discernable sense of humor in the barracks. Wulf's first night Yakov was the only one in the barracks who spoke to him. Wulf, shattered by the day's many stunning disappointments, was so touched by the young man's kindness, the first he had experienced from anyone for weeks on end, he wept silently in his bunk over it after lights out.

The barracks, it transpired, had never housed a pink triangle prisoner before. The other inmates were repulsed. They were angry as well. How dare the Germans shove such an abomination into their midst? Lights out came, and when Wulf climbed into his assigned bunk no one joined him. He lay awake all night in that space intended to accommodate twelve men, listening to the grumblings of the now even more overcrowded prisoners in the barracks.

The next night at lights out, without a word, Yakov climbed into the bunk beside him. He continued to share that bunk with Wulf for a full week, and every day Wulf listened sick at heart as the other prisoners berated him for sullying himself in this fashion. It was inexcusable to lie down next to a man like that. Surely God would strike Yakov dead. He could never expect, should he survive the war, to resume his studies. It would not be permitted for a man who had associated so willingly with a pervert like Wulf ever to be clean again or serve as a rabbi. A rabbi must be at all times a figure worthy of the deepest respect. He must not only proclaim the laws of the Almighty, he must be a shining example of complete obedience to each and every one of them. He must never even think of disgracing himself or his faith as he was doing. He was shameless and disgusting. He was despicable, a traitor to his people and his deity. With his actions, he spat in the face of every good Jew anywhere in the world and defecated on the graves of the great teachers and wise men of old. Indeed, he spat in the faces of the Prophets and even the Almighty Himself, and could expect to be judged accordingly.

Each day the argument raged, or rather the recriminations did, because Yakov never so much as attempted to defend himself against the overwhelming onslaught of ill will and criticism directed at him. And each night at lights out Yakov turned his back on his friends without a word and climbed into the bunk and slept at Wulf's side. By the end of the second week, apparently sick of the crowding caused by two men taking up the space intended for a dozen, two other prisoners had joined them. By New Year's the sleeping arrangements had completely evened themselves out again, though Yakov is still the only man in the barracks who will converse with Wulf, and many of the other prisoners refuse to have anything to do with Yakov any more. If Yakov minds this he gives no indication of it, and so he and Wulf sit together every night, and every night the conversation is the same.

"Any news of Hadassah?" Wulf asks.

"I had word of her just today," Yakov smiles shyly. "She is well."

"Thank God," Wulf mutters, recalling the smiling young woman whose photograph Yakov once showed him. Before the war she was studying to be a concert pianist. Now, even if she survives the camps, she will never play again. Not after having three of her fingers crushed on work detail and then amputated in the infirmary without any anesthetic. It's a miracle she wasn't transported after that accident, and he and Yakov both know it. Recovered now, she is back on work detail and as safe as anyone here can be.

"And Rudi?" Yakov asks.

"No news in two weeks now," Wulf says, the slightest of tremors in his voice.

"That is hard for you."

"Thank you for asking."

* * *

A few evenings later, on his way back to the barracks from the latrine, Wulf bumps into a prisoner he knows by sight but not by name.

"Rudi sends Wulf his warmest regards," the prisoner smiles. "Also, Heinrich and Manfred wish Johann a happy birthday, and Siegfried wants August to know that his foot is much better now."

"Karl sends Paul greetings," Wulf replies. "Martin wants Peter to know he is in good health. Lothar sends Wilfried his sincere apologies and begs forgiveness. And unfortunately, Walther has been transported."

The prisoner nods and Wulf smiles and they move off in their separate directions, the messages each has spoken already memorized by the other. There are other men in the camp whose stories are just like Wulf and Rudi's. Wulf realized this within the first twenty-four hours after their arrival. Before their arrests, these men did not molest or corrupt young boys, didn't produce or disseminate pornography, didn't prostitute themselves or others, didn't commit sex acts in alleyways or hidden in the thickets of the Tiergarten or the woods along the Spree. Wulf listened to them as they described commonplace lives of hard work and friendship and patriotism and above all love for and faithfulness to their boyfriends. Their accounts described exactly the feelings and experiences Wulf so vividly recalls from his life with Rudi. And the men told of being arrested, beaten, bullied, imprisoned, put on trial, convicted, sentenced. What this all meant was that his predicament didn't result from a horrendous error on the part of some nameless, faceless bureaucrat or some unfathomable animus nurtured against Rudi or him by some powerful, unknown individual, or any other of the elaborate explanations he'd imagined during his weeks awaiting trial. Article 175 really did apply, he finally comprehended, to exactly their situation, and what's more had been used all over Germany against men exactly like Rudi, exactly like him. Hundreds of them at least, but almost certainly thousands. He had long since learned to despise to the marrow of his bones the men who had abused and degraded them both, but on the day he realized that German law truly did make the love he and Rudi shared a crime he ceased to be a German. He became a citizen of some other country, one whose name no one seemed to know, one that had yet to be discovered, but one they all longed to find and settle and call home.

There are not many of these men. The camp is mostly full of Jews and communists. Even the Catholics and Gypsies outnumber them. But there are just enough of them, though no more than a handful in any one barracks, to keep the network alive that makes possible his tenuous communications with Rudi. He is part of that network himself. For every message he receives from Rudi or sends to him, he passes a dozen or more others along the line. He knows intimate details of the lives of men he's never met and has been in camp long enough now not to feel self conscious about those unseen men knowing the same kinds of things about him. The messages he relays are not always happy ones. But those messages of illness or death or transfer to another camp or transportation to the east have to be passed along just like the others. For wouldn't he want to know it if some misfortune befell Rudi? Whatever it was? And as soon as possible, whether there was anything he could do about it?

* * *

It's a very bad day. Three prisoners on Wulf's work detail have collapsed from the heat, and guards shot them in the head where they fell. Two others were crushed when the cart they were loading suddenly tipped over, sending a huge pile of stones cascading down on them. Now the detail is seriously short handed but has the usual quota of work to complete before they finish for the day. Despite the heat there is thick overcast. There can be no comforting sight of Allied bombers or their silver winged fighter escorts. There's not so much as the sound of their droning engines far overhead.

Wulf is more out of sorts than usual. He's had no word of Rudi in nearly a month and is beginning to fear some misfortune so awful that the network refuses to spread the news of it. He swings his pickaxe savagely, as if he's driving it deep into the hearts of a long parade of guards, kapos, officers, bureaucrats, and party functionaries that has miraculously been left to him to dispose of. And as he swings the implement tears run down his cheeks, making muddy rivulets on his dusty skin. He hears a sob and realizes a moment later that it has erupted from his own throat.

"Courage, Wulf," Yakov pants, moving like a shadow beside him. "Always courage. The eye of the Almighty sees all. His heart counts every tear shed by the oppressed. He comforts all who call on Him in their distress."

"He is your God," Wulf replies.

"He is Lord of all created things, Wulf. There is only one of Him. You are His child as much as I am. Never let anyone tell you otherwise. We are all His children."

* * *

The whole camp stands at attention on the parade ground. The prisoners wait silently, though they have no idea what for. Wulf assumes it's nothing good: it never is. They've been waiting for several hours. All work details have been canceled for the day. But though it seemed like it at first, this is no reprieve. The July sun beats down. There's not a breath of breeze. Many prisoners have fainted from the heat. They lie where they fell, unattended. No one dares assist them. Those who revive before the guards reach them scramble frantically back to their feet and resume, as best they can, the stiff backed posture required of them. Those who don't are being kicked and beaten into unconsciousness, possibly even death, by the guards. Their screams and moans come from all directions and are the only sound.

Sweat trickles down Wulf's forehead and into his eyes, stinging them. He doesn't lift a hand to wipe them clear. Prisoners who have fainted are not the only ones in agony on the ground. The guards are beating with clubs and rifle stocks anyone they catch moving a muscle. He doesn't dare even blink too insistently. Whatever the strange silence that blanketed the camp this morning means, the loudspeakers mute, the guards sullen, all regular activity at a standstill, he's certain of one thing. For whatever unknown reason, the margin of survival has just narrowed significantly, perhaps disastrously, for them all. He can see it in the faces of the guards, whose expressions transcend the ferocity he is accustomed to. They are furious far beyond anything Wulf has witnessed previously.

Everyone continues to wait. Prisoners continue to collapse. Prisoners cease their moaning and screaming and others take it up. The sweat continues to run into Wulf's eyes, burning like acid. He wonders if they'll recover, if he'll ever be able to see clearly again. He wonders what can have happened to bring about such orgies of violence among the guards. He wonders if his luck, or God forbid Rudi's, has finally run out.

After an eternity, the commandant rides onto the parade ground in the rear seat of his open Mercedes-Benz. During this distraction, Wulf finally feels safe enough to reach up quickly and clear his eyes. They still work. Looking around him he almost wishes they didn't. The car halts, and a guard opens the door for the commandant to step out. He strides to the microphone set on a stand in the middle of the parade ground. Even from this distance his agitation is apparent. He looks as if he's ready to kill with his bare hands. Wulf wonders for a moment if this is the commandant's actual intention, to have some prisoner brought to him so that he may beat the poor unfortunate to death while they all stand and watch.

"Prisoners, your attention," the commandant's gravely voice booms out of the loudspeakers. The amplified voice echoes off the barracks walls behind them, shattering into distorted, inhuman sounding fragments. No one moves. Wulf hardly dares to breathe.

"Prisoners. It is my duty to inform you that yesterday dastardly hoodlums who had infiltrated the highest echelons of the military, treacherous subhumans of the worst character imaginable, staged a cowardly attempt on the life of our beloved Fuhrer. This conspiracy involved hundreds, perhaps thousands, of individuals bent on nothing less than the complete destruction of the German Reich and the end of our way of life. Fortunately, the Fuhrer escaped with only minor wounds, but others of his party were killed or seriously injured. Many of those responsible have already been apprehended. Some have taken their own lives to avoid arrest. Others are awaiting summary judgment. The hunt continues for the remaining ones. And no stone will be left unturned. Rest assured that not one of these vermin will elude those determined to bring them to justice.

"Prisoners. Do not for one moment think to take comfort in the misfortune of our glorious Fuhrer. The German people are united behind him. Our forces are fighting courageously on all fronts. Our enemies are on the point of final collapse. The Reich will triumph over them all, and that triumph will come soon. Do not delude yourselves into believing otherwise or into taking any action indicative of disloyalty to our cause. All Germany expects you to continue your efforts on behalf of our glorious mission to redeem the world. Any failure to do so on your part will result in the gravest consequences.

"Long live the German Reich. All hail the noble German people, who will soon rule over all nations. Long live our beloved Fuhrer. *Heil Hitler.*"

The commandant's words die away, and no new sound replaces them in Wulf's ears. The commandant returns to his car, which then moves slowly back toward the administration buildings. The prisoners still on their feet continue to wait. Everyone knows without being reminded that until the order is given to dismiss, they must continue to stand at attention and maintain their silence.

* * *

Wulf trudges back toward his barracks. Around him, hushed, excited voices discuss the news. Hands slice the air with frenzied gesticulations. He ignores them. What has happened to the Fuhrer portends nothing good. It can, he believes, only make their lot worse. Let these idiots babble the day away. Let them waste their breaths suggesting otherwise, speculating that the commandant has not told the whole truth, that the Fuhrer may actually have died in the attack, that Goebbels, Himmler, and the others are attempting to consolidate their control over the country, that all this confusion will lead to the collapse of the Reich and an immediate Allied victory. That their deliverance may be days or even mere hours away. The fools. Haven't they learned anything from all they've been through, everything they've seen? Better they should be revising their plans and strategies for survival. After this it's going to be harder than ever to stay alive. Wulf is certain of it.

At the door to the barracks, the kapo stops him before he can enter.

"Here's your man," he says to two guards standing there.

"Prisoner von Riedel," one of them says, "you will come with us. *Schnell.*"

Wulf knows better than to ask where they're going. It doesn't matter. Whatever is going to happen will happen. He says nothing at all. He falls into step between the two guards. He doesn't allow himself to think, except of Rudi, offering up whatever prayers he can muster, heartsick at his powerlessness.

Guards stationed at the entrance to the main administration building pull open the doors so they can enter. Clerks and orderlies stare at them as they pass through the reception area and make their way down a bustling corridor. They stop outside a door at the very end of it, and one of the guards knocks. Wulf reads the sign on the door with mounting dismay in spite of his resolve. The horrible possibilities teeming in his brain continue their transformation into certainties. This is it. This is the moment he has been fearing for months.

"*Herein.*"

One of the guards opens this door. They enter a large office. Secretaries and clerks sit like automatons at their desks. Telephones ring. Typewriters clack. Messengers run in and out clutching envelopes, files, supplies.

"Prisoner von Riedel," one of his escorts announces to a black haired, reptilian man in civilian clothing who sits behind the largest of the desks.

"Wait," the man says, giving Wulf a look of such intense hatred he almost can't help shrinking from it. The man picks up the telephone on his desk. "The prisoner von Riedel is here, Herr Commandant."

Wulf watches as the man nods. For some reason he finds it comical that the man should nod like this as if the commandant can see his response. Is he going mad, to find humor in any aspect of this situation?

"Very good, Herr Commandant," the man says, nodding a last time. He looks up at Wulf's guards. "Take him in."

It's only a few paces to the door of the inner office. They cover the distance in the time required for Wulf's heart to beat fewer times than he can count on the fingers of one hand. One of the guards knocks, then opens the door and they step inside, right up to the commandant's desk. Wulf doesn't have to be instructed to stand at attention.

"Prisoner von Riedel, Herr Commandant."

"Very good," the commandant says, giving Wulf a withering glare. "Stand at ease."

The guards relax, but Wulf knows the commandant was not speaking to him.

"Prisoner von Riedel. I regret to inform you that your father, Field Marshal von Riedel, has just this morning taken his own life in Berlin. Apparently some traitor yet to be identified tipped him off that he was about to be arrested for his role in the plot against our Fuhrer. He has consequently escaped justice. Your brothers, however, are still being sought for questioning."

"Are all of them under suspicion, Herr Commandant?" Wulf can't keep himself from asking. The moment he speaks, he's certain that he'll be writhing on the floor in agony any second for speaking without permission. He feels the guards stiffen on either side of him.

"All of them."

"And my mother and sister?"

Still, incomprehensibly, no blows fall. No bullets smash into his skull.

"I have no information about them. As for you, Prisoner von Riedel..."

Wulf's heart pounds frantically. Why can't he master it? What kind of weakling is he turning into, in this hour when the other men of his family have behaved with supreme bravery?

"You are to be transported to the camp at Dora-Mittelbau. You leave immediately. There is a truck waiting. Guards, take him."

Dora-Mittelbau. Wulf has heard the name. Bizarre rumors have reached Bergen-Belsen about the place. Apparently, the entire camp has been carved into the side of a mountain. Deep below the wooded slopes, whole factories have been installed for the production of Hitler's vengeance weapons. Because of their location, the factories are impregnable to Allied bombing raids. They can go on producing weapons regardless of what happens above ground. The prisoners live under ground alongside the production machinery, never seeing the light of day. As bad as prisoners have it at Bergen-Belsen, conditions at Dora-Mittelbau are supposed to be ten times worse. Not that it matters. Worse than anything he has heard about the place is the knowledge that he is leaving Rudi behind. There's no time to send any kind of message. This, then, truly is the end.

They leave the office. Wulf can't believe it's not a trick. Surely they'll take him behind one of the buildings and shoot him. But he doesn't fall to his knees weeping hysterically and begging for mercy as he's seen so many others do. He doesn't stumble and have to be dragged along between his guards. He suddenly notices that he's taller than either of them. He holds his head high. He thinks of his dead father. He wonders if it's true that his father was involved in the plot. He hopes so.

Dora-Mittelbau: 1945

Klaus and Gregor cram themselves into the bunk on either side of Wulf. It's nowhere near lights out, but it's the only way to keep sick prisoners warm. And keeping sick prisoners warm is the only thing healthy prisoners can do for them. It's better than nothing, but not by much. It may have prolonged some lives by a few hours or days but it accomplishes little else. Wulf has done it himself many times. Warmed some poor wretch with his own meager body heat. Some prisoner or other is always sick. Klaus and Gregor, a Jewish physics professor and a Catholic priest, though he can't remember which is which, are doing the same for him. His chills this evening are so bad he can't stop shaking. He'll never get to sleep unless he can warm up. If he can't get some sleep he won't be able to work tomorrow. And if he can't work tomorrow that's the end of him. It's no use trying to get anyone to take him to the infirmary, though someone will if he asks. But until he's literally dying he won't be admitted, and once he is dying nothing they do for him in the infirmary will matter. So there's no reason to go there unless dying in an actual bed makes a difference to him.

He's been fighting the illness for three weeks now. Or is it four? He can't remember for certain. He heard some of the other prisoners talking about him tonight. Saying they've never seen anyone hang on so long. They seemed impressed with his determination to get better, or at the very least not get any worse. Well, good, if that makes them think any better of him, or men like him in general, though their opinion of him has nothing to do whatever with why he's fighting so hard to stay alive.

Dora-Mittelbau is a far more secure camp than Bergen-Belsen was, but even with access to the outside severely limited and the tightest of security in force due to the secret weapons factories here, news manages to ooze in. Things are getting worse by the day. The Allies have liberated Paris. They'll be to the Rhine, the very gates to the Fatherland, soon if they haven't reached there already. Back in December there were major engagements in Belgium that slowed the Allied advance for a time but at the cost of smashing blows against the *Wehrmacht,* which shows no signs of recovering and going back onto the offensive. In the east, things are even worse. The forces are in full retreat as the

Soviet hordes overrun kilometer after kilometer of territory that Wulf's father and brothers fought so hard to take from them in the first place.

Even the superweapons being manufactured in the factories Wulf and his fellow prisoners work every day to enlarge and expand don't seem to be helping. Britain has not been brought to its knees. The Allies have not sued for peace as the German people have been promised for years. There can be only one conclusion. It is inevitable now that Germany will lose the war. No one, not even the most pessimistic among the prisoners, argues otherwise any more. After five and a half years, the end—not the one Wulf would ever have foreseen back in his *Luftwaffe* days—is in sight. No wonder the guards are looking and acting like zombies. Whatever the prisoners know about the course of the war, the guards have to know more.

This in itself might or might not be enough to keep Wulf going. In his present state, he's not sure. But other news finds its way to them, too. To Wulf's surprise, he learned almost immediately upon arriving here that the network he and Rudi have depended on for news of each other extends far beyond the barbed wire and guard towers of Bergen-Belsen. It even reaches here. And just after New Years, a few weeks before Wulf's cough first came on in earnest, there was news of Rudi. Back then, however many weeks ago it is now, Rudi was still alive and well. As long as he doesn't hear anything to the contrary Wulf chooses to believe that Rudi still survives. And as long as Rudi survives, Wulf must too. They must live until the liberation, be reunited, pick up the pieces of their shattered life together, find some way to go on. He knows that if anyone can make all this happen, Rudi is the man.

But this *verdammte* cough. The racking chills and constant fever. The dizziness that plagues every waking hour. The diarrhea that saps his strength almost beyond endurance, that dehydrates him and makes his fevers even more severe. His symptoms grow worse every day. Each day he's less certain he can make it to the end of the shift. Each evening the struggle to the place where they are given food and then back to his bunk is more arduous. Tonight for the first time he's not sure he can do it any longer. Not even for Rudi. He's too ill to comprehend this heartbreak. He's too ill to shed a single tear over it.

"Rest, Wulfchen," Gregor—or is it Klaus?—whispers into his ear. "Rest now. We are with you. You will feel better in the morning."

* * *

When he awakens he thinks he must be dead. There is soft light, not the gloom of the barracks. He is warm and dry. He is lying on something soft. Is it a cloud? How can that be? How can he have gone to Heaven? He doesn't believe in God. And even if he did, he's pretty sure God doesn't believe in him.

* * *

He wakes again. Once more there is light, warmth, a kind of comfort he had all but forgotten the existence of. Ascending further into consciousness, he is aware that his chills are gone. He doesn't feel the insistent urge to cough. The tightness in his chest, like his ribcage is being confined in iron bands, is no more. His bowels are not cramping. He raises his head and attempts to see what sort of place this is. Even this minor exertion dizzies him, blurring what little vision he can muster. He can only get his head a few centimeters off the...*lieber Gott!* Is this a pillow under his head? Against his will his head collapses back onto it. His eyes fall shut. He exhales noisily. Then he hears soft footsteps moving quickly in his direction.

"Where am I?"

His feeble sounding croak shocks him.

"You're awake," a voice says, and the footsteps move nearer.

He'd speak again, but the effort of those first words exhausted him beyond trying. He forces his eyes open. He sees a face hovering over his.

"You're in the infirmary. Here, drink this."

A strong but gentle hand supports his head.

"Not too much. We don't want you choking. More? Well, all right, but only a little."

How, Wulf wonders, can clear water taste so much like a divine beverage of the gods?

"No, that's all right. Don't try to talk. We almost lost you, but you're getting better now. You'll be out of this bed soon. You'll see."

"How?" he manages to gasp.

"You have a friend."

* * *

"There," Josef the orderly says, propping him up against the pillows. "How's that?"

"All right."

"I've brought you some soup."

"Thank you."

"Do you want to try feeding yourself?"

"I don't think I can."

"Please try, Wulf. Just a spoonful or two. Here, I'll lay a towel over you in case you spill."

Wulf grasps the spoon with a trembling claw of a hand. He's sure there's no way he'll be able to keep any soup in the spoon long enough to get it to his mouth. He grunts in frustration.

"Easy now."

"I can't."

"Yes you can."

With a supreme groan of effort, Wulf steadies his hand. He grits his teeth and aims the spoon carefully at the soup bowl Josef is holding only centimeters away.

"That's better," Josef encourages.

He scoops up half a spoonful of soup. He feels sweat breaking out on his forehead from the effort. Gingerly he brings the spoon to this mouth, feels the warm liquid trickle over his tongue.

"*Wunderbar*, Wulf. Try another."

He feeds himself another, larger spoonful of soup. It tastes improbably like actual food. It nearly brings tears to his eyes. But that's all he can manage for now. His arm falls limp. The spoon clatters to the floor.

"Very good," Josef says. "I'll feed you the rest. Wait till your friend hears what you just did."

"My friend?"

"Ssh," Josef says. "Don't talk. We're trying to get him in here to see you tonight."

* * *

When he sees Rudi looking down at him, Wulf thinks he's dreaming. He doesn't speak. He simply smiles at the memory and prepares to sink back into deep slumber.

"Oh, *liebling*," Rudi croons, stroking his cheek.

It's a real hand and a real voice. A lump rises in his throat and his eyes fill instantly with tears.

"I'm sorry I haven't been here to see you sooner. But it's very dangerous."

"Is it really you?"

"Yes, my darling."

"How?"

"I was transported from Bergen-Belsen. I got here just after they brought you into the infirmary. We thought it was all over for you. But as you see, you're going to be fine."

"Oh, Rudi," Wulf sobs, kissing the emaciated hand that rests lightly on his shoulder.

"*Mach schnell,*" another voice hisses. "The guard will be back around any second."

"I'll see you again soon, Wulfchen."

"It's really you? You won't go away again?"

"I won't go away. You'll be out of here soon."

* * *

He improves rapidly after this. Messages of encouragement come from Rudi several times a day, though Rudi himself never appears at his bedside again. Still, this medicine, the only kind that can truly speed his recovery, has done its work. Inside a week he's up and walking, with assistance at first but soon on his own. He's eating solid food. He doesn't have to use a bedpan but can take himself down the hall to the toilet.

Now that he's feeling stronger he's awake much of the time. He observes the comings and goings in the infirmary. When he's thought about it at all, he's assumed that his treatment is the result of some change of heart on the part of the camp commandant, or at least the camp doctors, with regard to the treatment of prisoners. Perhaps they're trying to score points with the prisoners before the Allies arrive, hoping accusations of mistreatment won't be leveled at them later on. Not that a few weeks of good behavior is going to make anyone Wulf knows forget their barbarism during all the months and years before that.

But as he watches the doctors and orderlies with other prisoners, mostly helpless cases who have only been brought in to die, he realizes that nothing has changed. Somehow he is a special case. They treat him with the same deference they give the ailing guard two beds down. He can't help wondering why. Occasionally there are hints and these seem to center on Rudi. But theoretically Rudi has no more standing around here than he does. What can Rudi have done to get him this bed, the medicines that have saved his life, the warm regard of the orderlies, the unmistakable solicitude of the doctor treating him? It's a mystery. And since Rudi never visits again, it's one Wulf can't ask him about.

He offers up prayers of thanks for his survival and Rudi's continued well being and tries not to think about the prisoners still suffering and dying all over the camp, or the few he sees on the ward, ignored by the same doctor who's been so kind to him, neglected and sometimes even abused by the orderlies who are so friendly and helpful when they bring him his meals, change his bedding, help him wash every morning. Knowing first hand of the ordeals of the other prisoners, he can hardly force himself to enjoy his good fortune. But who wouldn't be seduced by such comfort after all he's been through?

* * *

He awakens to the sound of loud, angry voices in the corridor. There's a pistol shot followed by cries for mercy. He's not certain but he thinks he recognizes the voice that's pleading for mercy out there: his favorite orderly, the one who was on duty the first night he woke up. The one who brought Rudi to see him. What can this uproar mean? Have the Allies reached the camp? Are the Americans killing all Germans on sight?

Then he realizes he hears no English being spoken, just harsh Gestapo German. More shots ring out, so close he can smell the gunpowder. The guard in the bed next to him pretends to be asleep. Indeed, none of the patients on the ward make a sound. A final shot echoes down the corridor outside. After that there's no more shouting. No more cries for help, either. Just a long silence. Still no one on the ward says anything. It's as if they don't believe it's over yet.

And they're right. Suddenly the doorway into the ward is full of guards brandishing their weapons.

"Prisoner von Riedel," one of them shouts, "out of bed and come with us! *'Raus, schnell!*"

It's obvious they don't know which of the patients they're looking for. But Wulf doesn't even consider pretending to be someone else in the hope they'll grab some poor unconscious prisoner and take him away by mistake. It would only postpone the inevitable. They would discover the mixup sooner or later and he'd be in even more trouble, not to mention having the other man on his conscience.

"Over here," he says. "I'm coming."

"Nobody else move," a guard shouts. It's an unnecessary warning.

Two guards move to the sides of his bed as Wulf climbs out. They grab him by the arms and start to drag him away.

"There's no need for that," he tells them. "I'll do what you say."

But they ignore him. They manhandle him out into the corridor. He sees three orderlies and the doctor who's been treating him lying on the floor, their heads in pools of blood. Then they're out of the infirmary and heading across the parade ground toward the punishment block. He knows not to ask questions. If he's meant to know what it's all about, he'll find out soon enough. If not, it probably doesn't matter anyway. Not with only a few moments left. His only concern right now is Rudi. Is he still alive? Is he involved in this in some way? Wulf prays not, but he can't fight off his growing dread.

Soon he sees a knot of guards in front of the punishment block, surrounding another prisoner. He tries to look away, to convince himself that the fleeting glimpse of that other man only reminded him of Rudi. But of course he knows better. He stumbles along between his two guards. In a few more strides they've joined the larger group at the entrance to the building.

And now he can't help looking at Rudi, who has been stripped naked. Their eyes meet and in a split second he reads the whole story in Rudi's expression. Then, over Rudi's shoulder he sees the camp commandant.

"The prisoner von Riedel, Herr Commandant," one of his escorts shouts.

"And the orderlies and Dr. Lindemann?"

"Liquidated as you ordered, Herr Commandant."

"Very good," he nods. Then raising his voice, he addresses the crowd of prisoners lined up in ranks.

"Attention, prisoners. A plot has been uncovered in this camp. The prisoner Wagner, who you see before you, has bribed camp guards, a camp doctor, and orderlies working in the infirmary in order to obtain preferential treatment for his homosexual lover, the prisoner von Riedel. And as if the illegal and nauseating relationship between these two prisoners is not bad enough, do you know how the prisoner Wagner bribed these camp personnel? It was not with money, or goods obtained on the black market—yes, we know one is operating inside the camp, and you may be certain that we shall soon apprehend the parties responsible. Oh no. The depraved Wagner enticed them with none of those things, but with sexual favors. That's right, prisoners. He sold his own body to gain what he wished. He seduced them into doing his evil bidding so that this piece of human filth, von Riedel, would benefit. What could be more sickening, you ask? Their shocking acceptance of his favors and unbelievable acquiescence to his requests. All those camp personnel who have participated in this gross breach of camp discipline and who have in so doing broken the laws of the German Reich and betrayed their fellow servicemen have been liquidated, as you heard. At this moment they lie in pools of their own blood. Such vermin as these cannot be allowed to live. They deserve no other tribunal but the one that comes out of the barrel of a gun.

"But we are left with these two to dispose of. The prisoner Wagner, who is now guilty, in addition to the crimes which brought him to this camp in the first place, of corrupting loyal members of the Gestapo; and the prisoner von Riedel, who has benefited from these stupefying machinations. You will now see how the German Reich deals with incorrigibles such as these two. Let this be a lesson to any of you who have heard false rumors about Allied troop movements in this vicinity and who may be hoping for speedy liberation. Put any thought of plotting or resistance out of your minds for good. The German people will bow to no conqueror. They will fight to the last man, if necessary. Because of their determination in this sacred cause, the Reich is still strong. The Reich will be victorious. The Reich will continue to deal out the severest possible justice to its enemies.

"Guards, proceed."

Wulf watches as Rudi's arms are raised over his head and shackled to iron rings set into the stone walls of the building. Across the distance separating them, he looks into Rudi's eyes. There is no fear in them, nor any sign of regret. They burn with the purest, fiercest love Wulf has ever seen there. Tears begin to sting his own eyes. He blinks them away frantically, determined not to have his vision blurred, not to lose sight of Rudi even for a second. He knows what will happen to Rudi now. Nothing can save him. Nothing can save either of them. He knows what they will do to him after they finish with Rudi. At least the two of them will die within minutes of each other.

Whatever he must witness now he cannot allow himself to shrink from. Because when they come, his last conscious thoughts must be of Rudi. Of Rudi's love for him and this amazing self sacrifice. Of Rudi's courage even now, as the guards pause for a moment in their preparations and stare with loathing at him there with his bare back to the cold, damp stone. So Wulf will not lower his head or turn his eyes away. He will stare unblinking into Rudi's eyes until they close for the last time.

The beating starts. It goes on for a long time. The guards do not mean it to be fast. They are careful to avoid striking Rudi in the head or face. They do nothing to him that can result in unconsciousness. They beat him not to destroy him quickly, but to inflict the maximum pain for the longest possible duration. Before long, Rudi's body is a bloody mess from the neck down, while his face and head are nearly untouched.

But this is only the beginning. They continue. They torture every part of Rudi's body. Wulf moves only to blink away his tears. And his eyes never leave Rudi's, who, even after Rudi begins to scream in agony, continue to look deep into his own, sending out their desperate messages of undying love. When it is Wulf's turn, there will be no eyes like these for him to gaze into.

* * *

Wulf awakens in darkness. It takes him a moment to remember where he is. Then Rudi's screams begin echoing in his ears, and he curses the commandant for his treachery. His own punishment was not, as he expected, execution immediately following Rudi's death and in a similar fashion. He is in solitary confinement. There is darkness, so he sees nothing but Rudi's last agony repeating itself over and over in his mind's eye. There is silence, so nothing can interrupt the sound of Rudi's screams in his ears. There is nothing to keep him from remembering. No distraction of any kind. He knows from the expression of pure, white hot hatred on the commandant's face as he was led past him to this cell that he will not be allowed to die here. He will be fed enough to insure his survival. He will not be allowed to fall ill again. If he does, he knows the commandant will order whatever treatments are necessary to sustain his life. His punishment is to live on and remember until the commandant decides he has been tortured in this way for sufficient time. Only then will he be killed. He doesn't know why he is so surprised by this. It is exactly the kind of cruelty he has witnessed time after time from his countrymen. He should have expected nothing else.

* * *

Wulf wakes once again to silence and darkness. He has been trying to find a way to escape the commandant's cruelty, to outsmart the man and achieve the oblivion he so desperately longs for. For days now he has been refusing the food he is brought, flinging it against the stone walls of his cell as soon as the guards delivering it have slammed the door shut behind them. He has ripped at his bare mattress, urinated and defecated into it. He crouches naked on the bare floor of his cell, sleeps curled on the cold, damp stone every night—though he has no real awareness of time, has no idea when day dawns and when night falls. He is determined to starve himself to death, to bring on some illness which will kill him. He will not live without Rudi.

The Americans and British may be only a few miles away. They may be bursting into the camp even as he lies in his own filth. They may be moving through the camp rescuing his fellow prisoners. They may be in the corridor outside his cell door. He takes no comfort in this possibility. He has no interest in being liberated. He is determined to escape that, too. He will not live without Rudi.

* * *

Time passes. Wulf even refuses water now. But not only does he not die; he can't even make himself ill. He scratches at his arms and legs with now long fingernails until he draws blood, then rubs filth into the wounds, desperate to cause some infection, which, left untreated here, can't help but be fatal. Nothing works.

And still Rudi's eyes haunt him. Rudi's screams drive him to the brink of insanity, beyond which he would willingly go. What is it that prevents him?

* * *

When everything else fails he begins to pray for death. He prays with a fervor he didn't know himself capable of. He prays constantly for that one thing. To die. But apparently he's been right all along. There is no God to answer his pleas. What a time to finally have his suspicion proven.

* * *

Eventually, inspiration comes. Days or weeks later—he has no idea now long he's been wracking his brain for the answer to his predicament. Really, it's so simple he can't believe he didn't think of it before. He may lack knives, guns, anything to hang himself with, poison. He may somehow have become immune to starvation, dehydration, all known diseases. But there is the cell itself with its hard stone walls and floor. And there is his head, no more than a fragile eggshell containing his brain.

The first time he brings his head down onto the stone of the floor with all the strength he can muster he merely stuns himself, though he does feel a comforting trickle of blood from his scalp. He lies still for a moment to catch his breath. He will just have to beat his head against the stone more forcefully. He will have to find the strength somehow to do this. He concentrates on gathering every ounce of strength remaining to him. He says a final goodbye to Rudi, those loving eyes glowing at him from the darkness as he closes his own for the last time. Then, with a ferocity erupting from the inferno of his soul, he brings his head down against the stone once again.

* * *

He hears gunfire. He hears screams. He hears yells. He hears footsteps in the corridor outside his door that sound like thunder. Then there's a loud banging noise against the outside of the door itself. Finally the door bursts in and a torch beam strikes his closed eyelids.

"Oh, my God! Jesus, Mary and Joseph. The poor fucker."

These words are the first Wulf has heard in English since the afternoon in 1938 when he and his mother put Nanny Elderson on the Paris train. They had argued on the way to the station that afternoon about the outcome of Chamberlain's just concluded meetings with Hitler. Wulf had assured her that there couldn't possibly be war after that. England and Germany, he remembers insisting, would live in peace and harmony for centuries to come. She had just as fervently disagreed: war was now inevitable and she must return home to her own country and people. He should have known that day that she was right. She always had been. Indeed, no one in the von Riedel household could remember a single instance when Nanny was mistaken about anything, from her diagnoses of the illnesses of Wulf and his siblings to her predictions of Berlin weather, to her picks at the races, which she never bothered to bet on though she'd have made a fortune if she had. She had been right that afternoon; undoubtedly right to return to England and live with her sister, who ran a small hotel in Cornwall.

How strange that his first thoughts should be of Nanny Elderson.

The American's words—for it's an unmistakably American accent, not British—are accompanied by the sound of someone retching.

"Andy, come in here."

"No."

"You have to," the voice demands. "I think this one is alive."

Wulf hears more retching sounds.

"Well, at least go get a corpsman."

"In a minute."

"Andy, this guy needs help."

"Chip, if lying in that pigsty for God knows how long didn't kill him, another thirty seconds isn't going to make that much difference."

"Dammit, Andy."

"All right, already. I'm going. Poor bastard."

Wulf forces his eyelids open. The torchlight blinds him and he raises a hand to fend off the glare.

"Jesus, you are alive," the young soldier Chip says. "Don't be afraid. We're Americans. We won't hurt you. Just hang on, O.K? My buddy's gone to get help."

"Thank you," Wulf croaks, his heart plummeting as the hateful knowledge sinks in. God damn it. He's alive. And now the Americans are here. He's being rescued. Damn, damn, damn.

"You speak English?" Chip is astonished.

"We had an English nanny when I was a boy," he says, amazed to be conversing like this, as if with someone he met in a bar somewhere or on a platform waiting for a train. "Actually, she was more what you'd call a governess."

"Shit, man, you speak better English than I do."

"Corpsman's on his way," Andy calls from somewhere down the corridor. "Who are you talking to?"

"This guy speaks English."

"You're kidding."

"Swear to God."

"Oh, shit, here I go again," Andy says.

There's another fit of retching.

"Steady, bud," Chip says.

"I'm all right," Andy answers after one last spectacular stream splatters the corridor floor.

"Listen, I think we should get him out of this cell."

"Where you planning to take him?"

"Just out in the corridor. Jeez, Andy, he's lying in sewage."

"I don't think you should move him until the medic gets here."

"Andy, if what those God damned motherfucking Nazi pigs did to him didn't kill him, it won't hurt him to be moved five feet."

"O.K. Keep your shirt on."

"Listen, buddy," Chip says, "we're going to get you out of here, O.K?"

"All right."

"Let me know if we hurt you."

Wulf doesn't answer.

"I'll grab him under the arms," Chip says. "You get his legs."

"Hold on a sec," Andy says. Wulf assumes he's going to vomit some more. He can't blame him. "Just let me put down this blanket for him."

Wulf feels strong hands reach through his armpits and clasp in front of his chest. Other hands grasp him behind the knees.

"On three," Chip says.

"Ready."

"One, two, three."

They lift Wulf like he's a three year old.

"Hell," Andy says. "He hardly weighs a thing."

Being moved doesn't hurt at all, much to Wulf's disgust. The two soldiers lay him down on a blanket in the corridor. Andy throws another one over him. Wulf feels himself starting to cry. He doesn't want to, but he can't stop himself.

"God," Chip says. "They're never going to believe this back home. They're going to give us Section Eights the minute we open our mouths about it."

"I don't know about you, Chip," Andy says, "but we find any more like this one and a Section Eight is exactly what I'm going to need."

* * *

"Who did this to you?" the American doctor asks, peering at Wulf through steel rimmed spectacles and shaking his head in disbelief. It is the third time he has examined Wulf in as many days, and he still has that dazed expression on his face, is still obviously shocked by what he's seen here in the camp. Wulf doesn't understand the doctor's reaction. Or that of the G.I.'s who are working in the infirmary apparently on some kind of volunteer basis and the harried nurses who give them orders as they trot through the jammed wards. What else did the Americans think they would find here?

"Excuse me?" Wulf asks.

"We took some of the guards alive," the doctor explains. "They're all in custody and being investigated. If you don't know the names of the men who did this to you, you could at least give us their descriptions. I can guarantee you that if they're still alive they will be punished for doing these horrible things."

"You don't understand," Wulf says. In the last seventy-two hours he's come to realize that perhaps the most distinctive characteristic of these Americans, more so even than their compassion or generosity, is their innocence. They actually seem to believe that they can bring the murderers to justice, bind the wounds and treat the diseases of the prisoners and release them into happy, fulfilling lives in freshly liberated Europe, in the process repairing the damage the Nazis did all in a month or two. They honestly seem to think that the whole story can have a happy ending. Just like a fairy tale in which the wicked witch dies and the children are safely restored to their loving father. Their optimism is breathtaking, but also, it seems to Wulf, shockingly stupid. Still, would they have beaten Germany without such an attitude? And such faulty understanding of what they were up against? Maybe the only people on earth who could have defeated Hitler and his demons had to be even bigger fools than the Germans who followed them in the first place.

"I did all this to my self," Wulf tells the doctor.

"That's just not possible," the doctor says. "The scratches certainly. But give your head this kind of bashing up? How could you? I still can't believe your skull isn't fractured."

"The floor of my cell was very hard," Wulf explains as if to a child. "And I was extremely determined. Don't you know about us Germans by now?"

"Listen," the doctor says, lowering his voice so he won't be overheard by the orderly changing the dressings of the patient in the next bed, "you can level with me. I know how it is. Maybe in spite of yourself you got kind of friendly with these guys. Maybe they were nice to you once or twice and you started to believe they were different from all the others. So you don't want to get them in trouble. You figure you've been liberated and you're getting medical care and the war is all but over and they can't hurt you any more so why not let bygones be bygones. You just want to put it all behind you. Try to forget it ever happened as much as you can. I think I'd probably want to do the same thing if all this had happened to me. But you can't look at it that way. These people treated all of you worse than animals. They can't be allowed to walk away from it. They have to be punished. Made examples of. They don't deserve your protection."

"Please, doctor," Wulf says, "I'm protecting no one. I would never lift a hand to help a single one of those barbarians. You have my permission to hunt down every last one of them and shoot them like dogs. You may do any damned thing you wish to them and I will raise no objection. But I swear to you I did these things to myself."

"But why hurt yourself like that? Hadn't you heard that the war is nearly over? Didn't you know that we would be here soon to rescue all of you?"

"We had heard all those stories. Many of us even believed them. But it was too late for me, you see. You had already taken too long to get here. It is too long a story. You don't want to hear it, and I'm far too tired to tell it. Someday, perhaps."

"I'm sorry," the doctor says.

"You needn't apologize. You came as soon as you could. I don't expect you to understand a man like me not wanting to live."

"You don't seem to think very highly of our intelligence."

"Intelligence has nothing to do with it," Wulf says. "You haven't been through what we've been through."

"Granted," the doctor says. "But I'd submit to you that we've been catching up quickly since we got here. The two young soldiers who discovered you could hardly find their way back from the cell block. Their tears were literally blinding them. They brought you in here and we laid you on a stretcher for examination and they wouldn't leave you. They stood right by your stretcher and they cried their eyes out. These men fought their way across France and into Germany. They watched their friends die. They have seen the villages the German armies leveled to the ground. They have seen things no young man should ever have to see. But until we got here, we had no idea of what was happening or that places like this even existed. Not one of us has ever seen anything so horrible. We never even imagined such things were possible. We're all in shock. The men say they have no appetite after seeing these horrors. They have to be ordered to eat. And we have no idea what to say to any of you. We fall back on platitudes because we can't comprehend what you've all been through. Because we feel guilty that we didn't save you sooner. Because we're Americans and we always have to say something.

"I had to send those boys away. I had to order them to leave or they would still be here now. Every half an hour or so one or the other of them will come to me and ask how you're doing. Somehow it's as if you've become one of their own men. All over the camp the same thing is happening. Our men can't believe the horror. They can't cope with the things they've seen. They ask each other how God could have let such things happen, and since no one has an answer for that, they're terrified. They're not sure they want to live in a world where such things can happen. They're shocked and horrified and desperately hanging onto their sanity."

* * *

Wulf is evacuated to Buchenwald after eleven days in the infirmary. His head is still bandaged, but the dressings are much smaller now. The American doctor seemed very pleased with his progress. Wulf is carrying written orders that he's to report to the infirmary at Buchenwald daily to have his dressings changed and to continue having regular examinations until he's completely recovered. The trip from Dora-Mittelbau is shocking. Every village the truck passes through is like a ghost town. Bridges over even minor rivers and streams have been destroyed and replaced with rickety, temporary structures that threaten to collapse under the weight of the truck. Crashed aircraft litter the fields. Burned out railroad trains sit on silent tracks.

And everywhere he looks there are refugees with huge loads of belongings piled on handcarts or on their backs. Many of them are wearing bandages. Their eyes blaze with hunger and confusion. They and their children trudge along the sides of the shell pocked roadway. The men riding in the truck with Wulf are silent. None of these people on the road knew what they were enduring in the camps, it seems. But Wulf and his fellow prisoners never knew what these people were facing on the outside. The prisoners took it for granted that their nightmare was the only one. Only now as the truck rattles past these sights are they beginning to learn how widespread the terror has been.

* * *

Wulf notices the small prisoner watching him his first evening in the barracks at Buchenwald but is too tired from the journey to care who the man is or wonder why he's staring. Three days later the man is still observing him carefully, almost as if Wulf is some kind of laboratory experiment or animal in a zoo. There have been two new arrivals since Wulf, but the man has done no more than register their appearance before turning his hollow eyes back on Wulf, so it's more than novelty drawing his attention. It's nearly enough to annoy Wulf into confronting the man, but he has no stomach for it. The past weeks have drained all desire for conflict out of him. The strange little man will have to do something worse than stare before Wulf will do so much as acknowledge his existence. Nevertheless, the unwanted attention makes him uneasy.

They are all on edge. The relative comfort and cleanliness of their accommodations, the unaccustomed adequacy of the diet, their steadily improving health, the absence of arduous, exhausting labor; these things all disorient them, as does the shy, awkward kindness of the Americans. As they renew their strength, their confinement, benign as it now is, is all the more rankling. The small freedoms creeping daily into their existence merely whet their appetite for the walk out through those gates. To Wulf, the sudden absence of adversaries is the most disorienting thing of all. He finds himself growing more irritable all the time, though he is determined not to exhibit it to his fellow prisoners, each of whom, he knows, has his own sorrows, his own nightmare memories. Some tell one another their stories, huddling together on bunks or sitting in tight knots on the steps in front of the barracks. Wulf feels no interest in joining them. The others respect his solitude. It's not even remarked on. He's not the only one who keeps his distance.

His irritation continues to grow so that by the fifth night when the strange little man appears beside his bunk, his eyes glowing spectrally, it's all Wulf can do not to take a swing at him.

"Wulf von Riedel?" the man rasps through an adam's apple that's obviously suffered horrible injuries. The sound of it immediately banks the fires of Wulf's annoyance. He imagines the impact of those fists or truncheons on the man's scrawny neck and feels ashamed of himself. Should he have to have it explained to him that everyone in the barracks, this man included, has earned the respect due to all the victims?

"Yes," he says, "I am Wulf von Riedel."

"Heinrich Schlicker," the man says.

Close up, Wulf can see that the man is not as old as he had first thought.

"I would like very much to speak with you," Schlicker says.

"Oh?"

"Very much," the man repeats, his cadaverous eyes revealing nothing.

"All right."

"Would you like to walk outdoors?"

"If you wish."

"Let us walk, then."

They leave the barracks, Wulf self conscious about the difference in their heights. He towers at least twenty centimeters taller than Schlicker. He's glad now that he didn't give in to the impulse to bully. How would that have looked? And what would Rudi have thought of such a display?

It is still an hour until lights out. Groups of men dot the compound, talking together and sharing American issue cigarettes, the ends of which glow in the twilight like fireflies. A few individuals stand by themselves staring out into the darkness beyond the barbed wire and the guard towers, where Germany is still at war.

"Rudi Wagner is dead?" Schlicker asks.

It is a long time before Wulf is able to speak, but he senses no impatience on the part of the other man.

"Yes."

Another long silence follows this utterance. They continue walking, Wulf reminding himself to match the stride of this much smaller man.

"It is what I had heard. I suppose I've still been hoping there was some mistake."

"No mistake."

"I'm sorry."

They reach the end of the compound, the lights of the camp only a glow behind them. Ahead of them all is dark and silent. The fields beyond the fence lie sleeping in the spring evening. There is nothing recognizable of the horror.

"Were you there when it happened?"

"They made me watch."

They turn and walk along the barbed wire, far away now as it's possible to get from anyone else.

"You know what he did for you?"

"He got medical care for me when I became seriously ill."

"That's not all. He did the same things at Bergen-Belsen," Schlicker says, "to obtain his transfer to Dora-Mittelbau. He was determined to be reunited with you. We had all heard about that camp. We knew how much worse it was there. The diseases and constant deaths. But he insisted on going. You were there, and that meant he had no choice. So he did the only thing he could do to get there, you understand?"

"Yes."

"You can't think of him as being unfaithful to you."

"I don't."

"I particularly tried to talk him out of it. I saw no hope for you once you were sent there. We had heard about your father. We could imagine only too well what they had in store for you. I saw no point in his being there to witness it. I could see no reason why he should die as well. I told him as much. I was just trying to help him. I only wanted to save his life, but what I said made him so angry I thought he was going to kill me."

"Is this what you brought me out here to tell me? That you didn't want Rudi to come to Dora?" Wulf asks, fighting his anger. Wouldn't he have said the same thing to Rudi, if he could somehow have gotten the message to him? If he'd known what Rudi was planning? How can he blame this man for wanting to save Rudi's life, when that's all he had hoped and prayed for himself?

"No," Schlicker says. "I wish it were no more than that. I'm afraid it's far worse."

Hearing this, Wulf stops in his tracks. He doesn't speak. Suddenly he knows there is only one thing this man wishes to tell him, knows exactly what it is he has been led out here into the darkness to hear.

"You don't have to go on," he murmurs. "You don't have to tell me this."

"Oh, but I do," Schlicker insists. "We each have our own path to travel. The Americans think they liberated us, but they cannot. No one can. Some of us may be able to liberate ourselves in time. Though that will be very difficult. And I rather doubt I have the strength for it. So you see, I can carry the burden of it no longer. I must speak now, and it is you who must hear it."

"Go ahead then," Wulf says, steeling himself.

"You know how the Nazis were. I'll bet when they arrested you they got you to confess by promising to let Rudi go."

"Yes."

"And I know they tricked Rudi the same way. He told me they had. But I already knew the story. They did that kind of thing to almost everyone they arrested. All the people like us, you understand?"

Wulf doesn't speak.

"I'm sure you wondered how you and Rudi came to be taken."

"I assume we were denounced by someone."

"I was the one," Schlicker says. "There is no excuse for what I did. They didn't even come to me with threats. I went to them. I loved him so much. I was so jealous of you. I was such a fool. They listened to my story and promised no harm would come to him. Only you would be arrested. Only you would go on trial. Only you would be sent to prison. A regular prison. They said nothing of the camps. And even if they had, it would have meant nothing to me. We didn't know of such places. Until I reached Bergen-Belsen myself, I had no idea what they had done to the two of you. God forgive me, it's not bad enough that I would do such a thing. But to be such a fool as to believe them."

Schlicker begins to walk again. Wulf falls into step beside him. Is the man going to ask his forgiveness? He doesn't know if he can give it. If it were only his own sufferings to absolve Schlicker of, it would be different. But at the same time he doesn't know how he can withhold it.

"So in my jealousy I not only destroyed my rival for Rudi's love, I destroyed Rudi as well. And of course myself. The moment the two of you had been sentenced I was in custody also. But by then I knew I deserved whatever they did to me. And you must believe me when I say to you that I have lived until this moment for no other reason than to tell one or the other of you what I did."

"It's over now," Wulf says.

"You don't believe that."

"No."

"Then why say it?"

"One has to say something."

"Really?"

"In any case, nothing can be done about any of it."

"Indeed. But if you have to say anything, why not say you hate me?"

"I don't."

"No. I suppose you don't. The kind of man Rudi would sacrifice himself for wouldn't. I realized that when he refused to take my advice and insisted on being transported. I knew then that I didn't know you at all. I knew of your family, of course. Everyone did. And I had seen the films you and Rudi made together. I had seen your photographs in Rudi's apartment. I convinced myself you could be nothing more than a beautiful, spoiled young man. I had no reason to think that, but I desperately wanted it to be true and for you to be unworthy of him. How could you be so wealthy and so beautiful and have any character at all? Of course Rudi was wealthy too by then. And certainly beautiful. But I excused him because I loved him. You? You were nothing. Just an obstacle to my happiness with Rudi. As if that could justify what I planned to do. As if Rudi and I could have had the life together that I dreamed of, I was the one with no character or morals."

"Did you know him long?" Wulf asks.

"We were at *gymnasium* together. Long before he became famous and met you. Years later we met again in Berlin. We saw each other from time to time, but we were never really close. Still, whenever we ran into each other he was always friendly. He'd buy me drinks or take me to dinner. Always he would talk of you. And always at the end of the evening there would not be the invitation I hoped for. He would shake my hand and we would part with some vague promise about the next time we met and I would go home and dream of him. That is all there ever was between us. In all the years we knew each other as men, he never loved anyone but you. I hope you'll never forget that. Yet even that last night before he left Bergen-Belsen to go to your side I was still trying to tear him away from you, even though by then I knew it was hopeless.

"And now he is dead."

"Yes," Wulf grunts.

"And I have told you this story and you know what I have done. Now maybe I can begin to be a free man again. Come, let us go back. Unless you wish to be alone now?"

It is exactly what Wulf wants but he can't bring himself to say so. Somehow he feels he owes Schlicker a few more moments of companionship, awkward as it is for both of them. Tomorrow, he'll be glad he was silent. Because tomorrow when they find Schlicker's body hanging by the neck in the latrine, everyone will know that Wulf was in the barracks when it happened. There will be no question that it was anything other than suicide, not uncommon among the residents of the camp but baffling in the extreme to the poor, idealistic Americans. So Wulf's silence in that brief moment in the darkness beside the barbed wire buys him his alibi.

Later that same day they hear the news that Berlin has fallen and Hitler is dead.

* * *

The handsome young American officer smiles at Wulf. His thick black hair glistens with pomade, and his sky blue eyes behind the lenses of his steel framed spectacles are dazzling. The merest shadow of coal black beard is visible on his cleft chin. Really, he looks more like a movie star playing a soldier than the real thing. Wulf can't get used to the health and vitality of these Americans. They appear not to have been in a war at all, so clean, rested, and well fed they are. They also seem absurdly young. They remind Wulf of his schoolmates back at the *gymnasium*, in that lost life he sometimes involuntarily recalls.

On the wall behind the young officer's desk, a sign says "United States Army Internment Center Dachau." Wulf arrived two days ago.

"Herr von Riedel," the young officer says, rising halfway from his chair behind the heavy wooden desk that's had its Nazi insignia clumsily but effectively excised. "Thank you so much for coming. Please sit down."

Wulf sits. He finds amusing the manner in which the American makes it seem as if Wulf has done him a favor by appearing when summoned. Rather like

Wulf is an honored guest instead of a prisoner. And almost as if he hadn't been escorted from his barracks by a pair of armed G.I.'s.

"Cigarette?" the young officer holds out an elegant silver case, the kind of Art Deco piece Rudi used to carry, though of course he never smoked himself. He simply enjoyed offering cigarettes to others.

"No thank you, Captain," Wulf says. He is proud of himself for having deciphered the military insignia of the Americans within the first two days of their arrival at Dora-Mittelbau. He recognizes all their ranks and enjoys surprising them with invariably correct salutations.

"No?" the young officer asks. "Well, you're probably right not to. It's a filthy habit, I know. My coaches at Princeton always gave me holy hell over it. Horrible for the lungs. My father is a doctor back in St. Louis, and you should hear him on the subject. Regular crusader he is."

"Indeed," Wulf agrees, "smoking seems to do no one any good."

"Your English is very good."

"Thank you."

"Where did you learn to speak it?"

"At home. We had an English governess. And later I studied it at *gymnasium*. I think you call it a prep school. Or high school?"

"Either one," the young officer nods. "Our governess was French, though I wouldn't claim that my French is as good as your English. But now, don't hesitate to ask if you need anything translated during the course of our interview. Corporal Marx here," he indicates a strapping, curly haired, blond, Hitler Youth recruiting poster of a G.I. sitting in a corner reading a newspaper called *Stars and Stripes*, "is fluent. Though some of your people seem to think his accent is atrocious."

"It is atrocious," Corporal Marx nods, winking a smoky gray eye at Wulf, "because what I'm speaking to them is Yiddish. The Jews don't find it terrible at all."

"Anyway, that's Corporal Marx, and I'm Captain Lancaster."

"Pleased to meet you both."

"Now Herr von Riedel," Lancaster says, looking down at his notes, "I suppose you know why you're here."

"Not precisely."

"Oh. I assumed that some of the other men must have told you about these little interviews we're conducting."

"They have," Wulf admits. "But I'm still not sure I understand the purpose of them."

"Ah," Lancaster says, looking suddenly ill at ease. "Well, you see, we need to verify the identity and status of everyone still in our custody."

"Yes," Wulf says, "I've been told of that. But I don't understand why."

"Mm hmm," Lancaster nods, starting to blush now and looking more like a schoolboy called on the carpet by the headmaster than an army officer. "Gee, well, I guess by now word must have gotten around that there are to be no more general releases of camp residents. According to the records we have in our possession, the rest of you were originally incarcerated for crimes under the German penal codes, not because the Nazis judged you politically suspect or because you are members of certain racial groups or what have you."

In the corner, Marx snorts once behind his newspaper.

"And so we, the American authorities that is, have decided that as soon as it's practical you'll all be placed under the jurisdiction of the German civil authorities. It's our understanding that they'll probably wish to detain you until you've served out the full sentences passed on you by the courts."

"Yes," Wulf nods, "that has already been explained to us."

"Then just what is it?" Lancaster asks, obviously flustered now, "that you don't understand about this interview?"

"Why it is necessary," Wulf says, "since you have already decided what is to be done with us."

"Oh. I see. Well, it's simply this. We certainly don't want to detain anyone mistakenly, do you see? And that's why we need to verify the identity and status of each remaining resident. Just in case anyone was assigned to the wrong group. By accident, perhaps. Clerical errors sometimes occur. Does that clear things up for you?"

"Yes."

"Good," Lancaster says, looking relieved. "Now, Herr von Riedel, if you'll just answer a few questions, we'll get you out of here in plenty of time for lunch. Now first of all, what is your full name?"

"Wulf Robert Friedrich Andreas von Riedel."

He watches as Lancaster makes a notation on the file in front of him.

"Mother's maiden name?"

"Von Mangelsdorf."

"Place of birth?"

"Schoss Mangelsdorf, my great-grandfather's estate outside Konigsberg. That's in East Prussia. Or rather, what used to be called East Prussia. I have no idea what it's called now."

"And your great-grandfather was?"

"Joachim, the Graf von Mangelsdorf und Wallenstein."

"Your mother's family are Junkers?"

"Yes. My father's family as well."

Lancaster is obviously surprised by Wulf's pedigree, as well he might be. Wulf doesn't suppose the Americans have turned up many Prussian aristocrats in the camps. From what he's heard since the liberation, most of the members of his class who ran afoul of the Nazis didn't survive.

"Place of legal residence? Before you were arrested, of course."

"Berlin."

"Occupation prior to arrest?"

Wulf doesn't answer immediately. Will he be in even more trouble if the Americans know he was in the *Luftwaffe*? Is it even possible to be in more trouble than he already is? He wishes he knew these people better. They can't be as unsophisticated as they seem.

"Don't you understand the question? Shall I have Corporal Marx...?"

"No. I understand the question," Wulf says, sweating freely now inside his coarse clothing. "Before my arrest I was in the *Luftwaffe*."

"Seriously?" Lancaster's surprise has obviously increased further. "There's nothing about it in your file."

"I'm not surprised. They would have left that out, I suppose. Given the charges against me."

Lancaster considers this for a moment.

"I suppose there must be some way of verifying it," he says.

"There will be *Luftwaffe* records somewhere," Marx suggests.

"Might take quite a bit of time, even if they're ever found," Lancaster says. "What rank did you hold?"

"I had just been promoted to major when I was convicted."

"Major von Riedel, is it then? You should have corrected me when I addressed you improperly."

At first Wulf thinks Lancaster must be joking. He's not sufficiently accustomed to Americans to understand their humor or to recognize sarcasm when he hears it, but he's certain he's being made fun of.

"I mean it," Lancaster says, apparently reading his mind. "Please believe me, I intended no disrespect."

"It's all right," Wulf stammers, astonished at the apology.

"So you were in the *Luftwaffe*. Pilot?"

"Fighters. Messerschmitt 109's."

"And your rank was major."

"I was a *Staffelkapitan*. That's roughly equivalent to a squadron leader in your air force. My last posting was in France. Near Calais."

"I see," Lancaster says, scribbling more notes. "Hold on a second. Wasn't there a Field Marshal von Riedel who was involved in the August, 1944 plot against Hitler?"

"My father," Wulf nods. "I was told he committed suicide to avoid arrest. I never heard what happened to any of my brothers. I believe they were serving in the East at the time, though I was already at Bergen-Belsen and had no contact with them. Nor with my mother and sister in Berlin."

"So you really don't belong here with the others," Lancaster says. "In actuality you are a political prisoner, illegally detained and imprisoned because of your family connections. Is that what you're trying to tell me? That you were assigned to your prisoner category as some sort of reprisal?"

"Not at all. As I told you, I was already at Bergen-Belsen when the attempt was made on Hitler's life. I knew nothing of my father's activities until after the fact. And those events have nothing to do with my imprisonment, though it was the reason I was given for being transported to Dora-Mittelbau. But originally I was convicted of multiple violations of Article 175 of the German Penal Code. I'm sure it's all in the file somewhere. And it's correct."

Lancaster is blushing furiously now, and Marx has lowered his newspaper and is staring at Wulf in frank astonishment.

"So you need have no anxieties, Captain Lancaster, about detaining me unjustly. I believe you'll find that my sentence has over eight years left to run."

* * *

That same evening, just as he's about to climb the steps into his barracks, a prisoner he doesn't know approaches him and tells him someone wants to speak to him. He ignores the man at first. He's not interested in looking for trouble and he can't imagine what else such a summons can mean. Now that the only people left in the camp are criminals and homosexuals, it's gotten nearly as dangerous as it was under the Nazis. It's ironic that they traded one set of thugs for another, but to their credit, the Americans at least make an effort to keep things under control. The strange prisoner grows insistent, practically shouting out directions to where the mysterious individual can be found. Wulf decides to move off in that general direction just to shut the man up. He has no desire to be made more conspicuous than he already is by this stranger's hysteria.

So he walks out through the summer twilight toward the barbed wire, and soon he sees someone standing in the gathering shadows watching his approach. For a brief instant Wulf thinks he must be an already released camp resident who wants him to deliver a message to someone still inside. At the last second he recognizes the man. In civilian clothing and without his spectacles, Captain Lancaster looks even more like a schoolboy than he did in his office.

"Good evening, Major."

"Good evening, Captain."

"Cigarette?" Lancaster holds out a whole, unopened pack. "Oops, sorry. Forgot."

Wulf looks through the barbed wire at the younger man, who is perhaps two inches shorter than himself, slender but noticeably broad shouldered. An athlete obviously. He wonders what kinds of sports young men play in American schools.

"I wanted to speak with you again," Lancaster says. "Outside. You understand?"

"No."

"Well, I did. No reason, really. I just thought...uh, perhaps I could get something for you. I know you don't smoke, but I thought soap maybe. I know the stuff they give you in there is awful. Or tooth powder or canned meat or chocolate. Or some extra socks and underwear."

"No thank you," Wulf says, sensing a trap. Are the Americans trying to uncover black marketers in the camp? But how silly of them to send such a nervous young man on an errand of that nature. Even in the near dark, Wulf can see that he's about to wet himself. These Americans. How did they ever win the war? "We're really quite well supplied. You Americans are amazingly generous. And then there are also the Red Cross parcels. Truly marvelous. I don't suppose we'll continue to receive them, now that we're all criminals in here."

"Listen," Lancaster says, looking over his shoulder, "I just want you to know that some of us don't agree with what they're doing to you guys. I don't know if there's anything we can do about it, but, well, try not to give up hope, will you?"

"You are very kind," Wulf says. "But I'm afraid it's far too late for such advice."

"I guess it was pretty bad, huh?"

Wulf doesn't answer.

"You know, I've been doing these God damned interviews for five days now, and you're the first man I've spoken to who hasn't claimed he was assigned to your classification by mistake. You wouldn't believe the weird explanations I've heard. I've had men in tears, on their knees begging to be released. I've been offered bribes. Art works. Jewelry. Money in Swiss bank accounts. It's unbelievable the things they say they can deliver. But not you."

"I'm a German officer," Wulf says. "Not Nazi, but German. There is a difference, whether you understand it or not. The men in my family were Prussian officers long before that maniac was born. Before Bismarck, even. We're not trained to lie. And we're certainly not trained to beg. I have already disgraced my family enough. I have no intention of dishonoring them further by unworthy behavior. Even if they had no knowledge of it, I would."

"Is that it?"

"What do you think?"

"I don't know what to think," Lancaster says. "And you see, I can't help wondering what I'd do in a position like yours."

"I wouldn't waste any time on that."

"No?"

"You'd do much better to pray that you never are in a position like mine. I assure you, you don't know the half of it."

"I suppose you're right."

"Even if I'm not, you don't want to have to find out for yourself."

"Listen," Lancaster says, after a long silence, "are you sure there's nothing I can get you? Books perhaps? I don't know what you have to read in the barracks."

"A book?" When was the last time Wulf had a book in his hands? "Yes, I think I would like a book very much."

"What kind?" Lancaster asks eagerly. "A novel? A biography?"

"Shakespeare," Wulf says, thinking of it suddenly. "I used to love Shakespeare when I was in school."

"Oh, jeez. I don't know if we have any German language editions of Shakespeare."

"No," Wulf says. "Not in German. Bring me one in English. The German translations are all horrible. And it will be good practice, I think, reading in English."

"English it is, then."

"Thank you."

"Meet me here again tomorrow night? Same time? I'll try and have that book for you then."

"All right."

"Well, *auf Wiedersehen*, Wulf."

The use of his Christian name sends such a shock through him he can hardly speak.

"I...I'm sorry. I don't know your name."

"It's David. My friends call me Dave."

"Well then," Wulf says, "*auf Wiedersehen*, Dave."

"*Bis morgen Abend*. Is that how you say it?"

"I thought you didn't speak German."

"Marx is giving me lessons."

"I see."

"I really should go," Lancaster says with obvious reluctance.

"I also."

* * *

The next evening Wulf almost doesn't go to meet Lancaster. The idea of any further dealings with the young officer makes him uneasy. He's halfway expecting to be stood up and halfway expecting Lancaster will tip his hand, finally revealing whatever it is the Americans are trying to inveigle him into. But something he can't understand draws him toward the meeting place. Even as he sets off toward the barbed wire at the far corner of the camp he tells himself it's just a coincidence, just the direction he has happened to walk in to get some fresh air for a few moments before lights out.

Lancaster is waiting for him outside the barbed wire.

"Good evening, Major."

"Good evening, Captain."

"I was afraid you weren't coming."

"It's very crowded in the latrines this time of evening," Wulf explains. "You often have to wait quite some time for your turn."

"It must be terrible," Lancaster shudders.

For a moment, Wulf regrets having said it. The last thing he wants is this young man feeling sorry for him. But it's no more than the truth, even though it's not really the reason he was late.

"You get used to it," he says.

"I brought you a book," Lancaster says. "I'm sorry I couldn't get a copy of the plays. They were all checked out of the unit library. Who knew Shakespeare would be so popular with G.I.'s?"

"My father told me that the German infantry required three things to survive in the field."

"Oh?"

"Well made boots, simple, wholesome food, and Goethe."

"Really?" Lancaster laughs.

"That's what he said. Of course, he was a tanker by then. My brothers were tankers, too. I never heard any of them discussing what literature tankers found uplifting."

"Schiller, perhaps?"

"Perhaps."

"Anyway, I couldn't get you the plays right now, but I thought you might enjoy the sonnets."

"Sonnets?"

"Short lyric poems. Fourteen lines, iambic pentameter…"

"I know what sonnets are," Wulf says. "I didn't know Shakespeare wrote any."

"Yes. They're considered some of the best in the English language. I memorized lots of them in school. I don't know if I could actually recite one any more. It seems so long ago."

"Doesn't it," Wulf finds himself agreeing, as if his school days and Lancaster's had coincided.

"I marked some of my favorite ones in the book," Lancaster says, handing it through the wire.

"But wait," Wulf says, examining the slender, leather bound volume. "This is no library book."

"No," Lancaster admits sheepishly. "It's my own copy. I couldn't find another one."

"I couldn't borrow this," Wulf protests. "What if something happened to it?"

"I know you'll take care of it, Wulf. And I hope you'll enjoy the poems."

"I'm sure I will. Thank you."

"What did you do today?" Lancaster suddenly blurts in what Wulf recognizes as a transparent attempt to prolong their meeting.

"Today? Today I helped some men in one of the neighboring barracks repair their floor. They've had many sick in that barracks and haven't been able to make all the repairs we made in ours."

"I see."

"And you, Dave?"

"More of those God damned interviews. Jesus, I hate them. You know you're still the only guy in this place who's not going crazy trying to get out. What gives?"

"What gives?" Wulf repeats, trying out this new idiom. These Americans. They can't leave anything well enough alone. Not even their own language. "What gives? Well, I suppose you would have to say I don't see anything for me out there. There's certainly no demand for former *Luftwaffe* officers. I shouldn't think anyone will be looking for fighter pilots for a long time. I'll be far too old by then."

"Yes, but your family."

"Even if they are alive, I don't expect they'll want to have anything to do with me."

"Why not?"

"My mother and her Cousin Konrad were at the trial. They know I confessed to the charges. I know what they must think of me now."

"I guess I can understand your not wanting to face that. But at the very least you'd have your freedom."

"Freedom."

"Sure. To come and go as you please. To live where you want to and how you want to. To choose your own meals, for God's sake."

"Yes, freedom," Wulf replies. "I know what you are saying. But you see, even if I should leave here I will never be free again."

"Why not?"

"Please. You are a well brought up, clean living young American. A gentleman in every respect. You don't want to hear me speak of such things."

"You mean there was someone?"

"Yes. There was someone."

"And he's dead."

"He died at Dora-Mittelbau. He traded sexual favors to get medical treatment for me. I was all but dead, and it saved my life. Then what he had done to save me was discovered, and he was killed. They made me watch while they beat him to death. Afterward I was placed in solitary confinement. I was still there when you Americans arrived."

"I see."

There's a long silence.

"Was he your friend for very long?"

"Since I was eighteen years old. I am twenty-four now. You see, I've shocked you. It is better not to speak of such things."

"No, really," Lancaster protests.

"I must go now. It will be lights out soon."

"Meet me here tomorrow evening?"

"I don't think that's a very good idea."

"Why not? I enjoy our conversations a great deal."

"I too," Wulf admits. "But surely now there's nothing more to say."

"I'm still anxious to hear what you think of those sonnets."

"It would be nice to talk about poetry together," Wulf says, "but I shouldn't think your superiors would approve of such fraternization. It's not just that I'm a German, though that would probably cause you trouble enough in itself. I'm sorry, Dave, but it would make me very unhappy to think that I had compromised you in some way. I have enough on my conscience already."

* * *

Over the next week, Wulf ignores three requests from Lancaster that they meet. When the fourth comes, however, in the form of a note passed to him by a fellow prisoner, he thinks it over carefully. Is he doing something stupid, displeasing an American officer in this way? He really must avoid trouble at any cost. And why worry about protecting Lancaster? He's given him sufficient warning. No one can say he hasn't. Certainly enough to absolve himself of responsibility for anything that might happen. If Lancaster wants to take foolish risks associating with a German and a convicted homosexual, let it be on his own head. Wulf could use the company and would welcome another opportunity to practice his English.

So this evening he goes to the meeting, but warily, feeling like a cornered animal. As he approaches the fence, he realizes to his chagrin that he's forgotten Lancaster's book.

"Good evening, Major."

Wulf is unaccountably pleased to see the handsome young man.

"Good evening, Captain."

"You've been avoiding me," Lancaster grins uneasily. "I thought we were becoming friends."

"I thought we agreed that meeting like this was becoming dangerous for you."

"I don't remember any agreement," Lancaster says. "Besides, something's come up."

"Oh?"

"Listen, Wulf, I need you to tell me about your arrest and trial."

"Oh, please, Captain Dave, I would be much happier not to speak of that. Can we not talk about poetry instead?"

"I'm sorry. I didn't explain clearly. I'm not asking you to tell the whole story. I just need to know where your arrest and trial took place. I think you told me you were stationed in France at the time."

"Yes, but that is not where it happened. I was on leave in Berlin. They arrested Rudi and me in our own apartment."

"My God. I can't imagine how awful that must have been. But it was Berlin?"

"Why should it make a difference where it happened?"

"It just may be your chance to get out of here. I know you say you're not interested in that but you should be, because we Americans aren't going to be in charge of you forever. Before long we're going to be turning all of you back over to German authorities. And I have no idea what will happen to you after that. I mean, I'm sure we'll still hold them responsible for your treatment, but we won't be present on a daily basis to supervise. There's no telling what they'll let the real thugs in here get up to. Not to mention that you won't be receiving medical care from U.S. Army doctors, you won't be fed U.S. Army rations. It's going to be real different. You probably have a better picture of what it will be like than I do. And while I do understand your reluctance about being released,

I can't imagine you wanting to stay inside under the kind of conditions you'll be facing. So I want you to think very carefully about what I'm going to tell you now."

"Dave, I understand what you're saying. And I thank you for your concern. But what am I to do about it? You talk as though I have some choice in the matter."

"You do, Wulf, because Marx has come up with a plan."

"Marx has a plan, does he?" Wulf laughs. "It sounds like something the Nazis warned us about."

"Yes," Dave shares the joke. "But it's a good plan. I think it will work. And if it does it will mean freedom for you."

"Why should Marx want to help?"

"He had an older brother he idolized. You had older brothers, too, didn't you?"

"Yes."

"Was there one in particular who was special to you?"

"They were all wonderful. They were all heroes to me."

"Well, Marx's brother was his hero. And when Marx's parents found out about him—you know what I'm talking about—he killed himself. He hanged himself from a pipe in the basement. So when Marx first heard that there were prisoners like you in the camp, he was beside himself. And he's been trying to think of a way to help ever since."

"I see. And this plan he has made. It is something, how would you say it in English? Underhanded?"

"We're the U.S. Army. We'd probably say 'highly irregular'."

"Really? That sounds extremely German. So tell me. What about you, Dave? Why would you risk becoming involved in something highly irregular?"

There is a long silence before Dave speaks.

"I don't know how to explain it Wulf. It just seems wrong to me. What they did to you. What they're still going to do. How is it any different, really? The way you felt about your Rudi? Was that really immoral?"

"Morality is what people decide it will be, Dave."

"Which means it can change. Doesn't it?"

"I don't know. Perhaps."

"Well, anyway, just think about it in practical terms. Haven't you all been punished enough already?"

"You know how I would answer that."

"O.K. Well, you know of course that Berlin fell to the Russians. It was several days before we had any troops there. We're still far outnumbered in that part of Germany. And since the Russians were the ones to take the city and still virtually have a free hand there, all the files and records are in their control. Everything. Including presumably the records of your arrest and trial."

"I see. So?"

"They're not sharing. People don't realize it yet, but the alliance between the Russians and us barely survived until the end of the war. We're close to going to war with them right now. Some of our generals would already be on the way to Moscow if the politicians would let them. But we've still got the Japanese to beat, you know."

"We tried to be allies of the Russians, too," Wulf says. "That didn't work out either. So what about Marx's plan?"

"When we first got here, he grabbed a lot of forms and things. Stuff the Nazis used for record keeping. He has one of their typewriters, too. Not to mention that he's fluent in German and hardly anyone else in the unit speaks a word."

"So he is perhaps thinking about forging documents? Altering records?"

"Something like that. We can't do it for everyone, obviously. It would arouse suspicion if we let too many of you guys go. And of course, we have to assume that Allied authorities have access to the arrest records and court proceedings of prisoners whose offenses occurred in territories we liberated. We don't know this for a fact. The Nazis may have sent all the material to their central files in Berlin. But for safety's sake, we have to assume that stuff is still floating around somewhere and may eventually fall into Allied hands. If it hasn't already."

"I think I understand," Wulf nods. "You and Marx will only risk forging documents regarding persons whose cases can't be investigated by American authorities because the Russians won't let them see the records from Berlin."

"That's it. You've got it. Anyway, Marx had been cooking this up for days before we even started interviewing prisoners. So when you came along, well, we were both so impressed with you. Personally, I mean. And it doesn't hurt that your father was a member of the von Stauffenberg group that went up against Hitler. It makes it that much easier to pass our faked documents off as real, because our commander's bound to be more sympathetic to you than any other prisoner we would try to spring this way."

"Do you really think this will work?"

"I do, Wulf. If you agree to it, we can have you out of here by lunchtime tomorrow."

"All right, Dave. Tell me what it is I have to do."

"You'll do it?"

"I'll think about it."

"You'd better think fast. I've already made an appointment with the commander for first thing tomorrow morning. I'll show him the documents Marx has created for us. I'll explain to him about your father and how it's our conclusion that you were assigned to your classification as a reprisal. I'm sure he'll agree to your release. He'll probably call you in for a brief conversation. He may ask you questions. You'll need to pretend that you don't speak English well so we can have Marx translate. It won't take more than ten minutes, I'm sure. Then you walk out of there a free man."

"With nothing but the clothes on my back."

"Marx and I have organized some things for you. It's not a lot, but it'll get you started on the outside. You just walk out that gate and another friend of ours will meet you. He'll have a bag. Clothing. Canned rations. Chocolate. Cigarettes. I know you don't smoke, but people on the outside are using them as currency these days."

"You and Marx could be caught," Wulf protests. "You could be punished. I wouldn't want that on my conscience."

"Marx has a plan for that, too. Your actual release papers won't be forgeries. Once the commander has agreed to it, you'll be just as official as any other displaced person. You'll be able to go anywhere you want. But promise me one thing."

"What's that?"

"Don't go east. The Russians control basically all the territory east of the Elbe. And we've heard that they're rounding up able bodied German men and shipping them out to Siberia. So head west or north, but don't even think about Berlin, O.K?"

"I have no reason to go east anyway."

"Just don't forget it, promise?"

"All right."

"And remember, when you're called in tomorrow, you don't speak English. Let Marx handle it."

"I won't forget. I don't know how I can ever thank you."

"Don't think about that. Just go make a life for yourself. Maybe we'll meet again someday and you can buy me a drink."

"What is it you Americans say? 'It's a deal'?"

"That's what we say, all right."

"I should go now, Dave."

"Not yet."

"But it's almost lights out."

"Just a couple more minutes, Wulf. There won't be time tomorrow. We won't have a chance to talk like this again. You haven't told me what you thought about the sonnets."

"*Ach, scheiss'*. I forgot your book. Shall I bring it to you tomorrow?"

"Better not. We're not supposed to know each other. Keep it. It will be something to remember me by."

Buenos Aires: 1947

The *Prinzessin der Weser*, a forty year old freighter out of Hamburg, chugs through a light swell under a full moon. Alone at the rail Wulf stares up at the Southern Cross. Back home it's winter, the second since the end of the war. The bombed out buildings and shell cratered streets nestle under a mantle of snow that only partially camouflages the destruction and calls up faint, ridiculous recollections of prewar coziness. Here in the South Atlantic it's high summer, warm enough for him to stand on deck at midnight in nothing but a pair of stoker's shorts. Wulf knows his geography as well as the next man; better than most, actually, thanks to the expensive *gymnasium* he attended. He understands how far their voyage is taking them, can clearly see the map in his mind. But the afternoon they sailed, three weeks before Christmas, walls of sleet propelled by fearsome winds off the polar ice cap shot across their bows like machine gun fire, and the last thing Wulf would have imagined lying ahead of them was the warm, damp caress of this breathtaking night against his bare skin under this sky teeming with unfamiliar constellations.

The *Prinzessin*, forty-seven days out of Hamburg now and laboriously nearing Buenos Aires with her holds full of scrap metal, is practically a relic. It's nothing short of a miracle that she survived the war, ancient, wallowing tub that she is. By all rights an Allied bomber or submarine should have sent her to the bottom long before the end of hostilities. In other circumstances, a vessel of her decrepitude would have been scrapped years or even decades ago. But in post-war Germany nothing of any conceivable use is wasted. Things that once would have been thoughtlessly tossed aside are salvaged, jealously hoarded, put to uses totally unforeseen by their original creators. A seaworthy freighter like the *Prinzessin*, slow and small and profligate of fuel though she is, is practically worth her weight in gold. Her continued existence and operation means jobs for the crew members and food and shelter for their families. It means profits for the shipping line that have already encouraged investors and may eventually make possible the construction of her replacement. It means foreign trade for a Germany in ruins, transfusions of currency from all over the world that will eventually revive the nation's economy and make her the envy of her neighbors once again. And, incidentally, make possible the continued payment of reparations to Germany's victims.

To Wulf, on his first voyage as a merchant seaman, the ship also represents the greatest freedom he has known since before the war. She represents escape from the dispiriting realities of the life he has led since the night of his arrest. And she already feels more like home than any place he can remember since he last set foot in the apartment he shared with Rudi in Berlin. This new job means a real roof over his head, not a squalid hovel constructed of materials scavenged from the ruins, in a corner of the cellar of a bombed out apartment building. There is electric light in the forecastle where he bunks with his mates. There is running water. Even, luxury of luxuries, hot water for his—he can scarcely believe it—*daily* shave and shower. And there is food. Simple but plentiful. Three meals every single day. Not one every day or so when he can miraculously come by half a loaf of coarse bread, a couple of slices of gristly sausage, a moldy end of cheese. There is real, though weak, coffee every day. And he's no longer dressed in whatever rags he can find but in actual uniforms, newly made and reasonably well fitting. All this dazzling bounty is provided by the company, and wonder of wonders, there are wages in addition.

By almost any other standards, he and his shipmates live a spartan existence. But by the standards of Germany, January, 1947, they're practically sybarites. No wonder everybody covets their jobs. Even Wulf's position as a stoker, shoveling low grade Ruhr coal into the hungry, inefficient old boilers below, four two hour shifts a day, seven days a week while they're at sea. He can't believe his luck. There were hundreds of men lined up to apply for positions that day he was hired. He attributes his good fortune to genetics. He was the tallest, broadest shouldered man on the pier. He was all skin and bones, hadn't eaten in three days and felt weak as a kitten, but he looked fit enough, like he could handle the work. And he has. Strenuous as it is, it's far easier than anything he did in the camps. And despite the exertion, he's been putting on weight steadily ever since they sailed.

It is, of course, not in the least like the life he dreamed about as a boy, or even one he might have imagined as a young *Luftwaffe* officer. But it's the one he has. And in the new Germany nobody forgets the dead even for a moment, those who have no life at all, or the tens of thousands of men still in Siberian captivity who may never return. He stares out for a few minutes longer at the moonlight burnished waves. He takes a last, deep breath of the warm, tangy air. Then he heads below to report for his next shift.

* * *

The bus rolls down a wide, tree lined boulevard that reminds Wulf of Paris. With their ornately sculpted plaster and stonework the white buildings look almost like wedding cakes. Shiny automobiles dart in and out of traffic, their horns tooting, their tires squealing, their engines racing. The sidewalks are crowded with elegantly dressed and groomed, obviously well fed people. Wulf gapes out the open window, dazzled that such a clean, prosperous place as this actually exists. By what dispensation were this city and its residents spared the ravages of recent history?

Crammed into the seat with him, Karl yawns, lets out a stentorian belch, and starts to laugh.

"*Halt den Mund, Idiot!*" Helmut barks, standing in the aisle beside them. "Shut up, why don't you? Don't be such a pig."

He glares down at Karl, who belches again, even louder. Helmut gives him a good cuff to the ear.

"I don't know why I put up with you, you ignorant, uncouth swine," Helmut complains. "Wulf and I should have left you behind."

Helmut and Karl are the nearest thing Wulf has to friends on board ship. Or for that matter, in the entire world. They served together on a succession of U-boats. They survived the war by a series of miracles that rivals that of the Children of Israel in Egyptian captivity. They signed on as seamen on the *Prinzessin's* first voyage after the war ended. They bicker constantly, yet it's obvious to Wulf that they are closer than brothers; indeed can't imagine life without each other. Their wives, twin sisters, share a flat together back in Hamburg. Helmut and Inge have twin sons. Karl and Lotte have just one boy, the same age as Helmut and Inge's boys. Helmut and Karl's mother-in-law, whom they gleefully refer to at every opportunity as "the storm trooper" or "the Gestapo she devil", presides over the household. One big happy family. At least as long as Helmut and Karl are at sea, which is constantly, though this is their first voyage to Buenos Aires. Wulf isn't at all sure why they have adopted him. He's odd man out among the crew: from a prominent family, a former *Luftwaffe* man, and an officer and pilot to boot. But since their first day at sea the two of them have assumed that he has nothing better to do than listen to their bickering, exclaim over the photos of their wives and sons—they display these at every opportunity—sit with them at meals, drink with them, sun himself on deck with them during his off hours, play cards with them; be in other words their captive audience and all too frequent referee.

This afternoon they're on their way to visit Helmut's Aunt Johanna, Uncle Kurt, and Cousin Albrecht. Johanna and Kurt left Germany in 1930. Helmut and Albrecht haven't seen each other since they were boys. But until she died in an Allied air raid, Helmut's mother wrote letters every week to Aunt Johanna, and Helmut talks of his extended German/Argentine family as if he sees them regularly and seems thoroughly conversant with their comings and goings. Uncle Kurt owns a butcher shop, which Aunt Johanna helps him run. Albrecht works as a mechanic for the local Daimler-Benz distributor. He and his wife Luise have three sons. Luise's father is a Lutheran pastor. Wulf knows more about these people than he really wants to, but there's no avoiding it. It's about all Helmut's talked of the last few days.

They change buses twice more before reaching the neighborhood where Helmut's relatives live. They get off the bus on a street lined with small shops. Signs in the shop windows are in German. People on the sidewalks as they march toward Uncle Kurt's butcher shop converse in German. Other people sitting over lunch at sidewalk cafes read newspapers printed in German. Wulf has always known that there are many Germans living in Argentina, just as there are many living in the United States. But somehow nothing he has heard has prepared him for a scene like this, as if he traveled over ten thousand miles to find not a foreign country but a Germany where the war never took place.

"Here we are," Helmut says, pulling open a shop door.

Karl and Wulf follow him inside.

"Kurt Keller," Helmut bellows.

"What's this noise?" the stocky, gray haired man standing behind the counter demands. His white apron is bloodstained. Inside the glass display cases, Wulf sees heaps of beef and pork cuts. In Hamburg it would be worth tens of thousands of marks. "Who the hell are you, anyway? Who let this riff raff into my shop? *Raus*, all of you, before you scare off my paying customers. I'll call the police on you, just see if I don't."

"Fuck yourself, old man," Helmut snarls, reaching across the counter and grabbing him by the collar.

The gray haired man's right hand suddenly appears, clenching the handle of a gleaming cleaver. It looks like it could take a man's hand off at the wrist with one stroke.

"See this, boy?" he growls.

"*Ja.* So what?"

"So take your hands off me before I cut off your cock and balls and put them in this case."

"Just try, you old bastard."

Wulf's beginning to fear they've blundered into the wrong shop when a tall, skinny woman appears in the doorway from the back room.

"Shut your fool mouths, both of you," she commands. "You'll have the police in here in another minute. And I won't stop them. I'll let them cart you off."

The two men start giggling. Helmut drops his sea bag on the floor, vaults over the counter, sweeps the woman into his arms, gives her loud, smacking kisses on the cheeks while she tries to bat him away.

"So, Helmut," the man with the cleaver says, laughing and gasping for breath. "Look how you grew up. Just like your father. I'd know you anywhere."

"Indeed," the woman says, laughing now herself, "Martin never had any manners, either, may he burn in hell. *Ach, junge*, it's so good to see you."

"You, too, *Tante* darling." Helmut lets go of her and turns to the man. "And Uncle Kurt. You haven't changed a bit."

"*Nein,*" Uncle Kurt agrees, "I'm still a mean old bastard, and don't you forget it."

The men embrace and slap each other on the back.

"Who are your friends, Helmut?" Tante Johanna asks.

"Karl you already know of," Helmut says.

"Oh, this is Karl? Lotte's Karl?"

"*Jawohl*, Frau Keller," Karl says, standing up straighter than Wulf has ever seen him and reaching across the counter to shake her hand.

"*Ach, nein,*" she protests, "you must call me Tante Johanna as well."

"And this," Karl says, wrapping an arm around Wulf's shoulder, "is our most excellent friend and shipmate, Wulf von Riedel."

"Pleased to meet you," Wulf says, shaking her hand and then Uncle Kurt's.

"Boys," she says, shaking her head sadly, "you are all so thin. It's terrible to see you looking like this. Kurt, slice me some sausage. Come in back, boys. I'll fix some sandwiches."

* * *

They are still eating, drinking, and telling jokes when Albrecht arrives on his way home from work. A handsome, curly haired young man, he greets them all warmly and insists they come to his house, where Luise is preparing dinner. Wulf feels uncomfortable accepting so much hospitality from these strangers, but Helmut grins at him reassuringly and he follows the others out to Albrecht's car, a tiny, elderly Mercedes, which gleams like it is brand new.

"Who did you borrow this from, old man?" Helmut asks, shoving Karl and their two sea bags into the back seat, then crawling in himself.

"I borrowed it from no one," Albrecht insists in the strangely accented German Wulf noticed when they were first introduced. "It is mine."

"*Lieber Gott,*" Karl exclaims. "You own an auto?"

"Of course," Albrecht says, getting into the front seat beside Wulf and starting the engine. "Many people here own their own autos. This one is not new, certainly. But I take good care of her. She is fine German machinery. I think she will last a long time yet. This is a rich country, Cousin. Life here is good. You will see."

They drive a few blocks. Albrecht steers the car into a narrow street of tiny, brightly painted cottages. Flowers bloom in the yards. It looks as freshly scrubbed as a village in the Swiss Alps.

"Just look at this," Helmut says, as they pull up in front of a cottage half-way down the block. "How many families do you share with?"

"None," Albrecht says.

"You're joking," Karl mutters.

"*Nein.* No joke."

"But how can you afford to pay rent on a whole house for just yourself?" Helmut asks.

"We do not pay rent," Albrecht answers, climbing out of the little car. "Papa bought it for us and every month I pay him back. And my sons will live in even finer houses than this. Homes of their very own."

"*Ach, Scheisse,*" Karl grunts, heaving sea bags out of the back seat. "This Argentina."

The front door of the small house swings open and Albrecht's three boys burst out. Wulf stares at them. Children used to look like this, ruddy cheeked, energetic, strong limbed. Children used to laugh like these children laugh, used to screech just this way with high spirits and excitement. He remembers. But he also remembers the thin, pale, exhausted looking children he has grown accustomed to seeing on the streets of Hamburg in their pitiful rags, their skin grimy, their hair stringy and dull, their eyes forever starving. He feels a lump rising in his throat.

Albrecht's wife Luise follows the boys into the front garden. She's a lovely dark haired girl. She looks as if she's never had a sad thought in her life. She greets them all as if they're her own brothers. She says she hopes they like steak with fried potatoes and onions.

* * *

Helmut, Karl, Albrecht, and Wulf sit in the back garden drinking rich, dark beer of a quality Wulf has forgotten ever existed. The moon rises out over the River Plate. There is a faint tang of salt in the breeze. Wulf can hear Luise inside the house, getting the boys ready for bed.

"Everywhere here there is opportunity," Albrecht says. "Everywhere there are good German businessmen looking for workers to hire. Men who speak their language, you understand? Who share their beliefs. They are prepared to pay high wages to such men. Some of those businessmen may even make their protégés partners. I myself have just been promoted. I now supervise all the mechanics in my firm. There is much work repairing autos and trucks. We hope soon to be able to get parts from the plants in Stuttgart and Mannheim. Then there will be even more work. We could hire four or five men right now. But the boss doesn't want to hire any non-Germans. He would even be willing to hire men with no experience, because he knows Germans work hard and Germans learn fast. But we can't find any.

"And," he continues, looking at Wulf, "there are many German girls here who would like to find German husbands. Beautiful girls. Well educated and obedient. A German man in Argentina can take his pick."

"But now listen, Cousin," Helmut says, "say a man wanted to come out here from Germany. For the opportunity, as you say. How could he leave his family behind? He couldn't think of such a thing."

"We have many friends in the government," Albrecht says. "If such a man wanted to come to Argentina, once he had a job and his employer was willing to sign a verification that he was a worker, there would be no trouble arranging for his family to follow him into the country. His employer would probably even pay for their passage. This is a land of many opportunities. Why within a year at the longest, that man could be driving his own auto and living in a house just like mine. I tell you, Cousin, within five years he could own his own business."

* * *

When Wulf wakes, Fritz, Albrecht's oldest son, is staring down at him in his makeshift bed on the living room floor.

"*Guten Morgen,*" Wulf says.

"*Vati* says you were a fighter pilot in the war," Fritz chirps.

"Yes," Wulf says.

"*Vati* says you might tell me about it. It must have been wonderful, shooting down all those American and British bombers. Did you win many medals? I bet you did. Would you show them to me? Please?"

"Fritz," Luise calls from the kitchen, "leave Herr von Riedel alone. Go wake your cousins Helmut and Karl. Tell them breakfast is almost ready."

"But Mutti, Herr Wulf is going to show me his medals. From the war."

"Fritz, remember the lesson you learned at church school last week?"

"Yes."

"What was it? Tell me, please. I've forgotten."

"You know, Mutti."

"You must remind me, *liebchen.*"

"It was 'children obey your parents'."

"That's right. I remember now. Now leave Herr von Riedel in peace and go call Helmut and Karl."

"All right."

Wulf watches the child leave the room. He wipes the cold sweat off his forehead, then reaches into his sea bag and pulls out clean clothes. He slips into them quickly, then starts picking up his bedding and folding it.

"Leave that," Luise says from the doorway. "I'll take care of it later."

"It's no trouble," Wulf says. "I can do it."

"I'm sorry," Luise says.

Wulf isn't sure what she's referring to.

"Albrecht puts all kinds of ideas into their heads. Even before they could talk, he was telling them his stories. I wish he wouldn't do it. It gives them the wrong impression, I'm afraid."

"Does it?"

"It's all right," Luise says. "I'm not like everyone else around here. You don't have to pretend with me. I can see in your eyes that things were bad for you. I have some idea what it was like. I read all of the letters Johanna got from Helmut's mother. My mother got letters from her family, too. We never heard from them again after the fire bombing of Dresden. It must have been horrible. People here don't seem to understand. Argentina was neutral. Officially at least. We had no bombings. We had no rationing. What we had were both sides buying our beef and our wheat and making the whole country rich. And we had pro-German newspapers. We had films from before the war about the new Germany. And all those newsreels that claimed victory was right around the corner. Everybody here believed that. Nobody ever told us the truth of what was happening. I suppose I believed it all myself, at first. But when those letters came…"

"Yes?"

"Sometimes I have nightmares about them. I don't understand how anybody can feel the way people here do about the things that happened. It makes no sense to me. That's why I wish Albrecht wouldn't talk to the boys about it the way he does. Like it was all a game. Or some wonderful adventure. Nothing more than a stage play, with heroes and villains. He still believes…"

"Believes what?"

"Oh, you know," she sighs, turning away from him. "I hope you like steak with your eggs."

"Listen," he says, suddenly remembering his horror at the extravagant dinner she served them last night.

"Yes."

"Is what Albrecht says true?"

"What does he say?"

He can hardly bring himself to ask the question. It seems so indelicate.

"About what a good life it is here. I mean, forgive me, but can you really afford to be feeding us steaks again this morning? After all that food last night? A meal like that must have cost four months' wages."

"I knew it," she says, turning to face him. "What you just asked tells me more about what it's like in Germany these days than anything I've heard so far. Of course we can afford it. People in Argentina have steak at every meal. Even poor people have it at least once a day."

"You must be joking."

"Oh, I assure you, Herr von Riedel," she laughs, "it is no joke. This truly is the promised land."

* * *

After lunch at the butcher shop, Helmut, Karl, and Wulf catch a bus and ride out to the garage where Albrecht is the supervisor of mechanics. The building is brand new, large as an aircraft hangar. Over a dozen trucks and autos are

undergoing repair. Many others sit outside. The mechanics all wear neat overalls with their names embroidered on patches sewn to the chests. They greet the
visitors warmly, explaining the specific repairs they're making. Their tools are
dazzling, almost like surgical instruments.

Wulf recalls happier days helping Franz, the family chauffeur, maintain
the small fleet of family vehicles. He remembers more recent times tinkering with Rudi's magnificent Bugatti coupe under the watchful eye of Horst.
His fingers itch to pick up tools, to lean over the fender of that sleek looking
green cabriolet in the corner, expertly discover the malfunction lurking under
its shiny hood and rectify it.

"You saw outside?" Albrecht asks. "All those autos and trucks? Sometimes
their owners have to wait for months before we have time to make the repairs.
They are desperate to have their motors running again. They will pay almost
any amount. This business is a gold mine. But we must have more men. As soon
as possible."

Wulf sees Helmut and Karl looking at each other. He sees Helmut's slight
nod and Karl's answering grin. He feels Albrecht's eyes on him. Albrecht is
ready to offer all three of them positions here. The other workers know it, too.
He sensed it in their warm greetings. All he and his shipmates have to do is say
the word.

* * *

After dinner at Uncle Kurt and Aunt Johanna's, a meal which leaves Wulf
ready to believe what Luise told him about the consumption of beefsteak in
Argentina, Albrecht tells Luise that it's boys' night out. She smiles and wishes
them all good evening. Then she loads her protesting sons into the Mercedes for
the short drive home. Albrecht leads the three shipmates along quiet streets of
small houses and into a busy avenue. They walk past brightly lit shop windows
full of goods, past shiny cars crowded at the curbs to his favorite *ratskeller*.

"Now I will show you what we are about here," he says as he pulls open
the door and leads them inside. "Now you will see what the German men of
Argentina are made of."

They walk single file through a dark corridor. They can hear gruff male
laughter and music playing on a phonograph. The aromas of cigar smoke and
strong, rich beer drift out toward them. Wulf is the last through the doorway.
The small room is jammed. Dozens of men of all ages sit at the tables, lean
against the bar, stand talking to one another. The noise of their conversations

is deafening. A few faces turn to watch them come in. Several of the men greet Albrecht, who is obviously a regular here and apparently popular.

A table is emptied for them. The three of them sit down while Albrecht goes to buy the first round of drinks. Wulf fingers a wad of bills in his pocket, determined to pay for the next round. He's still embarrassed by the hospitality here. And he's about to feel even more beholden to his host, because before the night is out he plans to ask Albrecht for a position at the garage. He feels bad at the idea of jumping ship. But he can't resist the charms of this beautiful city and the opportunities it represents. His own car. His own little house. And who knows? One day there might even be a special friend to share it with. Someone who doesn't bear the scars of the war, who has no searing memories, who suffers from no guilt, who never wakes in the middle of the night screaming from nightmares of the camps.

That day may be sooner than he thinks, he realizes, as he notices a strikingly handsome young man staring at him. He looks back, just for a moment, and is shocked to see that certain look in the young man's eyes. It can't be. He looks again, and this time he's sure he isn't imagining it. While this is happening, he misses his chance to buy drinks. He looks away from the young man to see that Karl is already handing him a fresh stein. Oh, well. Next round for sure. He raises it and drains off half the stein in one gulp.

"Why don't you introduce me to your friends, Albrecht?" he hears someone say. Wulf doesn't dare look up from his drink. He knows it's the young man. His heart pounds. He knows the young man has come to their table to meet him.

"'N Abend, Otto," Albrecht says. "This is my Cousin Helmut, from Hamburg. And his brother-in-law, Karl. And their good friend Wulf."

"Pleased to meet you," Otto says.

Now Wulf has to look up. He can't ignore the young man. He has to return the greeting and the handshake. And in spite of himself, he returns the special look Otto again gives him. He can't believe Otto is doing such a thing right here in this tavern full of people. Don't any of them recognize what is going on?

"Please allow me to buy the next round of drinks," Otto says, already moving away from the table.

"Seems like a nice chap," Karl remarks.

"The finest," Albrecht agrees. "He's my boss's oldest son. And he's not some spoiled rich boy. He apprenticed in the shop. He's as good a mechanic as any in Buenos Aires. Now he works in the offices. He has a fine head for business. He will make a big success someday, I can tell you. I'll just get a chair so he can join us."

Otto returns with their beers. As if by magic, the chair Albrecht has brought for him gets shoved into place at the table right beside Wulf, who is giddy with the simple joy at being in the presence of such a lovely young man, excited at so obviously being found attractive, and tense with anticipation at what the night may bring. And the boss's son, to boot.

"So," Otto says, sitting down and moving his chair even closer to Wulf's. "Tell me about these gentlemen, Albrecht. They seem very interesting."

"Helmut and Karl were submariners during the war," Albrecht says.

"You must have some stories to tell."

"We have enough to last all night," Helmut assures him.

"And tomorrow night, as well," Karl agrees.

"And you, Wulf?"

Wulf finds himself dazed by the young man's frank stare. He grins back, unable to speak.

"*Ach,* that one," Karl grunts. "He's too modest. He'll never tell you."

"Tell me what?" Otto asks, leaning toward Wulf.

"Fighter pilot," Albrecht says.

"Really?"

Wulf nods.

"They are crew members on a freighter out of Hamburg," Albrecht explains. "I've been trying to convince them that their future is here."

"Have you?" Otto asks.

"Oh, he has," Helmut says.

"Very good," Otto says, not taking his eyes off Wulf. "It's absolutely true, of course. The future is here in Argentina. Have you offered them jobs with us?"

"Not yet," Albrecht admits. "I was hoping that we would have a chance to discuss it with them tonight."

"Well," Otto says, "it's certainly a good thing that I ran into you all. And let me assure you that anyone Albrecht recommends has a secure position with our firm. You can all start whenever you wish."

"How about tomorrow?" Karl asks.

"You look to me like you could use a few more days of vacation," Otto says. "How about Monday instead?"

"*Ausgezeichnet,*" Albrecht beams. "Excellent. It's all settled then."

Karl and Helmut grin at each other. Wulf sits transfixed, gazing at Otto's shining hair.

* * *

Much later, as the five of them sit at their tiny table, a tall, stocky man of about forty approaches. Albrecht leaps to his feet, nearly upsetting his beer. Wulf has lost count of the rounds and still hasn't bought drinks. Neither has Helmut. Every time they get ready, someone at another table comes by with more drinks for them.

"Herr Schlegelmann," Albrecht stammers. "What a great pleasure."

"*Guten Abend*, Albrecht," Schlegelmann says, looking at them in a way that suddenly makes Wulf's skin crawl. "Are these your friends I've been hearing so much about?"

"*Ja*, Herr Schlegelmann."

"I should very much enjoy meeting them. But it's far too noisy out here for an enjoyable conversation. Why don't you join us in the back room?"

"Why, yes, Herr Schlegelmann. That's extremely kind of you."

"You too, of course, Neubauer," the man says, nodding to Otto.

"Thank you," Otto says, "perhaps later. I must make a phone call first."

"I'll tell Bodo to expect you," Schlegelmann nods.

Wulf is torn. He'd much rather stay with Otto. But he doesn't want to embarrass Albrecht in front of this obviously important man. The others rise from their seats. He glances at Otto, who gives him a little nod. Its meaning is crystal clear. Wulf need have no fear. They will be seeing each other again soon.

They follow Schlegelmann to a doorway Wulf hadn't noticed before. Schlegelmann knocks twice. The door swings open. They follow him into a small room, and Wulf enters a waking nightmare. Men in brown shirts sit around small tables. They wear the hated regalia he had hoped never to see again. And covering the back wall, lit with spotlights, is that hated flag. Wulf feels immediately nauseated. He stumbles, falls against a table.

"Wulf?" Albrecht asks, looking concerned.

"I'm not well," Wulf says.

"I'll just take you back out," Albrecht says. "There's a toilet…"

"No," Wulf waves him off. "I'll be all right. Go visit with your friend."

"Are you sure?"

"Of course."

"Well," Albrecht says, "he is a very important man. One of the most in-fluential Germans in all of Argentina. He's a very valuable person to have look-ing out for you."

"I see."

"I hope you'll feel well enough to rejoin us."

"Maybe later."

Albrecht nods.

Wulf turns. The man at the door swings it open for him and he stumbles back outside. He hears it shut behind him. He sees Otto standing a few feet away. He steps toward him in desperation. In an instant Otto is beside him, grasping him firmly by the arm.

"This way," he says. "I didn't think you would like it in there."

* * *

"Feeling better now?" Otto asks.

"Yes, thank you," Wulf says. "I'm not used to drinking so much beer."

"That's not what made you sick," Otto says.

Wulf ignores the comment, which makes him uneasy.

"Where are we going?"

"My car's just down the block. I thought we'd go for a drive. Is that all right?"

"Yes."

"We can put the top down and get some air. Would you like that?"

"You have a cabrio?"

"A roadster, actually. A 1938 model 200."

"Ah," Wulf says, remembering Rudi's last car after he placed the Bugatti in storage. The very same model.

"You don't have to put on an act with me," Otto says once they're on the way. "I'm not one of them. I pretend to be, I'm afraid. It's not something I'm proud of, but I do it. My whole family does. But we're not like them. *Scheisse mensch*, we came to Argentina to get away from them. And now they're here. More of them every day."

"I don't understand."

"We had to come. Or at least get out of Germany. My grandmother—my mother's mother—is Jewish. And my father is a very smart man. He took Hitler at his word. From the very beginning he knew he at least had to expect the Nazis to annihilate his wife's family. Perhaps even his own children. We're one fourth Jew, after all. And he didn't believe that France was far enough away. So he talked his father out of some capital and bought the business out here. You know what they did to the Jews, don't you?"

"Yes. I was at Bergen-Belsen. And Dora-Mittelbau."

"I thought I heard you were *Luftwaffe*," Otto's voice hardens with suspicion.

"I was. What I meant was I was in the camps. I was a prisoner."

"*Gott in Himmel.* I didn't take you for a Jew. How did a Jew get into the *Luftwaffe* in the first place?"

"I'm not Jewish. Not even one fourth. Didn't you ever hear what they did to men...?"

"Yes?"

"Men like us?"

"Men like who? What are you talking about?"

"Like you and me, Otto."

"What are you saying?"

"They rounded us up. Just like they did with the Jews and the communists. Hundreds of us that I know of for certain. Probably tens of thousands. They took Rudi and me, just because we loved each other."

"You're joking."

"You haven't heard about it," Wulf shrugs. "Nobody has. We were just perverts, after all. Not innocent victims like the others. Nobody cares."

"You survived," Otto says, voice husky. "Rudi?"

"No."

"Then you do understand."

"Yes."

"So we're going away again. With people like Schlegelmann growing more powerful in Argentina by the day, it's the only thing we can do. He's not just influential among the Germans here, Wulf. He has many friends in the government. There's no telling how much longer it will be safe for Jews here. Even people like me, who are mostly invisible. Or just German immigrants who aren't Nazi sympathizers. So Father's sold the business and sent the money to Switzerland. That's a secret, by the way. You mustn't say anything to Albrecht. No one can know anything about this until we're safely out of the country."

"I don't think I'll be seeing Albrecht again."

"I thought you were staying at his house."

"Maybe you could drive me there so I can pick up my bag. I'll go back and sleep on the ship."

"Of course."

"You know the way?"

"I've been there many times. Mother likes to bring birthday presents to Albrecht's little boys. Not having any grandchildren of her own so far."

"Luise tried to explain it to me," Wulf says, "but I didn't grasp what she was saying. It just didn't seem possible. Not until I walked into that room and saw them. I thought that was all in the past."

"Luise is a fine woman. And her parents are good people. They'll probably be able to raise those boys right in spite of Albrecht and his friends."

"God, I hope so," Wulf shudders.

"I know. They're sick animals. They're the same people who…"

"Yes," Wulf cuts him off. "And you? Where will you go this time?"

"We don't know yet. Father made some friends in the British Embassy. They've promised him visas for all of us as long as we promise not to go to Palestine. It will either be Australia or South Africa. I guess that means learning English."

"It's not a difficult language."

"You speak it?"

"I learned it as a boy. My brothers and I had an English nanny, you see. Then I picked it back up again when the Americans came."

"Lucky you. Oh, God, Wulf. Why couldn't I have met you there? Wherever we're going, I mean."

Wulf can't answer. He's feeling the same thing.

"When does your ship leave?"

"Tomorrow afternoon."

"You'll go back?"

"I have to now. I thought it was so perfect here. I was ready to forget Germany forever. It's so terrible there these days. You probably wouldn't recognize it. But at least people there understand the mistake we all made."

"Do they?"

"Well, perhaps not completely. But we live with the consequences. We are surrounded by them every day."

"That should have some educational value."

"As you say."

"Here we are," Otto says, pulling up in front of Albrecht's house.

"Thank you for the ride. And the talk. I wish things had been different."

"Shall I wait for you?"

"What?"

"I could give you a ride to your ship."

"I couldn't ask you..."

"You could ask me for anything," Otto says. "Don't you realize that?"

Again, Wulf is speechless.

"Listen, Wulf. This is crazy. We can't just say goodbye like tonight never happened."

"But Otto, what else can we do?"

"I've got my own apartment. We could have one night, at least. I'll drive you to your ship tomorrow."

"Would you like that?"

"Wulf..."

"I see. I'll just go inside and get my bag."

"I'll wait here for you."

"Yes," Wulf says, climbing out of the car and staring at the young man behind the wheel through eyes blurring with tears. "Yes, Otto, please wait for me."

New York: 1949

As the *Prinzessin der Weser* chugs past the Statue of Liberty into New York harbor, lights are just coming on all over the city. Wulf stands at the rail, awestruck. This may be the most amazing thing he's seen in his entire life. All those huge buildings lit up like Christmas trees. He turns up his collar against the stiff December breeze and huddles more deeply into his pea coat. Dark clouds hang low over the twinkling canyons of Manhattan. The scent of imminent snowfall fights with the salt tang in the air.

It's three years now since his first voyage as stoker on the *Prinzessin*. Three years of steaming back and forth between Hamburg and Buenos Aires, with an occasional Hamburg to Cape Town or Hamburg to Rio run thrown in for variety. The second time they sailed to Buenos Aires he tried to find Otto Neubauer but quickly learned the family had already left Argentina. No one he asked could tell him where they had gone, and some he spoke to were openly suspicious of his questioning. From then on, whenever the ship landed in Buenos Aires Wulf never left the immediate vicinity of the docks. Even from safely on board ship, the city made him feel faintly ill. There was nothing he wanted to see there. His shipmates found this wildly eccentric, but Wulf's quirks were already well known in the company, so they just shook their heads and went on with their sight seeing.

The first time the ship sailed to Cape Town he tried finding Otto there, too, remembering what the young man had said about his father's plans. But no one he asked had ever heard of the family, and once again people seemed suspicious of a German asking questions. After that there didn't seem to be any hope of ever seeing Otto again so he tried to put that magical night out of his mind. But in spite of his determined efforts, it still haunts him.

Germany is slowly recovering. The cleanup of the cities is agonizingly slow. People's lives are terribly hard, especially now, in winter. But they're not content to freeze to death in their apartments or starve. They want to work. They're willing to take any job. And more factories reopen every day. More goods are produced every succeeding week, and with most Germans hardly in a position to buy the shiny new products themselves, the goods go overseas. The shipping line Wulf works for now operates a fleet of seven vessels. Five of the others are more or less like the *Prinzessin*, sturdy but aging veterans of hundreds of voyages to every corner of the globe, painted up and repaired and their long overdue retirements indefinitely postponed. They are slow and ungainly, their boilers transform astonishing quantities of Ruhr coal into depressingly little forward motion, and their quarters are cramped and seem less inviting with each succeeding voyage, though Wulf can remember a time when he thought of the *Prinzessin's* forecastle as roughly on a par with a suite at the Adlon. But they are sturdy little ships, capable of standing up to the worst of weathers, seemingly immune to serious mechanical malfunction, apparently indestructible.

The seventh ship in the fleet, the *Imperatrix*, is currently on her maiden voyage. She is the line's new flagship, its first all new, purpose-built vessel since before the war. Compared to the *Prinzessin* and her sister ships, the *Imperatrix* is a sleek racehorse of a vessel. She can make Hamburg to Buenos Aires and back in twenty-three fewer days than the others while carrying three times the cargo. She burns diesel oil, not the low grade Ruhr coal Wulf has shoveled by the ton into the *Prinzessin's* ravenous boiler over the last three years. The owners offered Wulf a transfer to the new ship. They told him they would pay for his training to become a diesel engine mechanic. They appreciate the fact that he's one of only a handful of seamen who have stayed with them. He receives regular pay raises and more time off than anyone in the company below the rank of an officer. Wulf has seen crew members jump ship on every voyage, in every port of call. Sometimes he wonders if there are any able bodied men his age left in Germany. Those who survived the war and didn't get carted off to Siberia by the Russians seem hell bent on leaving the country as soon as possible and by any means available to them. Germany is fast becoming a country of women, children, and old men. He hears the ship's officers joke at least once each day about operating a passenger liner that just happens to carry a little freight as a sideline.

Wulf appreciated the offer to join the crew of the new ship. He took it as a compliment to his dedication and an acknowledgement of his industriousness. This was welcome, since his self respect is still in short supply. His fear of exposure and reimprisonment as a homosexual is more or less constant. For though the Nazis are all gone—at least that's the official version of the state of things in Germany these days, though only a slow witted child could be expected to believe it—Article 175 remains on the books and continues to be enforced in all the zones of occupation. Men are still arrested and imprisoned for nothing more terrible than loving each other. Men he knew in the camps are still there serving out the remaining years of their terms. Men who somehow managed to get out are afraid to associate with others like themselves or tell anyone their stories for fear of new charges being brought against them. Imprisoned or free, they still have the status of criminals, every last one of them. And this injustice rankles unbearably. As a result, Wulf is obsessed with earning the good opinion of everyone he encounters, as if a sufficient accumulation of it might save him from disaster. When that good opinion has been expressed to him, however, he finds himself incapable of trusting it, searching instead for ulterior motives on the part of the individual praising him. So he didn't risk the transfer to new duties on the new ship, which seemed to him to present as many opportunities to fail as to succeed, as many chances to earn censure as praise. The *Prinzessin*, shabby as she is, feels like home to him. He knows the work. And nothing bad ever happens to him as long as he stays on board her. So she's a lucky ship as far as he's concerned. With the *Imperatrix* now permanently assigned to the Buenos Aires run, the *Prinzessin* will now sail the North Atlantic only, traveling to ports in the United States and Canada.

This has brought him to the United States for the very first time this Saturday a week before Christmas. Wulf takes a last long look at the unbelievable skyline and wonders how anyone could ever grow tired of such a sight. Then he hurries below out of the cold. Crew's quarters is chaotic. Everyone is excited about shore leave in this city they've all heard so much about. There is a line for the showers. Men stand in twos and threes at the basins shaving or combing and recombing their hair. Wulf waits on his bunk for the worst of the rush to subside. Nothing about his plans requires him to be first off the ship.

* * *

After Wulf's painstaking shave and a long, relaxing shower, crew's quarters are deserted, so he takes as long as he wants in front of the mirror, brilliantining his hair into glistening perfection. Then he pulls on a blindingly clean set of whites he's been saving for months. He's going to have an adventure. Since that one night with Otto, his sex life has been confined to furtive contacts in alleyways and washrooms with complete strangers, after each of which he's more, rather than less, frustrated. But tonight is going to be different. A few weeks ago, sitting in a *ratskeller* he frequents when in Hamburg, he overheard a couple of businessmen talking about a place they had visited in New York. From their conversation there was no question what sort of place it was. And

besides, Wulf had once accepted thirty marks from one of the men for consent-
ing to have his cock sucked, which knowledge reinforced his certainty as to how
their remarks should be interpreted. Knowing he'd be sailing for New York
soon, Wulf listened so hard as the men described the place he thought his brain
might explode. He wrote down its name and location on a napkin the bartender
handed him response to his frantic gestures.

He checks himself a last time in the mirror. His skin is tanned and flawless. His eyes are clear and bright. His teeth gleam. His hair is combed exactly
as he wants it. He pulls on his pea coat, rushes up the companionway. He's the
last crewman to leave the ship.

* * *

Hours later, back on board the *Prinzessin* and huddled under his blanket,
Wulf struggles to fight off his bitter disappointment. The club hadn't been at all
what he was expecting. There was no laughter. There were no friendly smiles.
There were no jolly looking groups of men standing around talking and joking,
buying each other rounds of drinks and playing interminable tournaments of
darts. None of the images he recalls so vividly from the clubs in Berlin in the
old days. There was nothing more to see than a few middle aged men sullenly
smoking and a flock of tough looking youths dressed only in t-shirts and dun-
garees despite the cold outside talking loudly among themselves and ignoring
the middle aged men staring at them so avidly. No one in either group caught
his eye, though he could feel that he was attracting the attention of some of the
older men. They bought him several rounds of drinks: horrid American beer
that tasted like a cross between ammonia and dishwater, so nasty he nearly
choked on his first swig of it. Beer like that, in the richest, most powerful nation
in the world. Inconceivable.

But no one attempted to converse with him. They just issued a steady
stream of desperate sounding pleas, which he finally grew so tired of listening
to he ended up assenting to a particularly unattractive gentleman's offer to suck
his cock in the alley.

Just like back in Hamburg, except that the man paid in dollars.

Why had he even bothered?

* * *

Wulf sleeps most of the next day. He skips breakfast and refuses his shipmates' invitations to join them exploring the city. Claiming to feel ill, he begs to
be left alone. And late in the afternoon as his shipmates return, he ignores them

as they recount their amazing adventures, pulling up his blanket and muffling their voices with his pillow. He is ill, he tells himself: the most dread illness of all. He is sick at heart. Is there nowhere he can go in the whole world to find the kind of friendships he longs for? Is there never again to be anyone like Rudi or young Otto?

As evening falls, it's once again noisy and crowded in crew's quarters, but only briefly as his shipmates shower and change into clean clothing and then leave for the evening. Once the place clears out, Wulf gets out of the bunk, dresses quickly, and leaves the ship just long enough to find a liquor store. He spends the money the American gave him the night before on whiskey, which he takes back to the ship. By nine p.m. he's thoroughly drunk and out like a light.

* * *

"He's not sick," Albert insists, reaching under the covers and yanking on Wulf's shoulder. "Smell that? He's just sleeping off a binge. Come on, Tonio, help me roll him out of here."

"And then what?"

"Leave me alone, *verdammte schwein*," Wulf growls. Ordinarily this would be sufficient. Wulf's reputation as a solitary character stretches far beyond the decks of the *Prinzessin*. Indeed, it's a legend throughout the shipping line. Old-timers respect it and youngsters are intimidated. But these are extraordinary circumstances, with the towers of Manhattan looming over their decks.

"*Nein, nein*, Wulf," Albert says. "You're going to have a shower before you stink up the whole place. Then some breakfast and after that we'll talk about what else we've got in store for you. We can't let you miss all the fun."

"I say, go away," Wulf snarls. "Go suck the devil's cock, both of you."

"I think he's feeling better," Tonio observes.

"On a count of three," Albert says. "Ready. One, two, three."

* * *

After all Albert and Tonio's efforts, Wulf knows it would be ungracious to refuse their invitation to explore the city with them. So he meekly allows himself to be dragged along. They tramp through the city streets, gawking, pointing, amazed by something on every block, whether it's the expensively dressed, well fed businessmen hurrying along with their briefcases or the elegant women getting into and out of taxis, or the tall buildings rising dizzyingly into the sky, or the streams of large, shiny automobiles speeding past. Wulf has never seen anything like it and is almost glad he came along.

They ride the subways, gape from the railings of the observation deck atop the Empire State Building, take a boat ride out to the Statue of Liberty. Looking around him, Wulf thinks it is no wonder the Americans won the war. If they could build a city like this, they could do anything. Truly, Germany never stood a chance against a nation like America.

By nightfall he tells himself he's had enough and resolves to stay on board again for the evening. He's still smarting with the disappointment of his first night in the city. But once crew's quarters has emptied out again, he finds himself restless. Not sure why he's bothering, he showers and shaves, taking as much care over his appearance as he did on his first evening in the city.

Nine o'clock finds him back at the club, once more hoping against hope.

* * *

"Hello, sailor," the dark haired man says almost as soon as he's made his way to the bar, which is lined with men tonight. "What can I buy you to drink?"

"Whiskey and soda, thanks," Wulf says, looking the man over. He's in his thirties, expensively dressed, tall and a little paunchy. He must have been very attractive not too many years ago. He could easily be again if he took up exercise and gave up the heavy drinking that has left such obvious marks on his complexion. His brown eyes are slightly blurred, starting to be bloodshot. Wulf can smell whiskey on his breath.

"Coming right up, my friend," the man smiles with perfect teeth. "Charlie, a whiskey and soda for my new friend here and the usual for me."

"Coming right up, sir," the bartender calls back, raising a curious eyebrow at Wulf, who's attempting to communicate telepathically that he wants his drink mixed weak.

"I haven't seen you in here before," the man says. "We always appreciate new faces."

"My ship is just here for a few days."

"Say, you're not American, are you?"

"German."

"You guys invading again?"

"I beg your pardon?"

"Sorry. Bad joke. Your English is very good."

"Thank you."

"So this ship; what do you do on it? No, don't tell me. You're the second mate, right?"

"Stoker," Wulf corrects him.

"That's a good one," the man laughs.

"No, really," Wulf says. "It's an old freighter. Very old, very slow. And I am a stoker."

"God damn," the man says, shaking his head in disbelief. "I do believe you're serious."

Wulf nods, raising the drink the bartender has set down in front of him.

"Well, that would explain those shoulders. You're a very big boy. What? Six feet tall? And easily over two hundred pounds."

"I don't know your American measurements that well."

"Well, tell me in metric then."

"One hundred eighty-three centimeters. One hundred and two kilos."

"My God. That's over two hundred twenty pounds." He lays a flabby hand on Wulf's shoulder, and Wulf notices the bartender shaking his head with disapproval. "And I bet you're hard as a rock, aren't you?"

Wulf shrugs.

"Another drink?"

"Please," Wulf says, astonished at how quickly the man has downed his rum and coca-cola, "let me buy the second round."

"Wouldn't think of it," the man says. "Name's Denny, by the way."

"I am Wulf."

"Pleased to meet you, Wulf."

* * *

"So," Denny says some time later, "you ready to get out of here?"

"I beg your pardon?"

Wulf sees a momentary flicker of alarm in Denny's eyes. Good. He doesn't want this to seem too easy. As if there's no question of his acquiescence after having accepted those drinks. After all, he offered to buy his share of rounds. It wasn't by his choice that Denny refused the offer every time, and he doesn't want Denny thinking it gives him the right to make any claims.

"I'm sorry," Denny says, looking faintly alarmed and backing away. "I thought we understood each other."

"Oh," Wulf says, acting surprised. "Are you asking me to go somewhere with you?"

Denny blushes.

"I must apologize for my English, it seems," Wulf says. "It's not always as good as people think."

"Really," Denny says, still ill at ease.

"Well, you actually seem very nice," Wulf says, "but perhaps I should go back to my ship."

"Oh, please, Wulf," Denny says, looking crestfallen, "don't do that. Come with me instead."

And now that Denny has made it a request rather than a *fait accompli*, Wulf is happy to oblige. It's what he came looking for. Not to be bought, simply to be wanted. Denny could be more attractive, it's true. But his conversation is intelligent and he's certainly companionable. Besides, Wulf isn't looking for someone to fall in love with.

"Yes," Wulf says, smiling, "I think I should like that very much."

"Terrific," Denny grins, relief almost comically apparent in every muscle of his body. "Just give me your ticket and I'll get our coats."

"No," Wulf says, asserting yet more independence. "Give me yours."

"Well, all right," Denny says, looking dubious.

"What is wrong?"

"Nothing," Denny shakes his head. "You're just not like the guys I usually meet in here, that's all."

"Well, of course not," Wulf laughs. "What did you think? I am myself only."

*　*　*

Outside there's a light dusting of fresh snow on the sidewalk, and Wulf is happy not to be making the long walk back to the docks or trying to find a taxi. Denny is obviously very well off. He will surely know how to get a taxi at this time of night, though the street seems completely deserted.

"The car's this way," Denny says. Wulf falls into step beside him. They stop beside a sleek silver gray roadster he noticed earlier when the taxi driver let him out a block from the bar.

"*Scheisse mensch*," he grunts as Denny shoves his key into the door. "Is this your auto?"

"Like her?"

"She's magnificent."

"First one you've seen, I take it?"

"*Ja*. What make is she?"

"New Jaguar XK120 model. You haven't heard of them?"

"No."

Now that he looks more closely, the car, with its flowing lines and slender, oval shaped, vertical air intake, reminds him a little of Rudi's old Bugatti coupe.

"They're British," Denny explains. "Fastest things on the market just now."

"I can certainly believe that."

"Would you like to drive her?"

"*Ach*, Denny. I couldn't. I haven't been behind the wheel in years."

"Hell, Wulf, it's just like riding a bicycle. Once you know how, you never forget."

"No, please. Not in this weather. Such an expensive auto. I'd surely have an accident before we went a block. Then you'd send me right back to my ship and our so nice evening would be over."

"As if I won't have an accident myself after you got me so drunk," Denny laughs, shoving a lock of hair back off his forehead.

"Please, Denny, open the other door so I can get in."

"Suit yourself."

* * *

Denny's apartment is in a tall building a fairly long ride from the bar. Wulf has no idea what part of the city they're in. There is garaging in the cellar of the building. After parking the car, they ride upstairs in a silent elevator, then walk along a deeply carpeted corridor. Inside, Wulf notices the apartment seems to be on two floors. The rooms they pass through are large and expensively furnished. Wulf recognizes Monets, Dalis, Picassos, and a Degas hanging on the walls. Either they're real or they're excellent copies.

"This way," Denny says, taking him by the hand and leading him toward a staircase. Upstairs there are several more rooms, all as breathtaking as the ones below. They enter a large bedroom.

"There's just one thing," Denny says, pulling Wulf's coat off and laying it carefully across the arms of a maroon leather club chair.

"What?"

"Don't take offense, Wulf. I'm honestly not criticizing your hygiene. You look clean enough to eat breakfast off of. But I really like to have a man fresh from the shower. Do you mind?"

"Certainly not," Wulf smiles. It was the way Rudi always liked him best.

"The bathroom is through that door. Feel free to use anything you see in there. And take as long as you want. I'd like you to get ready just like you did tonight before you came to the bar."

"All right."

"There's a robe you can put on when you're ready to come out."

Wulf nods.

The bathroom is a marble lined temple to cleanliness. It's positively dazzling. He's seen nothing like it since the good old days back in Berlin. He starts the water in the shower and then undresses quickly. When he thinks back to this night, he will remember his amazement that the shower head is high enough that for once in his life he doesn't have to stoop to get underneath it.

* * *

When Wulf wakes, Denny is smiling down at him, wearing the bathrobe from the night before.

"Henderson sent me to ask you," Denny says, "how you like your eggs."

"Scrambled," Wulf says, mildly surprised that he remembers the English word for it.

"With a little Swiss cheese mixed in? And freshly grated black pepper?"

"The Swiss make cheese?"

Denny looks flummoxed for a moment. Wulf can't contain his chuckle. These Americans are too ready to believe that foreigners are unintelligent.

"You..." Denny laughs.

"The eggs sound delicious," Wulf says.

"And he also wants to know would you like bacon, ham, or sausage. Oh, never mind. I'll just tell him to fix you double portions of all three. A big breakfast for a big boy. A big, hard working boy. And never mind getting out of bed. He'll serve us in here."

* * *

"So do you have any plans made for today?" Denny asks, as Wulf pulls on his clothes from the night before. They have been laundered and perfectly folded.

"Nothing really."

"Good. We'll go for a drive in the Jaguar," Denny says, as if he's just thought of it, though Wulf believes he knows better. "I know, I'll teach you how to drive it."

"You really want that beautiful auto wrecked, don't you?"

"Nonsense," Denny laughs. "You'll pick it right up. It's Sunday, Wulf. There'll hardly be any traffic in the city. And the snow has melted off. The streets are perfectly clear. It's a beautiful, sunny day. What do you say?"

Since he first saw it the night before, Wulf's been itching to climb behind the wheel of Denny's beautiful roadster. He might as well admit it.

"All right. Yes. I would like that very much."

* * *

"You see what I told you?" Denny laughs. "You're a natural."

Wulf is not sure what makes him think that. They've gone less than a block, and he's only in third gear. But it's a magnificent feeling, steering the powerful machine down the road, trying out its many controls. And suddenly it feels like just yesterday when he last drove a car.

"All right," Denny says. "Take a left up here. I'm going to give you an A number one New York City tour."

* * *

"What would you like to do now?" Denny asks several hours later, as they sit in the Jaguar in its garage stall, the motor purring quietly. "Come upstairs? I could go for a second helping of last night's menu."

So could Wulf, but he feels uneasy being away from the ship for so long.

"I should really go back to the ship."

"It's not leaving already, is it?" Denny asks, sounding horrified.

"This evening."

"You know, on second thought, perhaps we should go to your ship."

"*Ja*," Wulf says. "I think that's best."

"Yes," Denny nods. "Absolutely. I'll wait with the car while you collect your things. Then we can come back here and get back to work. If you're receiving my signal."

"I'm sorry," Wulf says, confused. "What is it you're talking about?"

"You know," Denny giggles, "last night."

"*Ja*, of course. But what was that about collecting my things?"

"Perhaps you'd better turn off the engine."

Wulf does.

"Now I want you to listen to me carefully. And I don't want you to interrupt. I just want you to listen until I've completely finished what I have to say. O.K?"

"All right," Wulf says, even more confused.

"Wulf, here's the thing. I've just lost my sixth chauffeur. Since Labor Day—um, I mean the first of September. I have to have a chauffeur, and I can't seem to keep one. Now I know I can trust you. And I think you'd be happy with the job. I think you'd stay around for a while. You'd have your own suite of rooms. A bedroom, a sitting room, a private bathroom. I'll provide all your uniforms. I'll provide all your meals. You'll have Tuesdays off every week and one Monday a month. I have three cars. You can use any of them when you're not driving me. I'll pay for your membership at a gymnasium near here so you can keep up with your exercise. I'll buy you a radio for your rooms. Hell, a television too, if you want. In addition, I'll pay you a salary of one hundred dollars a week. I have friends in Washington who can take care of all the immigration business, so there's nothing to worry about on that score. You'll have resident alien status by the end of the week, and in five years you'll be eligible for citizenship. If you have any family or loved ones you want to bring over, I can arrange that, too. Though I can't allow them to live in the apartment with you. And even though you're some of the very best sex I've ever had, you don't have to sleep with me unless you just want to. Which I hope you will, of course. Occasionally at least. But that's not a condition of the job. I don't want you to think that for a minute. You can have all the boyfriends you want. Or girlfriends. For all I know you go both ways, and that's O.K. too. You can even bring them back to your room. As long as they behave. So what do you think?"

"This is a joke, *ja?*" Wulf says, flabbergasted.

"Oh, Wulf," Denny sighs, shaking his head. "You're too good to be true. You know that?"

"I don't understand this expression," Wulf says, sure that he's being made the butt of some joke and not at all happy about it. "What does this mean, too good to be true?"

"It means a guy who's so wonderful you can't believe he's real," Denny says.

"But how can you say that about me? We met for the first time last night. You know nothing of my life. I could be some terrible person."

"I know a great deal about you," Denny says. "For instance, this. You're a stoker on a German freighter. You told me you've worked for the shipping line for three years. Now in all that time you can't tell me you haven't seen crewmen jump ship in every port you visit. I know conditions have improved over there, but why else are most guys going to take a job as merchant seaman, if it's not because they're trying to find the easiest, quickest way out of Germany?"

"It's true," Wulf says. "I even thought about it once. In Buenos Aires."

"What stopped you?"

"It doesn't matter."

"Tell me, Wulf."

"I found that the city was full of Nazi sympathizers."

"So what?"

"Denny, how can you say that? Don't you know how horrible the Nazis were?"

"Of course. But did that matter to the men who did decide to jump ship there? There had to be some."

"There were."

"Plenty, I bet. But not you. So you've got a moral code that won't let you have anything to do with certain types of people. That's one thing I know about you, and it's a very important thing. Then there's loyalty to your employers. And your willingness to work hard."

"But everyone must work hard," Wulf protests. "That is the way life is."

"I don't work hard. I don't work at all, if I can help it. I'm lazy and undisciplined and dissipated and corrupt, and I'm just damned lucky that Mommy and Daddy are zillionaires and don't bother asking questions about my life. Otherwise I'd probably starve to death. I'm not kidding. I'm telling you, Wulf, there are a lot of terrible individuals out there. The world is chock full of them. Anyway, you know what else I know about you?"

"What?"

"Last night, in a bar with a particularly bad reputation, I met the handsomest man I've ever seen in real life. Somebody who can have anyone he wants. Somebody who can ask practically any price for it. I took him home with me to my apartment full of expensive artwork and antiques. I left expensive jewelry and my wallet with two thousand dollars cash in it lying on top of the dresser all night long. I left him alone in the bedroom several times during the night and again this morning. Now I know he's poor, and he has a very hard job that probably doesn't pay very well. And a man in his situation wouldn't have to be a criminal to have slipped something—one little thing—into his pocket. Something I'd probably never have missed.

"And what do you suppose happened?"

"Nothing happened, Denny. I would never..."

"That's the point Wulf. Absolutely nothing. That handsome man didn't beat me up. He didn't cut my throat. He didn't strangle me to death, which he's certainly strong enough to do. He didn't rob me. He didn't ask me for money. He didn't steal the keys to my car, even though he obviously admires it a great deal, and drive off in it never to be seen again. And those things happen all the time to people like me. Some of them actually have happened to me in the past. But you never thought for a single moment of harming me. I know you didn't because I've been with some really dangerous characters, and frankly I'm a pretty rotten sort of individual myself and I can smell it a mile away. So whatever you think, I do know quite a bit about you. And you really and truly are too good to be true. Now will you please take the job?"

New York: 1953

Wulf stows Denny's suitcases in the trunk of the Rolls-Royce, then opens the rear door for Denny to get into the back seat. They're friends now and off and on lovers, but in public, or when Denny's friends are around, Wulf is scrupulous in his observance of the appropriate punctilio. None of his parents' servants back in Berlin ever behaved one iota more properly than he does. He's determined that no one be able to guess from anything he says or does that he's anything more than Denny's chauffeur. And only a few among even Denny's closest friends are in on the secret. So they're safely in the car and pulling into traffic in front of the station before Wulf addresses Denny informally.

"How were things in Washington?"

"Hectic, as usual, Wulf."

"You testified in the senator's hearings?"

"Yes. And I think I did rather well. Everybody said so."

"And how was your friend, Mr. Cohn?"

"The usual. He sends his regards. I think he was rather annoyed with me for not bringing you along."

"That would hardly have been proper," Wulf says.

"He's a very powerful man, Wulf. The usual rules don't apply in his case."

Wulf doesn't believe this for a moment. He's been in America long enough now to know that men like Denny and Mr. Cohn are only a little better off here than he and Rudi were under the Nazis. They can be, and frequently are, arrested and imprisoned. Their bars are raided by the police on a regular basis. Their families can sign papers to have them committed to mental institutions, where they are sometimes subjected to surgical procedures and other experiments aimed at "curing" them. They are hounded from their jobs, turned onto the streets by their landlords, disowned by their parents. He has heard all this described by Denny's friends, many of whom have experienced such things first hand. He seriously doubts whether even Mr. Cohn could escape such misfortunes if anyone really wanted to pursue him. He wouldn't be the least bit surprised to wake up one morning and find the man completely disgraced, abandoned by the powerful friends Denny sets such store by. But discretion is not really his reason for wanting to avoid the man. The one time he slept with Mr. Cohn, as a favor to Denny, he found the man boorish and hateful. He'd just as soon avoid any possibility of a return engagement.

"And your friend, Mr. Hoover?" he asks. "Did you see him also?"

"Yes, and Clyde as well. We had quite a party, I can tell you. Some of their F.B.I. men are absolute stunners. And very willing to please, if I make myself clear."

"I see. Are there more hearings scheduled?"

"There's no end in sight, Wulf. The things they're uncovering in these hearings would curl your hair. It's a wonder the country hasn't collapsed already, with all these communists and fellow travelers everywhere you look. Hollywood's full of them, which is bad enough. But they've completely taken over the universities, too. And even parts of the government. The State Department is positively crawling. I swear to God, every last filthy one of them is hell bent on selling us out to the Russians."

When Denny talks like this it makes Wulf's blood run cold. He has heard the same kinds of ranting in the past. It's hard to believe that the Americans who seemed so compassionate when they liberated Germany could hold beliefs so similar to those of the Nazis. But there's no doubting it: it's all over the newspapers these days. It's so upsetting he's almost given up on reading anything but the sports page. He never discusses his misgivings with anyone. As a resident alien, he doesn't feel he's in a position to express his opinions openly. And besides, maybe the Nazis were right about this one thing. Perhaps the Russians are as bad as people are constantly saying. Three of his brothers are still in Siberian prison camps. Only Willi has ever made it back to Berlin.

"I'll probably be going back to Washington in a week or two," Denny says. "While the hearings are in recess, they want to interview me about some more people I knew at Harvard."

"I see."

"I tell you, it breaks my heart, Wulf. To think of my own close friends betraying our country like that. Do they really believe they'd be better off under communism? Hell, the first thing the communists will do when they take over is shut places like Harvard down for good. And the second thing they'll do is round up all the Harvard men they can find and shoot us. You'd think anybody smart enough to graduate from an Ivy League school would understand that."

The rest of the way home, Wulf listens to Denny's bitter, unending ruminations. He doesn't much like Denny when he's in one of these moods, so he tries his best to ignore what he hears.

* * *

Wulf trudges slowly up the corridor, exhausted from his workout. The guys at the gym are all the time telling him he should enter physique contests, that he'd be a sure winner. From the photos he's been shown of the winners of some competitions, he thinks they might be right. But he doesn't want to risk the notoriety, and he knows Denny wouldn't be pleased by it either. He already attracts too much attention for his own comfort just walking around the city. It's enough for him that he's as strong as he is and looks like he looks. Not to mention that he still keeps improving bit by bit. He doesn't have to compete against others to take pride in this. Rudi always used to insist that competing against himself was the greatest thrill of all, and Wulf has finally come to understand what he meant by it.

At the front door of the apartment he reaches into his pocket for his keys. Then he notices that it's slightly ajar. That damned Denny. He's probably been out on the town, come home falling down drunk and left the door open. Again. Wulf can't remember how many times he's reminded Denny about this. It's not safe. Something terrible could happen just because of this drunken absent mindedness. Wulf goes inside, locking the door behind him. From the foyer, he can hear the television in Denny's bedroom upstairs. It seems like almost every night he has to go in and turn off the set after Denny passes out. He thinks this is an unconscionable waste of electricity. He goes into the kitchen for a drink of water, then heads upstairs to make sure Denny is properly settled for the night.

Denny's bedroom is dark except for a bedside lamp and the glow of the television screen. Wulf crosses the room and turns off the set. He leaves the lamp on in case Denny wakes up in the night, though that isn't at all likely. Denny usually doesn't move a muscle until noon or later after he's been on a serious drunk, which this one smells like. Wulf is shutting the bedroom door behind him when he realizes that he doesn't hear Denny's usually stentorian snoring. Uneasy, he re-enters the room and moves quickly to the bed. He's heard of people choking on their own vomit in their sleep or suffering other fatal reactions to the massive ingestion of alcohol and suddenly fears the worst.

Sure enough, Denny's not breathing. Wulf checks for a pulse and finds none. He's reaching for the bedside phone to summon help when he sees the marks on Denny's neck, ugly and livid even in the dim light, and the sight stops him dead. Denny has been strangled. He can't remember how many times he's warned Denny about the kind of guys he brings home. He can hardly count the late night trips to the emergency room he's made with a bloody, beaten up Denny. He's feared this exact thing almost since the beginning.

Denny's been strangled. It's the cook's night out, and Wulf's alone in the apartment. He knows he should call the police but he's afraid to. They'll surely think he did it. Even if there's not enough evidence to convict him, he's bound to stand trial. Even if he's acquitted, it seems certain he'll be deported, and, once back in Germany, thrown back in prison. He briefly considers going to his room, packing a bag and taking off into the night. But he understands full well the impression of guilt that would create. And after all Denny's done for him, he can't just leave him here like this. He has to do something. He mentally runs down the list of Denny's friends. Mostly they're just like Denny. Rich, lazy, useless in an emergency. They drink too much, smoke too much, gossip savagely about each other, steal each other's boyfriends and servants. He can't imagine any of them being much help right now.

Then it comes to him: Barry Zuckerman. Not a member of Denny's inner circle—Jews seem to make them nervous. Wulf has never once seen Barry drunk. Barry has never tried to get into Wulf's pants. Barry has never repeated gossip in Wulf's presence. And Barry is a successful attorney. If anybody can help right now, Barry is the man. And if anybody Denny knows will actually be willing to help, Barry is that man too.

Wulf brushes a lock of hair back off Denny's forehead. He goes downstairs to the study to make the call, feeling it would be improper to have this conversation in the presence of Denny's body. Denny's address book is in its usual place. He finds Barry's number and picks up the phone, glancing at his wristwatch as he does so. Ten o'clock. He has no idea what kind of hours Barry keeps, though if he's at home this time of night that's one more thing he doesn't have in common with Denny's crowd. Wulf listens with mounting dismay to the ringing on the other end. He doesn't know what he'll do if Barry doesn't pick up.

"Hello."

"Mr. Zuckerman?"

"Speaking."

"This is Wulf. Denny Blackford's chauffeur."

"Good evening, Wulf. What can I do for you?"

"Mr. Zuckerman, I just arrived home from the gymnasium. And I…I'm afraid I found Denny dead. I think he's been strangled."

"That damned fool," Zuckerman explodes. "If I've told him once I've told him a thousand times, sooner or later one of his cheap hustlers was going to cut his throat. Damn it to hell."

"I know, Mr. Zuckerman. I warned him too. So many times I can't tell you. I wish he had taken our advice. It's a terrible thing. And I didn't know what to do. So I called you."

"Good man. Have you called the police?"

"I was afraid to. I'm sure they will believe I did it."

"Right. Just hang on a moment while I think this through."

"All right."

Wulf holds onto the phone like a man overboard grasping a life preserver.

"Wulf?"

"Yes, Mr. Zuckerman?"

"First of all, I want you to call me Barry, O.K? Mr. Zuckerman is either my father or my grandfather."

"I'm afraid Denny wouldn't like that."

"That really doesn't matter now. And even if he was still with us, it's none of his business what I want you to call me, right?"

"If you say so."

"I do. Now tell me, when did you get back to the apartment?"

"Not more than ten minutes ago."

"Did anyone see you come in?"

"No. I came in through the service entrance."

"There was no one on the elevator with you?"

"It's self service after eight p.m."

"I don't just mean the attendant. Was there anyone at all on it with you?"

"No one."

"You're absolutely certain?"

"Yes."

"All right. I want you to get out of there. Right this minute. Don't touch anything, you hear? And don't go to your room and pack a suitcase or anything like that. You say you just came in from the gym?"

"That's right."

"Did you have anything with you?"

"A small bag. My workout things."

"Take that with you. Leave quickly. Take the emergency stairs, not the elevator, and make sure no one sees you."

"But where am I going?"

"You know that place down in the Village Denny has you take him to sometimes?"

"Yes."

"Go there. And once you get there, don't leave. I'll call the bartender when it's time for you to come back. Don't be concerned if it's an hour or more, understand?"

"I think so."

"Good. I'll take care of everything."

* * *

It's after one a.m. when Wulf returns home. There are police cars and an ambulance in front of the building. Two uniformed officers stand at the entrance, flanking the doorman.

"Evening, Carswell," he says to the doorman, trying his best to appear no more than casually curious. "What's going on?"

"Evening, Wulf. There's been some trouble up at Mr. Blackford's place. His attorney Mr. Zuckerman is there with the police."

"But what is it? What has happened?"

Carswell glances at the officer on his right, who shakes his head.

"I'm sorry, Wulf, that's all I can tell you. Mr. Zuckerman said I should tell you he wants you to come up."

"All right."

He races through the lobby to the elevators, giving the right impression, he hopes. Once on the twelfth floor, he hurries to the apartment. Two more police officers are guarding the door, which stands open.

"Whattaya want, buddy?"

"I live here," Wulf blurts. "I am Mr. Blackford's chauffeur. Can someone tell me please what has happened?"

"It's all right, officers," he hears Barry Zuckerman's voice from inside. "Let him through."

"Is that you, Mr. Zuckerman?" Wulf asks, stumbling past the officers. "Where are you?"

"In the living room."

"But what has happened? Has Mr. Blackford been robbed?"

He enters the living room. Barry Zuckerman sits on the sofa facing the fireplace. Two middle aged men in badly tailored suits sit in club chairs at right angles to him. They look up at Wulf.

"Who's this, then?" one of them asks.

"Mr. Blackford's chauffeur," Barry tells them.

"Please, Mr. Zuckerman, where is Mr. Blackford?"

"Perhaps you'd better sit down, Wulf."

Wulf drops his small duffel bag and sits down on the sofa beside Barry. He feels better already, seeing Barry there and obviously in charge of the situation. He cautions himself not to look relieved.

"I'm afraid I have some bad news. Denny, I mean Mr. Blackford, is dead."

"But how? Was he taken sick? I wouldn't have gone out this evening if he had complained of not feeling well."

"He was strangled, Wulf. The doorman let two gentlemen in just after eight o'clock. Denny told him it would be all right to send them up. The door-man never saw them come out again. Denny had called me earlier to come over for a drink at ten thirty. When I arrived, the doorman couldn't get Mr. Black-ford to respond on the house phone. So we came up and found him dead in his bed. And no sign of the visitors. They must have gone out the service entrance."

"But it can't be," Wulf says, shaking his head and hoping against hope his appearance isn't arousing any suspicions on the part of the two men in suits.

"Wulf, these gentlemen are Detectives O'Reilly and Fitzpatrick. They want to ask you a few questions."

"All right," Wulf says, trying not to sound nervous.

"Don't worry," Barry smiles, "I'll be here the whole time."

* * *

"I'm sorry it's so small," Barry Zuckerman says, looking down at the sofa bed he's just finished putting sheets on. "I'm afraid you'll be awfully uncomfortable."

"It's just fine," Wulf says, still shaken. "I've slept in much worse places."

"I know," Barry nods.

"What?"

"That tattoo on your arm. I've seen them before. I know what they mean."

"Oh."

"We lost a lot of relatives in the camps. But two of my cousins survived. They're over here now."

"I was in Bergen-Belsen," Wulf says. "Then Dora-Mittelbau."

"It's all right if you don't want to talk about it. That's not why I brought it up. I just wanted you to know that I know. I've known for a long time."

"You never said anything."

"It wasn't any of my business. But when you called tonight so frightened of the police, I knew you had to be thinking about that."

Wulf nods.

"You do trust me, don't you?"

"Yes."

"And you believe what I told you? The police have no reason to think you had anything to do with this?"

"I suppose."

"It's the truth," Barry says. "You have nothing to worry about."

"Perhaps not from the police," Wulf says. "Because of your help. And I know it's terrible of me to think of it at such a time as this. With poor Denny dead. But I now have no job and no home."

"Didn't I tell you on the phone I would take care of everything?"

"Yes."

"Well, I meant it. Everything. Tomorrow morning I want you to go back down to that place in the Village where I sent you tonight and have a talk with Charlie the bartender. Tell him I sent you and that you need a job."

"Charlie is the boss? He can hire me?"

"Not exactly," Barry grins. "I'm the boss."

"You?"

"That's right."

"It's very kind of you, but I'm afraid I know nothing about working in a bar."

"Charlie can teach you everything you need to know. It's not that hard. And he'll be glad of the help. Business is booming lately. You saw it last night. Cram packed, Charlie said it was. On a Tuesday, yet. Charlie has been begging me to hire somebody, but I didn't want to take just anybody off the street. I wanted somebody I can trust. Like I do Charlie. So it's perfect, you see? And when you've finished talking with him, you'll go around the corner to a little apartment building I'll give you the address for. There's a fifth floor walkup that's just been redecorated. It won't be what you're used to, but you'll be able to afford it, and it's convenient to the bar."

"You know the landlord?"

"I am the landlord."

"But why?"

"Why what, Wulf?"

"Well, you are an attorney. Very successful, Denny always said. Making lots and lots of money. I'm sorry, but you know how he and his friends talk about rich Jews."

"Yes."

"So why do you own a bar and an apartment building?"

"Because regardless of what Denny and his friends say about me, I'm not rich like they are. If I get in trouble I can't just go to my family and ask them to write a check. I don't have a trust fund that pays me a quarterly allowance so that I don't have to work for a living. I'm like you. I have to work to support myself. And I'm not stupid either. I'm a homosexual. The state of New York could revoke my privilege to practice law tomorrow. Then where would I be? So instead of buying fancy cars and giving huge parties and traveling in Europe for months on end like some people I know, I buy up businesses and properties. The bar and the apartment building you'll be living in aren't the half of it. Later on, when I'm completely independent and no one can ever destroy my life because I sleep with men, there'll be plenty of time for extravagance."

"I see."

"Makes sense, doesn't it?"

"Absolutely, but…"

"But what?"

"Why are you helping me like this? Denny's friends are always offering to help me, but they always want things in return. You know what I'm talking about."

Barry nods.

"But you never act like you want anything from me. Even now, you are making up this bed instead of just taking me to your own bedroom."

"You and I are a lot alike, Wulf. Oh, I know, you're not Jewish. You're not a doctor or attorney or a stockbroker. Nobody will ever describe me as handsome, and I could spend the rest of my life in a gym lifting weights and I'd never be put together like you are. I'm not talking about superficialities like those.

I'm talking about other things. Things that really matter. And I guess the easiest way to explain it is just to say that I believe that I'm not doing anything for you that you wouldn't do for me if our situations were reversed. And if you did help me in such a way, you wouldn't expect a thing in return."

"But…"

"Stop right there. I've watched you take care of Denny the last three and a half years. I know better than anyone what a mess he was, so you don't have to feel disloyal talking frankly about him. I know it can't have been easy for you, keeping him out of scrapes. I know about all the guys you threw out of that apartment when they threatened to hurt him. I know about a lot of other things you did for him. Way more than any normal employee would have bothered to do. Hell, do you have any idea how many chauffeurs he'd gone through before you showed up? Well, all that may not seem like much to you. Knowing you, it probably doesn't. But that bastard owed you."

"He didn't owe me anything. He paid me very well. He provided me a home. He gave me a chance to be in America."

"Don't you see? You just proved my point about you," Barry says. "You're so focused on everything he did for you that you don't understand what you did for him."

"I did what he needed me to do. What he paid me for."

"You just don't get it. And what's ironic is how little he deserved it. Regardless of how he treated you, he was a pretty rotten guy all around. I know, I know. It's wrong to speak this way of someone so recently departed. But it's also wrong to be dishonest. To pretend you liked and respected someone just because they're gone now. That kind of hypocrisy nauseates me more than I can tell you. I won't dirty myself with it. You know why this happened, don't you?"

"He found the wrong hustlers," Wulf says. "What else could it be?"

"You know, Wulf, that's just what the killers want the police to think. It's obvious they knew Denny pretty well or they wouldn't have gone about it this way. And who knows? The police are so ignorant when it comes to people like us that they just may believe it. But those men weren't hustlers. I can guarantee you that. That much is obvious from the way Carswell described them. He's seen enough real ones come and go to know the difference."

"It's true," Wulf nods.

"It's this business in Washington. You know about it?"

"With Mr. Cohn? And Senator McCarthy?"

"Exactly."

"I know only what Denny told me about it. I didn't understand it very well."

"They've been destroying the reputations and careers of perfectly innocent people."

"Denny says those people are communists."

"Wulf, back before the war times were very hard in America. And a lot of people became convinced that the communists were the only ones who understood or cared about the plight of the working people."

"I have heard of this. It was the same in Germany. Before Hitler."

"Yes. Well, here in America there was no Hitler. There was democracy, real democracy, and millions of Americans exercised their choice and became members of the Communist Party. We didn't know about Stalin then, or a lot of the terrible things the Soviets did, and the communist program seemed to make sense. The American communists didn't hate our country. Many people joined the party because they sincerely believed that the communists were our best defense against the Nazis. At the time nobody else was speaking out against the Nazis. Many Americans believed the propaganda about how Hitler was reviving Germany until it was too late to stop him without going to war. Others joined the communists because they thought there was a chance to make a better world for everybody, not just the rich. In those days it was perfectly legal to be a party member. And as far as that goes, it isn't just the real communists Senator McCarthy and that bastard Cohn are going after. It's socialists, too. You know the difference?"

"Of course."

"Well, O.K. After the war was over we started to figure out what an animal Stalin was. Just as bad, in his own way, as Hitler had been. And it became obvious pretty quickly that we couldn't consider the Russians our allies any longer. So people's feelings about communism changed over night. But these people that Denny has been implicating are just as horrified by Stalin and the Soviets as anyone else. They're as loyal to America as Denny is himself—I mean was. He's hurt a lot of people who didn't deserve it. And he's made a lot more people angry. I told him he should never have gotten into bed with Roy Cohn. I knew Cohn was just using him because of his money and his social connections. Denny was too egotistical to see that. And I knew sooner or later something like this would happen. Frankly, he was asking for it."

"So you think someone actually tried to get revenge on him? For testifying in the hearings?"

"Either that or they wanted to stop him before he could hurt anyone else. McCarthy and Cohn are far from finished."

* * *

Wulf is standing behind the bar polishing glasses when Barry comes in.

"Evening, Wulf," he says, stepping up to the bar. "How's things?"

"Fine, Mr. Zuckerman."

"Wulf," Barry shakes a finger at him, "what did I tell you?"

"Sorry," Wulf gulps. "Barry. What can I get you?"

"You'll soon figure out that my usual is a Virgin Mary," Barry grins. "Not a very appropriate drink for a Jew, but it suits me in other ways."

"Coming right up."

"Make it a triple," Barry says. "I feel like raising some hell tonight. And bring it to me back in the office, will you?"

Wulf pours out the tomato juice and garnishes it, then carries it back to the tiny office where Barry sits slumped behind the desk.

"Thanks, Wulf," Barry says. "Close the door, O.K? And pull up that chair. We need to talk."

"Is it bad news?" Wulf asks. "Something about Denny?"

"It is about Denny," Barry says. "And it depends on what you consider bad news."

"They haven't found the killers yet? But it has been six weeks already."

"No, Wulf. They haven't found the killers. And I don't think they're going to."

"But why not? Surely the police..."

"They're not really looking."

"But they must find the men who killed Denny. It's their job."

"Listen, you heard the questions they asked you."

"Yes," Wulf says. "About Denny's hustlers."

"That's right. You see, they're convinced that's what happened. Denny just got mixed up with the wrong boys."

"But you were sure it had something to do with the senator's investigation."

"That's right, but I haven't told the police that."

"Why not?"

"Because Mr. Cohn and Senator McCarthy are extremely powerful men. They'll be very unhappy if word gets out that one of their star witnesses was killed as revenge for his testimony. It might stop other witnesses from cooperating with them, you see. They wouldn't appreciate that at all. It might even occur to them to take it out on me. And I'm just a little guy."

"Surely they wouldn't do such a thing."

"Trust me, Wulf. They would. Anyway, that's pretty much beside the point. The police aren't going to listen to me in any case."

"Why not?"

"I'm a defense attorney. The police distrust me on priniciple. And I'm a Jew besides. You've been in the States long enough to know that being a Jew is still a big deal to a lot of people."

"Yes."

"So the police think a couple of hustlers killed Denny, and they've apparently said as much to Denny's parents. Now the Blackfords are very wealthy and influential people. The last thing they want is for the police to make an arrest and have the D.A. bring a couple of hustlers to trial. Can you imagine the publicity? So what I think has happened is that Denny's father and uncles must have suggested to the police that it might be best if Denny's killers aren't pursued too vigorously."

"But can they do that? Just let it drop?"

"Of course they can do it. Anyone who's rich and powerful enough can do that."

New York: 1956

Wulf glances at his watch. Eleven twenty-five p.m. Just over ten minutes have passed since the last time he checked. He sets down the glass he's polishing and leans on the bar. His eagle eyes sweep the room and see exactly what they saw two minutes ago. Rain is falling, audible each time the door opens to admit a dampened patron. It's too early yet for anyone to think seriously of leaving. Judy Garland and Edith Piaf sing in mournful alternation on the jukebox. No fan of either singer, Wulf, whose taste runs to symphony and opera, sometimes wakes in the middle of the night with the words to these songs on his unwilling lips. A pall of cigarette smoke hangs overhead like a bank of clouds, its fug almost obliterating an underlying reek of stale beer and after shave.

It's the usual Tuesday-and-every-other-night crowd. In their nondescript clothing, johns sit along one side of the long, narrow space ignoring each other, nursing their drinks and pretending not to stare across the abyss with their big, hope starved eyes. Along the other side of the room, hustlers in t-shirts and levis so tight they seem certain to cut off circulation preen and boast to each other just loud enough to make certain they are audible to the johns of their fantastic exploits, some of them violent, some of them even criminal, all the while pretending not merely to be unavailable but not even to be aware of the presence of the johns in the same room with them. Both groups studiously act bored with the whole routine, though Wulf is certain that secretly every last one of them, john and hustler alike, is as deeply engrossed in the proceedings as if what they're performing is the final scene of *La Traviata*. It's just like every other night he has worked here since Barry Zuckerman swooped down like his guardian angel and rescued him from the rubble of Denny Blackford's mysterious demise. The murderers are still at large over three years later. Barry was right: nobody wanted the case solved.

Sometimes Wulf despairs of there being anything in store for these men other than this dire scene repeating itself endlessly. What he observes taking place here is certainly nothing like what he and Rudi thought it meant to be gay, though he has to admit that there were plenty of bars just like this one back in Berlin. He and Rudi just never went to places like that. At least not to stay for more than a few minutes while they greeted friends and gulped down a quick drink. Perhaps that's the point. This is America, where all things are possible, and nearly a generation has passed since those days; why hasn't anything changed? Why isn't there anything more to their lives than this depressing and futile ritual to observe every night and to dread participating in when he gets older? And the chilling corollary to that question: why aren't there any attractive gay men his own age who want more than a quickie in the alley behind the bar? Where are the true love stories, the Rudis and Wulfs of today?

Just then, the man he's been watching surreptitiously for the last several weeks comes in. Tall and broad shouldered, he sports expensive clothing of invariably flattering cut, sleek black hair that Wulf feels an almost uncontrollable urge to bury his nose in and inhale deeply, and glasses that make him look uncannily like Clark Kent just before he steps into the phone booth. Obviously neither john nor hustler, he's been coming to the bar several nights a week for the last month or so. He'll order a drink or two, tip unusually well, speak to no one, sit for half an hour or so, and leave. Well versed now in the arcane etiquette of barroom seductions, Wulf finds himself unaccountably flummoxed when this man appears. Why can't he just go up to him, make a little small talk, and arrange a date? He's done exactly that with dozens of men, perhaps hundreds—though he doesn't like to admit to himself that there have truly been that many—since he first came to New York. If there's such a thing as an expert at it, it's got to be Wulf. He knows people whisper of his conquests all over the city.

The man walks over to the bar, gives Wulf his usual friendly, non-provocative smile, orders a drink, leaves a tip equivalent to its cost, and goes to find his regular seat in the otherwise deserted no man's land between the johns and the hustlers, where he resolutely ignores both groups, gazing just often enough to both dismay and intrigue Wulf, in what might be his direction.

* * *

At the university the next morning, the department chairman's secretary sends a note to Wulf's first class. The chairman would like to see him at eleven o'clock. This summons makes it impossible for Wulf to concentrate during his next two classes. He squirms and doodles through the lectures, one eye at all times on the creeping second hand of his watch. He arrives at Professor Riordan's office early for the appointment, unable to find any worthwhile way of occupying his time elsewhere.

"Good morning, Mr. von Riedel," the secretary says, peering cheerfully up at him through eyeglasses with rhinestone encrusted frames.

"Good morning, Mrs. Feldman."

"Pretty day, isn't it? It looks like spring is finally here."

"Yes," Wulf agrees.

"You know, it seems as if the winters get longer every year. I was just saying to Mr. Feldman this morning at breakfast that I can't ever remember a winter lasting as long as this one has."

"You could be right."

"Mr. Feldman blames it on those sunspots," she continues, "but do you know what I think?"

"What?"

"It's all those A-bomb tests," she says, lowering her voice self consciously. "The explosions have caused the poles to shift and upset the climate."

Her chatter may be frightfully inane but it's somehow comforting all the same. Wulf envies Mr. Feldman, a man he's never met, the companionship of this woman, not because she's a beauty or possessed of a sparkling personality or great intellect, but for the simple reason that she's a living, breathing human being. These days Wulf often thinks he'd give up almost anything, perhaps even sex, just for someone to talk to for more than a few minutes at a time. He's still musing over this when the door to Professor Riordan's office opens and a terrified looking student slips out. The expression on the young man's face makes Wulf's blood run cold. And it's his turn with Riordan next.

"Abby."

"Yes, Professor."

"Is Mr. von Riedel out there?"

"Yes, he is, Professor. We've been having such a lovely chat."

"Send him in, please."

"He's on his way, Professor Riordan," she chirps, nodding at Wulf, who's already on his feet and heading toward the office door.

"Ah, von Riedel, come in, come in," Professor Riordan grunts, emptying his pipe into a wastebasket. "Close that door behind you, won't you?"

"Certainly, Professor."

"Do have a seat. Be right with you."

Wulf sits across the desk from the professor, now busily engaged in refilling his pipe.

"Nice day, isn't it?" Riordan asks.

"Very nice," Wulf agrees. Over six years he's been in this country now and he still isn't used to these people's inability—or is it unwillingness?—to come straight to the point.

"About time spring showed up," Riordan mumbles, puffing away like a steam locomotive.

"Indeed."

"Now Mr. von Riedel, I've just been looking over your file. Most impressive, I can tell you. Most impressive. It's not often we have a student of your caliber in the department. Your professors have only the highest praise for your scholarship. And to be finishing up your degree in only six semesters; most impressive, as I say."

"You are very kind," Wulf says.

"That brings us to the subject of your graduate school application."

"There's not a problem, is there?"

"Problem? Certainly not. We'd be crazy not to admit you. You're exactly the kind of candidate we're trying to attract here. It's just that I heard a rumor, never mind where, that you've also applied to Columbia. Now tell me, is there any truth to that?"

"I did apply there," Wulf admits. "Just in case. I didn't want to—how do Americans put it?—put all my eggs in one basket."

"Yes, yes, of course," Riordan nods. "I'd probably have done the same myself if I had the brain you seem to have. Well, we certainly wouldn't want to lose you to them, so in order that there's no misunderstanding about it I wanted to explain to you exactly what we're going to be offering you. You'll advance to Ph.D. candidacy immediately, no M.A. required. We've assigned you a teaching assistantship of two sections of World History survey per semester, for which you'll be paid the standard stipend. We've assigned you an office which you'll share with three other graduate students. We've also assigned you a carrel in the library. You'll be eligible to teach upper division courses as soon as you successfully complete your comprehensive examinations. All tuition and registration fees will be waived. In addition, you'll receive a textbook and supplies allowance of two hundred and fifty dollars per semester. You'll receive a grant of one thousand dollars for foreign travel, good next summer and renewable for each summer after that. Now how does all that sound?"

Wulf is astonished. He hasn't dared to hope for anything like this.

"Wonderful, Professor."

"I suppose you'll need a few days to think it over. But I need a definite commitment from you by, oh, let's say the fifteenth of the month, shall we?"

Wulf is tempted to accept the offer on the spot, but he knows what Barry would say about that. He has to keep Riordan hanging for at least a day or two or he'll never hear the end of it.

"That won't be a problem."

"Very well, then," Professor Riordan says. "I hope you'll give the matter your most careful consideration. It's a very good offer we're making. I think you'll see that when you think it over. I seriously doubt anyone will be able to better it."

* * *

As soon as Professor Riordan's office door is closed behind him, Wulf rushes off to find a phone.

"Zuckerman, Fenstermacher, and Cline."

"This is Wulf von Riedel. Is Mr. Zuckerman in?"

"One moment please."

Wulf counts to five before Barry picks up.

"Wulf? Is anything wrong?"

"Not a thing in the world. Listen, I apologize for calling you at the office, but I just couldn't wait to tell you. It's the most wonderful thing."

"You've finally found Mr. Right."

"Sorry, not that wonderful."

"Damn. I tell you, Wulf, there's nothing like settling down with someone nice."

"Honestly, Barry, you don't have to sell me on it. Just find me the guy, would you?"

"If you were really trying to find somebody it wouldn't take you two minutes. So what's up?"

"I'm admitted to graduate school. I just saw the department chairman. They're offering me an assistantship and stipends and travel grants, you name it. It's like Christmas. Oops, sorry."

"No offense, pal. Didn't I tell you Jeremy is a WASP?"

"That's right, you did. Presbyterian, was it?"

"Yep. Well, Wulfele, what terrific news."

"Isn't it?"

"Yes indeed. Congrats, my friend."

"It's all thanks to you. If you hadn't made me start college in the first place, this would never have happened."

"I saw the potential, that's all."

"That's all? All? Hell, man, you gave me a new life."

"So go thou and do likewise."

"Right," Wulf says. "I've never forgotten that sermon."

* * *

Wulf would like to celebrate his good fortune, but it's Charlie's night off. Charlie would trade with him, but Charlie does him so many favors already he'd hate to ask. So Wednesday finds him in his regular place behind the bar, even more frustrated than usual, promising over and over to treat himself to something really special on his next night off. No matter how he chooses to celebrate, he knows it will be a disappointment because there's no one special to share it with. This isn't his first stroke of good fortune, after all. He knows how the whole thing works.

It's rainy again tonight, but not a soft shower like last night. It's coming down in sheets outside: a real downpour. This brings more hustlers in from the street, which in turn animates the johns even though the boys are more bedraggled than usual. Still, whatever the boys look like, the johns are ecstatic. They have more to choose from. And no matter how blasé they seem, the boys are desperate for warm, dry places to spend the night. The prices negotiated will be below the usual. As with everything else in this country, the law of supply and demand is in force. Tonight's conditions point to a buyers' market.

The unaccustomed noise and commotion have Wulf a little on edge. He barely notices when the black haired man slips in a little later than usual and makes his way through the crowd to the bar.

"Evening," he says, smiling that smile that seems terrifyingly sincere.

"Evening," Wulf returns the greeting, staring wistfully at the usually immaculate but now touseled, rain shiny hair and wishing he had the guts to just yank the guy over the counter and plant a deep, juicy one on him.

"Wet out there." The man's sky blue eyes sparkle behind the lenses of his glasses.

"And in here," Wulf grins, tilting his head toward a couple of soaked to the skin hustlers who've sidled up right beside the black haired man with the apparent intention of actually buying drinks for themselves. Their sodden t-shirts are dripping onto the bar. "Your usual?"

"Yes, thanks."

Wulf pours the drink, and as he does his radar goes off. After nearly three years working here he can smell police raids, and this one's about to start. He should have known to expect it with the place this packed.

"Listen very carefully," he tells the man, not looking up from what he's doing.

"Beg your pardon?"

"There's about to be a bit of trouble here," Wulf says, not daring even to mouth the word "raid" because of the panic that might ensue. "No, don't turn around. Please, it's very important that you do exactly as I say. If you do, I can probably get you out of here. Now, move down to the far end of the bar with me."

"What's this all about?"

"I can't explain," Wulf says, already moving. "There's no time."

He notices with relief that the man is moving along with him. He swings up the hinged section at the end of the bar, grabs the man firmly by the upper arm and pulls him through the opening.

"Christ, what are you doing?"

Wulf shoves him through the doorway into the hall leading past the office and to the alley exit. He can already hear a commotion in the front part of the bar.

"See that door back there? Go through it. It'll put you in the alley. Once you're outside take a left, not a right, and keep going. Stay in the alley for at least two more blocks. And whatever you do, don't come back tonight."

Wulf slams the door on the man and hopes for the best. There are half a dozen uniformed officers inside the bar now, cuffing people, johns only as always, and taking names. It's time to call Barry.

* * *

Like always after a raid, they're open the very next night. Most of the johns are back, some of them sporting black eyes and other assorted bruises like badges of honor. All of the hustlers are there, too, just like nothing happened. Individually or as a group they don't look particularly brave, but what else can it mean that such mistreatment as they've so recently been subjected to hasn't deterred them? Wulf doesn't see why the police don't get the message. The place is here to stay and so is its clientele. Why waste their time and the taxpayers' money harassing them? Why not just leave them alone? It's not like they're doing anyone any harm.

He's ruminating over this when Charlie emerges from the office carrying a dozen long stemmed roses stuck into the mouth of a carafe.

"Roses? Here? What, did somebody die?"

"They were delivered this afternoon. I just now remembered they were in back. There's a card addressed to 'Blondie.' That sure as hell ain't me. Who do you suppose they're for? Whoever could it be?"

He hands Wulf the card.

"'Thanks for last night'," Wulf reads aloud.

"Looks like you've landed a live one," Charlie says. "You must have fucked him so good."

"Nah," Wulf says, figuring it out. "It's just some guy I helped sneak out the back way during the raid."

"God, Wulf, don't let Barry hear about it. You'll catch hell. You know the rule. They have to take care of themselves. Otherwise it's obstruction of justice charges for the bar owner and a possible loss of liquor license."

"I couldn't help myself," Wulf says. "This guy's different. I mean, he's kind of a regular. But he's not really like the johns, and he's definitely not a hustler. He comes in alone and he leaves alone. I know you've noticed him. My height. Probably about two hundred pounds. Black hair. Glasses."

"God, yeah," Charlie nods. "That movie star type. Pretty boy mug and those big, big baby blues."

"That's him."

"Man, those shoulders. If he's the guy you sneaked out of here last night, I don't blame you one bit and neither would Barry. But there is something I don't understand."

"What's that?"

"Why you haven't had him already. I mean, shit, boy, you nail everybody halfway decent that ever comes through that door. You hardly have to try—it just happens. But I've been watching you look at that guy and I know you haven't made your move yet. So what gives?"

"I don't know," Wulf says, hanging his head. "Too classy for me, I guess."

"You're an idiot. You know that?"

* * *

As Wulf is locking the front door a few nights later, he sees the black haired man standing a little way down the sidewalk.

"Evening," he says.

"Morning, you mean," Wulf corrects him, yawning. "I'm afraid we're closed."

"Oh, that's all right," the man says. "I didn't really come for a drink."

"Well then, thanks for the roses."

"You got them. Good. I didn't know whose name to put on the card."

"You didn't have to do it, you know."

"The hell I didn't. I get my name in the papers like that, I can kiss my job goodbye. I know you know how that works. No, you really saved my life, buddy. I have to tell you, the whole thing gave me a hell of a scare. I swore I'd never come back here again. But, well, then I got to thinking I'd like to thank you in person."

"That's very nice of you," Wulf stammers.

"So, um, thanks," the man says, offering Wulf his hand. "Thanks very much."

Wulf shakes the man's hand and feels something like an electric shock running up his arm.

"Listen, I was thinking maybe..."

"What?" Wulf asks suddenly breathless.

"Naw, it's awfully late. You've been working all night. You're probably beat."

"Not really," Wulf says, stifling another yawn. "Did you have something in mind?"

"Nothing special. Cup of coffee somewhere. That is if you know of a place that's open."

"Sure," Wulf says. "I'd like that."

"You would?" the man sounds surprised. "Well, that's terrific."

"I know just the place," Wulf says. "Great coffee and they're open all night. Pie, too, if you're hungry. The lemon meringue is really good."

"Sounds great."

"Follow me."

They fall into step together and a sudden feeling of warmth washes over Wulf. Damn if he hasn't got a lump in his throat. And only because this handsome stranger with beautiful manners wants to have a cup of coffee with him.

"Listen," the man says, halfway down the block, "I feel really stupid about this: my name's David."

"My name is Wulf. Pleased to meet you."

"My God," the man says, stopping in his tracks and staring hard at Wulf. "No, it couldn't be. That would be too much of a coincidence."

"What would?"

"I knew a man named Wulf once. Right at the end of the war."

"Come over here," Wulf says, heart pounding. They step into the brightly lit circle of sidewalk under a streetlight. He stares into the sky blue eyes behind the lenses of David's eyeglasses, and it's the infinite kindness he sees there that he finally recognizes.

"I can't believe it," the man says, astonishment on his face and in his voice. "It is you."

"Yes," Wulf nods, eyes filling with tears.

"What was it? Von Riedel?"

"Dachau," Wulf chokes. "1945. And you're Captain Lancaster."

"Not any longer. I've been a civilian since they demobilized me in 'forty-six. God, so you actually got away."

"With your help," Wulf says. "I worried for months afterward that you might have gotten into trouble."

"No," David says. "Nothing ever happened to us. We helped several other guys after you. You're the first one I've ever run into. And here you are in New York, working in a queer bar."

"That's just temporary," Wulf says.

"Oh?"

"I'm graduating from NYU next month."

"No kidding. What are you studying?"

"History."

"I studied history myself."

"Oh, yes?"

"At Princeton. Boy, this is a damned shame."

"What?"

"There's not a bar still open in the whole city. We should be drinking to this meeting, not christening it with pie and coffee."

* * *

"That Clark Kent guy never showed up again, did he?" Charlie remarks one evening a few weeks later. "Raid must have scared him away for good. Damn shame, that. He sure did give the joint some class."

"I guess," Wulf mutters.

"Hold on there," Charlie says. "What's that blush about?"

"Blush? What blush?"

"You know I'll torture you if you don't talk, so 'fess up."

"I…well, I've kind of been dating him."

"Hot damn," Charlie gives his left deltoid a slap that stings. "So what's he like in the sack? Good as he looks? Or even better? Those matinee idol types, oh my God. I fucked one once and I wasn't right for a month. Swore I'd never do it again. They're just too damn dangerous."

"I honestly don't know."

"Don't bullshit me, son."

"I'm not. It's the truth."

"Well fuck me raw," Charlie says, looking amazed.

"We haven't done anything. Not a God damned thing. Not even a goodnight kiss."

"And now long has this been going on?"

"Since the week after the raid. I've been seeing him three, sometimes four times a week."

"Well hell. If you're not fucking the man silly, just what do you do to while away the hours?"

"We try out new restaurants. We went to the opera once. We take long walks through the city. He just moved here a few months ago. He likes me to show him places. The parks. The buildings."

"Unbelievable."

"I know."

"So tell me, why are you still seeing him if he don't put out?"

"Come on, Charlie. You know why."

"Well, damn me, I guess I do. Never thought I'd see the day when somebody got to you that way, big boy."

New York: 1969

Wulf signs the papers and hands the clipboard back to the driver.

"See you in San Francisco," the man says, climbing into the cab.

The truck seems ridiculously large. It's hard to imagine something that size being required to transport the contents of two small apartments, but that's what the moving company sent. Wulf steps to the curb. The engine of the truck rattles to life. Its roar reverberates off the walls of the buildings lining the narrow street. Smoke erupts from the exhaust stacks. There's a sound of gears grinding, and the truck lurches into motion. With the traffic this afternoon, there's no telling how long it will take for it to reach Dave's building just a few blocks away. Wulf will get there faster on foot.

* * *

It all started a couple of years ago. They'd been to Europe on vacation so many times they were a little bored with it, and Dave suggested San Francisco instead. Neither of them expected to fall in love. Wulf was downright cynical about it. The place simply couldn't live up to its hype. Who knew it would exceed expectations? They extended their stay three times. On the flight home, they discussed moving. Wulf can't remember who brought it up, but there wasn't much argument. They had both fallen and fallen hard. It was easy for Dave. His career was portable. Wulf had to send out his vita, attend conferences and hiring fairs, sacrifice a goat or two. It took time. But now it's all worked out. He'll start his new position at Berkeley in the fall.

* * *

It seems crazy at their age, starting from scratch in a new city. Most people in their late forties are getting ready to start that long downhill coast toward retirement. Most people in their late forties are intent on playing things safe. Most people in their late forties are at least a little bit bored with each other. To liven things up they buy new furniture, have an affair, take up an eccentric hobby. But this? Well, God knows there's no cure for complacency like burning down the house around you. Wulf can't believe he isn't terrified. In middle age, he's become absolutely fetishistic about security. But here he goes, avidly stepping out onto the tightrope no more than a couple of strides behind Dave.

* * *

When he stops to think about leaving the city Wulf feels like an unfaithful husband. It is New York, after all, that gave him his new life. It made room for him when it seemed there wasn't a safe place anywhere. It gave him opportunities he never would have dreamed of. It brought Dave and him together. It seems ungrateful to turn his back on the city now, after all that. It has offered him nothing but good, and here he is leaving it behind.

He makes detours on his way to and from classes at the university to revisit sites he wants to imprint more clearly on his memory. Wherever he goes during these weeks he forsakes the subway for the streets, avid for details half forgotten or never before discovered. The city, which over the years he has learned to take for granted, springs vividly back into his awareness in all its chaotic glory. A thousand vignettes teem in his dreams each night.

In those streets it's full blown spring, as glorious a New York spring as he can recall, but there is something strangely autumnal in Wulf's heart, a sense of things ending.

* * *

A poster of brightly painted Victorians in the window of a travel agency. A busker on the sidewalk across the street from Central Park playing "I Left My Heart In San Francisco" on his saxophone as night falls. A postcard that says "Greetings From Fisherman's Wharf" lying in the gutter in front of Wulf's apartment. The "Rice-a-Roni" jingle playing on the TV in the living room while Wulf stands in the kitchen doorway watching Dave dish up his world famous *coq au vin*. A shot of the Golden Gate Bridge on the cover of a coffee table book he spies across the room at a cocktail party. A feature on the city in an ancient issue of *National Geographic* he finds in the waiting room at his doctor's office. A toy cable car on the mantelpiece at a friend's apartment. The City By the Bay won't leave him alone. It seems as if everywhere he turns there's some reminder. And each time it happens, for just an instant he catches his breath. A moment later he knows exactly what they're doing and why.

* * *

Dave and he are like small children waiting for Christmas, or third graders marking off the days until the end of school. With each passing hour time seems to slow itself down. Each item they check off the list of things that must be done prior to their departure brings satisfaction—but only for a moment. It is as if the list magically accumulates two new tasks for every one they complete.

* * *

Their last night in New York, they go out to dinner with Barry Zucker-man and his newest boyfriend, Jay, a youngster who looks like he shouldn't be allowed out of the house after dark without his mother. Wulf must have looked that young himself once, he thinks, remembering those evenings in Berlin with Rudi when he was still a schoolboy.

As they leave the restaurant and walk up the sidewalk side by side, he moves as close to Dave as he can without actually touching him. Just so he can feel Dave's warmth beside him in the darkness. He and Rudi used to walk hand in hand, but that was a different time and place.

It's a stifling summer night. Humid, and without any air stirring. The streets of the Village are awash with the scruffier varieties of humanity. Sirens wail several blocks away. Barry and Jay chatter behind them like a couple of teenagers.

"I won't miss this climate," Wulf says.

"I won't miss those damned sirens going at all hours."

"They have sirens there, too," Wulf says.

"Let me dream," Dave insists.

"I won't miss the crowds," Wulf says. "And I know what you're about to say. I get to dream, too."

"I won't miss these smells," Dave says. "I know San Francisco doesn't smell like this."

A police car screams past. A second follows it.

"Local color," Barry chortles. "Welcome to Greenwich Village."

"I wonder who those pigs are after," Jay muses.

"I told you," Barry says, "you shouldn't call them that. They're just doing their jobs. This city would be a fucking jungle without them. It wouldn't be safe to walk the streets at night."

"Like it is now?"

"Don't lets have this argument, O.K?"

"Uh oh," Dave mutters. "Trouble in paradise."

"I give it exactly two more weeks," Wulf says. "Not a minute longer."

"Poor Barry."

"It's his own damned fault. There are plenty of men his own age who would kill for a husband like Barry. But will he so much as look at one?"

"That's my point," Dave says. "I feel sorry for any guy who can't be happy with what he can get. Of course some people would say it's easy for me to talk."

Another squad car speeds past. Then two more.

"Does anybody smell smoke?" Barry asks.

"As a matter of fact, yes," Dave says, sniffing the air.

Wulf can smell it, too.

"Since when does it take all those police cars to fight a fire?" Jay asks. "And they wonder why people call them pigs. Always showing up where they're not needed. They're probably doing everything they can to get in the fire department's way and fuck things up."

Suddenly two men run around the next corner.

"It's a riot," one of them yells. "Go back."

"A riot?" Barry asks.

But the men are gone.

"What did they mean, a riot?" Barry asks. "Who ever heard of a riot in the Village?"

A moment later there are more running footsteps. But these are coming from behind them. Wulf turns to look over his shoulder. Three or four men are running full tilt up the block toward them. They stand aside to let the strangers pass.

"Hurry up," one of them shouts. "The cops are calling in units from all over. We need reinforcements."

"What are you talking about?" Barry demands. "Reinforcements? What's that supposed to mean? Are we being invaded?"

One of the men stops. He moves back down the sidewalk toward them. He's panting. His long hair is matted with sweat. He's got a crazy grin plastered across his face like he's just heard the best joke ever.

"It's the pigs, man. They raided a bar. One of our bars, you know? And damn if the guys inside didn't fight back. Have you ever heard of such a thing? But they did it. Now they've got the cops trapped inside of the bar, and it's on fire. But more cops are coming from all over. It's starting to get really crazy, man."

Two more squad cars race past, their sirens and lights bouncing off the walls of buildings all the way up the street.

"What bar?" Wulf asks.

"The Stonewall."

"The Stonewall?" Barry says. "That pigsty? They should just let the cops have it."

"Come on," the long haired man insists. "We need everybody we can get. We've got to show the pigs they can't go on treating us like shit."

"Oh, please," Barry mutters.

"Chicken," Jay taunts. "Barry Zuckerman is a big fat chicken."

"I am not."

"Let's go have a look," Dave suggests.

"Seriously?" Wulf asks.

"What can it hurt?" Dave says.

"I'll tell you what it can hurt," Barry says. "At the very least, you can get arrested. And if it's as bad as this guy says, you could get your head cracked open but good. You know what the cops are like, Wulf. You remember the old days at the bar. Well, nothing has changed. Not one damned thing. Let's get out of here."

"So we can get arrested, can we?" Wulf asks, filled suddenly with a strange exhilaration. "That's O.K. We've got our attorney with us."

"Yeah, Barry," Dave says, "let's go."

San Francisco: 2008

In the beginning there was Stefano Fabiani. An illustration by Tom of Finland became flesh and dwelt among us, full of swagger and authenticity. Serene, unconflicted, devoid of ambiguity, his advent in the city signaled a new dispensation. No longer would gay men bow down before the false idol of trade. They would transform themselves instead into the into the object of their desires. They would find within themselves the manhood so long denied them by the breeders and would stand and say to the world, "we are not the misfits and freaks you call us—we are men as much as anyone". No longer would stereotypes reign: the drag queen, the hairdresser, and the interior decorator would live on, but only in their rightful place as constituents of a broader, more comprehensive community. No longer would nellie and camp be the obligatory styles. They would persist only as items on a menu of possibilities stretching into infinity.

Thus would Tristan Bentley speak today, if Tristan were allowed to speak today. Once again negotiations with the bishop have been unavailing. He is allowed to stand before the crowd in full vestments looking on as Judge Will Crawford officiates, but he may not by word or deed communicate any overt support for the ceremony or its participants. The bishop is not an evil man. Indeed, he is nearly as passionate as Tristan himself on the subject of justice. He is not his own master any more than Tristan is. We do what we can when we can, sufficient unto the day. Or not, as the case may be.

This afternoon, watching as the tribe Big Steve founded and led assembles in the Lundquist-Montgomerys' garden, Tristan senses his late husband's absence like an amputee senses a phantom limb.

* * *

All Big Steve ever wanted was to live his life exactly as he pleased. In that respect he was no different from millions of other men of his generation. But the reality was that he was different from those millions in a way that made such an aspiration nothing less than radical. When in the history of the human race had gay men ever had the option of living exactly as they pleased? Aware of this reality but not obsessively so, not that he'd have been dissuaded by history in any event, he set about his quest. Because he had enlisted in the Korean War era military at an illegally tender age (thanks to the machinations of his Auntie Violetta and Father Rodrigo, the family priest), he found himself retired at a non-commissioned officer's pension at thirty-five. Recuperating from combat injuries at a military hospital on his return from Viet Nam, he found himself enchanted by the San Francisco skyline outside his window. He knew he couldn't live the life he dreamed of back in Brooklyn, surrounded by generations of busybody neighbors, friends, nuns, clergy, and family members, but what about there? The more he stared out that window, the more his choice seemed to make sense. Upon his release from the hospital and separation from the service he had made a brief trip back home to put his affairs in order. On his return to San Francisco, a ridiculously snooty realtor, the kind of homosexual he had no intention of ever becoming, had sold him his house in Eureka Valley. A senior officer right out of a Nazi propaganda film had sworn him in as a member of the San Francisco Police. The stage was set. But aside from Big Steve himself, where was the cast?

* * *

City, home, career: these were the foundation on which Big Steve would build his dream. Because that's how he had always understood it: a dream was not something that happened. A dream was meaningless until you made it real. A pair of Labrador Retrievers filled out the picture. Soon he found a congenial gym, a serious, unpretentious place that catered to true hard core bodybuilders and suffered posers and hangers-on with thinly disguised contempt. Paradoxically, because the focus of the establishment was anything but social, he found that the socializing which actually took place was marked by exactly the sort of casual, low key, guys having beers and shooting the breeze camaraderie he remembered so fondly from the service.

* * *

Sex had never been a problem for Big Steve. He had always found it easy enough to gain satisfaction of a sort with women if that was all that was available, so he rarely felt seriously deprived. He thought of being with women as a rather expensive and complicated form of masturbation rather than real sex, but it was better than nothing. And with his looks and physique, there was no shortage of women, ever, except to the extent that his life in the military limited his access to them. If he had a nickel for every time some gym buddy or pal or barracks mate expressed admiration at his long list of conquests, he'd have been a very wealthy man. Later on, when self styled experts asserted that this aspect of his history made him bisexual, he told them there was no such thing; and if that didn't convince them to at least curtail the discussion, he'd advise them that such logic meant that every man who'd ever had sex with another man in prison must be considered bisexual as well. On occasion, someone would respond to this with the argument that prison life was completely different from life on the outside. To that, Big Steve would reply that it was only different for straights, because everyday life was a prison for gay men. And more than anything, gay was not what you did or didn't do with your body or someone else's. It was what went on in your head.

What he had learned about himself was that regardless of how many women he slept with and how satiated he was thus able to keep his body, sex was a matter of the heart and brain, and in those localities no woman would ever truly please him. Only a man could bring him what he most deeply craved. There were men, too, over the years, though this was of necessity less frequent and a great deal more problematic. Unlike some men of his generation, he found nothing aphrodisiac about the dangers involved. The idea that he could be thrown out of his beloved army, could end up in prison, in a mental institution, or even dead, didn't add any thrill to sex. The risks associated with his kind of sex just made the status quo more intolerable. Moving to San Francisco constituted a major improvement in that respect, but not as big a one as might have been expected. There were plenty of available men. That much was true. And there was even a kind of grudging tolerance of the whole thing. But the appearance of freedom masked an unpredictable reality. The quality of specimens in the pool was uneven at best while their psychology was often questionable. But Big Steve's vision was of a time when his satisfaction could be nothing less than perfect, and he confidently awaited further developments.

* * *

What a man needed, in addition to a city, a career, a home, his faithful dogs and plenty of sex whenever he wanted it made a short list indeed. A lot of men would have looked at what he had already accumulated and called it good. Such was the level of expectations which obtained among gays in those days: there was a general reluctance to ask for too much. Fantasize about it, yes. But seriously aspire to it? Not really. The social context was so oppressive that making any effort at all seemed to be tempting fate. You could lose what little good there was about your life in a heartbeat, so why ask for more? Big Steve had never been one to limit himself to what other men accepted as sufficient, however. What he still lacked were, to his way of thinking, the true essentials: a man to love and a man to be his best friend. Without these, the rest seemed pointless.

He had already selected the first, though it would take some time for Tristan to find him. Still later, Nick Romanovsky would come on the scene, and the components of Big Steve's own particular version of the American Dream would be assembled.

* * *

That could have been the whole story: Big Steve's dream comes true and they all live happily ever after. Except that history had other intentions. Big Steve, Tristan, and Nick weren't just three guys. They were members of a species that evolution was forcing to migrate into a new environment to which it was better adapted. That's how Ned Westerleigh explains it to this day. Their experiences were individual and specific, certainly, but had important collective implications. Big Steve, it turned out, was far from the only gay man in San Francisco who had his particular dream. He was simply one of the first to actualize it so ideally and so visibly. People looked at him with his job and his home and his dogs and his lover and his best pal and thought, "why don't I have that?" or, increasingly, "how do I get that?" Some of them were so bold as to ask him how he'd done it. He hadn't thought of it as any particular accomplishment, but this curiosity indicated to him that others did. He was happy enough to talk about his experiences, but only when asked. He didn't give advice, just shared stories. That was enough. Some people are born gurus, some achieve gurudom, some have gurudom thrust upon them.

* * *

That's how it started. Big Steve never aspired to lead a movement, much less a cult—though that specific accusation was made, more than once, generally by some drunken queen in a fit of pique at having been turned down by Big Steve, or Tristan, or Nick, or all three of them simultaneously. All around them gay San Francisco was inventing itself in a phantasmagoria of fabulousness. Big Steve didn't disapprove of this in principle, though he found certain aspects of it questionable in the extreme. His fundamental argument with the way gay was manifesting itself far and wide was that no alternatives were being presented. It was one big fraternity party. It was a cult of Dionysus, with, paradoxically, a code of dress and behavior as stylized and rigorous as a Byzantine mass. Everyone was either a drag queen, a go-go boy, a hustler/pornstar, a leatherman, or some other fantastic species. Where were the regular guys? Life was one long, drug and alcohol fueled soiree. Conspicuous consumption and outrageous display were obligatory. All of which was—well, a matter of taste, as far as Big Steve was concerned. People could do or be whatever they wanted, as long as their wanting it was authentic and not just a pose or an accommodation to a degree of peer pressure he found astonishing. It was the imperative codifying and enforcing and regimenting the nascent culture that he objected to. It smacked of the schoolyard with its bullies and its tattle tales. Because his orientation was fundamentally libertarian/anarchistic, Big Steve refused to play in that particular sandbox. And though he never considered himself a crusader, he invariably encouraged others to abstain as well, if they felt like it. He didn't swim against the tide, he merely shrugged it off. He was anarchism personified, with the muscle, looks, and ego strength to back it up. The high priests and their acolytes never forgave him for disregarding their hegemony.

* * *

One of the city's most formidable queens once invited Big Steve to a soiree she was giving. She was such a notable personage that an invitation was the gay equivalent to an invitation to Buckingham Palace. Her parties were legendary. People clamored for invitations. People paid exorbitant bribes. People were even rumored to have attempted suicide as a result of having failed to be included on her guest list. Refusing to attend was unthinkable. No one had ever snubbed her majesty that way, the consequences being generally accepted as too dire to contemplate. There was just one problem—the dress code for the evening specified drag, and no one could ever remember an exception having been made to one of the queen's fiats. No exception, ever, for anyone.

Thus did the arbiters and oracles rule the city and thus did they attempt to bring Big Steve to heel.

He didn't go to the party. He might have considered experimenting with drag though he would almost certainly have decided against it, but the second someone tried to make it an imperative he put the possibility out of his mind forever.

The queen broke one of her own rules. She spoke to him about it afterward. That was how serious an infraction Big Steve committed staying home the night of the party. But it was also a sign of what a trophy he would have been and might still be. He could be denigrated, he could be designated taboo, but he couldn't be ignored any more than gravity could. People knew what he had done and that presented too serious a challenge, not just to her, but to queendom generally. It couldn't be left unaddressed.

"Your problem," she told him, "is you take yourself too seriously. You'll never be worth knowing until you get in touch with your feminine side. No gay man ever is."

Big Steve responded by telling her that he'd consider taking her advice on one condition—he'd make a serious effort to get in touch with his feminine side if she would make an equally serious effort to get in touch with her masculine side. Supposing, of course, that she actually had one.

Of such exchanges lifelong feuds are born.

* * *

Big Steve was called everything: dinosaur, Uncle Tom, barbarian, muscle fascist, assimilationist, frump. Him, with his sixty inch chest, thirty-two inch waist, and eight per cent body fat—a frump. Him, with that head of hair his barber worshipped and that complexion his dermatologist said wasn't possible in a man his age—a frump. He was accused of self loathing, being anti-sex, aping the heterosexuals. It was all too ridiculous to bother reacting to. Ironic as well, being vilified by his own people when the real enemy, as he constantly pointed out and everyone should have taken the trouble to ponder carefully, was the straight majority. Still, living well was the best revenge, and nobody lived better than Big Steve. Tristan and Nick seethed, unable to match his Olympian imperturbability. To please Big Steve, Tristan spent what seemed like half his life biting his tongue. Nick, eligible bachelor par excellence though he was, was thrown out of more than one elegant soiree for defending his buddy, or on occasion just for knowing him.

* * *

Big Steve's position was a minority one. He didn't have to have that explained to him. He didn't consider it a position at all. He simply lived his life as he chose. He understood that his way of life wouldn't have suited a lot of men even if they'd known they had the option. But though the majority of gay men in the city played for the other team, not all of them did. Without an effort, without any intention at all, Big Steve attracted a surprising number of adherents. It turned out that not everyone felt compelled to be fabulous. It turned out that his dream, hopelessly mundane and old school though it was labeled by the activists, pundits, and brunch table philosophers, was more compelling than any of the high priests had reckoned on.

* * *

The tribe coalesced slowly at first. Mostly they saw each other at the gym. That's where Big Steve articulated his philosophy and shared his wisdom. The rest of the time they traveled their own paths. Nick was on a more or less permanent rampage through the sex clubs and the back rooms of the city, laying waste to all and sundry on his quest for a Tristan equivalent and amassing a fearsome reputation as a sexual athlete in the process. Jared, still known as J.B. at the time, entertained visions of being adopted by the glamorous pack of go-go boys, part time hustlers, and collegiate-gymnast-and-wrestler types that constituted the Jules de Croteau stable, headquartered in that notorious wedding cake style mansion in Pacific Heights. Matt's flight schedule with the airline and Ashby's medical school classes kept them incommunicado for weeks on end. Kirk stayed busy juggling wife, sons, and boyfriend and spending the quarterly allowance from his trust fund as irresponsibly as he could manage. Cooper served the realm as prince consort to one of the city's reigning queens, and dined, brunched and attended the symphony and the opera in the company of his coterie of young drag queens of a decidedly relentless temperament. Others weren't even in the city yet: the Lundquist twins had yet to make their Fire Island debuts; Buzz still dreamed of someday, somehow escaping the desert and the closet; Sean was playing semi-professional rugby in Toronto and considering giving Australia a try. Griffin dreamed away his life in deepest, darkest Kentucky.

Meanwhile, what seemed like the entire remaining gay population of the city continued its crazy sarabande, donning its chosen finery and lurching from brunch to tea dance to drag show to gallery opening to dinner party to opera gala to opening night at theatre to symphony concert to wet t-shirt contest to orgies both organized and impromptu to black party to white party to underwear party and then to the after party beyond; dishing, dancing, drugging: divine, dizzy, delirious.

For his part, Big Steve lived a life that was the modern day gay analogue of medieval monasticism. He went to work, went to the gym, walked his dogs, washed and waxed his Maseratis, and spent the rest of his time lurking in the house like a Viking warrior in the off season. There was the family diet to attend to: planning menus, shopping, cooking. There were his and Tristan's bodies to maintain. Working out was only the tip of the iceberg: shaving Tristan's chest properly required amazing concentration and a surprising amount of time, for instance, and his own body was substantially larger and more resolutely hirsute. Late at night, with his lover and the Labrador Retrievers safely tucked in upstairs, he passed the wee hours watching old Steve Reeves and Gordon Scott movies on the late, late show, plotting to get his buddies appropriately married off, and thinking up new and amazing ways to fuck the living daylights out of Tristan, who must certainly have been the most thoroughly satiated gay man on the west coast in those days.

* * *

Gradually, the distractions of high gay fabulousness lost their allure, or at least their novelty, and the fundamental verities that Big Steve embodied shone more and more brightly and compellingly against their fading background. The men who had heretofore been little more than gym buddies sought out each other's company more and more frequently and exclusively. They consciously began to emulate Big Steve, quote him, adopt his attitudes, regard him as more than just a source of workout or diet or posing pointers—as an authority on a whole universe of subjects, in fact, including how gay life was best lived. He was Big Steve, their mentor, prophet, and guide. He was the warrior-prince leading them to their destiny.

* * *

By then Big Steve and his crew had attracted the attention of an older generation. These men, survivors of the bad old days of fearsome oppression and the eternal closet, observed this new evolutionary stage with varying types of interest. Many disapproved of everything new in gay, as the old always disapprove of the young, and labeled Big Steve's gang ruffians for no other reason than their unapologetic masculinity and their disdain for unnecessary refinement. Others found the ostentatious seductions of the newly visible mainstream inviting as a sort of youthful fantasy come to life just in time for them to witness it during their waning years. But a steadfast few, like Ned and Wulf and Dave, understood and appreciated what Big Steve's people represented and offered their patronage, thus becoming revered elders of the tribe.

Ned Westerleigh was the youngest son of a British nobleman whose pedigree made the royal family look like a litter of mongrels. He was one of those handful of men in every generation who would be remarkable in any company. He had served during World War II in British intelligence. His exploits had provided the inspiration for more than one writer of espionage fiction—they were too remarkable for treatment in a documentary style—and they kept him from returning to Jolly Olde for several years after hostilities had officially ended.

Unwilling to marry some plutocrat or other's heiress daughter to make his fortune, he'd left the United Kingdom permanently in the aftermath of one of
those spy scandals the British were so good at during the Cold War years, his
cover blown sky high. He'd come to America aristocratic almost beyond description but basically penniless. This was a species Americans had a particular
fondness for, and he made the most of the opportunity that fondness represented. He'd made his fortune several times over but lived relatively modestly.
Philanthropy was perhaps his favorite activity. In his own words, he'd been
everywhere, seen everything, and been introduced to everyone at least once.
He had an encyclopedic knowledge of history, politics, and the arts. His greatest
gifts were his unshockability, his discretion, and his refusal to indulge in judging
others. He had been for many years a bosom companion and sometime lover of
Tommy Yayle, had subsequently become Cooper Luxemberg's patron and mentor, and ended up more or less adopting Big Steve's whole gang. He admired
them for their athleticism and their manners. In these qualities they reminded
him of his days at Winchester and Oxford. They were beautifully behaved when
the occasion warranted, but without any of that stuffiness or over refinement
that so many American gays seemed to consider *de rigueur*. They were a robust,
high spirited crew, and their gatherings brought to his mind the Old Boys' din-
ners of his young adulthood.

     Wulf von Riedel loved Big Steve's tribe because they redeemed his youth.
They were fulfilling the dream he and Rudi had shared in those far off days. It
was as if the Nazis were finally being defeated. The rest of the world had been
liberated in 1945. Now, well over a generation later, it was the turn of Wulf's
own people. He loved them for their earnestness and the courage they showed
daily in this fight. It was a courage he believed was empowered by their devotion for each other, couple by couple and as a group. Observing them as they
fell in love, moved in together, pursued their careers and built their lives, he
recalled his all too brief time with Rudi: here at last was the promised land he
had believed they were entering together. These glorious young men were his
friends and brothers reincarnated as middle class Americans, and he adored
them and all they did, watching over them with solicitude and patience. He
was Scott Bailey's uncle but adopted that role with the entire tribe, becoming
in the process, though he'd have been shocked to realize it, a role model second
only to Big Steve himself. And with Dave Lancaster by his side, he gave them
a glimpse of what it could be like to grow old with the man you loved. As a

couple they represented a possibility neither society nor most of the gay world acknowledged the existence of.

* * *

When Big Steve was shot, Tristan would have given anything to be the one bleeding out onto that sidewalk in the Tenderloin. He didn't want to live in a world where such a thing could happen. He didn't want to live in a world where a man like Big Steve could be anything less than indestructible. His life lost all meaning: he simply couldn't go on. Over the bitter days and weeks that followed, his friends lent him the faith and courage he couldn't muster. Big Steve had taught them how to care for one another, and they gave Tristan his life back.

Officially the case is still open. Tristan and Nick are the only ones present who know any better.

Two decades later, the rest of the tribe is here this afternoon.

* * *

Music weaves through the garden. Guests enter, greet each other, find their seats. It's a large crowd. Tristan watches them take their places. He can't help it if he's taking roll. There's Quinn Duckworth, looking more like his father Matt by the day. There are Maya Czerny's sons with their fiancées. There are Lance and the Duchess, greeting Ned Westerleigh. There's Kirk's ex-wife Yvette with her latest beau.

There's Scott's cousin Johann. There's Will's Uncle Harris, accompanied by the formidable Captain Volk. They're more than guests at a wedding, they're actors in a play coming onto the stage. Except this play is history: Tristan's, theirs, and that of a whole people. Four generations now, from Ned Westerleigh through tiny Nikolai Romanovsky III, bouncing excitedly in his grandfather's lap. It's geography, as well: four continents are represented among the guests.

* * *

After Big Steve died no one succeeded him as acknowledged leader of the tribe. There was no jockeying or politicking—there was simply an unspoken consensus that since he could never be replaced there was no reason even to try. Individually and collectively they had come of age by then. They no longer needed a warrior prince leading them, advising them, inspiring them. It's all ad hoc these days. Individuals step forward as events unfold and needs arise. When strategies and tactics are called for, everyone looks to Nick. When swashbuckling is required, they all know they can depend on Cooper. When clarity is the issue, Tristan's always ready with the appropriate analysis. When it's a matter of patient, unassuming strength, Jared's constantly prepared. When it's prophecy they need, who better than Wulf, with the wisdom of his age and experiences? When there's a question about history or culture, they have Ned, who knew Carpenter and Forster and corresponded with Isherwood for decades, who visited Hirschfeld in Berlin, and whose Uncle Alistair just may have dallied with Wilde once upon a time. When it's poetry they crave, Will is their man, with his publication history and his library of a memory. Collectively, their resources are comprehensive. That is Big Steve's legacy. And his monument.

* * *

Will Crawford rises from his front row seat and takes his place at the center of the dais. A moment later Tristan joins him. If only Big Steve could see this. Tristan knows he's not the only one in the crowd sensing this regret. At the keyboard, Duncan "Trey" Wakefield begins to play, and after the first statement of the ground the string quartet joins in. Pachelbel's "Canon" may be a cliché, but that doesn't keep it from being an ideal wedding number. Particularly in an instance where "Here Come the Bride" isn't relevant. At Will's signal, the guests rise. Arm in arm the two couples begin their long awaited march down the aisle.

Wulf and Dave move slowly but stand straight as soldiers. They are a living reminder that old age is for the strong, not the weak, and that the only true failure in life is giving up hope. Behind them, Jared and Scott are dignity personified. Wulf and Dave have been together for over fifty years. Jared and Scott for over thirty. It seems incomprehensible that only now are they free to do what they're doing this afternoon. Certainly no one could have stopped them at any time in the past if a mere ceremony was all they had wanted. But only now can it mean what their hearts have always told them.

San Francisco: 1976

Scott is pulling up his jeans when the blond man with the mustache approaches him. He looks like he's probably in his early thirties. He's perhaps an inch taller than Scott and outweighs him by thirty pounds—all of it firm, ripped muscle. He's handsome to a degree that shouldn't be allowed in real life. Guys like this are the reason why half the gay men in the world are moving to San Francisco these days and the rest are considering suicide because they're sure they could never compete here.

"Hey," the man growls.

"Afternoon," Scott says, woozy at the thought of this guy watching him dress. Scott had noticed him earlier, doing bench presses with what struck him as an apocalyptic fervor.

"My buddy and I have a bet going," the man says.

The buddy, standing halfway down the row of lockers, is black haired, equally handsome, and even taller and more built, though it hardly seems possible. At least of mere mortals.

"Yeah?" Scott feels like a second grader being shaken down for his lunch money but is damned if he'll let his vulnerability show.

"I say you're the mystery man in Zane Stark's suicide."

This is the last thing that Scott wants to hear, but he's not really surprised. He's known it was just a matter of time. Those photos have been all over the news for weeks now. The resemblance to Scott is strong but superficial. So far the "mystery man" has been sighted as far away as Sydney, Paris, Johannesburg, Tel Aviv, and New York.

"And what does your buddy say?" Scott asks, keeping his voice steady. It's possible, of course, that these guys work for one of the tabloids, but in this gym, in this neighborhood, they're more likely just to be gossip queens. For that matter, in this gym, in this neighborhood, it could be a pickup line.

"He says even if you are, it's none of our business."

"Sorry," Scott grins, "Mr. Universe wins."

"Damn."

"So what was the bet for?"

"Loser buys drinks all around," the blond guy says, poking himself in the chest with an index finger he manages to make look like a weapon.

So. A pickup line it is. This may or may not be the lesser of the two evils.

"I don't really drink."

"Neither do we. Much. I'm Nick, by the way."

"And your buddy?"

"Stefano. More commonly known as Big Steve."

"Yes," Scott says. "He would be. I'm Scott."

"The suicide note was addressed to 'S.'," Nick says. It's definitely an accusation but apparently a good natured one.

"Was it? I'm afraid I haven't been paying attention."

"Cut it out, Niko," Stefano finally speaks. It's a Brooklyn truckdriver's growl. Somehow Scott had been expecting exactly that. "After a while, that shtick isn't funny any more."

"Whatever you say, Big Steve."

"You're the third guy he's used it on this week," Big Steve explains.

"Got it," Scott grins, his anxiety ratcheting down another notch or two.

"And don't call him Niko. Only I get to do that."

"So finish dressing, baby face," Nick says, "and we'll get out of here. I owe you a drink, and Big Steve gets testy if he misses a feeding."

"I'm not sure I've got time to join you," Scott says. He's more than a little reluctant to be picked up by a pair of demigods playing hooky from Mount Olympus. He's been down that road before. But really, if escaping that fate had been his primary goal why the hell did he come to San Francisco of all places? Or this particular gym, for that matter? The Aleutian Islands. That would have been a better choice. Except given Scott's luck he couldn't have stayed out of trouble there, either. Besides: in broad daylight? In a semi public place like this locker room? What does he think there is to be frightened of? He can't spend the rest of his life being afraid of his own shadow.

"Of course you have time," Big Steve says.

* * *

Their idea of drinks turns out to be iced tea in a greasy spoon down the block. Hardly the modus operandi of a pair of sexual predators. They seem as likely to be Sunday School teachers out recruiting for The Kingdom. Crammed into a booth with the two of them, Scott feels inexplicably safe.

"So are you two...?"

"What?" Nick asks.

"Don't play dumb," Big Steve says. "He wants to know if we're a couple."

He was actually wondering if they were gay. The way they came on to him at the gym he'd assumed that they were. But then Big Steve slipped into that police uniform, which threw Scott completely off. And on the walk down the block their patter was so totally un-gay he began to think he might have been mistaken. They're so different from the muscle queens he knew back in West Hollywood that it's hard to be certain. On the other hand, nothing about them seems straight. Nothing at all. Even that SFPD uniform, which could just as easily be a costume the way Big Steve wears it. Scott memorizes the badge number anyway, just in case it's real.

"We're not together," Nick says. "Big Steve's other half is named Tristan, and he's working day shift this week. I, on the other hand, am available."

"Rampantly," Stefano agrees. "Also, inexcusably. But enough about us."

Which is what Scott was hoping to avoid.

* * *

The man in those notorious photos that the tabloids have been featuring on their front pages is Rick Rutherford, aka Dewey Norman, aka Calvin Plimpton. Just days before Zane's suicide, he vanished. Or just after Zane's suicide, depending on which tabloid you read. His apartment near the Chateau Marmont had been cleaned out, and Zane's Maserati Spyder, which what's his name was said to be accustomed to driving, showed up back in Zane's garage complete with a full tank of gas—and, strangely, not a single fingerprint anywhere on it. As far as Scott is concerned, anyone who can leave a car that clean is a professional criminal. As Zane's personal assistant, the mystery man had apparently embezzled a cool half million of Zane's hard earned dollars. There's also the matter of some missing jewelry and a painting or two: details of these items have been sketchy because Zane's grieving widow can't remember for certain what there had been in the collection. There's been no sign of him or the loot, which is now thought to be in Switzerland, if it's not in Israel—or perhaps Fiji. And despite the fact that Zane's suicide note was addressed to "S.", everyone seems convinced it was meant for this man. The current hypothesis is that Zane was addressing him by another, as yet undiscovered, alias.

Angelica's family tried to suppress the contents of the note, but as nearly always in cases the tabloids have taken an interest in, were unsuccessful. So now all America believes that Rick, or Dewey, or Calvin; or Steven, Sean, Seymour or whoever, was Zane's homosexual lover. And all America is fascinated and re-volted by this. Not to mention astonished that a guy like Zane could be a queer. The guy who had been described in print more than once as a real man's man turned out to be exactly that, albeit in a totally novel and unexpected sense of the cliche. And now in addition to being shocked, outraged, and secretly titil-lated, all America is on the lookout for the lover/embezzler whose cruelty drove the heretofore beloved television star to kill himself. So far, there have been sightings in twenty states and seven foreign countries. None of them confirmed.

The photos in question are not of very good quality—at least as they've been reproduced in print. It's possible to tell from them that the subject is tall, blond, broad shouldered, muscular. The facial features aren't very distinct, but they're clear enough that no one who gave them more than a cursory examina-tion would mistake the man for Scott. Which is ironic in the extreme, since there's no possible mistake about it: the "S." of the suicide note is unquestion-ably him. It's just a matter of time, he expects, until someone puts two and two together.

* * *

That's what he's still mulling over when he gets to his apartment and finds a letter from a law firm on Wilshire Boulevard. It's almost as if his think-ing about the whole thing has somehow attracted their attention. The letter requests that he contact them in connection with the estate of Zane Stark. He wants nothing to do with the whole thing, but he dealt with enough attorneys during his years as Zane's personal assistant to know they're not going to leave him alone now that they know where he is. He'd better find an attorney himself.

* * *

"Is your name Scott, by any chance?"

The man is a couple of inches shorter than Scott and has apparently spent his entire adult life in the gym. His unfashionably short blond hair is oiled to a standstill. The part is ruler straight. If there was ever an Eagle Scout who never outgrew it, this has to be the guy.

"Who's Scott?" Scott asks, loading his workout things back into his gym bag.

"Because if you're Scott, I'd like to apologize to you on behalf of my husband and our friend Nick. Neither of whom should be allowed to talk to strangers."

"You must be Tristan."

"At your service. Come on, let's get out of here. Big Steve has got me restricted to egg whites, tuna, and skinless chicken breasts this week, and I'm likely to kill someone if I don't have a burger."

* * *

"So how bad were they?" Tristan asks, pulling pickles off his burger. "Too much sodium. It makes you retain water. Then you look like the Michelin tire man."

Scott thinks Tristan looks about as much like the Michelin tire man as Ethel Merman looked like the Statue of Liberty.

"I can't imagine why you would assume they weren't perfect gentlemen," Scott laughs.

"Only because the minute my back is turned they misbehave," Tristan snorts. "They bring out the worst in each other."

"Always? Really?"

"Without fail. When I heard Nick had used that horrible line about that dead actor I was ready to spank him. Honest to God. Trouble is, Big Steve would have to tie him up first, and Nick would only enjoy it."

Something about Tristan makes Scott feel like confiding in him. Maybe it's the straight arrow persona that somehow manages to veer unexpectedly off course, maybe it's the cornball southern accent. Maybe it's just that he's been finding his secret oppressive, particularly since the Viborg attorneys are now on his scent.

"You know," he says, "they weren't that far off course."

"You're just being nice," Tristan says, either missing or ignoring his hint, "that's what they said about you, you know. 'He's not just a smoking hot muscle boy, he's really nice'."

"In that case, bad behavior isn't their biggest problem," Scott says. "More like lack of judgement. I'm not nice at all."

"I notice you don't deny being the smoking hot muscle boy."

"That speaks for itself, I believe. Obviously neither of them has seen an optometrist lately. They really should, you know. Big Steve is likely to fail his next police physical based on his poor eyesight. Assuming he really is a cop, that is."

"Do I look like a man who would marry a fake cop?"

"I really have no idea how to answer that."

"All right, I'll answer it for you," Tristan says. "I don't."

"Well, in that case, he should certainly know better than to describe me as nice."

"Why do I sense a confession looming?" Tristan asks, looking uneasy. "Nick's the prosecuting attorney. Maybe you should save it for him, whatever it is. I grew up Baptist. I know nothing about being a father confessor. Or even a sister confessor."

"I knew Zane Stark," Scott says. "I'm the mystery man. 'S' is for Scott."

"I suppose that means you've got the missing half million in your gym bag," Tristan grins. "You can pay for this burger. Let's see, what else would I like this afternoon?"

"That would make me the personal assistant," Scott shakes his head. "I'm just the boyfriend in the suicide note."

"I thought they were supposed to be the same person."

"When did the tabloids ever get anything right?"

"I take your point. It's an interesting proposition, that the mystery man and the personal assistant might be two different people. It would certainly make a better screenplay. Is that the treatment you're planning to pitch? Who do you see playing Zane Stark in the after school special?"

"You think I'm joking."

"Aren't you?"

"You wouldn't happen to know a good attorney, would you?"

"Jesus, you're not joking. I so wanted you to be joking."

"I just didn't feel like spilling my guts to your buddies."

"That shows great discretion on your part, I must say. But then you go and ruin it. I'm even less trustworthy than they are."

"I bet you aren't."

"Couldn't you at least pretend to believe me?" Tristan asks. "Can't I be the intimidating one for once? Why do Nick and Big Steve get to have all the fun going around scaring people?"

"They didn't scare me."

"Sure they didn't."

"And for the record, I didn't take the money."

"That's good, because I'd have to arrest you if you had."

"You're a cop, too?"

"Guilty as charged."

"Then you must know a good attorney."

* * *

By the time his appointment with Maya Czerny rolls around, Scott has received a second letter. This one is far more specific and detailed than the first, which he hasn't yet responded to. In return for signing a document waiving any and all rights to Zane's estate, he's to receive a cash settlement. The amount they're offering would buy him a house. He places both letters on the desk in front of Ms. Czerny, a titian haired knockout in a navy blue suit.

"I thought you said you'd received one letter," she says, putting on a pair of reading glasses that make her look like Raquel Welch playing a secretary just before the boss loosens his tie and says "why, Miss Jones, you're beautiful".

"I did say that," Scott says. "The second one came yesterday."

"I see," she nods. "Well, let's have a look."

While she reads, Scott feels his bowels churning. The whole thing seems like a trap to him.

"Interesting," she says, placing the letters back into their envelopes. "Appears completely straightforward."

"What should I do?"

"I can't tell you that."

"Well then, what are my options?"

"I wouldn't advise it, but you could just ignore the letters. When we spoke on the phone, you indicated that you'd prefer to have no dealings with Mr. Stark's executors, and that's certainly an option."

"And they can't do anything?"

"No. They can't force you to waive your rights to a portion of the estate, assuming you actually have any," she says. There's a questioning look in her eyes, like she's not sure what to make of him.

"I'm sure I don't."

"You've seen the will, then?"

"No. I just can't imagine Zane including me in it. Why would he? He had a wife."

"Yet the suicide note was clearly not addressed to her. I read the tabloids like everybody else. Not that I'm proud of it. But everybody in America knows about the suicide note. And you say you're the one it's really addressed to."

"I'm sure of it."

"In that case, maybe it's not surprising that the executors are trying to pay you off. You have no legal standing to contest the will of course, but there would certainly be publicity if you tried. I'd say they've had enough attention in the press already. You might be of the opinion that Mr. Stark's reputation has suffered all it possibly can already, but I assure you it could get lots worse. The executors certainly understand that."

"I have no interest in any involvement with this. I cared deeply about Zane, and I wouldn't do anything to cause difficulties. Money from his estate won't make me any more likely to behave like a gentleman."

"No. But it might be easier in the long run just to take it."

"Why?"

"When we spoke on the phone, you indicated a desire to get this matter behind you. Accepting their offer is certainly the fastest way to do that. It ties everything up nice and legal. They get the assurances they apparently want, and you get left alone. If you don't accept their offer, they can never be entirely sure of your silence. I can guarantee that you'll keep getting letters. Not to mention that the longer it goes on, the greater the likelihood of the tabloids getting wind of it."

"So I should just take the money and run?"

"That's the simplest thing to do, legally speaking. Of course I have no idea what your personal stake in this is."

"Half the time I wish I'd never met him."

"And the other half?"

"I wish I'd never left him."

"Sorry," she smiles, "I can't help you there. I'll tell you what. Let me make a call on your behalf. I'll see what I can find out."

"Would you do that?"

"It'll cost you," she grins.

"What's your percentage?"

"For making a phone call it'll just be an hourly billing. If it turns out that negotiations are required, then we'd discuss percentages."

"All right."

"It would help if you could leave these with me."

* * *

"Thanks for that referral," Scott says, leaving the gym the next day.

"Oh, did you have your meeting with Maya?" Tristan asks. "Did it go all right? No, don't tell me. I don't want to know anything about it. I don't want to have to arrest anyone today. I hate when I have to do that. The paperwork alone is enough to make a grown man cry."

"It went just fine, thanks," Scott says. "That Maya's a pistol. And you can keep your handcuffs in your pocket. I don't think anybody's going to get arrested."

"That's a relief," Tristan says. "I have to say, I don't generally use my handcuffs in a professional capacity. They're more for weekends. Now before I forget; dinner at our house Friday night. And if you don't show, I'll sic Nick and Big Steve on you."

"Don't want that," Scott says. "Although I probably ought to. Can I bring anything?"

"Your sense of humor," Tristan says. "I think that would be a good thing to have with you."

* * *

This is something new to Scott: two middle class guys—because what's more middle class, really, than a couple of policemen?—living together as a couple, complete with a house full of furniture and a pair of Labrador Retrievers. Thank God he's not the only guest for dinner. He'd probably end up begging them to adopt him. That Nick is here, for one. Then there's Cooper, a guy a couple of years younger than Scott. He's medium height, big shouldered, big armed, big chested. Tristan and Big Steve apparently don't know anybody who isn't a gym rat of some kind. Cooper is the kind of handsome that people commit suicide over—if he had been Zane's personal assistant, the whole thing would make sense. His accent is a perfect match for Big Steve's. Though he has the eyes of a superstar of porn, he actually sells real estate. Scott recalls seeing his ads in the bar papers. The other man present, J.B., is almost exactly the same size and build as Nick. He has a thick mat of close cropped, shining silver hair that's a fascinating contrast with his youthful, ruggedly handsome face. He doesn't say much. When he does speak, he gives the impression that he chooses each word very carefully. Looking at him makes Scott feel giddy, which is always a bad sign.

* * *

"You're supposed to be out there getting yourself married off," Tristan says, handing him a plate to dry.

"Obviously."

"Not my idea. I just want you to know that."

"It's all right. Really."

"Big Steve has this vision, is the thing. All the gay men in America pairing off and moving in together and buying furniture. If you're going to be a member of the family, you have to understand how it all works."

"I didn't know I was going to be a member of the family."

"Thus spoke Big Steve."

"Does he always call the shots?"

"More or less."

"And the vision apparently includes a couple of Labrador Retrievers," Scott chuckles.

"You know, you really are a nice guy. I wonder why you try so hard to seem like an asshole."

"Do I really?" Scott is so accustomed to thinking of himself as invisible that it's always interesting being reminded he isn't and hearing people's impressions of him.

"Only a little bit," Tristan grins. "You're not very convincing. It doesn't fool anybody in this crowd, rest assured."

"I'm curious," Scott says. "What does Big Steve's vision say about the gay men of France and Germany?"

"Oh, they're included. Big Steve's ambitions are global."

"He may be on to something," Scott says, determined not to tip his hand. "I could really go for that Cooper."

"Cooper is a kept boy," Tristan says.

"I thought he sold houses."

"Out of his boyfriend's agency," Tristan explains. "Though boyfriend really isn't the most accurate term for Tommy Yayle. He's got to be at least fifty. Big Steve doesn't approve of Tommy. The feeling is mutual. Big Steve is planning for someone to come along and distract Cooper enough to break them up."

"Is that why I'm here tonight?"

"It might be one reason," Tristan says. "Possibly. But I didn't tell you that."

"I'd have thought your friend Nick could bust up a marriage with one hand tied behind his back."

"He has been known to," Tristan says. "Though not recreationally. He requires more motivation than that. In the case of Cooper and Tommy, he doesn't have it."

"Why not?"

"Same reason Nick hasn't asked you out."

"I didn't know I was a prospect."

"Well, you were. Past tense, you notice."

"Not up to his standards, huh?"

"Please. This is San Francisco. Nobody's impressed by false modesty around here."

"I didn't know it was false."

"Really," Tristan says, peering at him intently. "You really expect me to believe that? You become more intriguing all the time. Well, you see, Nick's problem is that he wants a wife with a cock. But he's only really attracted to super butch types like you and Cooper. It's like one of those 'Hidden Picture' puzzles you see in *Highlights* magazine at the dentist's office."

"I guess I'm supposed to take super butch as a compliment."

"I'd be perfect for Nick, of course," Tristan says, "except I'm taken."

"That's putting it lightly," Scott laughs. "But you don't really seem like anybody's wife."

"You have no idea."

* * *

There's something awfully familiar about Maya Czerny, Scott thinks, facing her across the desk. He wonders what it is and why he didn't notice it before.

"I called the attorneys handling the Zane Stark estate," she says. "He died without a will. This is California, so his wife gets everything."

"Well, doesn't that settle it?"

"It settles the estate, yes. But as I suggested to you at our last meeting, it's really not about keeping you from getting your hands on more money. It's about buying your silence. I'm certain of that now that I've spoken to them."

"I told you before I don't want anything from the estate except to be left alone. They have absolutely nothing to fear from me."

"Well, they apparently don't know that. They've doubled their offer."

"What?"

"Five hundred thousand if you sign away any and all claims. And there's language about not talking to the press about your relationship with Zane."

"Jeez. Do you think that agreeing to it will make them leave me alone?"

"According to this document, it will."

"What should I do?"

"That depends. If you honestly want this behind you, take the money and run. If you think you can get more out of them, you can certainly try. But you'll have to get yourself another attorney."

"Why's that?"

"Because it would mean you lied to me about your interests when we first talked, so I'd have to fire you."

"I'm not that honest, as a rule," Scott says, "but I haven't lied to you."

"Then why don't you sign right here, and I'll ship this back to them. There's a space under your signature for you to indicate where you'd like the payment sent. I'd suggest a direct transfer to your bank account."

"Got it."

* * *

When J.B. called to ask him for a date, the last thing Scott wanted was to say yes. But Big Steve and Tristan had been so hospitable he felt a little obligated. And for that matter, he had always been able to resist anything except temptation. So against what he thinks of as his better judgment he said yes. Neither of them has much to say over dinner. Scott finds himself with an almost irresistible urge to reach out and stroke that thick mat of gleaming silver hair. J.B. passes the time staring at him with famished looking eyes. It seems both awkward and quasi pornographic, and Scott regrets everything about it. When J.B. asks him back to his apartment, it's all he can do to say no. But he doesn't dare have sex with a guy he could actually fall for.

"You're a nice guy," Scott tells him. "Very nice, from what I can tell. And I'm pretty rotten all the way around. It's not a good idea."

"It's the limp, isn't it?" J.B. asks.

If J.B. had meant this as a manipulation, it would be pathetic. But Scott believes he knows better. Besides, it's not that bad a limp. Whatever's wrong with the leg certainly doesn't slow J.B. down at the gym. He's an absolute beef monster.

"I hope you can believe me that it isn't," he says. "Honest to God, it isn't."

The look J.B. gives him makes him want to crawl into a hole and never come back out.

San Francisco: 1977

Scott steps into the classroom just before the bell rings. He drops a sheaf of papers onto the lectern, gives the class the briefest of glances, and turns to the chalkboard. In precise, teutonic block letters he writes, "German 107a: Reading German Poetry and Prose" and then his name, office location, telephone number, and hours. Finally, he turns to address the class.

"*Guten Tag. Willkommen ins Deutsch 107a. Ich heisse Scott Bailey. Jetzt werde ich die Namen aufrufen. Antworten sie bitte.*"

He reads down the list of names. It's a small class. The course prerequisites are completion of the Beginning and Intermediate German courses with grades of C or higher. Since those courses complete the foreign language requirement for graduation from the university, very few people enroll. Typically these are German majors or minors, who are a rare breed in this neck of the woods. Those present are here for one reason and one reason only: they want to be. He has been told to expect them to be interested and highly motivated, a welcome change from the freshmen and sophomores who frustrated him so thoroughly last year. So even though he hasn't taught the course before, it should be a piece of cake. When he reaches the end of the list, he realizes he has called twelve names but there are thirteen people sitting out there looking at him with varying degrees and types of expectancy. And though he's been trying all through roll call not to stare, he knows exactly which one is Mr. No Name.

He's sitting in the back row, in the corner to Scott's left. His glossy brown hair begs to have hands run through it, and he's sporting a mustache that he might have pilfered off Errol Flynn's upper lip. He's got a jaw line out of a detective story, eyes fit to make the heroine of a Jane Austen novel swoon, probably repeatedly, and a cleft in his chin just made to lick marmalade out of. His cheekbones could inspire either sonnets or haiku and almost certainly have. And that classically handsome face sits atop an upper body, clad this unseasonably warm afternoon in a gray tank top, that could have stridden purposefully right out of a drawing by Tom of Finland. If such things ever happened. Which here in San Francisco they, or at least rough approximations of them, do with what Scott considers astonishing frequency.

Scott does not subscribe to the cliché he hears repeated endlessly in this city which asserts that all the attractive men one encounters are gay: his own daily observations refute it categorically. So this man, despite his "let's get out of here and find someplace where we can play hide the sausage" smirk, is straight. End of story.

"*Gibt es sonst noch jemand?*" Scott asks, looking up from the roll sheet as if he doesn't know the answer too damned well for his comfort. And on cue, the vision raises his hand. Scott gets a breathtaking shot of exquisitely sculpted armpit, one of his favorite parts of a man, lightly fringed with silken hair.

"Curtiss, Jeff. That's Curtiss with two s's. I just added this morning."

"*Auf Deutsch, bitte,*" Scott corrects him, sure that his answering grin is a hopelessly silly one.

"Sorry," Curtiss, Jeff, answers. "My conversational skills are really rusty. But my reading is just fine."

"*Also gut,*" Scott says, resigned.

* * *

Scott spends the forty-eight hours until the next class trying to recall where he's seen Curtiss, Jeff with his two s's, not to mention his everything else, before, determined to convince himself that he has never laid eyes on the man and only thinks he has because he wishes he had. The mystery seems destined to remain forever unsolved, however, as there's no sign of him when Thursday comes around and the group gathers. And Scott spends the entire hour and twenty minutes mentally berating himself for being so disappointed by the man's absence. He's trying his best to observe his rule about not getting himself hung up. And getting involved with a student, while par for the course for a fuckup like Scott, is not in his best interests. Still, he's so preoccupied that by the time the bell rings he's not sure what, if anything, he's taught his students.

He's surprised to find Curtiss, Jeff waiting outside the classroom when he emerges into the corridor. Wearing vintage 501's and that *Bundeswehr* tank top that's all the rage lately, he's leaning against the wall and looking, Scott thinks, downright pornographic.

"Hi," he says, smiling that incendiary smile of his.

His eyes, Scott notices, are the color of iced tea.

"Herr Curtiss," Scott says, running up his defenses with all possible dispatch. "What can I do for you?"

"Wanted to let you know that I dropped your class."

"Oh? Why did you do that?"

"Because I could tell just looking at you that you weren't the type of guy who'd even consider dating one of his students," he grins. "So how about it? Dinner tomorrow night?"

This is so exactly what Scott's trying to avoid these days that it's probably inevitable.

"Oh, God. I got it wrong, didn't I? I'm usually right on target. But you're not gay, are you? There's probably a cute little wifey at home taking care of a couple of even cuter kids. I'm so sorry about this. I make it a rule never to hit on straight guys, honest. And here I've gone and embarrassed you."

"No, wait," Scott stammers at his retreating backside, "I'd love to have dinner with you."

"Seriously?"

"I'm always serious about a dinner invitation."

* * *

"So," Jeff says, spearing a chunk of lemon chicken with his fork and punctuating his interrogation with it. "What's a guy like you doing teaching German—for shit pay I'll bet—at San Francisco State?"

"Working on a Ph.D. What else?"

"Somehow I don't see you as a university professor," Jeff rolls his eyes.

"I don't plan to teach long term. It's just until I can break into translating. Literary stuff. I've done enough technical translations to last a lifetime. That's how I got my foot in the door. Right now I'm working on a novel by Erika von Kleist-Metternich. For Random House. It could get my career off the ground."

"The painter's daughter?"

"You've heard of her?"

"I'm an art history major," Jeff says. "In fact, my old man has a couple of his paintings."

It's Scott's turn to be surprised. He would have figured Jeff for general studies.

* * *

"Where do you like to go dancing?"

"I don't have a regular place," Scott says.

"Well, there's this new club a few doors up. But you'll have to lose that t-shirt."

"I suppose that could be arranged."

He watches Jeff leave a generous tip and then they're out on the crowded sidewalk. Not quite halfway up the block Jeff grabs his hand and drags him through a narrow doorway into a dark corridor. Jeff sheds his flannel shirt and ties it by the arms around his waist. Inside the bar it's smoky and dimly lit, but not so dark that Scott can't see the hardware Jeff's sporting: a frighteningly authentic looking set of military dog tags hanging on a foot long length of chain slung from a hoop run through his pierced left nipple. That's where he's seen Jeff before: he's the model in an ad for a local levi and leather bar.

Jeff catches Scott staring and laughs. Scott makes a grab for the dog tags, and Jeff feints to his left.

"Come on," Jeff says. "Let's dance."

* * *

"So what's it going to be?" Jeff asks a couple of hours later as they stand on the sidewalk outside the bar sweating profusely despite the late evening chill.

"What?" Scott asks, a little deafened from the music.

"Your place or mine?"

Scott's been anticipating the question all evening. Ordinarily it's no big deal, but Jeff is anything but ordinary. Scott wants to play this exactly right, because the last thing he needs is to get involved in something with the potential for complications.

"There's just one thing," he says.

"What's that?" Jeff asks, grin fading just enough that Scott notices it.

"I'm not looking for a boyfriend right now."

"Cool," Jeff says, looking relieved. "I've already got one."

Perfect, Scott thinks.

* * *

"That's some piercing," Jeff says. "Must have hurt like hell. I know I nearly passed out when I had my nipple done. But that? Jesus. I'd have ended up in the hospital."

"Don't remember," Scott says, looking down at himself. "The guys who did it to me had slipped me a mickie. I woke up with this thing stuck in my cock."

"Shit, man," Jeff says. "So if you didn't want it in the first place, why keep it?"

"To remind me to choose my friends more carefully."

* * *

"His name's Tommy Yayle," Jeff says. "He broke up with his last boyfriend a few months back. He sells real estate. You've probably seen his ads. They're on a lot of the bus stops. He's got this huge place down in Hillsborough. He's an older guy, you know, but very charming."

Scott doesn't really want to hear Jeff singing the praises of his new boyfriend, but it seems ungracious to object. What he'd really like to do right now is either track down that Cooper guy or go to sleep.

* * *

"You sure you're not looking for a boyfriend?" Jeff asks one night a few weeks later.

"You want me to throw you out of this bed?"

"Not me, silly. It's just, you know, Tommy has some really nice friends. I could set you up if you wanted. I mean, this gig I've got is really cushy. Believe me, you could do a lot worse for yourself."

"Is that why you're here right now?" Scott asks, irritated, "because you're so happy with Tommy?"

"I am happy with Tommy," Jeff insists. "I think he's about to rent an apartment for me. The last boyfriend had a place on Nob Hill. And a Jaguar. Can you believe it?"

"Really."

"Honest to God."

"But."

"What do you mean, 'but'?"

"I hear you about to hedge," Scott says. "Admit it. You're happy, but you're not that happy."

"Tommy's nice, a lot of fun, and very, very generous. He's just not very good sex," Jeff says.

"You're welcome," Scott laughs.

* * *

When Maya Czerny called him to say that Angelica Viborg wanted to arrange a meeting, Scott was dubious. But Maya assured him that it seemed kosher, and he reluctantly agreed. He took the money, after all. Her money, and lots of it. So he guesses that gives her a right to call the shots. This was exactly what he was afraid of in the first place. First she wants a meeting. Next time, who knows what she'll ask for? He knows exactly how demanding she can be, and taking her money must have given her the idea she can make demands. Why else would he be here in an elevator on his way up to the presidential suite or whatever it's called about to pee himself? What can she possibly want with him?

His feet sink into deep carpet in the private elevator lobby. He taps on the door, hoping nobody will hear and he'll have an excuse to walk out. But no such luck. There she is, peering out at him.

"Scott," she gives a little yelp of surprised pleasure, as if she wasn't expecting him. "Oh, Scott, it's been too long."

She offers him her cheek for a kiss. He gives it the lightest possible brush with his lips.

"Scott, darling, you look wonderful."

"And you look amazing," he says. "As always."

"I do not." She makes a face. "I'm jet lagged to death."

"How long are you in town for?"

"You know, I haven't the faintest. You'd have to ask my P.A. If you can find her. Wretched girl. Oh, that's right, she's walking the dogs. Let's go into the sitting room. I ordered tea."

Scott follows her into a room that looks like backstage at Versailles. They sit facing each other. He had forgotten how much Angelica can sound like a duchess. It seems incongruous for a Southern California girl. But she did go to finishing school in Switzerland.

"I was surprised to hear from you," he says.

"Nobody's supposed to know I'm in San Francisco," she says, either deflecting, or more likely simply oblivious to, his implication. "I'm between jobs and I want some privacy. Just for a day or two."

"Your career certainly has been keeping you busy," he says, "if the tabloids are to be believed."

"Which they're most definitely not," she snorts. "But work is simply the best therapy there is, don't you think?"

"Definitely."

"Tea?" she asks. "Or something stronger?"

"Tea is fine," he says.

"Of course. I remember. You never did drink, did you?"

She pours tea and hands him the cup.

"I seriously thought about taking up the habit the last little while."

"It's been a terrible time," she says, finally acknowledging it. "Simply awful. That whole year. The pregnancy. Then the boys. Then Zane. It was like some book from the Old Testament. The Plagues of the Viborgs."

"I'm sorry I wasn't there for you."

"How could you have been?" she asks, wide eyed at the idea. "The situation was impossible. Anyway, you did what you could."

"Stay away, you mean? Keep my mouth shut?"

"It was the best thing."

"It was the easiest thing."

"Two birds with one stone, so to speak," she smiles. "You mustn't feel guilty. You were right to get out when you did."

"Still, it certainly seems as if you got the short end."

"Ah, but I'm used to it," she says. "It's my lot in life. I have to say I was a little disappointed that you didn't hold out for more money. Daddy certainly expected you to. I was prepared to go as high as a million. Any more than that would have been hard to keep hushed up."

"I really loved him, Angelica," he blurts. "I swear to God I'm not just some heartless, gold digging..."

"Of course you're not, Scott. We all know that. I mean it. We were surprised, of course, when we realized what that suicide note meant. But, well, perhaps not that surprised. It certainly made sense. It filled in the blanks, so to speak. I'd have been happier, of course, if Zane had told me about himself, but, well, I guess a girl can't have everything."

"I hope you know that keeping it a secret was never my idea. I never thought it would continue at all once you two were married."

"Zane always did exactly what he wanted," she says. "Nobody knows that better than I do. No, it was more of a surprise, really, when Zane told me about your arrangement with my brother."

"It was hardly an arrangement," Scott protests.

"No, you're right," she says. "I shouldn't have used that word. Dylan and Stewie were never really organized enough for that."

"One of the last times I spoke to Zane he said that if I hadn't left, the boys would still be alive."

"He didn't," she cries. "That asshole."

"I'm not making it up."

"My brother and his friend were very dirty little boys. They were going to end up in deep, stinky shit sooner or later. You mustn't take what Zane said seriously, darling, you mustn't. I certainly don't."

"Does the rest of the family know? About me and the boys?"

"I never told them. What good could it possibly have done? Anyway, your activities with them aren't really relevant. They were tied up in their own apartment by a psychopath who molested and then strangled them. How the psychopath got there in the first place isn't the issue."

It seems to Scott that it's exactly the issue, but he doesn't say so.

"The police still haven't caught the guy."

"Mummy and Daddy have hired whole platoons of private investigators, too. They're far better than the police, those guys. It's quite a job keeping them from telling the rest of the story."

"I'm sure you're up to it," Scott observes.

"I'm very good at doing what has to be done."

Scott shrugs.

"Zane's death has been even more problematic," she says.

"Oh, God, Angelica. I'd give anything if someone could tell me he had an incurable disease or something—anything so it doesn't have to be because of me. I just can't understand it. I mean, it's not like he actually loved me."

"Of course not, darling," she agrees. "He didn't love you any more than he loved me. What he loved, if he loved anything, was having everything he wanted. For a man like Zane, nothing could be worse than having *almost* everything he wanted. That's all it was, really. I'm convinced of it."

"I'm sorry," Scott says, "but I'm not buying it."

"Oh?"

"I'm just not that special. There are guys like me everywhere. Zane only had to get off his ass and pick out a replacement."

"That might have been true at one time," she muses, "but once he got that series, everything changed. After that, he could never be sure again who was in it for love and who was in it for everything else. That's what made you special, Scott. You could give him the one thing nobody else could—the certainty that you were there for him and nothing else. He always knew where you stood. You proved it when you left. That's what killed him."

"If that were true, Hollywood would be a ghost town."

"Not necessarily," Angelica says. "The city is full of cynics who don't care that they have to buy love if it's pretty enough. But Zane was a true romantic. That's what doomed him."

* * *

Angelica's parting shot is a copy of the coroner's report that shows up in Scott's mail a few days later. It makes pretty sensational reading. Scott can't imagine how much it must have cost to keep the details out of the tabloids. And it's no wonder Angelica didn't tell him about it herself.

Before Zane committed suicide, he sexually mutilated himself.

* * *

"God, that was great," Jeff says, hoisting himself off Scott and rolling onto his side.

Scott braces himself. Jeff's always chatty after sex, while all Scott ever wants to do is take a nap.

"It's going really great with Tommy, you'll be glad to know."

"Will I?"

"Why wouldn't you?"

"No idea."

"I've just about got him ready to take me apartment hunting."

"Great," Scott says. "I mean, if that's what you want."

"I could use a little help, though."

"I don't know what good I'd be," Scott says. "I don't know a thing about apartment hunting in this city. You'd know that if we'd ever gone to my place. It's an absolute disaster."

"Not that," Jeff giggles. Giggling is his most unattractive mannerism. "I mean help with Tommy."

"What do you mean, help with Tommy?"

"He's been hinting that he'd like to watch while somebody gives me a real good going over, if you get my drift."

"I suppose I do," Scott says.

"So what do you say? We could put on a real show for him. I'm sure he'd give me anything I ask for after that."

"You know," Scott says, "I'd really hate not to help you out, but I don't think I can do that."

"Why not? I think it would be really hot."

"Undoubtedly. But I just can't. You should really try to find somebody else. I'm sure you won't have any trouble."

"But you'd be so perfect. Tommy's been talking about blond muscle guys so much lately. It's turning into an obsession."

"Aren't you afraid I might take him away from you if we did that little performance?"

"You'd never do anything like that, Scott. I know you better."

"Well, thanks for that," Scott says. "You know, the last few months have been a lot of fun, but I don't think I can see you any more."

"You're joking."

"No."

"Just because I suggested…"

"No. Not because of that."

"Then why?"

"Because it's time, Jeff. That's all."

"That makes no sense."

"Life almost never does."

* * *

It is time, Scott thinks on his way home from the squalid little studio apartment Jeff is so intent on moving out of. He didn't realize he meant it when he said it. He thought it was just a flip remark born of annoyance. When he gave a peeved Jeff that little peck on the cheek as he left he was already composing his apology for the next time they met. But repeating it somehow makes it manifestly true. He has spent his entire adult life trying not to turn into his father, but he realizes now he's been going about it all wrong. It wasn't his father's drinking that was the problem. So staying sober isn't the answer Scott has always believed. It's what drove his father to drink that Scott should have been looking out for. And he's failed miserably at that. He certainly won't avoid turning into his father by drifting through life hooking up with beauties who turn out to be catastrophically flawed or even just terminally trivial. Or by simply reacting to life as it happens to him. A more active approach to the problem is undoubtedly called for.

So yes, it's time. Not just time to cut Jeff off, but time to ditch his current gym, with its high concept décor and ridiculous crop of straights posing and preening. He's only been going there to avoid Big Steve and company. It's time to accept the fact that they're his natural element—the brotherhood of

the gym. Time to stop worrying about their matchmaking, which is well inten-
tioned and basically harmless. He can stand his ground with them if he really
wants to. He can make his own choices. And God knows he could use some
friends like them: simple, uncomplicated gays with no discernable attitude.

* * *

"Welcome back, stranger," Tristan greets him from the lat machine.

"Thought you'd fallen off the face of the earth," Nick says, leering.

"No, you didn't," Scott laughs. "I know better. Big Steve's spies are everywhere."

"He's onto you, Nick," Tristan laughs.

"God, I missed this place," Scott says.

* * *

"Now that you chased Nick away," Tristan says, eyeing a plate of french
fries on a neighboring table, "he thinks we're here talking about him."

"I didn't chase him away," Scott says. "All I said was I wanted to speak to
you privately."

"He's a prosecuting attorney," Tristan says. "The word 'privately' doesn't
mean the same thing to him as it does to normal people."

"Well, I'm sure he'll eventually figure out that this song is not about him,"
Scott says. "What's his deal, anyway?"

"Oh, Nick's all right. He's just got a bad case of the wedding bell blues."

"You'd think guys would be lined up around the block to apply for the
position," Scott says.

"Tell me something," Tristan says, still gazing at the french fries. "You've
seen my abs quite recently. Is there anything wrong with them? Anything at
all?"

"The word washboard comes to mind."

"Thank you."

"For what?"

"Reminding me why I'm not stealing that guy's fries. So what's up?"

"Once upon a time you and I had a talk about the Gospel According to
Big Steve," Scott says.

"That wouldn't surprise me. I'm disciple number one."

"That stuff about guys pairing off and buying furniture for their Labrador
Retrievers. How the hell does it work?"

"Huh?" Tristan says.

"You heard me."

"Well," Tristan says. "Mostly I guess nature just takes its course."

"Is that all?"

"Isn't it enough?"

"Well, these guys, do they fall in love, or what?"

"Oh, I get it. You want to talk about the L word."

"It's not that I want to talk about it," Scott says. "I just want to know how I'm supposed to go after it. I've been batting a negative one thousand for so long."

"I wouldn't worry your pretty head about it too much."

"Just let nature take its course?"

"Big Steve doesn't really believe in love," Tristan says. "I mean those guys with the Labrador Retrievers do love each other, but that's not what brings them together in the first place."

"I suppose that would be where the sex comes in," Scott says. "That's not the answer I was hoping for."

"You're too cynical, that's your problem," Tristan explains. "It's not about sex, either."

"Now I'm really confused."

"Big Steve is a great believer in destiny," Tristan says.

"Really."

"The man you're looking for is out there looking for you. And when you're both ready, bingo."

"That's all?"

"Yep."

"You really believe that?"

"Hell, boy, I'm living proof."

* * *

On his way to pick up some Chinese takeout a week or so later he runs into Maya and J.B. on Castro Street.

"How did your meeting go?" Maya asks. "With what's her name."

"Fine."

"I assumed that," she says. "Otherwise you'd have called me. 'Fine' doesn't really answer my question, I'm afraid."

"Well, I have a question, too," Scott laughs. "How do you two know each other?"

"Jared and I go way back," Maya says. "We're cousins."

"'J' is for Jared, huh?" Scott says. "I'd have put money on James. So what's the B for?"

"Bartok," Jared says.

"Jared Bartok," Scott says. "That's funny. I took calculus with a guy named Jared Bartok. Santa Monica College, about a million years ago."

"My God," Jared says. "I must have been fucked up worse than I thought back then if I don't remember you being there."

"You'd never have noticed me," Scott says. "I hadn't had my growth spurt yet. Hell, I was barely pubescent."

"Unbelievable," Jared shakes his head. "I was such a mess in those days. I'd only been back from 'Nam for a few months."

"You know," Scott says, "you and I really should go out again. I think I fucked up last time. In fact, I'm sure of it."

San Francisco: 1979

Wulf stares at himself in the mirror. It's a nightmare he'll never wake up from. He goes to the gym four times a week. He takes obsessive care of his appearance. He doesn't smoke or drink. He doesn't eat red meat. Indeed, Dave is fanatical about every aspect of their diet. And here looking back at him is the result. Sure, he can pass for ten, maybe twelve years younger than his true age, but that still leaves him looking like a man in his mid to late forties. There's no getting around it. A middle aged man is a middle aged man. He will never again look or feel as good as he has always taken for granted. It somehow figures that he'd only really start to care about his looks once they began to go.

And damn Dave's monthly business trips to New York. Damn them to hell for all eternity. Because as long as Dave is around, Wulf doesn't worry that much about growing old. Dave is all the reassurance he needs, and one touch from Dave is still enough to make him feel like he's twenty years old again. Or thirty, at worst. But when Dave's away it's pure agony. He can hardly stand to show his face outside the house. He envisions himself as an elderly, shabbily clothed, decrepit man wandering the streets of Telegraph Hill alone, mumbling to himself distractedly, supporting himself with a cane, leading a pair of mangy, equally aged dogs on leashes. Whenever he describes this vision to Dave, Dave just laughs and reminds him that by all rights neither of them should have lived past the age of twenty-three, that they're both still decades away from the tottering senility Wulf imagines so vividly and describes so melodramatically, and that considering everything that Wulf has been through in his life, old age is likely to be a picnic. They will, Dave assures him, be fabulous oldsters.

Wulf finishes drying his hair and goes into the bedroom to dress. These clothes in his closet: are they too young for him? Do they make him look like a ridiculous old queen trying desperately to hang on to a youth already long gone? Do people see him wearing things like these and think how pathetic he is? Or laugh behind his back? Every day he sees other men his age making fools of themselves with their unsuitable wardrobes and hairstyles. He has always promised himself he would never be like that. Has he ended up like them without even knowing it?

Damn it all. He sits on the bed and forces himself to take slow, deep breaths. The first hour after he gets out of bed is always the hardest. The last day of Dave's absences always finds him near prostration. He wonders for a moment what happened to the resilience that kept him going through the times that were truly hard. When and how did he grow so soft? It's faintly nauseating. But outside the bedroom windows it's a lovely morning. The sun is shining, the water of the bay is like liquid jewels, the city is the same paradise he's loved passionately for over a decade now. He'll put the top down on the Mercedes and drive to work with the wind in his still luxuriant though now silver hair. By the time he's on campus he'll be starting to feel all right again. There he'll be surrounded by hordes of gorgeous twenty year olds, which is terrifying of course, but he'll also be in the company of his faculty colleagues, most of whom, even several who are quite a bit younger than Wulf is, look a good deal worse than he does. He knows it's vain of him to take such comfort in that.

Dave will be back tomorrow. He'll have stories to tell and plans for the weekend, and Wulf will be sprung from this purgatory once again.

* * *

Wulf's research assistant is a twenty-four year old doctoral student named Ryan Laughlin. A Yale graduate, he is part of the unending exodus of gay men to this city from all over the globe. He's on the phone when Wulf gets to the office, talking ninety miles a minute. Ryan is built like a first string tight end for the Raiders. He's got eyes the color of coffee and a huge head of dark brown, Pre-Raphaelite curls. His skin is like antique porcelain. Dave used to have skin like that. Smooth and soft like an infant's. Lovely to touch, like honey to taste. Horribly susceptible to sunburn of course, but there's a price to be paid for everything beautiful.

"Yeah?" Ross drawls a Boston born and bred vowel into the receiver. He didn't get into Yale because of family connections or money, and he sounds exactly like you'd expect the son of a long line of bus drivers and assorted other municipal workers to sound. "Call me as soon as you hear anything. You know I'll kill you if you don't." He slams down the receiver.

Wulf knows him well enough by now to know that this signoff doesn't signify violent emotion. Ryan just makes loud, sudden noises and gestures no matter how he feels or what he's doing. Wulf applauds his energy, as a matter of fact. He's known far too many overly genteel gay men in his time and welcomes the brashness of Ryan's generation. It's nice to see and be around men not afraid of acting like men. He knows this may not be a politically correct sentiment, strictly speaking, but he can't bring himself to care.

"Morning, *Herr Doktor Professor.*"

"Good morning, Ryan."

"Heard the latest?"

"The latest about what?"

"The Dan White jury may be bringing in a verdict sometime today."

"Ah," Wulf says, shuffling through the mail Ryan has arranged on his desk. Somehow Ryan has gotten the idea that secretarial duties are part of his responsibilities. Wulf is ashamed of himself for not disabusing Ryan of this notion. But the attention feels nice.

"You don't seem very interested. I thought Milk was a friend of yours."

"Harvey was more of an acquaintance. Convicting his murderer won't bring him back. So I don't guess I'm interested in this circus of a trial."

"How can you say that? This is big. I'm telling you, it's history happening before our very eyes."

"I seriously doubt it," Wulf says. "Now if there was the ghost of a chance they'll convict the man, that might be historic. But they're not going to convict. They're going to acquit. And an acquittal will simply reaffirm society's long standing tradition of approving the eradication of gay men by whatever means are available."

"I can't believe you still think he'll get away with it," Ryan grumbles, shaking his mane emphatically. "It's an open and shut case. He was caught red handed. There were witnesses. And not just any witnesses. The list of people who testified for the prosecution is like a directory of the city government."

"Just wait," Wulf says. "You'll see."

"Care to bet on it?"

"I'd feel guilty taking money from a struggling graduate student."

"Patronizing bastard," Ryan snorts.

Wulf laughs. What would his colleagues say if they knew he let his research assistant talk to him that way? But what the hell? It's the Seventies. Academicians don't walk on water any more. Not that they ever did, but they certainly enjoyed giving that impression. The mystique is long gone, thank goodness. But all too many of his peers aren't aware that times have changed. And this is an inexcusable lapse on the part of a department full of historians.

"If that's the worst thing you can think of to call me, you must be in a pretty good mood. Did anything special happen overnight?"

"Actually, yes," Ryan says, blushing. "I met this guy. His name is Erik. He's a Latin American Studies major. Not here. At State. And gorgeous? I nearly came in my 501's just staring at him. I never in a million years would have thought he'd want to dance with me."

"Why ever not?" Wulf asks, searching his desktop for the manila folder with this morning's lecture notes. He's sure he laid it out the last time he was in the office. "I'd certainly dance with you if you asked me. Hell, if I saw you in a club I'd probably ask you to dance myself. Of course, then you'd have Dave to contend with."

"No thank you," Ryan says. "Dave's a nice guy and all, but sometimes he scares me half to death."

"He can be rather possessive."

"Not that I blame him, Prof. I'd be the same way if I had a living legend for a boyfriend."

"Living legend? Don't talk nonsense."

"Listen, Prof, not to change the subject, but just what is it you're looking for there?"

"My lecture notes for this morning. I thought I put them right here. You haven't seen them, have you?"

"Oops, sorry," Ryan says. "They're in my book bag. I had them down in the photocopying room."

"These things? Whatever for?"

"Because, Prof, you're a world renowned historian and the best lecturer in the whole university, and somebody needs to be preserving these things for posterity, because knowing you you'll just get frustrated someday and throw them all out. So over the weekend I decided it was high time I got my ass in gear and started an archive."

"Oh, please, Ryan. Even you can do better for a lame excuse than that."

"No, really," Ryan insists. "I mean it."

"Then you're an even bigger fool than you are a liar," Wulf chuckles, glancing at his watch. "Better get a move on if I don't want to be late."

"Don't forget the meeting of the tenure review committee this afternoon."

"Oh, yes," Wulf says. "Thanks for reminding me."

* * *

Wulf has just put down the receiver after talking long distance with Dave when the phone rings. He's tempted to let the machine pick up and go to the bathroom for a long soak in a good hot tub but picks up instead.

"*Herr Doktor Professor.*"

"Ryan."

"The very same, your handmaiden and acolyte. Have you heard the news?"

"What news?"

"The verdict is in, oh mighty and revered one. And we were both wrong."

"Oh?"

"Yeah, they convicted that bastard like I told you they would. But what they convicted him of was voluntary manslaughter. So they might as well have acquitted him just like you said they'd do."

"So how does that make us both wrong?" Wulf asks. "It sounds more like we were both right."

"I suppose you could look at it that way."

"I'd much prefer to, if it's all the same to you. Listen, where are you anyway? There's an awful lot of noise on your end."

"I'm down here on Castro Street. And you might want to get yourself over to Civic Plaza. I think something's going to happen."

"Really?"

"Yeah. They're already starting to march from here. That Cleve guy seems to have organized it all ahead of time. Looks like we might get some actual history out of this after all."

"Oh? Well, I might go have a look."

"If I were you I wouldn't miss it."

* * *

By the time Wulf is able to work his way through the crowds milling around Civic Plaza and finds himself in the middle of the street in front of City Hall, it's obvious to him that Ross was right. This many angry gays and lesbians all in one place at the same time does have some kind of historical significance. Has there ever been such a gathering before? Of course there was the march on the night of Harvey's death. It seems to him that crowd was larger than this one. But its character was completely different. Tonight's crowd is spoiling for a fight. Its chanting borders on savagery. He can sense blind fury seething just below the surface. These people are not here to mourn. They're here to make somebody pay for the injustice that has been done. Wulf is frightened and exhilarated at the same time.

He can't help but recall the scene in New York, not quite ten years ago,
when a ragtag assemblage of drag queens, street people, eccentrics and loonies
took on the entire NYPD. The Stonewall Inn had hardly seemed worth fighting
for at the time. The "uprising" had bemused Dave and Wulf even as they played
their token part in it that night, "obstructing" officers in the performance of
their duty. No one present could have foreseen a gathering like this: hundreds,
perhaps thousands of times as big and just as angry. Half a generation later, here
are doctors and lawyers, teachers and nurses, engineers and airline pilots intent
on justice. "Out of the closets and into the streets" had been Harvey's message,
and tonight is his legacy. Just like that other night, after this one nothing will
be the same.

Suddenly he hears the sound of breaking glass. It's begun. The crowd
surges toward the steps of City Hall. Wulf struggles against the tide, not wanting to get any closer to the melee he can hear gathering force all along the front
of the building. He makes it to the opposite side of the street, then stops to
look back at what's rapidly developing into a full scale riot. He can hear police
bullhorns and angry shouts. The crowd continues to chant, to press toward the
building like an irresistible force intent on testing its strength against an immovable object until the laws of physics are violated in some new, unimaginable
catastrophe. Sirens wail in the distance. The sound comes from every point
of the compass. The police must have called in reinforcements. But are there
enough police in the entire city to quell a disturbance this large and tumultous?
Silly question. Wulf knows there are always enough police. It's a fundamental
law of the universe.

Wulf's impulse now is to run. Police are arriving from all directions, faces full of contempt, truncheons ready. But someone has to witness this. Someone has to stand still and watch. Someone will need to tell this story. He stands
his ground and the riot ebbs and flows around him like riptides. Police and civilians alike stagger past him, bleeding. Camera crews dodge rocks and bottles and
keep filming the action around them, their lights casting bizarre shadows across
the seething human maelstrom. And now he smells smoke. Down the street,
he sees a line of police cars in flames. He moves toward this amazing spectacle.
And suddenly his attention is focused on one vignette.

A police officer stands over a crumpled figure, swinging his club onto the inert form over and over again, while a desperate man attempts to pull him away. Wulf can't stop himself. He breaks into a run. In no more than two dozen paces he's right behind them. He catches a flash of pale gold as a stray beam of light from a camera truck sweeps over the hair of the man on the ground. Hair exactly the color and texture of someone Wulf saw beaten to death long ago. He hears a savage yell erupt from the sea of noise around him and realizes an instant later that it's reverberating in his own chest.

The next thing he knows he has grabbed the police officer by the neck from behind. He wrenches the officer's head as if he wants to snap it clean off, and the officer does down. The other defender yanks the club from the officer's grasp, then stands frozen. Wulf grabs it from him and drives it into the officer's gut. The officer's eyes are full of terror. He struggles like a drowning man to get his breath back.

"Take off his helmet," Wulf hears himself yell. He bends over the officer, brandishing the club while the other man unsnaps the chin strap and lifts the helmet away from the officer's head.

"This is America, God damn you," Wulf screams into the officer's up-turned face. "What the hell do you think you're doing, you fucking pig, trying to beat a man to death on the street? Who do you think you are, acting like that? He's a human being, not some animal. It's time for somebody to teach you a lesson."

He swings the club down onto the officer's skull with all his might. He feels the jolt all the way up to his shoulder joint as the club makes impact. The thud he hears is sickening. The officer's eyes snap shut.

"Help your friend," he tells the other man, who's staring at him in aston-ishment. He looks down at the cop. He notices with redoubled fury the square of black electrician's tape covering the badge number. He rips it away and mem-orizes what he sees underneath. Then he delivers a hard kick to the cop's ribs and one more for good measure. He turns to where the man is crouched over his friend. Blood seeps into the thick blond hair from a scalp wound.

"He's unconscious," the man says.

"We'd better get him out of here," Wulf says. "Just a moment and I'll help you."

He turns back to the cop. He can't do anything about the dozens of other officers he sees assaulting civilians, but he wants to make sure this one thinks twice before he ever hurts anyone again. Wulf kicks him again, harder than before, and thinks he can sense the cracking of ribs. He kicks the cop once more just to make sure. That should do it.

* * *

It's chaos in the emergency room. Ambulances wail outside. Police and civilians are arriving in a steady stream, most on their feet, but a few, like the blond young man, have to be carried in. There's nowhere left to sit in the waiting area. Wulf stands with the blond man's friend and looks closely at him for the first time. He's tall and enormously broad shouldered. His thick mat of close cropped hair is silver, but his face is the face of an eighteen year old. Tears are streaming down his face, and his gym pumped body is wracked with sobs.

"He'll be all right now," Wulf says as orderlies wheel the blond boy's gurney into an examination cubicle and pull the curtains closed.

"He'd better be," the young man shudders, "that fucking cop was trying to kill him."

"I know."

"He would have if you hadn't come along. I tried to stop him, but I couldn't."

* * *

Wulf stands in the doorway to the hospital room. The silver haired young man slumps in a chair at the head of the bed.

"I brought you some soup."

The young man looks up.

"I thought you left."

"Here," Wulf says, handing him the styrofoam cup.

"Thanks."

"How's he doing?"

"The same," the boy sighs. "The doctor says she doesn't think there's any serious injury. But he still hasn't come around."

"My name's Wulf."

"I'm sorry. I didn't even think. I'm Jared."

"Pleased to meet you."

They shake hands. Jared's grip is weak. His hand is clammy. He's probably in shock himself.

"And this one?"

"Scott."

"Scott," Wulf repeats reaching down and smoothing a lock of golden hair off the deeply tanned forehead. "He looks like a tough one. I think he'll survive."

"What time is it?"

"A little after two."

"You should go home, Wulf."

"I think I'll stay around. You really shouldn't be alone here."

"Oh, God," Jared sobs, "I was hoping you'd say that."

Wulf finds a blanket in the cupboard and tosses it around Jared's shoulders.

"You really should try and get some sleep."

"I can't. Not until I know Scottie's going to be all right."

"Is he your lover?"

"Yes."

"How long have you been together?"

"About a year and a half. I've heard people talk about love at first sight all my life, but I never really believed in it. But one look at Scottie and I was hooked. He wasn't interested in me at first, but he finally came around. It's been really good. Until this."

"This will be over soon. Don't worry."

"You know, there's something awfully familiar about you," Jared says, looking at him closely. "Are you sure we haven't met somewhere before?"

"Absolutely certain," Wulf smiles. "I promise I would never have forgotten meeting someone as stunning as you."

Jared's blush is charming.

"Forgive me. I didn't mean to embarrass you."

"It's just that Scottie's the good looking one."

"Don't be silly."

"Oh, God, Scottie, if you'd just wake up."

"He's going to be all right, Jared."

"How can you be so sure?"

"Because you're here with him. He knows that. And he knows how much you love him."

Just then Scott stirs.

"*Nein, nein! Bitte, nein!*"

"He's waking up," Jared says, grabbing Scott's hand and squeezing it. "I'm here, sweetie. It's O.K. No one's trying to hurt you."

Scott settles down but doesn't open his eyes.

"Just a nightmare. I thought he was waking up."

"I'm sure it's a very good sign," Wulf says. "Tell me, that was German Scott was speaking, wasn't it?"

"His mother was from Germany. He learned the language from her. His father taught it at a university. Scott works in literary translating."

"Have you met his parents?"

"They're both dead. Scott's mom passed away when he was only three. He hardly remembers her. His dad died when he was in junior high."

"Really. What's his last name?"

"Bailey."

"My God."

"What's wrong?"

Wulf is speechless. He can hardly believe it. He stares down at the handsome young face. It's simply not possible. But why else would Scott look so uncannily familiar? Just like Wulf's brother, Georg.

"Nothing. I just feel very tired all of a sudden. I'm not young and strong like you and Scott."

"Tell that to the cop you almost killed," Jared grunts. "For a minute there I thought you really meant to."

"I think I did."

"What stopped you? He deserved it. He would have killed Scott if you hadn't stopped him."

"I felt like doing it. But I couldn't. I promised myself a long time ago I'd never let them make me into something like themselves, and tonight I almost did."

* * *

Wulf drops the coins into the pay phone and dials Ryan's number.

"Hello? Do you have any idea what time it is, whoever you are? Come to think of it, I don't care who you are. I'm hanging up and going back to sleep."

"*Achtung*, Ryan, *achtung!*"

"*Herr Doktor Professor*, is that you?"

"It is I, Ryan. Your mentor and guide. Listen, I need you to meet my seminar this morning, if you will. Take notes over their discussion. I don't particularly care to know what the students say. Unless there's some bizarre accident it'll be dreary and inane. But it would really help to have some idea of who did the assigned readings and who didn't. Think you can handle it?"

"Sure, Prof. What's up? You sick or something?"

"Just never made it to bed. And you've got no one but yourself to blame. You're the one who told me I should go to City Hall last night."

"So you were there. What did you think?"

"I'm still not sure. Tell me, Ryan. You and your friend Erik. You're both all right?"

"Oh, hell yes. After he torched a couple of squad cars, we got our asses out of there."

* * *

"No offense, sweetheart," Dave says once they're in the car leaving the airport, "but you look like death eating a soda cracker this morning. What the hell have you been up to?"

"You heard about the verdict in the Dan White case."

"Slimy bastard. They should have given him the death penalty. I would personally volunteer to strap him into the chair and throw the switch."

"Well, there was a march on City Hall last night. It ended up turning into a riot."

"I'm not surprised."

"Dave, I may be in a lot of trouble."

"What are you talking about?"

"I assaulted a policeman."

"My God."

"He was beating this young man. I mean really beating him. The boy was already down on the sidewalk, and the cop was just berserk. He was going to kill that boy. And Dave, I couldn't help myself. I only got a glimpse of that boy, but for a moment he reminded me so much of Rudi. I just went insane. I meant to hurt that cop. And I did."

"That's understandable under the circumstances."

"There's more. I spent the night at the hospital sitting up with the boy's lover."

"Is he going to be all right?"

"They think so. There don't seem to have been any injuries beyond a concussion and a couple of fairly serious gashes to the scalp. You know how badly wounds like that bleed. It always looks much worse than it is. But he hadn't regained consciousness as of an hour ago when I called. I'd really like to stop there on our way home. Just to check. Is that all right?"

"Couldn't it wait? You look completely bushed. I feel like throwing you into the shower and scrubbing the skin off you and then putting you to bed for about a week."

"No, Dave, it can't wait."

"Why not, Wulf?"

"Because either I'm losing my mind, or that boy, the one who got beaten up, is my nephew."

"What?"

"My sister Amalie's child."

"But what makes you think it's this guy?"

"Well, for starters, his name is the same. Scott Bailey. And he's about the right age."

"There's probably more than one of those floating around."

"I know. But with a German mother who died when he was a small child? With a father who was a university professor?"

"You're right. Too many coincidences. And you're not going to relax until you know for sure, are you?"

"You know me."

"All right, the hospital it is."

* * *

Scott is sitting up in bed when they walk into the room. Jared is nowhere to be seen. Wulf takes one look at the young man and stops in his tracks. Even with the bandage on Scott's head it's like looking into some kind of weird combination of mirror and time machine.

"Oh, my God," Dave mutters, "I see exactly what you mean."

"Scott?" Wulf says. "How are you feeling?"

"Head still hurts like the dickens. But I'll live. You must be the angel of mercy Jared told me about."

"Where is he?"

"Our friends showed up and took him for something to eat. Poor baby was a wreck. They should be back any time."

"He loves you very much. But you already know that."

"He'd better," Scott says. "Because I don't know how I'd go on living without him."

"I don't think you have anything to worry about."

"Listen," Scott says, "I'm really sorry. I know Jared told me your name, but my head's still pretty muddled."

"Wulf von Riedel. And this is my husband, David Lancaster."

"Pleased to meet you, David," Scott says, shaking Dave's hand. "This guy is some hero, to hear Jared tell it."

"I've always thought so," Dave smiles.

Scott's eyes close for a moment and he shakes his head.

"I'm sorry, Wulf. I really must be out of it. I could have sworn you said your name is...no, that can't be, because..."

"Von Riedel," Wulf says. "It was your mother's maiden name, wasn't it?"

"Did Jared tell you that?"

"I didn't ask him."

"What a weird coincidence."

"Actually, I don't think it's a coincidence at all," Wulf says. "I think your mother must have been my little sister, Amalie."

"Oh, shit," Scott says. "That cop really fucked up my brain. I'm starting to hallucinate. Oh, shit."

"It's all right, Scott," Wulf says, taking Scott's hand. "There's nothing wrong with your brain. And believe it or not, that cop did both of us a favor. Don't you see? I'm your uncle."

Scott stares at him for a long time. Then he nods.

"Jared said there was something familiar about you. He said he felt like he'd known you for a long, long time. I guess it's some family thing."

"Perhaps."

"I never really knew her," Scott says, a single tear running down his face. "I was only three when she died. But I have photographs. She was very beautiful. Very beautiful and very, very sad. Daddy always said horrible things happened to her during the war."

"Wulf," Dave says, "you really ought to let him get some rest. You need some yourself."

Scott looks at Wulf.

"I don't want you to go away."

"Wulf, Scott, please," Dave insists, "you're both exhausted."

"I know," Scott says. "That's not what I meant. I know you were here all night babysitting Jared. Of course you need to go home. I'm going to sleep some more myself. But I haven't had any family since my father died. Wulf, please..."

"I'll be back this evening," Wulf says.

"We both will," Dave promises. "Here, I'm leaving you our card. I'm putting it right here on the bed stand. Make sure Jared puts it in a safe place when he comes back."

"Don't worry, *liebchen*," Wulf says, bending down to kiss Scott on the forehead. "Now that we've found each other, I won't let you slip away."

San Francisco: 1982

Wulf stares down at the stack of papers and shakes his head in disbelief. It's the most recent chapter of Ryan Laughlin's dissertation. He's never seen a poorer piece of writing from a doctoral candidate. Or indeed from any graduate student. It's so different from the previous chapters Ryan has completed that he can scarcely believe it was written by the same person. And it's not just the quality of the writing that is substandard. The assertions Ryan presents are questionable at best. The arguments he uses in supporting them are flimsy and poorly developed. The research is nothing less than inexcusable. If he had received something like this on April first, he'd know it was a practical joke: a parody of bad academic writing. That's exactly the kind of thing Ryan is capable of, but not something Wulf believes he would waste his time on at this point in his program. So it must be an honest effort, and that's not good. Because it's not at all the kind of work Wulf has come to expect—take for granted, even—from Ryan. And it's not the kind of work he dares show to anyone else on Ryan's committee. Something is seriously wrong.

He hadn't wanted to chair Ryan's committee in the first place. He had feared their close friendship would prove an impediment in providing appropriate guidance to Ryan in the process of his research and writing. Now he's glad he caved in to Ryan's nonstop wheedling. As chairman, he's the first to see this chapter. He can run interference for Ryan. He can speak with Ryan about the current fiasco before anyone else on the committee has to know about it. He can take care of this unfortunate matter, leaving the other committee members none the wiser and Ryan still on track. All nice and neat and no damage done to Ryan's sterling reputation in the department.

So why is Wulf dreading their conference so much?

* * *

"*Herr Doktor Professor*, I know," Ryan says the minute he comes into the office and sees the manuscript pages lying on Wulf's desk. He flops into the old armchair he dragged into the office one day years ago from some thrift shop or other which has stayed right there ever since over Wulf's repeated protests. "It's awful, isn't it?"

"Thank God," Wulf says. "I was afraid…"

"Oh, I knew it was shit," Ryan says, hanging his head. "I shouldn't have given it to you in that shape."

"Why did you?" Wulf asks, noticing with concern the dark rings under Ryan's eyes and an instant later the bloodshot eyes themselves.

"I didn't want to disappoint you," Ryan says. "I promised you that chapter by the fifteenth and I was determined to produce it come hell or high water. Stupid, huh? As if turning in that load of shit were actually better than turning in nothing at all. If you'll give it back to me, I'll get cracking on it immediately. And I promise not to bring it back until it's right."

"Ryan?"

"What?"

Wulf looks at the matinee idol face for a moment. The skin tone is bad. There are lines he doesn't remember seeing before. And the eyes refuse to meet his. Is it drugs? Alcohol? Ryan wouldn't be the first doctoral student to turn to something like that to help him through his dissertation.

"Is everything all right?"

"Why do you ask?"

But Ryan's expression is all the answer Wulf needs.

"What is it? You can tell me. You know whatever you say will stay in this room."

"Honestly, Prof," Ryan insists, making a valiant but totally unconvincing attempt at bravado, "I have no idea what you're talking about."

"Ryan, don't do that. I know you too well. Don't shut me out. I only want to help."

Ryan looks at him like he's giving this the most serious possible consideration.

"So?"

"It's no big deal, really. Erik's been a little under the weather, that's all."

"Flu?"

"Uh, yes, flu."

"Ryan."

"Prof?"

"I want to help you."

"I know," Ryan says. "I appreciate it. I really do. And I'm sure Erik's going to feel better soon and I'll get right back to work. You'll see."

"Flu, Ryan? Erik's flu is so serious that it makes you do something like this?" He picks up the pages and shakes them. "What kind of flu is that, pray tell? I have seen many kinds of flu in my time. I have had many kinds of flu. Not one of them made Dave do something like this."

"Stop, O.K?" Ryan chokes. "Just let's not get into this, please?"

"Stop what? Trying my best to help the most brilliant graduate student I have ever worked with? Excuse me, but I'm afraid I can't just pretend to believe you and leave it at that. You should know better."

"All right," Ryan says, exhaling noisily. "All right, so it's not flu."

Wulf waits for him to continue, but he doesn't. Instead, Ryan starts to sob.

* * *

"Hello?"

"Matt, it's Wulf. Is Ashby there?"

"No. Is something wrong?"

"I need some information. Can you have him call me when he comes in?"

"Sure, Wulf. But maybe I can help. Doctor's wives know all kinds of things. You'd be surprised."

"I'm sure. Now tell me, has Ashby said anything to you about his new disease?"

"New disease? Listen, Wulf, are you and Dave all right?"

"We're fine. It's one of my graduate students. Or rather his boyfriend. He's in the hospital with some weird kind of pneumonia. Ryan is afraid he's dying."

"Wulf, I hate to tell you this, but he may be. We may all be."

* * *

Wulf stands outside Erik's hospital room holding a bunch of roses he cut from Dave's prize bushes. A sign on the door says "No Visitors." Another sign instructs anyone planning to enter to put on sterile gloves, gown, and mask and dispose of them in the bin by the door immediately upon leaving. This is worse than he'd expected. But worst of all is the coughing he can hear inside the room, a sound which takes him right back to the camp at Dora-Mittelbau.

Footsteps approach down the corridor.

"Are you here to see Mr. Velasquez?"

Wulf turns. The nurse is a tall, strong looking woman in late middle age. Her smile is warm and grave at the same time.

"Yes."

"I'm afraid he can't have any visitors today. But his friend is down in the waiting room. I'm sure he'd be happy for some company. What gorgeous roses. Those didn't come from any florist."

"No," Wulf says. "My, um, friend grows them."

"Lucky you," she smiles, "and lucky Mr. Velasquez. I'll make sure he gets them."

"Thank you," Wulf says, surrendering them to her.

"The waiting room is just down the corridor. Second door on the left."

Wulf walks toward the waiting room in a daze. That cough haunts him. Men in the camps who coughed like that seldom had more than a few hours to live. Of course this is a hospital with all the most up to date equipment. There are doctors and nurses here ready and willing to help. There are drugs no one had dreamed of back during the war. Perhaps, like so many other illnesses these days, it sounds worse than it really is. Then he remembers Ryan's tears yesterday in his office and the great, wracking sobs that shook Ryan's tall, athletic frame like a rowboat in a hurricane. Fearless Ryan, who sets police cars on fire. No, this is every bit as bad as it sounds.

In the waiting room he finds Ryan sprawled out on a sofa, snoring. Not wanting to disturb him, he almost turns to leave. But he'd hate for Ryan not to know he's been here. Almost as much as he hates the idea of Ryan keeping this vigil alone. He sits down in an armchair and leafs through a three month old issue of *Newsweek*. The fawning tone in which they write about Nancy Reagan makes him want to vomit. It sounds almost exactly like his mother used to when speaking of her great friend, Magda Goebbels. And is Mrs. Reagan really so different from that notorious Nazi wife? If so, Wulf has yet to see any indication of it. Why are his fellow citizens so deluded these days? Why are they so blindly and stupidly following this demented cretin, lapping up his deranged nonsense like cream? And why are so many things today calling up memories of things he'd much rather leave half forgotten?

Ryan stirs, rubs his eyes. Sits up. He looks around for a moment like he doesn't remember where he is.

"Prof?"

"I came to see Erik."

"They won't let you."

"I know. The nurse I ran into seemed very nice. I thought I'd sit with you for a while."

"I owe you an apology."

"No, you don't."

"I should have told you earlier," Ryan says. "I would have. But with this thing you never know how people are going to react. Your closest friends find out you have it, or even know someone who does, and they won't have anything to do with you. It's unbelievable."

"You know me better than that," Wulf says. "You have to by now."

"You're right," Ryan says, "as always. So, apology accepted?"

"Absolutely not. I refuse to accept an apology from a man who's done nothing wrong. I'll have to spank you if you keep talking like that."

"God, Wulf, you're a saint. You know that?"

"Hardly."

The tall nurse comes into the room. She has Wulf's roses in a vase.

"Mr. Laughlin, I'm sorry to interrupt you. Dr. Altman says you'd better come."

"Is it…?"

The nurse doesn't answer.

"Oh, God, no," Ryan says, lunging to his feet.

Wulf follows him down the hall, helps him into the gown, the cap, the mask, the gloves. When they're through, Ryan looks like a cross between a mummy and a spaceman.

"I'll be right here," he says.

* * *

"I know it's awful for you," Wulf says, watching Ryan push evil looking green beans around his plate. In Wulf's lexicon, "hospital food" is an oxymoron. "I wish there was something I could say. I know there's not."

"You know, Prof, you're the first person either of us knows who has bothered to come here."

"I can't believe it."

"It's true."

"In that case, I wish I'd come sooner."

"I wish I'd told you. I could kick myself. Well, it's too late now."

"Listen, is there anything Dave and I can do? Help with arrangements?"

"There's nothing to be done. Erik's family is in charge of everything. As far as they're concerned I don't exist."

"You mean he never told them about you?"

"Oh, he told them all right. They just didn't want to know anything about it. If his doctor and the hospital folks hadn't ignored them I wouldn't have been allowed to see him at all."

"That's outrageous."

"I'm not sure I dare show up at the funeral."

"You'll dare, all right. Dave and I will be there right beside you."

* * *

Wulf slips into the pew at the back of the sanctuary and sits next to Scott.

"Thanks for coming," he says.

"Jared knew him," Scott says. "He came with me. He's parking the car."

"I guess it's what we have husbands for. They're our private parking attendants. Dave always complains about it but he complains even worse about the places I park the car when it's my turn."

"My friend Jeff knew Erik, too."

"Will he be here today?"

"He's in the hospital."

"My God. Dave and I had read about this, but it's different when people you know are involved."

"Right."

"How well did Jared know Erik?" Wulf asks, wincing at the unintended meaning the minute the words are out of his mouth.

"Relax," Scott says, with a bitter little smile. "He was just another guy Jared couldn't get to first base with. There were dozens of them apparently. I guess we should both be thankful."

"You know, I've never understood it," Wulf says. "I think your husband is spectacular."

"Guys saw the silver hair and the limp and didn't look any further."

"Ridiculous."

"You don't have to sell me on him. I was crazy about him from the first minute."

"That's not the story I heard."

"You listen to the wrong people. The problem with Jared was he was devastating," Scott says. "He terrified me. In those days I liked them pretty but forgettable."

"I see."

"It seems like ancient history," Scott says, looking over his shoulder. "Ah, there are our husbands now. Ryan's with them."

* * *

They stand a little way off from the grave giving Erik's family the privacy they so obviously believe is their due. Ryan is next to Wulf, frightened to move closer. When Erik's mother saw him at the church she went into hysterics. Two of Erik's brothers, aided by the priest, tried to get the whole bunch of them to leave. Then Stefano and Tristan arrived, and one of the Velasquez cousins recognized them as fellow officers. A compromise of sorts was reached, but it left no one happy.

Wulf surreptitiously holds Dave's hand, mentally taking roll. Hardly any of them actually knew Erik, but they're almost all here. All of Wulf's extended family, which is now Ryan's family, too. Stefano and Tristan, of course. Nick and Dario with their infant son, Dario, Jr. Dario's appearance created a stir among the female Velasquezes. He's constantly being mistaken for that Mexican movie star whose name Wulf can't ever quite remember. Cooper and Griffin are here. Cooper, always pugnacious, looks like he's spoiling for a fight. Forrest and Morgan have Forrest's cousin Jimmie Lee with them. Just out of the hospital himself, he's obviously not well at all. Morgan's brother Nelson and his boyfriend Sean have come, too. Ashby is here by himself: Matt's on a long haul San Francisco to Paris this afternoon. Will and Evan have brought their friends Kirk and Yvette. Elizabeth and Ned stand with Buzz and Trevor. Jared's cousin Maya and her girlfriend Renee are sitting on a bench over to the side: Maya is pregnant, and her morning sickness sometimes extends well into the afternoon. And there's Jamie Altman, Erik's doctor and gym buddy of half this crowd: how many funerals of his patients has he been to this last month?

All these beautiful, strong, brave, smart young friends of his and Dave's— is anyone safe? Who will be left in a few months time when Maya's twins are born? Who will be left next summer when the parade flows down Market Street? Will there be anyone left to parade down Market Street?

Yes, Wulf thinks, they have to survive this. They've survived so much already. This can't be the end: it can't all have been in vain.

* * *

Wulf pounds on the door of Ryan's apartment. He knows Ryan is in there because the downstairs neighbor said he could hear him walking around. After a long time, he hears footsteps coming toward the door. But it doesn't open.

"Whoever you are," Ryan yells hoarsely, "go away and leave me alone."

"Ryan, it's Wulf."

"Go away, Prof. I mean it."

"You'd better let me in. You know what a stubborn old German I am. I'll spend the night out here if you make me. I swear to God I will."

"Jesus."

Wulf picks up the bag of groceries at his feet. The door swings open and he charges in before Ryan has a chance to change his mind. Ryan's appearance shocks him but he doesn't let himself think about that.

"Which way is the kitchen?"

"Over there."

"When's the last time you ate?"

"I don't know. A couple of days ago."

"When's the last time you took a shower?"

"Last week sometime."

"Go. Clean up while I heat this chicken soup Dave made. And I'm going to fix you a sandwich with this Siberian Soldier's loaf he baked specially for you."

"You sound like somebody's grandma."

"Good. Go. Or do you want me to strip you naked myself and scrub your skin off? I'll do it, you know."

                                        * * *

Ryan wolfs down the food.

"I'm going to tell you a story," Wulf says. "This happened back during the war. And don't make any smart remarks about whether it was the Second Peloponnesian or the Third Punic. I only look that old."

"Aye, aye, Captain."

"Well, I lost someone I loved with all my heart. We had been lovers for nearly six years. The camp guards made me watch while they beat him to death. After that I didn't want to live any more. I simply couldn't go on. I tried my best to kill myself. You wouldn't think that would have presented any great challenge in a Nazi prison camp, but I couldn't manage it.

"So I lived. It took a long time, but I finally realized there were things I had to do. It would have been much easier not to, but I did them. One foot in front of the other. One day and then the next. Slowly but surely the pain eased. I found love again. I found my life's work. None of that would have happened if I had given up as I ached so desperately to do. Do you hear what I'm trying to tell you?"

Ryan looks up from his soup bowl. There are tears running down his cheeks. He rivets Wulf with horrendously bloodshot eyes. He unbuttons his flannel shirt and pulls it open. He points to three purple blotches on his chest.

"You see these?"

Wulf nods.

"Do you know what they are?"

Wulf shakes his head.

"They're cancer lesions. Kaposi's sarcoma. Erik had them. If the pneumonia hadn't killed him, the cancer would have in time. Do you hear what I'm trying to tell you?"

"Yes."

"It's over, Prof. Finished. You don't have to worry about my dissertation any more, because I'm not coming back to school. I'm not going to live long enough to finish my doctorate anyway."

"You don't know that."

"You can't tell me I'm wrong."

"No, I can't"

"So what's the use?"

"Neither can you tell me for certain that I'm wrong, Ryan. As long as you're still alive, there's still a chance. And you have things to do."

"Such as?"

"Three more chapters and your dissertation will be finished. I know you've done the research already. There are probably rough drafts of those chapters around here somewhere. So perhaps you will decide not to finish the degree. Maybe it would be a good idea not to put yourself through the ordeal of the oral examinations. Don't even bother submitting the work to the committee. Maybe that's the only possible choice under the circumstances. Maybe in your position that's what I would do myself. But you must at least finish the writing."

"What the hell for?"

"Because if you finish it, I promise you I will submit it to my publishers. I give you my solemn oath I will see that they publish it. And then there will be something left when you're gone. Something that you did. Something nobody else could do. You're a scholar, Ryan. A very fine one whether you ever earn your Ph.D. or not. One of the finest I have known. Ten years from now, or twenty or thirty, I want people to see that book on a library shelf somewhere and take it down and read it and know that you were here and what you were capable of. I want them to be as amazed by your intellect and scholarship as I have been all these years. And most of all I want them to read the page where you dedicate the book to Erik and know that he was here too. And that you loved him."

"Prof," Ryan sobs, "I can't do it. I swear to God I can't. Please don't try to make me."

"I know you can. If I have to move in here with you, if I have to type it out from your dictation and Dave has to come in every day to cook your meals and do your laundry and cleaning, and if I have to make my Scott and Jared come over and help us nurse you, I will. Because you will do this. Do you understand me? If this terrible thing is going to take you from us before your time, if that truly is going to be your fate, you must at least go down fighting."

Berlin: 1985

The airliner banks and begins its final approach. Wulf stares out the window, eyes peeled for familiar landmarks.

"When was the last time you flew into this airport?" Scott asks.

"Summer of 1943," Wulf says. "It was at night and the city was under a blackout because of the Allied air raids. You couldn't see a thing. We might as well have been in the middle of the Gobi Desert. I was a pilot myself, of course. I had made many landings here. I took my first flying lessons here, as a matter of fact. But that night I could hardly believe that the men flying that plane were able to bring us in safely. It was an old Junkers trimotor: we called the type *Tante Ju*. It was a humbling experience, I can tell you. We fighter jockeys always thought we were the best pilots in the sky. But when those boys landed that old crate in the dark that night, well, it knocked me down a notch or two."

"I thought you came back here in the 'Fifties."

"I did," Wulf nods. "Three different times. I was researching my book on the plots to assassinate Hitler. But on those trips I always took the train from the American Zone. It was the height of the Cold War. There was air service into Berlin but I wasn't sure it was safe."

"I read that book when I was in junior high," Scott nods. "Daddy had told me about my grandfather being executed for his role in the plot, so of course I was interested. I remember I would stare at his picture trying to figure out if I looked like him."

"It sold better than anyone expected," Wulf says. "And it made me a little money. Nobody gets rich in academic publishing. But my committee at NYU woudn't accept it as my dissertation. They said my personal association with the events prevented me from being sufficiently objective in my scholarship. So I came back to Germany and did more research and wrote a book about the Weimar Republic. It wasn't nearly as good a book. I'm not sure why my publishers accepted it. Probably because of how well my first book had done. I don't suppose anyone read it. But it earned me my Ph.D. And Columbia offered me a lectureship that eventually turned into a tenured position. By then I'd learned my lesson and never wrote about World War II again."

"Why not?"

"The academic community in America simply wouldn't trust the word of a German of my generation on the subject of modern German history. They still haven't gotten over that. It's the same reason the first serious academic studies of homosexuality had to be done by straight people. Of course back then, a gay man who had any aspirations to a tenured position wouldn't have dared to be open about himself. People would automatically have thought he had nothing more on his mind than dragging cute students into the bushes and corrupting them."

* * *

Scott handles the rented Volkswagen like a native German taxi driver, a rarity in these days of Turkish immigration. It's as if he has a map of the city wired into his brain. He doesn't take a single wrong turn between the airport and their hotel. All those trips he's made working with authors, Wulf supposes. He's content to slump in the passenger seat. Hardly anything he sees rushing past the car windows looks at all familiar. It's as if he's visiting a strange city for the first time. He finds this comforting. The less he recognizes, the less this is going to hurt. He wonders if this reaction is typical of émigrés or his alone.

"You O.K?"

"Yes."

"Jet lag is a bitch."

"I did everything Jamie Altman said I should, and look at me."

"What do doctors know?" Scott snorts. "Don't get me wrong. Jamie's a wonderful man. I'll keep trying to set people up with him until I get him married off. But doctors might just as well all be voodoo practitioners from what I can tell. Every time I go to see Jamie, who anybody will tell you is the very best there is, he sits quietly while I diagnose myself and tell him what he should prescribe."

"Does that actually work?"

"Look at me. I'm not dead yet."

Wulf stares at this beautiful young man who's so uncannily like himself at that age, right down to the arrogant streak that would do justice to a Prussian nobleman. He's sure the family will find Scott fascinating.

"The minute we get to the hotel," Scott says, "I'm putting you straight to bed. Pardon the expression. I promised Dave I'd take good care of you."

* * *

"So how many times did you come over in all?" Scott asks the next morning over breakfast in their hotel room.

"Four."

"And you never saw your family?"

"No. The first time I came I tried to. That was in nineteen fifty-seven. I had written to tell them when I'd be arriving and where I'd be staying. They sent my oldest brother, Willi, to meet me at my hotel. He gave me news of them all. Georg had taken his family to Sydney. Jurgen and Heinrich had finally returned from Siberia. Your mother had died a few months earlier. He showed me some pictures of you that she had sent. Everyone agreed that you were a von Riedel down to your toes. They never saw her again after she left for America with your father, you know. Anyway, Willi and I had coffee and he explained quite clearly that none of them wanted anything to do with me. They felt sorry for me, of course. They knew it wasn't my fault I was a pervert and a degenerate, but I simply wasn't welcome to visit them at home. And it was apparent from what he said that they didn't particularly appreciate the letters I'd been writing. So on my next trip I didn't bother trying to contact them. And I stopped sending them letters except at Christmas. By the last time I was over here, the wall had gone up and they were living on the wrong side of it. It was very tense in those early days. There was no question of trying to cross. Nothing like now, with people traveling back and forth from one side to the other like it's commuting between Manhattan and Brooklyn."

"So except for Willi, you haven't seen any of them since the war?"

"That's right."

"Are you nervous?"

"A little. But I think you're probably more anxious than I am."

"You've got that right. They still blame Dad, don't they?"

"I don't know. Maybe not so much any more."

"We'll see."

* * *

"This is incredible," Scott says, the shutter of his camera clicking away like automatic weapons fire.

"It is," Wulf agrees. As far as the eye can see the wall is covered with graffiti. But not just any graffiti. This stuff is highly political in content. And there's no question about the talent that it required. Some of it is museum quality art.

"You know, the two of us should really do a book together about this," Scott says, stopping just long enough to change rolls of film.

"I expect someone already has."

"Do you think?"

"Look around you," Wulf says. "Don't these West Berliners seem every bit as entrepreneurial as anyone you'd see in New York or Los Angeles?"

"Yes," Scott says. "So?"

"You don't imagine nobody around here has figured out yet how to exploit this thing for profit. It would be like the French never making a nickel out of the Eiffel Tower. Or our friends back home deciding that the Golden Gate Bridge is nothing more than a way to get from point A to point B."

"I see your point," Scott says. "Come on. It looks like there's some really good stuff down there."

* * *

The next morning there's a long line of cars waiting to cross at Checkpoint Charlie. Volkswagens, B.M.W.'s. Opels, Mercedes. Tens of thousands of West Germans have relatives in East Berlin. And things have changed since the worst days of the Cold War. Traveling to the Eastern Zone seems to have become routine. Though traveling in the other direction is still an impossibility for just about everyone but artists on official cultural exhanges and Olympic athletes.

Wulf and Scott are on foot. The car rental company doesn't allow taking the Volkswagen across. They walk through the gap in the wall and it's like entering another century. Here's the Berlin Wulf remembers. And very nearly as shabby as it was the last time he saw it. It's as if only the most rudimentary of reconstruction has taken place in the forty years since the war ended. The buildings are in an obvious state of slow decay. The pavement is cracked and potholed. Ground floor windows of the buildings they pass are bricked up. It's like one of the run down areas of New York City.

"There's a tram stop up ahead," Scott says as if he's the native guide and Wulf the first time tourist. "How are you holding up?"

"Would you please stop asking that? You make it sound like I'm eighty years old and you're expecting me to keel over any second."

"Sorry," Scott says. "It's a bad habit, I know. It comes of having to babysit your own father practically from the time you're in kindergarten."

"Was it that bad?"

"Yes. Exactly that bad. We'd never have had a hot meal if I hadn't cooked it. We'd never have had a stitch of clean clothing if I hadn't done the laundry. He'd never have gotten out of bed in the morning if I hadn't rolled him onto the floor. And you know what? I adored him. Everybody who knew him did. And what's crazier than that is I didn't think there was anything out of the ordinary about all I was having to do to keep us going. I thought all kids had to handle their parents that way. At least until I got to know the next door neighbors."

"It wasn't his fault, Scott," Wulf says.

"You don't have to tell me. I've had plenty of time to figure it out."

"She was a very sick woman. I don't know if anyone could have helped her. It must have been hell for your father watching her suffer the way she did. After being gang raped for forty-eight hours straight by the Russians. They raped your grandmother, too. But she was a middle aged woman by then and she had been through a lot. She was just tough enough to stand it. But poor Amalie was only sixteen years old."

"Nobody ever told me she had killed herself," Scott says. "They just said she had gone away to be with Jesus. You know those country Baptists. Or maybe you don't, come to think of it. Anyway, do you know when I finally realized the truth?"

"No. When?"

"When Zane Stark killed himself. I did a lot of soul searching about whether I could have stopped him if I'd gone back. For some reason it started me thinking about Dad, and I didn't know why. What could he have to do with my feelings about Zane's death? Then it just came to me."

"That makes sense," Wulf says.

"I still don't know how she did it."

"Gas," Wulf says. "She pulled your father's car into the garage and sat in it with the motor running. She had left you with the woman next door. She said she had to go run some errands and she didn't want to take you with her because she was afraid you were getting sick."

"Really."

"That's the story Willi told me."

"That old Buick?"

"I have no idea."

"It must have been. It's one of my earliest memories. Why did Daddy go out and buy a new car the day after Mutti went to live with Jesus? It seemed like a strange thing for him to do. Of course, I was a tiny little kid. Lots of things seem strange to a kid that age."

"Indeed."

"Aha, here we are. Tram stop."

"It's likely to be a long wait," Wulf says, looking down the long, empty street.

* * *

Wulf's hand shakes slightly as he knocks on the door of Willi's apartment. The corridor is dimly lit and smells of sausages and cabbage. He hears footsteps inside moving toward the door.

"No turning back now," Scott mutters.

The knob turns and the door opens.

"Wulf?"

"*Ja.* Here I am. You look just like *Vati.*"

"Well, don't just stand there like an old cow chewing her cud in a field," Willi grunts. "Come in, come in."

Wulf and Scott enter the small apartment.

"So," Willi says, "you are our Amalie's boy?"

"Yes," Scott says.

"Well, you look like a von Riedel all right. No question about that. Look at him, Wulf. Doesn't he look just like Kurt?"

"Yes, he does."

"And really very much like Georg's oldest son, Rainer. That Georg. He had the right idea. Getting out of here while there was still a chance. He's become a very rich man out there, let me tell you."

"What do you hear from him?"

"*Ach.* A heart attack last month. But he's on the mend now. Juditha says those Australian doctors are wizards. Now I ask you, Wulf, where the hell would Australians learn anything about medicine? It doesn't make any sense to me. When she called us I told her she should bring him back to Germany. For the doctors, you know? Just until he's truly recovered. But she laughed at me."

"How is Ursula?" Wulf asks, watching Scott wander around the small living room looking at photographs on the walls like he's in a museum.

"She visits her mother this afternoon at the old people's home. She will be back soon."

"And how is Mutti?"

"Sleeping. Ursula will wake her up when she comes. Ursula will want to make her ready before you see her. Come, sit down both of you. I will bring beer. And Ursula has left us some sandwiches. You must tell me about your California. Is it like what we see on television?"

"You get American television programs here?" Scott asks, astonished.

"Ssh," Willi grins. "Not so loud, *junge*. Nobody is supposed to know that we tune in to the West Berlin stations. Everyone does it, of course, but nobody admits it. Ah, life in the Democratic Republic."

* * *

Wulf enters the tiny bedroom with Scott behind him.

"Is that you, Wulfchen?"

She's sitting up in bed, a tiny, fragile creature, hardly recognizable. But he'd know that voice anywhere, still velvety and musical at the age of ninety.

"*Ja*, Mutti."

"Come closer so I can see you. My poor old eyes are not so good."

He moves to the side of the bed and bends down. Surrounded by that ruined face, her eyes are bright and vibrant. He brushes a wrinkled cheek with his lips.

"*Ach, mein lieber Kind.* It has been far too long. Such a terrible shame. And who is this with you? What a handsome young man. He reminds me of someone."

"Didn't they tell you I was bringing Amalie's son with me?"

"Silly me, so they did."

"He speaks German as well as I do, so be careful what you say in front of him."

"Really? Come here, child. Give a forgetful old woman a kiss."

Scott bends over her.

"Oh, my darling," she says, stroking Scott's cheek with a claw of a hand. "How beautiful you are. Do you know, Wulf, he looks exactly like your father did when I first met him? I thought he was the handsomest man in the world. I nearly fainted when he kissed my hand that afternoon in *Tante* Luise's drawing room. I was only fifteen. Unfortunately, he only had eyes for my cousin Felizia. I could have killed her for hogging him like she did that day. But I promised myself I'd marry him in spite of her. And I kept my promise, didn't I? Child, you have your dear mother's eyes. So clear and so extraordinarily blue. Oh, it is so wonderful to see you at last."

"I'm very happy to be here, Grandmother."

"And my Wulfchen, too. My dear, dear Wulfchen. Sit down, both of you. Sit, please."

Wulf pulls up chairs and they sit down, one on either side of the bed.

"I was so happy, Wulfi, when you wrote to tell us you had found this boy. Not just because my daughter's child had been restored to our family, but because it had been such a long time since there had been any word of you."

"I'm sorry."

"No, no, I'm not blaming you. It was my fault, I know. Oh, Wulf, I have spent so much of my life being a fool. I understand it now, and I think about it so much. How else should I spend my time? I cannot go out of the apartment on my own. I'm not strong enough. I can no longer see well enough to read. And I hate that infernal television. So stupid. So boring and vulgar. Such a waste of time. So all I have to help me pass the time is remembering. I sit here for hours trying to decide what is the worst thing I ever did out of my hopeless foolishness. I don't know. There are so many things to choose from. It is much easier to decide what were the few good things I did. I enjoy thinking about those."

"Mutti," Wulf chokes, "stop it. There's no need for such talk. It's not why Scott and I came to see you."

"You think not? Well, you are wrong. There are things I must say to you. Who knows if there will ever be another chance? Do you think I want to go to my grave with these things still on my conscience? I may be nothing but a silly old woman now, but even I know better than that. No, Wulf, you will hear. You must hear. If I am strong enough to say these things, you are certainly strong enough to hear them. And you, my grandson, you will hear. Because my foolishness cost your dear mother her life, and you must know the story so that you can remember her properly."

"Oh, Mutti," Wulf sighs.

"It was that bitch, Magda Goebbels. 'How kind of her', I thought every time she returned one of my calls. I knew not to expect her to see me again after your father's trouble. Who could blame her? But she would still talk to me on the telephone as long as I promised to tell no one of our friendship. 'Bless her', I thought. 'How noble', I thought. 'Such an important woman and here I am so disgraced, the widow of a traitor to Germany'."

"He was not a traitor to Germany," Wulf insists.

"Of course not," she says. "I know that now. I understand it all now, when it is too late. But you must understand how it was at the time. And how stupid I was. Well, anyway, that Magda Goebbels, damn her to hell. And damn me for listening to her. Even that very last day before the Russians came she was still saying, 'Oh my dear, there's no need to be so frightened. The *Wehrmacht* has fought the Russians to a standstill. They can hold them outside the city indefinitely, and soon the Americans will come and everything will be fine again. There is no need for you to flee. There is no need to fear for your sweet Amalie or your lovely home.' Stupid, stupid me. After what they had done to your father. What they would have done to your brothers if they had been able to capture them. I was spitting on the grave of my husband every time I spoke to her. But did that stop me? No. So I did as she said. I stayed put. Made no preparations to leave or to protect us from the Russians. Not knowing of course that that woman was already in the bunker. Or that she was already planning her own suicide. Wulf, I trusted her. A woman who would poison her own children. I shouldn't have listened to her. I should have taken your sister and left the city. How God can ever forgive me for such stupidity—I simply don't know. I had plenty of money. I had my jewels still. We could have gone anywhere. We had many friends in the west. I had cousins in Sweden. It was not as if I had nowhere safe to take your sister. But we sat in that house and we listened to the ridiculous lies they were telling on the radio and just let it all happen to us.

"And after the Russians came there was no question of leaving. They took everything they could get their hands on. And soon we were too sick and weak to think of traveling, even if that had been possible. And then it was soon obvious that Amalie was pregnant."

"You mean my mother had another child?" Scott asks, astonished.

"They were stillborn. Twin boys. She was too young. Too weak. And she had suffered so much. What little food we had in those days was terrible. When we had food at all. Those babies would certainly have had many health problems if they had lived. There were many children like that after the war, with such tragic defects. So very, very sad. It was a mercy that she lost them. But it was so terrible for her. In spite of how she had come to conceive them, she still mourned them with all her heart. She thought God was punishing her by taking those children away. Now what would God have been punishing her for? What had she done wrong, I ask you? And how could anyone have been as stupid as I was?"

"Mutti," Wulf says, "that was all so long ago. Why upset yourself like this?"

"Wait," she interrupts. "There is more you must hear. You must both hear how cruel I was to her when she met this boy's father. How I told her if she left us she must never think of coming back again. How I said I would never forgive her if she married that young American. I told her he was a lazy good for nothing. I told her he would never take care of her properly. I told her he was a drunkard."

"He was a drunkard," Scott says.

"Perhaps so. But she believed he loved her. And all the young men were dead. Or maimed. Or in Siberia, like her brothers. Where was she going to find a husband if she didn't marry that American? And a chance to go to America? It was like a dream of heaven, I tell you. A dream of heaven. I must have been crazy, trying to stand in her way like that. I should have been happy for her to have such an opportunity. So she went away from here thinking I didn't love her. That she had disappointed me. I might as well have held a gun to her head and pulled the trigger. I might as well have given her poison to drink, like Magda Goebbels did with her children. And because of it she was miserable all the time and this lovely boy had to grow up without a mother. Oh, the shame. The horrible shame.

"And then you, Wulf. How could I have believed the horrible things the Nazis said about you?"

"It was true, Mutti," Wulf says. "I was a homosexual. I was Rudi Wagner's lover."

"I don't mean that. I mean what they said about how filthy and depraved you were. I knew better. You were my child, not some degenerate, some animal. And I knew Rudi. I loved him like my own son. But I listened to what they said and I didn't disagree with them and I stood by and let them put you in prison without lifting a hand to help either of you."

"It would have done no good."

"I could have insisted that your father write the court a letter from the front. A decorated war hero and field marshal: they would not have dared to hurt you after that. I could have hired a better attorney than the one they gave you. I could have begged Magda Goebbels to intercede on your behalf. But all I could think of was my own embarrassment and the way our family was being disgraced. And then to go on for years and years continuing to think those horrible things of you. What kind of mother was I? To ruin the lives of two of my children that way?"

"Stop," Wulf says. "I won't listen to any more of this. What's done is done."

"I know that. I know nothing can be done to change it. But you must give me a chance to show you that I know better now. That I'm sorry now. Surely that must mean something to you, that I'm sorry."

"It means everything, Mutti," Wulf chokes.

"And you my grandson?"

"We're all human," Scott says. "We all make mistakes. We all need forgiveness now and then."

"Oh, my dear ones. Now we understand each other better, *ja*? Now I can have some peace of mind. Not much, I'm afraid, but it will be enough."

"I hope so," Wulf says.

"Child, go over to that cupboard and open it."

Scott does as she tells him.

"There are two boxes, one large and one not so large."

"I see them."

"Take them out."

"All right."

"The not so large one is for you, my grandson. When your mother left us, she went practically empty handed. She refused to take anything I had ever given her. She said she didn't want any of it. Under the circumstances you can hardly blame her. There are things of hers that you must have. I have kept them all these years just in case. She needs you to remember her. Perhaps these things will help."

"Thank you, grandmother."

"The large box is for you, Wulf. The day after you and Rudi were arrested, Rudi's servant came to me with a suitcase full of things he had taken from the apartment. I was able to hide them from the Russians. I have saved them all this time. I apologize for keeping them so long. I was stupid. I kept thinking you would change and come back to us, and I would give them to you then. Well, you will have it all now."

Wulf looks at the cardboard box, stunned.

"Now you will both go. I am very tired. Ask Ursula to bring me some tea, please."

* * *

"Do you want me to leave you alone?" Scott asks. "I can go take a walk."

"That's all right, Scottie," Wulf says, pulling open the flaps of the box. "Actually I'm glad to have someone here with me. This all has to be looked over before we take it through customs. I would rather not do that alone."

"I'm still surprised we were able to get the boxes through the border crossing," Scott says.

"Willi knew what he was talking about."

"Do you have any idea what's in here?" Scott asks, sitting next to him on the bed.

"I couldn't even begin to guess what Hans thought he should try to save. Or what the Gestapo may have left in the apartment. In addition to their other qualities they were horrible looters. This may be nothing but junk."

The box is tightly packed. Scott had to carry it most of the way because of its weight. Each item is wrapped in cloth that looks like it started life as bed linen. Thin strips of material are knotted around each bundle. The cloth is old and practically disintegrating. Wulf fusses with a knot.

"Why not just cut it?" Scott suggests, reaching into his pocket and pulling out his Swiss Army knife.

"Good idea." Wulf takes the knife and gingerly cuts through the tie. He unwraps the bundle. Inside is a small leather case, the kind jewelry is packaged in. He opens the hinged lid. It's the bracelet of heavy gold links Rudi gave him for his nineteenth birthday.

"God, how gorgeous," Scott breathes. "It must be worth a fortune."

"Prewar German gold? No kidding."

"She never sold it," Scott says. "And I'm sure she could have used the money."

"Indeed," Wulf says. "That speaks volumes, don't you think?"

"Was it yours or his?"

"Mine. A gift from him."

He closes the case and sets it down on the bed. He pulls out another bundle. He fumbles with the knife.

"Here. Let me do it."

"Please."

Inside the bundle is a small, flat, highly polished wooden box. Wulf knows without looking what it contains.

"What is it?"

"One of Rudi's bronze medal from the Olympics. He was a decathlete, you remember."

"Holy shit, you don't see those every day."

They continue opening the bundles. Hans seems to have known about every piece of jewelry either Rudi or Wulf owned. Except for the matching gold rings they had been wearing when they were arrested, nothing is missing. There is even Rudi's heavy gold toilet set. Wulf remembers leaving his own matching one behind in France and wonders what ever happened to it. There are his own *Luftwaffe* medals, which he had always left in Berlin with Rudi for safekeeping. As they dig toward the bottom of the box, the bundles get larger. A highly polished wooden box contains the hand made scale model Rudi ordered for Wulf of the Bugatti coupe. A pasteboard box contains a portrait photo of Wulf in his brand new *Luftwaffe* Captain's uniform.

"Whoa," Scott mutters, "you were quite the hunk, weren't you?"

Wulf shrugs. The picture might as well be of a stranger. He can hardly remember what it was like to be that smiling young daredevil. There are only three flat bundles left and two larger items he's sure are the photo albums. They open the smallest of the flat bundles. It's an autographed publicity photo of Rudi.

"God," Scott says. "He was a beauty, too."

"This was taken before I ever met him," Wulf says. "Mutti's Cousin Konrad got it for me. He was Director General of UFA, where Rudi was under contract. This is just a standard publicity photo. I suppose it must have been taken in 1935 or 36."

"Man, you two must have made an absolutely stunning couple."

"Everyone said so," Wulf nods. "You couldn't tell it to look at me now, of course."

"Nonsense. You look pretty terrific."

"For a man in his sixties, perhaps."

"You could pass for fifteen years younger than that."

"Still," Wulf says, "unless you die young, you're middle aged or old for a lot longer than you're young and beautiful."

He pulls out the next bundle, a publicity photo of Rudi taken during the filming of *Die Schwimmbad Spionage*. The antique frame, heavy Prussian silver, is hardly tarnished. The inscription, unlike the one on the previous photo, is a personal message. Wulf still remembers watching Rudi write it as he lay in Rudi's bed in the aftermath of their first night of lovemaking.

"It's unbelievable," Scott says reverently. "Both of you so gorgeous. And looking enough alike you could almost be twins."

"We played brothers in the movies."

"You were an actor, too? You never told me."

"I wasn't really an actor. They only used me because of how much I looked like Rudi. We made five films together in all."

"Amazing."

Wulf turns to look at Scott. He wonders if Scott realizes how much he looks like the men in those photos himself. Probably not, he decides. Scott seems as oblivious to his own beauty as he was himself in his time. Wulf grasps the last of the bundles with a shaking hand. This, he's sure, is the photo he's been dreading since first laying eyes on the box.

"You unwrap it," he tells Scott.

"Mother of God," Scott says, gazing at the photo in its art nouveau frame. "Didn't I just say you two must have been magnificent together? When was this taken?"

"Fall of 'thirty-nine. Just after the invasion of Poland."

"I didn't know Rudi was in the *Luftwaffe* too."

"He wasn't. That's another publicity photo. From *Return of the Spy Brothers*."

"*Return of the Spy Brothers*," Scott nods. "What was it about?"

"It was a sequel to our first film together, which was a smash hit. They rushed it into production almost immediately. We played brothers who were *Luftwaffe* officers. We busted up a Soviet spy ring and kept the location of our top secret fighter plane base from being discovered."

"I'm sorry to say it, but it sounds awful."

"Oh, it was. They were all awful, the films we made. Such contrived plots and bombastic dialogue. Pure propaganda. Not art at all. Rudi was always much better than his material."

"But look at the two of you."

"Yes," Wulf sighs.

"What's left?" Scott asks, peering into the box for more treasures.

"If it's what I think, it's a couple of photo albums. Rudi was a fanatic about taking pictures. Every vacation trip. Sitting around the studios waiting for the crews to set up for the next scene. Wherever we went he took dozens of photos. It used to infuriate me. I really didn't enjoy having my picture taken."

"Let's see."

"Look at them if you like," Wulf says, suddenly overcome. "I need to rest."

San Francisco: 1988

"Mr. von Riedel?"

The doctor seems ridiculously young, but Wulf supposes it's mostly because he feels so old and decrepit.

"Yes."

"We've got Mr. Lancaster stabilized. We're sending him up to cardiac I.C.U. You'll be able to see him there. There's no hurry. It'll be about thirty minutes."

"Thanks."

"I have to warn you, sir. He could have another attack at any time. The first twenty-four hours are crucial in these cases. We've got a full cardiology workup scheduled for first thing tomorrow."

"Thank you."

Wulf wasn't planning to call anyone at this time of night. But he realizes now that there's no way he can sit this vigil alone. He finds a pay phone and gets the small slip of paper out of his wallet. He doesn't trust himself to remember Scott and Jared's number.

* * *

"How is he?" Jared asks. He's got a spectacular crop of five o'clock shadow that makes him even sexier than usual. In a black sweatshirt and jeans, he looks like a Hollywood cat burglar.

"Holding his own."

"How long have you been here?"

"We got to the emergency room about midnight."

"You should have called sooner."

"I didn't want to disturb you."

"What are you talking about? I still owe you for the night you sat with me when Scott was assaulted by that cop."

"You don't owe me anything."

"I left a message at his hotel."

"His hotel?"

"He's in Berlin."

"That's right," Wulf says. "I forgot."

* * *

"Mr. Lancaster is awake now," the critical care nurse says. "You can go in and see him."

"I'll be right back," Wulf tells Jared.

He walks into the tiny cubicle. Machines hum, buzz, and beep, keeping Dave alive, at least for the time being. He threads his way through a maze of stands, cords, tubing until he's hext to the bed. He bends over and kisses Dave's forehead.

"How are you feeling?" he asks.

"Like I'm dying."

"You're not going to die," Wulf says. "I won't let you."

"Good."

"Is there anything I can get you?"

"Just don't go away, huh?"

"Don't worry."

"I hate to put you through this."

"It's all right. Jared's here, being my wingman."

"You'd better call Nick Romanovsky."

"There's no need to disturb him."

"In the morning, I mean."

"Dave, nothing's going to happen. You'll be fine."

"Just call Nick, please."

* * *

"I've brought breakfast for both of you," Tristan says, looking ridiculously chipper. "Takeout. The stuff they serve down in the cafeteria will kill you."

"Bless you," Wulf says.

"Thanks, bud," Jared grunts, half asleep.

"How is he?"

"Holding his own. We're waiting to see the cardiologist."

"Nick called. He'll be by just as soon as he drops the boys off at Montessori."

"All right."

"And I'm supposed to remind you to go vote sometime today."

"Oh, God," Wulf says, "it completely slipped my mind."

"The end of the Reagan era," Tristan says. "I can't wait."

"Don't count your chickens," Jared says. "If that halfwit Bush wins, nothing will change."

* * *

There's barely room in the cubicle for Dr. Chang, the cardiologist, and Wulf.

"You're quite lucky, actually," Dr. Chang tells Dave. "It could have been much worse."

"Yeah, doc," Dave says. "I could be dead right now."

"You did everything right. You apparently called at the first sign of the attack. That's key. You're improving by the hour. But I'd like to do a bypass procedure as soon as possible."

"Bypass?" Wulf asks.

"Triple, most probably," Dr. Chang says.

"What does 'as soon as possible' mean?" Dave grunts.

"This afternoon."

"So soon?" Wulf asks.

"The sooner the better," Dr. Chang says. "The chances of full recovery increase markedly if the procedure is performed within the first seventy-two hours of the original attack. We could wait a day if you insist, but I'd prefer to go ahead."

"You're the doctor," Dave says.

"I see that Dr. Altman is your personal physician."

"That's right," Wulf says.

"I've got a call in to him. He'll be by sometime this morning to answer any questions you have. If you're not prepared to go on with the procedure after talking with him tell the nurse, and we'll cancel for today."

"Thanks, Doctor Chang," Wulf says.

* * *

"Morning, gentlemen," Cooper says. As always, he's a walking advertisement for a hard core exercise regimen and expensive personal care products. "What's the word?"

"Triple bypass surgery this afternoon," Jared says. "Tentatively at least."

"Right," Cooper says. "Who's the cardiologist?"

"Dr. Chang."

"Jewish wife. Three kids. I sold them their place in St. Francis Wood. English Tudor. Oops, sorry about the redundancy. Don't tell Griffin, please.

Wulf, I know Dave will come through it like a champ. I've got a rotation set up so Helen of Troy and Guinevere get walked and fed."

"Thank you so much."

"Sorry I can't stay," Cooper says. "I'm meeting clients in twenty minutes. Showing a Mediterranean in Pacific Heights."

"Go get 'em, boy," Jared yawns.

"Griffin will be by after school. If it's convenient, Wulf, he'll take you to go vote. Gotta show those bastards who's boss."

"Which bastards would those be?" Wulf asks.

"Any and all Republicans."

* * *

"I'm sorry, Nick," Wulf says. "I know how busy you are with the boys. But he insisted on seeing you."

"Damn right," Nick says. "How ya feelin', champ? Not so hot, huh?"

"I've been better," Dave says.

"What can I do for you?"

"About my will."

"Oh?" Nick glances at Wulf, alarm flickering in his eyes.

"Just tell me everything's in order. I don't want there to be any glitches."

"Well," Nick says, "of course there's nothing to worry about. I'm sure the surgery will go just fine and you'll be back on your feet before you know it."

"The will, Nick."

"Yes, Dave, the will. The will is airtight. Maya and I went back over it just a couple of weeks ago during our annual review. You can rest easy."

"I told you, Dave," Wulf says.

* * *

Jamie Altman arrives, looking like an Arrow Shirt ad. It's one of Wulf's greatest regrets currently that Jamie and Wulf's old research assistant Ryan Laughlin weren't able to make a go of it. What a catch this man is. With a bedside manner like his, he could get away with murder.

"So how's our patient this morning?"

"I'd be a lot happier if this meeting were taking place on the golf course," Dave says.

"I'll bet. But since I don't golf, I guess I'd have to be your caddy."

"I'd like to see that," Wulf laughs.

"What kind of doctor doesn't golf?" Dave grumbles.

"One who paints water colors," Wulf says, grinning at Jamie, whose work has won awards.

"I've spoken with Dr. Chang."

"What's his hurry?" Dave asks. "Is business that slow this month?"

"Business is business," Jamie shrugs. "Seriously, Dave, I think he's right about this. If you really don't want to have the procedure, there are other things we can do for you. But your recovery will be slower."

"Slower than after major surgery?"

"That's right. And without the procedure there's a far greater chance of another attack. This is the best we have to offer right now."

"See, Dave," Wulf says.

"All right, Jamie," Dave says. "I have to trust somebody."

* * *

Wulf always finds it disconcerting when he sees Tristan in uniform. He looks like a kid dressed up for Halloween, not a real policeman about to go on duty.

"How are you holding up?"

"Not well," Wulf says. "I'm terrified I'm going to lose him."

"I could say all kinds of things to try and make you feel better," Tristan smiles. "But it's true. You might lose him."

"How did you get through it?" Wulf asks. "When you lost Big Steve?"

"I honestly couldn't tell you," Tristan says. "Mostly it had to do with having lots of really good friends."

* * *

"How long has he been in surgery?" Griffin asks.

"Just over two hours now," Jared yawns.

"I can't imagine what Wulf must be going through."

"He's a tough old guy," Jared says. "But this has hit him pretty hard. Even if Dave comes through it O.K., they're going to need lots of help."

"You can count on Cooper and me."

* * *

Wulf stands in the tiny cubicle staring at the ballot. It's hard to see the point. Bush is almost certain to win. Can they stand another four years of this Reaganite insanity? He keeps trying to convince himself that it's nothing like the old days back home. But the anti-intellectualism of that whole party terrifies him. Their answer to everything seems to be to turn back the clock. As if that were actually possible. When he first came to America, he almost convinced himself that Americans were different from everybody else. Now he knows they're not. They just drive bigger cars, live in bigger houses, and eat too much red meat.

No reason to linger over this. He made his choices weeks ago. By the time he gets back to the hospital, Dave should be out of recovery.

* * *

Jared comes into the waiting room looking a little less haggard. Wulf tried to send him home for the night, but all he would agree to was to go home just long enough for a shower and change of clothes.

"Have they let you see him yet?"

"Any time now," Wulf says.

"It's going to be all right, Wulf."

"If we can just get through the next twenty-four hours," Wulf says. "That's what they tell me."

"And of course the twenty-four hours after that."

"Yes."

"I spoke to Scottie. He's trying to get an earlier flight back."

"There's no need."

"It's what he wants to do," Jared says. "And he gave me a message for you from your mother."

"Oh?"

"She's praying for you and Dave."

* * *

"I'm here, my darling."

"They tell me I'm still alive."

"The doctor said you came through with flying colors."

"They also said that motherfucker won."

"I don't care about that."

"I don't think I do either. But now I've got one more reason to survive this. I refuse to die with a Republican in the White House."

San Francisco: 1992

Scott sits in the dark living room listening to the hypnotic ticking of the mantel clock and the beating of his heart. He has been sitting motionless, tie unknotted, collar open, jacket slung across his knees, for hours. The certainty has been growing for weeks, transforming itself from the faintest suspicion to this huge, snarling, razor fanged monster. Today on the train ride home from a meeting with his agent, the panic he's been fighting all day finally overcame him. He was nearly screaming by the time he emerged into the twilight on Castro Street. Now it's well into the evening, but he can't move. He hasn't so much as stirred himself to turn on lights. He sits in the darkness drowning in his misery, the silence of the house broken only by that damned ticking and the fainter sound of traffic on the street outside.

He sits licking his wounds and beating himself up. This isn't how it's supposed to go. He promised himself this would never, ever happen. He replays the last fifteen years, frantic for the warning sign that must have been there. What he did to bring them to this point isn't the question. And he can't bear to think about the how and why. So he concentrates on when. When did he let himself get so lazy? When did he let down his guard and start to drift in this disastrous current? When did he start taking things for granted?

He wonders if it's all over. Can this marriage be saved? He has no idea. All he's certain of is it's not up to him. Jared will make that decision for them both, if he hasn't already. What will he do if Jared says there's no hope? He knows he'll never be able to cope on his own. He can't imagine starting over with somebody else. Even if anyone would have him after this. Why would anyone take a chance on a guy who would let someone like Jared slip though his fingers? He sits in the dark wondering what to do, but no solutions occur to him, and the clock ticks, and against all his expectations—and perhaps hopes?—his heart keeps beating. The silence all around him is excruciating. After all this time, not to have known better. There's simply no excuse.

He's still sitting paralyzed when the rattle of Jared's key in the front door rouses him, ratcheting his already insupportable anxiety up another notch. But he doesn't move. It's as if his backside has been welded to the cushions of the sofa. The front door opens and he hears Jared step into the dark entry hall. The light flashes on in there, and he hears Jared leafing through the mail, whistling "Don't Cry for Me, Argentina" like it's just another evening *chez* the Bailey-Bartoks. Jared's footsteps come closer. He hears Jared slap the dimmer. The wall sconces flash on, and he's no longer safe in the darkness.

"Jesus Christ," Jared exclaims. "You startled me. What the hell are you doing sitting in the dark like that?"

"Thinking."

"Thinking in the dark is never a good idea," Jared grins. "You could at least have turned the lights on. What were you thinking about? Couldn't have been good. You look like a boy who's lost his puppy."

"Jared, we have to talk."

"Oh?" Jared asks, looking at him like he's suddenly not sure who it is sitting there on the sofa, his husband or an armed and dangerously unhinged stranger.

"Sit down, please."

"All right."

"Jared, I know you know."

"Know what?"

"Jared, don't do that."

"All right," Jared says, voice suddenly husky. "I know."

"Who told you?"

"Isn't that beside the point?"

"Probably," Scott admits. "But I'd like to know."

"Nobody told me."

"You're kidding."

"No."

"You mean to tell me you just figured it out."

"You'd know. Believe me you would if I had an affair with somebody."

"Fair enough," Scott says. "You didn't say anything."

"I didn't know what to say."

"Anything. Say you hate me. Tell me to get out of here."

"But I don't hate you, Scottie. I don't want you to leave."

* * *

"I wish you'd talk to me," Jared says, moping across the dining table.

"I don't know what to say." Scott pokes at his lasagna with his fork. Jared isn't eating either. Why did he bother fixing dinner? What earthly use is doing something like that at a time like this?

"Well for starters, who is he?"

"I thought you already knew."

"I need to hear you say his name."

"Why?"

"Please."

* * *

Trace Jensen is a laughing, gray eyed, classically handsome, chestnut haired twenty-something Michelangelo's David, with an IQ over 180, a major trust fund, a vintage Jaguar, and fabulous condo on Russian Hill that Cooper Luxemberg sold him. And all that's just for starters. More relevant at the moment is his widely disseminated reputation as perhaps the most ingenious of all the practitioners of safe sex in this city crawling with guys who'd win Nobel Prizes for it if there were such a category. No doubt about it, Trace Jensen is a poster child for nineteen-nineties gay style. And for hot in any decade. Or century, God damn him.

How could Scott have thought that just one lunch date would be harmless? That's just like saying one hit of heroin won't do you any harm. Or, "it's just a little nuclear device."

* * *

"Thank you."

"You know who he is?"

"Everybody in the Bay Area knows who he is," Jared says.

Staring at Jared, Scott thinks he's aged at least ten years just since he came in the front door.

"Well?"

"Well what?"

"Shouldn't you be saying something along the lines of 'stop seeing him right now or I'll break your neck'?"

"I have no interest in breaking your neck," Jared says. "Besides, what if I said that and you told me you wouldn't?"

"Is that what you're afraid of?"

"That's one thing I'm afraid of," Jared says. "I don't think it's what I'm most afraid of, but it'll do for starters."

"All you have to do is say the word and I'll break it off."

"As if it's that simple."

"What's that supposed to mean?"

"That's not how it works. You don't break up with the other guy because your husband tells you to. You only break up with people you want to break up with. You only do it when you're good and ready."

* * *

"You'd better have a very good explanation for that long face," Wulf says, wielding his chopsticks like surgical instruments.

"It's that obvious, huh?"

Wulf nods.

"I've been having an affair."

"With Trace Jensen," Wulf nods. "I know."

"Jared told you."

"No, Jared didn't tell me. Jared has been refusing to discuss the matter with anyone. But he knows, and we all know he knows. Come on, Scott. You can't keep an affair with a guy like Trace Jensen a secret. You need to accept that. It's all over the city. Everybody knows."

"Everybody?"

"If by that you mean all your friends, yes. Poor little Griffin let the cat out of the bag in front of Jared several weeks ago. He was mortified when he realized what he had done. But Jared already knew. The wife may always be the last to know, but Jared's definitely not anybody's wife."

"No kidding."

"He's handling it pretty well, I think."

"You've discussed it with him?"

"As recently as breakfast today."

"Jesus."

"Let's leave Him out of this, shall we?"

"God, and now you're quoting Ned Westerleigh."

"A most quotable man."

"You seriously think Jared is taking it well? Because I heard him crying himself to sleep last night. I spent the night in the guest room, but I know I didn't imagine it."

"He told me about that."

"I could kill myself," Scott says.

"Don't exaggerate," Wulf warns him. "It's not helpful."

"All right. But I feel bad about this. Really, really, really bad."

"As you should. And don't think I'm being an auntie about it. I know people have their little liaisons. I'm not stupid. But you really are treating Jared badly. You shouldn't have kept it from him for so long. You should have tried to work something out."

"Work something out? What the hell does that mean?"

"He should have heard about it sooner, that's all. And from you. You left him with nothing to go on but his suspicions. That's when the local gossips are able to do their worst. And they have. Believe me. I'm surprised you haven't heard the dirt about yourself."

"I'd give anything for it never to have happened."

"Yet you go on seeing that young man."

"I really am a shit."

"Yes, I'm afraid you are, right at the moment."

* * *

If Wulf is right, Jared has known almost since the beginning. Scott knows Wulf must be right about this, because unless he was absolutely certain he'd never have said anything about it. So why hasn't Jared said or done anything? There are all kinds of things a man in Jared's position could have done. He could have murdered them both. It happens all the time. He could have walked out on Scott. He could have smashed all the tchotchkes, razor bladed all the art, thrown Scott out of the house, and changed the locks. He could have stalked them, caught them *in flagrante* and pitched a scene. Of course grand opera is not Jared's style. But this complete silence? Can it really be as simple as Jared closing his eyes and hoping that when he finally opened them again the whole sordid thing would be over?

* * *

"What can I get you to drink?" Jared asks.

"We've been together for fifteen years and you've all of a sudden forgotten what I drink?"

"Don't be silly. I only thought you might want something else for a change. Just this once, you know?"

"Club soda is fine."

Scott watches as Jared navigates his way to the bar. He's still a scorchingly attractive man. He's still in fantastic shape. His dense helmet of silver hair shows no sign of thinning. His skin is smooth and flawless. He turns heads wherever they go. When he walks down Castro Street in a tank top he practically causes traffic jams. So what the hell is Scott's problem?

"Here you go." Jared sets a drink down in front of him and resumes his seat.

"What are we doing here?"

"I thought, you know, neutral territory," Jared says.

"Was that Wulf's suggestion? I know you saw him this morning."

"May have been," Jared says, sheepish. "I can't recall for certain."

"I see."

"I was afraid you wouldn't come."

"I almost didn't."

"You slept in the guest room last night, Scott. That's the first time you ever slept in the guest room."

"You cried yourself to sleep."

"I need you to tell me what I did wrong."

"What?"

"You want me to say it again?"

"No. I heard you."

"So?"

"Oh, God, Jared. This isn't about you."

"Of course it's about me. We're a couple. Anything you do is about me. Please tell me what it is that I've done or haven't done that's made you so unhappy that you had to go off…"

"Stop right there," Scott says. "Just stop, O.K?"

Jared sulks.

"You haven't done anything to cause this. You're the perfect husband, all right? Is that what you want to hear?"

"What I want to hear is the truth. And I can't possibly be the perfect husband or this wouldn't be happening to us."

"Not true," Scott says. "Listen, big guy, I'm damaged goods. I told you that when we met. My mother killed herself and my father was a drunk and a womanizer. With a pedigree like that, I don't need any help at all fucking up my life. That's it. That's what I know and that's all I know. So please stop playing the martyr."

"I'm not."

"No, you're right. That wasn't fair."

"So what can I do to help?"

"I think I need to be alone for a while," Scott says. "I need to get away."

* * *

The bars on Folsom Street aren't Scott's usual stomping ground. Since he doesn't want to run into anybody he knows, any one of them should be safe enough. As safe as picking up a man in a bar can ever be these days. He pushes open the door of the first one he comes to and steps inside. It's exactly like he imagined it would be. He never thought this would be pretty. He looks around for a moment to get his bearings, and a cute boy leaning against the bar grins at him.

Can it possibly be that easy?

He smiles back, then realizes who it is. He waits tables at a restaurant Scott and Jared go to at least once a month. He's in a deeply scooped white tank top and tight, faded jeans. All the waiters at that restaurant are gorgeous, all bodybuilders, all apparently under twenty-eight. Scott pretends not to recognize him as he steps up to the bar.

"Out by yourself tonight?"

"What?"

"You left the silver fox at home."

"I'm sorry," Scott says, turning to look at him. "I think you must be mistaking me for someone else."

"No, really," the young man insists. "Don't you remember me? I work at *Menudo*."

"What's that?"

"A restaurant on Market Street. I wait tables."

"I don't know what you're talking about," Scott says. "I just got in from Chicago this afternoon. I've never been in San Francisco before. I'll certainly try that place if you'll tell me where it is."

"This is amazing," the young man marvels. "You really do look exactly like this guy who comes in all the time with his lover. They're both incredible hunks. Heavy tippers, too."

"What a charming compliment," Scott laughs. "What's that you're drinking?"

"No. Let me buy."

"Thanks," Scott says. "I had no idea guys here would be so friendly."

* * *

In the elevator on the way up to the room, Mickey shoves his hand in Scott's back pocket. Scott turns and smiles at him, inhaling unfamiliar cologne and something else that just smells young and hot. He might even enjoy this, though he wouldn't lay odds on it. Anything, though, to get Jared off his mind tonight.

No, scratch that. Anything at all to take his mind off Trace.

* * *

The next night it's another bar, and the man he meets there claims he flies fighter planes in the Argentine Air Force. This strikes Scott as too exactly like something he'd expect to read about in a "fiction selection" in a porn magazine to take seriously.

But Mateo is in his early thirties and luminously beautiful. His shoulders are truly awe inspiring, so Scott swallows his skepticism.

When they get to Mateo's hotel room, they spend twenty minutes looking at the chillingly authentic photos: Mateo in uniform, Mateo in a flight suit, Mateo sitting in the cockpit of a jet.

* * *

The next night Scott meets a young graduate student who's just moved to the city from Boston. They ride the cable car to the boy's tiny, California Street studio apartment, where they soak for a long time in a tub full of bubbles in a bathroom awash in candle light.

* * *

The next night it's the headmaster of a boys' school in Gloucestershire. He sounds like a refugee from *Masterpiece Theatre*. He looks like Princess Di's cousin. His hotel room is one floor up from Scott's, though Scott doesn't mention this.

* * *

The night after that Scott meets a glossily handsome businessman with an eighty dollar haircut and three hundred dollar loafers, who confides that he always votes Republican and claims to have a wife and children in Pacific Heights. They drive in the man's Porsche cabrio to a condo on Nob Hill the man says he borrows from a friend when he goes on what he calls adventures. Once inside, the man begs Scott to handcuff him to the bed, attach alligator clamps to his nipples, incarcerate his cock in a bizarre cage-like apparatus of chrome rings and leather straps, drip molten candle wax on his bare skin, and terrorize him with a bullwhip. Scott obeys these requests with only the briefest hesitation.

The role comes to him so naturally he terrifies himself more than he terrifies his partner, but he makes sure not to let on. The businessman begs for his phone number "for return engagements, dude".

"You'll just have to come find me if you want that again."

* * *

If Scott had stopped to think about it, he might have been surprised by the continued existence of bathhouses in the city, with the plague still raging. But he didn't think about it, and he still doesn't as he hands the desk attendant his money, signs the register and receives a locker key. Ten minutes later he's stripped and wrapped in a towel and sitting in a pool of his own sweat in the steam room. It's not long before he feels hands on him, which he pushes away.

He doesn't want it in here, shrouded by these thick, fetid clouds. He wants it later, after stalking the corridors, after being seen and desired by as many men as possible. He doesn't want to be an anonymous collection of shadowy parts. He wants nothing less than to be an iconic manifestation.

* * *

Scott lies on the bed in his hotel room, completely dressed. Outside the open windows it's twilight. He hears clanging bells and the rattling rumble of wheels on rails as the cable cars trundle back and forth past the entrance to the hotel lobby.

He's sick of eating in restaurants, which is saying something in a city where excellent food can be found on practically every block. He's sick of trying to sleep in this strange bed, too large, too comfortable, too empty no matter who's with him. He's sick of wondering in spite of himself what Jared and Trace are doing in his absence. He can't get either of them out of his mind. That's the bottom line.

Whatever this experiment has been about, the results are inconclusive. No diagnosis has been arrived at, no cure found. No state of oblivion has been achieved. No epiphanies have burst upon him. No state of satiety lasting more than an hour or two has been reached. He could have been exactly this confused and miserable without ever leaving home, without maxing out a single credit card, without making a damned fool of himself.

* * *

"I wasn't sure I'd ever see you again," Jared says as Scott enters the living room.

"I'm sorry. I should have called."

"It's all right. Wulf and Dave kept me updated. Every time you called them, they called me. I still worried, but not like I would have if you had really disappeared. So where were you?"

"One of those little hotels off Union Square."

"So they were telling the truth about you not being at their place," Jared nods.

"I didn't even ask them if I could stay there. They're your family, too. I wouldn't have put them in the middle of this."

"Thank you," Jared says. "Incidentally, what is 'this'?"

"Hell if I know," Scott says. "To be honest with you, I'm not sure why I'm here. And it's only fair to warn you I'm not sure if I'm staying."

"Duly noted," Jared says. "Anything else?"

"This thing with Trace."

"Wulf and Dave said you haven't been seeing him."

"That doesn't mean it's over."

"I see."

"But for what it's worth, it isn't going to last forever. I know he's going to dump me sooner or later. He's just not the marrying kind. And even if he was, well, I have no illusions about that. I know damned well it wouldn't be me he'd settle down with. He knows exactly how many good years I've got left, and it's not anywhere near enough. So it's just a matter of time until I walk through that door with my tail between my legs. I suppose I've known that since the beginning. And I still couldn't stop myself. That's my disease.

"When that happens, I'm going to need you like I've never needed anybody in my whole life. And if you're not here, I don't know how I'll get by. I know exactly how selfish that sounds, but you know as well as I do that sometimes you just can't help it. I'd break it off with him if I could. I'd go pick up that phone over there and just get it over with. But I can't. You told me I couldn't the first time we talked about this, and you were right. And I've spent this whole damn time just hoping and praying that when he finally does get around to cutting me loose, you'll still be here. I know I don't deserve it, but it's the only hope I've got. Nobody has the right to ask such a thing, but God help me, this is the best I can do. I'll beg if you want me to. I'll get down on my knees, I swear."

San Francisco: 1997

Dear Scott,

Your godson, Boone, will be getting out of the Marine Corps in a few more weeks. He has informed Marty and me that he will not be returning to Bloomington. He has decided to relocate to your neck of the woods. On the phone last weekend, Marty asked him why he wanted to live in the land of fruits and nuts. He told Marty not to be dense. I am not sure what that means, though Marty has a theory.

Anyway, I am hoping that you will be kind enough to help us out by keeping an eye on him. I have not said anything to Boone yet because I don't want to commit you to something without asking you first. But it would really set my mind at rest to know that you're looking out for him. He is my baby boy, after all. He is a very responsible young man, but he has never lived anyplace bigger than Bloomington, and I'm not sure he understands what he's getting himself into by moving out there.

In the Corps, he was trained as a firefighter. I didn't know they had firefighters in the military. That is the kind of work he's hoping to do out there. I don't know if you have any contacts in that field. Marty says Boone will have to watch out in San Francisco because all the gay guys there have the hots for firefighters, but when he talks about things he doesn't understand he just sounds like an idiot.

Anyway, please write (or call—we're so up to date in Bloomington these days we have telephones, ha ha ha) and let me know what you think. It would also be nice to hear from you for old times' sake—double ha ha ha!
Your friend,
Annie Browne (formerly Horstmann)

* * *

"What do you think?" Jared asks.

"I want nothing to do with him."

"He's your godson," Jared says, "which is weird, incidentally, because you're not Catholic or Anglican. As far as I know."

"A long miserable story," Scott says, "that I have no interest in revisiting."

"Good," Jared says. "So we'll do it. We'll write and tell her to have him get in touch with us when he arrives."

"What are you talking about?"

"You have to, Scottie."

"I don't think I do."

"Well, you're going to. And if you don't write and tell her, I will."

"You crazy bastard."

* * *

"Just so you know," Jared says a couple of nights later over Chinese take-out, "I wrote to Annie. I told her we'd be happy to help Boone in any way we can. I told her he's welcome to stay in the guest room while he looks for a place."

"I know I can't stop you," Scott says. "But I wish you hadn't done it."

"He's your godson, Scott."

"His father was the rottenest person I've ever known."

"It was over twenty years ago. It's time to let go of it."

"Right."

"I'm serious"

"Just remember, I'm scheduled to go to Berlin in another couple of weeks. If he shows up while I'm gone, you're on your own."

"Don't you think I can handle it?"

"As long as you don't forget that his father and grandfather were both psychopaths, you should be O.K."

* * *

Every time he comes back to Berlin, Scott is struck by the constant state of change that marks the place. It has accelerated noticeably since reunification. Massive construction projects in the city bespeak its restored status as capital of a wealthy, powerful nation. But it's more than simply the new buildings, the heavier traffic, the ever more prosperous looking people. It's the process of change itself that intrigues him, as if the city is a living organism and change is the air it breathes. The last time he was here with Wulf, they got lost on an excursion to find Wulf's old *gymnasium*. Scott feared that this signaled some loss of mental acuity on the part of his uncle, but a brief conversation with the concierge at their hotel set his mind at rest. Even long time residents find themselves disoriented by the city's transformation.

* * *

Scott is working with a new author. The novel, *Vita Brevis, Historia Longa*, is monumental, the longest book he's ever worked on. It's a compelling saga, told in clear, naturalistic style. The simplicity of the prose and narration has made translation remarkably straightforward. Beginning in Prussia in the years immediately preceding the Great War, it chronicles the story of five generations of a German family. The last section, apparently autobiographical, is about the struggles of a young gay man living a closeted existence under communist rule in East Germany and his eventual liberation after the Soviet collapse. Scott would like to believe it's destined to become Germany's equivalent to *War and Peace*, but he isn't sure.

After two decades working as a literary translator, he's usually a pretty good judge of a book's quality. But not in this case. He's too close to the work to view it objectively. This is because the novel is the lightly fictionalized account of his own family, and the author is his cousin, Johann. He'd only been vaguely aware of Johann's existence until couple of years ago when Wulf came back from a visit here raving about the young man and insisting that Scott translate this, his yet unpublished work. Scott was reluctant at first. Translation is his living, and unpublished works by unknown authors can be disastrous investments of time and effort. But after reading a couple of chapters of the manuscript Wulf had brought back with him, Scott was hooked. He suspects it will fall to him to find a publisher for it, but so be it. With his contacts, it won't be hard. If nothing else, it will make Wulf happy.

Johann lives in Leipzig, where he is a professor of literature, specializing in, of all things, Arthur Miller and Tennessee Williams. Under the communists, Miller was very highly regarded, and Johann's monograph on *All My Sons* and *Death of a Salesman* made his career in academia. His love for Williams, whom the communists considered the epitome of bourgeois decadence, stayed in the closet for about as long as Johann did. Raised and educated under the communists, he remains a communist philosophically but is pragmatic enough to enjoy the fruits of the new regime. When Scott first met him he experienced a bizarre, Alice-through-the-looking-glass sensation that has never completely dissipated in the course of their subsequent encounters. Johann is enough like Scott to be his twin. Their similarity goes far beyond physical appearance. They have similar mannerisms, and, to a great extent, tastes. Because of this, Johann's life experiences represent a kind of parallel universe for Scott—what his life might have been like under other circumstances—that he finds endlessly fascinating.

Scott has finally completed the translation of *Vita Brevis, Historia Longa*. He air freighted a copy to Johann in Leipzig several weeks ago. This morning's meeting will determine whether he is finished with the book or not. Authors can be amazingly picky about how they want their work to "read" in another language. If Johann suggests alterations to the draft, Scott will certainly consider them. But he sincerely hopes Johann will sign off on the work in its present form. He walks the few blocks to Johann's hotel, which is older and less ostentatious than his own. It is exactly the sort of place you'd expect a communist professor of literature to choose: utilitarian is the word that comes to mind. Scott admires its honest unpretentiousness and thinks he would enjoy staying there. He has to remember to tell his travel agent about it.

* * *

Johann is sitting in the lobby reading *Frankfurter Allgemeine*. He's wearing an outfit almost identical to Scott's. Registering this coincidence-which-really-isn't, the two start to laugh even before they've greeted each other.

"I'm so happy with your work on the book," Johann says, once the preliminaries are out of the way.

"I'm glad you like it."

"I speak fluent English," Johann says. "I read the language almost as well as German, and I write it well enough to publish academic papers. But I can't imagine doing what you do. It seems to me it's an art just like writing itself, but perhaps even more difficult when you consider the restrictions inherent in starting from a text which already exists."

"It's not for everyone," Scott admits.

"There's something about how the book reads in English," Johann says. "I don't know how to explain it."

"German is an incredibly precise language," Scott says. "English is less verbose, and no matter how hard you try you end up with something I think of as more impressionistic than what you have in the German original."

"Yes," Johann agrees, "that's it exactly. You know, it's fascinating how it makes the book profoundly different, but in a way that's somehow totally faithful to the original. I almost think I like it better."

"That's the highest praise you can give a translator," Scott says. "But I'm afraid I can't take complete credit for it. Uncle Wulf made several suggestions which proved to be crucially important."

"Did he? Well, bravo to Uncle Wulf," Johann says. "Still, the final product is a tribute to your artistry. And also, I think, to our affinity as men."

"That helps, certainly," Scott agrees. "I don't often experience this sort of meeting of minds with an author."

"I should think not."

"And as for how the book reads in English, well, English is apparently a very kind language to authors. Or maybe that's the wrong word. Maybe I should have said inspirational. Conrad said he didn't think he could ever have been a novelist if he hadn't learned the language."

"And he was a genius," Johann says. "Every time I reread *Heart of Darkness,* I feel I develop a new understanding of what literature is for. You know, speaking of our book, I had the devil of a time with those last few chapters. I had no idea how much more difficult it would be to write about peace than about war."

"Tolstoy knew about a thing or two about it," Scott says. "'Happy families are all alike'."

"Yes," Johann nods, "to introduce a novel about a singularly unhappy family. It certainly helped that you sent me those books by Aksyonov, so that I could see how he dealt with the problem."

"You must think I'm a raving Russophile."

"Not at all, cousin," Johann nods. "I think you're a pragmatist. There's a time honored family trait for you. Not to mention a German one. You know, I believe you're as much of a German as I am. As a matter of fact, I've been doing a lot of thinking lately about the persistence of such traits across generations, almost in defiance of external influences."

"Sounds like heresy, coming from a communist."

"Like everything else, communism is subject to historical forces," Johann laughs.

* * *

"I met Aksyonov once, you know," Johann says as they walk side by side up the *Kurfurstendamm.*

"Really."

"I was in Leningrad—back when it still was Leningrad—for a conference. I skipped out on one of the evening sessions to sneak away and meet him. My colleagues were horrified."

"I can imagine."

"It seems ridiculous," Johann muses, "how little it took to make one an unreliable element in those days."

"I think it's something Americans really don't understand," Scott says.

"You're probably right," Johann says. "Freedom of thought and freedom of expression appear to have become so internalized in the American psyche that you seem to have lost the capacity to comprehend any other condition of existence."

"Interesting theory."

"But now, just look around you. Berlin, finally at peace. For the rest of the world the war ended in 1945. For Germany, it really wasn't over until reunification. Think of it: from the Hitler coup until just a few years ago—literally generations of conflict and disruption only now at an end. We Germans can finally get back to being Germans."

"A lot of people would find that observation troubling," Scott says.

"Yes, they'd think it smacked of some frightening hypernationalist tendency," Johann grins. "And next would come the conspiracy theories about Hitler living underground in Argentina and plotting his return, and Speer secretly pulling strings at the U.N. from his cell. Acknowledging the new Germany in any overt way seems distasteful at best and positively frightening at worst. How do Americans describe such an idea? Politically incorrect, that's it. It's a politically incorrect sentiment to approve of reunification except as confirmation of the death of the Soviet Empire. But let me tell you something. The real reason people would object to what I just said is that it's true."

* * *

"Should we stop for lunch somewhere?" Scott suggests.

"We already have plans for lunch," Johann says. "I know a wonderful little place just a few blocks from here. The sauerbraten melts in your mouth. And I have a surprise for you. We're meeting someone there."

"You're finally seeing someone? That's great."

"Unfortunately still no," Johann smiles. "I do keep hoping that it's not too late for me."

"You come to San Francisco," Scott laughs. "Wulf and I will have you married off in no time at all."

"An American boyfriend. Perhaps not a bad idea. If you're not careful, I'll take you up on that. Or perhaps I should say, call your bluff."

"Well, if it's not a new boyfriend we're meeting for lunch, then who is it?"

"All in good time, Scott, all in good time."

* * *

When Scott first notices the young man step into the restaurant it's like seeing himself as he was when he first arrived in San Francisco.

"There they are now," Johann says.

"Is this the surprise?" Scott asks, staring at the young man and his friend, an exotic looking black haired beauty.

"Are you surprised?"

"Astonished."

"In that case yes, it is the surprise."

"Who is he?"

"Another von Riedel. Our cousin Karl-Heinz's son Peter, from Sydney. As you see, the family resemblance is remarkable. Whenever we are together, I feel like I'm looking at myself twenty years ago. Of course the boys all have such interesting haircuts these days, but other than that he's an absolute *doppelganger,* isn't he? Peter's on leave from the Australian Navy, so there's another family trait he shares. Our generation was the demilitarized one, Scott. Now it's back to business as usual. Peter and his boyfriend are here on vacation. We agreed to meet for lunch today and surprise you."

"I can hardly believe it," Scott says. "It's uncanny."

"Peter, Klaus," Johann calls. "Over here."

* * *

"To be honest," Peter says in that incongruous Australian accent of his, "Klaus here is the one who speaks German. I never learned word one. Too lazy, me. Those umlauts make me go crosseyed."

"Actually," Klaus says, "it's the separable prefixes that do him in. Those and the irregular verbs."

"Make that all verbs," Peter laughs. "If I never had to do anything, or talk to anyone about doing anything, I could probably become fluent."

"Klaus's father is Chinese," Johann explains, "but his mother is German. They met when she was doing graduate work in Shanghai."

"My mother and Mrs. von Riedel are best friends," Klaus says in perfectly accented German. "They were in primary school together. After the war, their families left Shanghai and went to Australia. Mom was Maid of Honor when Mrs. von Riedel married Peter's dad. When I broke up with my fiancé two years ago and came out to my parents, my mom and Peter's mom decided to play matchmaker for us."

"If you're going to talk about me," Peter says, "I wish you'd at least do it in a language I understand."

"Is that true?" Scott asks Peter. "About your mother and his mother setting you up with Klaus?"

"I almost didn't go on the date," Peter says. "Who wants to be set up by his own ma? It hardly seems decent somehow. It's a damn good thing I listened to her for once."

"You see, Scott?" Johann laughs. "I told you peace had broken out. If that's not proof, I don't know what is."

* * *

"Turn in at that gate up on the right," Johann says. He has brought them to a quarter of the city Scott is not familiar with. The roads are winding and narrow. Through stands of trees as dense as a forest, glimpses of lakes and rivers can be seen. Large, stately homes sit serene in grounds extensive enough to be called estates. Scott signals for the turn and steers the rented Volkswagen in between two stone piers grand enough for the gateway to a castle. The drive curves between parallel lines of poplars. At its head sits a Romanesque villa.

"What is this place?" Klaus asks from the back seat.

"Is it what I think it is?" Scott asks almost simultaneously.

"The house of the von Riedels," Johann says. "This is where your mother grew up, Scott. And Wulf. And my father. Your grandfather Georg, too, Peter."

"Who lives here now?" Peter asks.

"No one," Johann says. "It's closed up. The Russians took it from us in 1945. Later on, they transferred ownership to the Democratic Republic. Since reunification, the Federal Government has owned it. During the time of the Workers' Paradise, it was a home for retired railway workers. But no money was ever spent on maintenance, and it's practically falling down now. I wish I could show you inside, but even if we could get permission, it's not safe."

"It's remarkable," Scott says.

"The grounds are open to us, however," Johann says. "Park the car over in that shady spot, why don't you?"

* * *

Johann leads them around one side of the house. To its rear, broad lawns slope gently to the lake shore.

"Just imagine the scene," he says. "The boys swimming. Or rowing. You can see the ruins of the boat house over there in that cluster of trees. Your mother and her governess doing schoolwork on the veranda."

"My mother's family wasn't nearly so grand," Klaus says.

"No?"

"They dug coal in the Ruhr. My grandfather eventually became a union official and a communist. He had to leave Germany when Hitler came to power. He went to Russia first and then later had to run away from Stalin. That's how they ended up in Shanghai."

"A true son of the proletariat," Johann laughs, "and look at you now; the medical student. While this one merely plays around with boats."

"I'll have you know it's a guided missile frigate," Peter protests.

"The curse of the von Riedels," Johann laughs. "Obsessed with big guns."

* * *

On a low rise overlooking the lake, a small classical style pavilion sits shaded by towering trees. They approach it through thick grass almost too green for belief. Scott finds the idyllic aspect of the scene overwhelming. Seeing it for the first time, he feels he can almost understand his grandmother's near fatal attachment to the place.

"This is the spot I most wanted you all to see," Johann says. "Look."

Affixed to the forwardmost of the Corinthian columns is a simple bronze plaque inscribed in both German and English.

"'In memory of Field Marshal Wilhelm von Riedel, 1887-1944,'" Klaus reads aloud. "'He fought to save the nation from Nazi tyranny.'"

"The government has promised not to allow it to be removed," Johann says. "Like so many others, he was late to recognize the mistake Germany had made. But at least he was willing to take action once he did."

"The family didn't try to reclaim the property after reunification?" Scott asks.

"Many other families got their properties back, of course. But Grandmother wouldn't hear of it," Johann shakes his head. "We took the cash settlement the government offered instead. She would ask us to bring her out here to look around every now and then. But she never wanted to come back here to live. Renovations and upkeep would have been prohibitively expensive, of course. But that wasn't the reason for her reluctance. 'Bury me there next to Wilhelm and let that be an end to it,' she always said. 'Those days are gone. We must look forward instead of back'."

"She was a remarkable woman," Scott says. "Every time I visited her, she said something or other that surprised me."

"Everyone who knew her said that the war cured her of triviality."

"What will happen to the house?" Peter asks.

"She hoped this place would be put to use as a home for children with disabilities," Johann says. "She never forgot your half brothers, Scott. And it looks like the government is finally about to make her wish come true. The ministry responsible has promised to name it after her."

"She'd be pleased," Scott says. "She mentioned those babies to me more than once."

"She and Grandfather are buried over there," Johann motions to an obelisk shaped marker fifty feet or so away.

"It's a lovely spot," Scott says. "I know Wulf and Dave will want to visit it when they come in October."

"I saw her the day before she died," Johann says. "We all knew she was going. She better than anyone. She was quite clear about it. She told us, 'the past is a country where no one lives any more. Let the ghosts have it. We must concern ourselves with the future only'."

"That's a lovely sentiment," Peter says.

"I'm not sure it was original," Johann says, "but there was no questioning her sincerity."

* * *

It certainly is turning into a season for doppelgangers, Scott thinks, stepping from the jetway into the waiting lounge. He didn't leave them all behind in Berlin. Except for the haircut, which seems frighteningly *au courant* for a young man just out of the Marine Corps, Boone Horstmann is a dead ringer for his father—more clone than son, in fact. That sturdily handsome Boy Scout face, those hulking shoulders and arms, those confrontational pecs. Standing next to him, Jared might as well be invisible. If he wasn't so jet lagged, Scott would run away screaming.

"There he is now," Jared says.

Next thing Scott knows, he's in that familiar bear hug and receiving a discreet little peck on the lips. If only that could be the whole homecoming right there, instead of whatever drama is impending.

"Welcome home, sweetheart."

"Thanks."

"This is Boone."

"Yes, I see."

They exchange manly handshakes.

"What are you two doing with motorcycle helmets?"

"We rode out on the bikes," Boone grins.

"You didn't...?"

"No," Jared shakes his head. "Boone owns two B.M.W.'s"

"A K100RS," Boone says. "And an R100S."

"Really."

Boone might as well be speaking Serbo-Croat, Scott thinks. He used to keep up with motorcycle arcana but let it go long since. This must be yet another sign of middle age.

"That's a real sweet old R90S you've got in the garage," Boone says. "You ought to get her fixed up so you can ride."

"Right. And how am I supposed to get home?"

"Well," Jared says, "we've got an extra helmet here. You can ride with one of us. Or in case you're too beaten up from the flight, Wulf brought the Benz. He's waiting in baggage claim. He can drive you in."

* * *

"He's an extremely charming young man," Wulf says, peering ahead at traffic. "Everybody has remarked on it."

"Everybody?"

"Everybody," Wulf nods. "He was a great hit at brunch last Sunday. Even Cooper approves."

"Brunch last Sunday. My, you all have been busy."

"Pull in your claws, Scott."

"Is that safe?"

"Why wouldn't it be?"

"I seem to recall something about either learning from history or having to repeat it."

"You're not going to repeat history."

"You seem awfully sure of that."

"He's not his father," Wulf says.

"That remains to be seen."

"Incidentally, you never said anything about him being gay."

"Is he? Really?"

"Absolutely."

"It's news to me."

* * *

"Where is he?" Scott asks as Jared comes into the kitchen.

"Putting away the bikes."

"What else have you been up to while I was away?"

"We've been surfing a few times."

"He surfs?"

"He spent the last year and a half at Camp Pendleton. I'd have thought it was obligatory there."

"Jesus."

"And we've been renovating the basement apartment. New paint and fixtures. I thought it would be nicer for him."

"He's moving in?"

"He is," Jared says, with a glint in his eyes that brooks no argument.

"I thought you didn't believe in renting the place out to devastatingly attractive young men."

"We're not going to have that discussion right now," Jared says, patting Scott on the ass. "When you're jetlagged, you're an absolute bitch. Go upstairs and shower. I'll come up later and tuck you in."

* * *

In the two weeks since he returned from Germany, Scott has realized that the one way in which Boone is different from his father is his charm. He's positively incandescent with it, while Clay never made any particular effort in that regard, relying instead solely on his physical attributes. Scott considers it the cruelest possible irony that the one distinguishing factor between father and son only makes the son more dangerous. Scott refuses to be taken in. He may eventually succumb—if Cooper Luxemberg has, no one is immune—but he's not about to make it easy.

* * *

"You need to lighten up on Boone," Jared says.

"Why? Have I said anything? Have I done **anything**?"

"No," Jared admits. "But your disapproval is deafening."

"Jesus," Scott says. "What does that even mean?"

"You have to stop blaming him for being Clay's kid. It's not his fault."

"Well, it's certainly not mine."

"Scottie, stop this. For your own sake as much as his."

"Huh?"

"Don't play dumb. You know you've been holding on to it for far too long. It can't hurt you any more."

"Shows how much you know."

"Sweetheart, do you think I would let anyone do anything to harm you? Really?"

"Finally," Scott says, allowing himself to be hugged, "someone talking sense around here."

* * *

"Thursday night," Boone says, loading his blender carafe into the dishwasher. He does his own dishes in his apartment, but this vessel, in which he mixes his protein shakes, must be disinfected as apparently only a Robert Bosch dishwasher is capable of doing. "I'm taking you out for your birthday. Just the two of us."

"It's not my birthday," Scott says.

"I know."

"Did you put him up to this, Jared?"

"No. Scout's honor," Jared says, crossing his heart.

"You weren't a Boy Scout, as far as I know."

"Scottie," Boone says, "I owe you. You never missed a year sending your godson a birthday present. You should have seen how jealous my brothers were. Of course, their godfather was in prison during most of their childhood. Anyhow, now it's my turn to treat you."

"Say 'thank you', Scott," Jared instructs.

"Thank you, Boone."

"My pleasure."

"And don't you dare stand him up," Jared says.

"That's right," Boone says. "We've got business to attend to."

"That sounds ominous," Scott says, hoping it sounds at least halfway like a joke.

"Make sure you look sharp," Boone grins, "'cause I'm taking you some-place really spiffy."

* * *

Scott has to hand it to the kid. Hair in glossy perfection, tailor made suit fitting him like he's a runway model—albeit an oversized one—and that devas-tating grin: Boone is a faggot's wet dream of a date. His manners are beautiful, he knows exactly which fork to use, and he can order in French. Somewhere in this city somebody's dying to meet him. He even limits himself to one glass of wine with dinner: somehow he managed to borrow one of Big Steve Fabiani's old Maseratis from Tristan Bentley for the evening, and he obviously doesn't want to bend it. Scott senses the crossed fingers of the whole gang behind what-ever is supposed to take place tonight, and he feels unworthy of their good wishes. They must see something in Boone that he doesn't. Or won't.

* * *

"I think this is my favorite place in the whole city," Boone says. "Jared brought me here the night after I got in. He told me about the crazy rich lady creating a monument to the firefighters of '06."

"It's a great story," Scott says.

"You know, Scott," Boone says, absurdly young face looking all the more serious because of his boyishness, "I get it. You might not think so, but I do. My dad was a real bastard. And I'm sure I don't know the half of it. But a guy who'd give his wife and unborn baby AIDS is capable of anything. Mom nursed that girl until the day she died. Brought that baby home with her and she and Marty took care of him till he passed away, too. I'll never forget that little guy. Mom's the only hero of the whole story. Clay never lifted a finger to help. We never even saw him until it was all over. He always said he got it from sharing needles with his workout buddies, shooting up those 'roids. Swore he wasn't gay, ever. So anyway, I really mean it when I say I get it. He was so totally rotten whatever went down between the two of you had to have been just awful."

"Boone, we don't have to go into it."

"Sure we do," Boone says. "We're never going to be O.K. with each other if we don't. And I really like your friends, you know? They already feel like my family. It's all so perfect for me here, except there's just this one thing standing in the way."

"I'm sorry about that."

"I guess you can't really help it."

"Don't say that. It makes me sound helpless. Like a victim."

"I repeat, Clay Horstmann was a grade A bastard. He'd have gone to prison himself except that he agreed to testify against that doctor and the priest guy. And mom says he really put you through hell."

"Jared says I'm supposed to at least try and get along with you."

"That's all I'm asking for, really."

"Why? Because you figure your charm and good looks will do the rest?"

"I guess that's the way he operated, right?"

"I'm sorry," Scott says. "That wasn't fair."

"I do try, you know," Boone says. "It's not that I want to be like him. And anyway, he wasn't really my father. When somebody says the word father, Marty Browne is who I always think of. Clay was just this guy who came around now and then and upset Mom and my brothers."

"But not you."

"I was too little when he left us. He hardly meant anything to me. It's just this, what do you call it, irony? That of the three of us I'm the one who looks most like him?"

"Life can be funny that way."

"Well, I've never been able to laugh about it. Sometimes I think I'd give anything to wake up some day and have it all be different. But you can't change the past."

"My grandmother died recently. The one in Germany."

"I know," Boone says. "Jared told me."

"When I was there last month," Scott says, finally realizing what the message is supposed to mean to him, "my cousin Johann told me about something she said the day before she died: 'the past is a country where no one lives anymore. Let the ghosts have it. We must concern ourselves with the future only'."

San Francisco: 2008

"I never liked this house," Morgan says, staring at the numbers on the offer Cooper just handed him. "I didn't want it in the first place. I told Forrest it was ridiculous for two men to buy something the size of a fraternity house. That was exactly the wrong thing to say. Because it just made him want it more. 'That's what everyone will call it,' he said, 'the frat house. When they see us out in the clubs they'll say, "Look, there are those guys who own the frat house".' After that, there was no stopping him. That's the way our whole marriage went. Somehow I always knew exactly what to say to make him do the opposite of what I wanted. My greatest regret from those days is I never learned how to talk to him."

"What were you at the time?" Buzz asks. "Twenty-three?"

Morgan nods.

"Ask Griffin here," Buzz says. "He'll tell you. It takes years for couples to learn to communicate effectively."

"Who says?" Cooper demands. "I never have trouble communicating with Griffin, do I, sweetheart?"

"It's a work in progress," Griffin sighs.

"That's my point," Buzz says. "You never stood a chance, hon. Nobody under thirty does."

"Seriously, Morgan," Cooper says, "it's a good offer."

"I see that," Morgan says, handing the paper to Buzz.

"Full asking price, furniture included," Cooper says. "Cash purchase, short escrow. I've verified their financials. Couldn't be better."

"Right."

"And we're waiving the commission. That's another two hundred fifty thousand you'll pocket."

"I don't want you doing that, Cooper," Morgan says. "Not with business as bad as it is. It's way too much. If you want to do something, discount the commission to three per cent. That's more than fair."

"Buzz has been with the agency for nearly thirty years and we've never paid him what he's worth. It's not negotiable."

"He means it, Morgan," Griffin says.

"All right."

"So why the long face?" Cooper presses.

"Hon," Buzz says, "if you're not ready to sell, it's O.K. We can hold onto the place for now. Cooper's always thought we should wait for the market to come back."

"It's not that. I'm ready to sell, all right."

"Then what?"

"This is going to sound crazy after the pissing and moaning I've done all these years," Morgan says, "but now that it's actually happening I'm just not ready for the party to be over."

* * *

Matt never thought about it at the time. You don't when you've just fallen in love. He was a married man with nearly grown sons, but he'd never been in love before and the shock of it had knocked him on his ass. One look and he hadn't been able to help himself, and he was fortunate that it had been Ashby, kind, ambitious, pure hearted Ashby, and not just some little piece of bar trash who'd have taken advantage of him, wrecked his marriage, and then gotten bored and left. It had seemed like a fairy tale. And for all practical purposes they had lived happily ever after. But there are definite drawbacks to marrying a man young enough to be your son. It's all right when you're in your late thirties and can pass for ten years younger than that. When you can still look at yourself in the mirror and be almost totally content with what you see there, and when all your friends look at the two of you and say things like "what a divine couple you make". Even Eleanor said they took her breath away. What are you supposed to think when your not yet but about to be ex-wife says a thing like that? You certainly don't second guess it.

Surely he must have known better. He was an airline pilot at the time. His job was to be prepared for all eventualities, no matter how rare or unlikely. How could anyone not have anticipated this? You plan for natural disasters, serious illnesses, sudden death even—all manner of catastrophes. You buy insurance, you keep your affairs in order, you work out at the gym, you watch your diet, you maintain your roof and gutters and foundations, you change your oil on a rigorous schedule, you floss. You calculate odds as routinely as you tie your shoes and comb your hair and you make every reasonable effort to be prepared for what you think of as the worst, but you blind yourself to the surest thing in life, the passing of time, until reality won't allow you to ignore it any more. Now here they are almost forty years later. Ashby is in his prime—not yet sixty. But there's no getting around the fact that Matt is an old man. Sure, he left his cane in the car tonight. He didn't embarrass them on the dance floor. But what must people have been thinking?

He knows that is a ridiculous thing to worry about when you've led the kind of life he has. But self consciousness is the least of it. It's the position he's put Ashby in that disturbs him most. He was so proud a provider and protector. There was nothing he wouldn't do for his brilliant, beautiful young partner. Nothing he wouldn't give him. Now there's precious little he's capable of doing or giving. He's been transformed into a recipient, and every fiber of his being rebels at that. He wants to lash out, to smash things, to make it like it used to be. But there's nothing to be done and no one to blame but himself.

Ashby won't even let him do that much.

* * *

Nick had never been interested in babies. They were something other people had and took for granted you'd be as fascinated by as they were. Worse, their parents expected you to tolerate the chaos and disorganization which accompanied them wherever they were present—no, not merely tolerate but accept as evidence of the superiority of their parents to anyone who hadn't engaged in the fundamental human activity of procreation. As if every species in the universe didn't perpetuate itself in one way or another. So no, he wasn't interested in babies, but he couldn't claim to be uninterested either, such was his revulsion, not to the babies themselves, who could be charming and pleasant or evil and monstrous as their natures inclined them, but to their parents. Parenthood more than anything else was emblematic of the ubiquitous and unmitigated noxiousness of heterosexuals, and he found it impossible to approve of anything associated with it.

So when Dario came off the plane from Mexico City that afternoon carrying Dario, Jr. in his blanket, Nick found it all but impossible to view the situation objectively, much less in the rosy light he knew was pretty much expected of him as the stepfather. And the fact that he'd spent the previous several months being subjected to—well, campaigning wasn't too strong a word for what Maya had been doing, all for the purpose of convincing him to join the ranks of the breeders: that didn't make it any easier, finding room in his heart for the tiny, funny looking interloper. But he didn't second guess Dario. Not for a second. In his heart he thought of himself as pledged to Dario for life, sweet, charming, transcendently beautiful Dario, who in certain neighborhoods and supermarkets was mistaken for the Mexican actor, Jorge Rivero. No, Dario could do no wrong, so the baby would be all right. He'd get used to the baby because there was no alternative. And he certainly saw Maya's point. He could well understand that a woman's instincts were different than a man's in regard to reproduction and that it would have been ridiculous to expect that Maya's lesbianism might cancel out that reality. He had read all the articles she sent him in which the long term health benefits of pregnancy and childbirth were described. Really, he couldn't have been more sympathetic to her quest. He just wasn't sure that making a contribution to the gene pool of her as yet hypothetical child was a response he wanted to embrace. It was that age old question of theory versus practice. And that was a question, he knew, that had stymied better men than him.

He loved his boys. There was no question about that. Dario, Jr., Nikolai, Jr., Stefano. He was a passionate father and by all accounts an exemplary one. Meanwhile, his misgivings about parenthood never abated. Indeed, they informed the way he executed the mission in profound ways. Nobody ever tried harder to balance being a good father with being an authentic gay man than Nick, who'd seen one trump the other more times than he could count and was determined to send the message that to accept that in oneself was to just give up.

It hadn't been easy. When Dario died suddenly leaving him alone with three toddlers, he'd come closer than at any point in his life to giving in to despair. Everyone had rallied around, especially Tristan and Big Steve, who weren't only his best friends but providentially his next door neighbors. A "manny" was found, schedules constructed, routines established. He knows surviving that first year was one of the signal achievements of his life. It was a slow motion miracle that unfolded only over interminable weeks and months. Then, a suitable period of time after Big Steve's death, Tristan moved in and unexpectedly as that, Nick found his life was complete. He was raising his sons with the love of his life. If he hadn't been such a fervently lapsed Catholic, he would have said it was heaven.

The boys were everything any father could have hoped for. Strong, healthy, athletic, smart, talented, fearless—perfect little renaissance men in the making. He was as attentive as it was humanly possible to be, always present at recitals, concerts, performances, parent-teacher conferences, and games, games, games. Dario, Jr., with whom he had no biological relationship at all, he had no difficulty raising as a Romanovsky in everything but name. Stefano was his spit and image. Perversely, Stefano's fraternal twin, Nikolai, Jr., took after Maya's mother's family, the Bartoks—he looked exactly like his cousin Jared. If it had occurred to a documentary filmmaker to tell the story of the perfect gay family, he couldn't have found better subjects than the Romanovsky-Bentley household.

When Dario, Jr. graduated from college *summa cum laude* and went off to Stanford Law, Nick couldn't have been prouder. When Stefano married a young Englishwoman whose father was a millionaire philanthropist distantly related to both Ned Westerleigh and Rupert FitzMerlin and went off to Africa with her to volunteer in an AIDS clinic, Nick couldn't have been prouder. When Nick, Jr. and his partner Rolf decided to have a child by means of Romanovsky sperm and a surrogate Maya located for them, Nick reminded himself of all the reasons he'd been dubious of procreation in the past and promised himself not to buy into the whole phenomenon, which raged unabated all around him.

And when in the fullness of time Nikolai III was born, the last thing Nick expected was to fall in love.

But he did. More or less at first sight. So much so that he very nearly kidnapped the infant from the hospital and took him home to raise under his own roof. Nicky is eighteen months old now, walking—a little clumsily, and talking—barely intelligibly. Not even Tristan himself has ever aroused in Nick the mindless, unbridled passion he feels for this flesh of his flesh and bone of his bone. It is the most sublime yet terrifying emotion Nick has ever experienced. And wonder of wonders, the adoration is mutual. Nicky is a happy, gregarious child, friendly and open with everyone, but Papa Nick is his true and best and special friend. Everyone recognizes the bond between Big Nick and Little Nicky. This led to a little friction with Rolf at first, whose maternal instincts are highly developed. But even Rolf has come around, especially since there's now another little Romanovsky in the oven.

For the wedding Nicky sported a tiny outfit of white shirt, slacks, and striped tie that Nick has spent the entire duration of the event trying to maintain the perfection of. They have gone hunting for frogs in the remoter regions of the garden. They have washed their hands repeatedly in the ornamental fountains in front of the house. They have taken to the dance floor to wow the onlookers with their hot moves. They have visited the Lundquist-Montgomery Labradors in their kennel. They have cadged special treats from the caterers. They have toasted each other and the happy couples sippy-cup clinking (actually thudding faintly) against champagne flute. They have posed for photos Nick knows will break his heart in a few years when this perfect baby turns into a boy and then a man.

* * *

"That man there, Westerleigh. There's a man with a guilty conscience if I ever saw one."

Tristan almost jumps out of his skin, but it's only Griffin with a fake British accent. This is the zany side of Griffin hardly anyone gets to see. Griffin is embarrassed if it's mentioned publicly, and Cooper invariably glowers.

"Jesus, you nearly gave me a heart attack," Tristan laughs. "Who are you supposed to be anyway, the Real Inspector Hound?"

"At your service, accompanied as always by my faithful sidekick, prophet, and mentor, Westerleigh."

"What are you talking about? Ned left over an hour ago."

"Westerleigh is always with us," Griffin insists, "though often he appears to be invisible. To the naked eye, at least."

"How much have you had to drink?"

"I'm not drunk," Griffin says, snapping out of the accent into his natural born Kentucky dirt farmer drawl, which isn't much more realistic sounding than the fake British one and certainly doesn't represent an aesthetic improvement. "My husband doesn't allow me to drink."

"What the...? Cooper doesn't allow you to drink? Since when?"

"Since always. You're not very observant for a cop. Even a retired one. That's club soda I've been guzzling all these years."

"But why?"

"Alcohol and I don't mix. One drink and I'm silly, two and I'm flat on my ass. And as if that weren't bad enough, when I drink I have an unfortunate tendency to fall asleep at the most inopportune moments."

"You mean?"

"Precisely."

"Cooper certainly wouldn't like that."

"There," Griffin says, back in character, "I've told you my guilty secret, now you tell me yours."

"I hate weddings."

"Then I have to tell you Westerleigh and I are of the opinion that you made a singularly inappropriate choice of a second career. Who ever heard of a man of the cloth who hates weddings?"

"You disappoint me, Inspector. I'm afraid that's not at all the response I was expecting from you."

"It isn't?"

"What you should have said was, 'stop trying to throw us off the track, you dastardly cur'."

"You were? I mean, I was? I mean—what do I mean, Westerleigh? You don't know either? Then how are we ever to get to the bottom of this?"

"Because what you really want to know is *why* I hate weddings."

"Well, at least Westerleigh does."

"I'm sure you'll relay the information," Tristan says, "if he should happen not to hear me."

"Of course."

"Good."

"Double plus good."

"You're sure you haven't been drinking."

"Sober as a judge," Griffin says, holding out his left hand, himself again. "You see? Steady as a rock."

"That's two too many metaphors."

"Similes."

"Please excuse my error," Tristan says. "Unlike you, I have been drinking. You see, they make me feel guilty."

"Good. Because you are guilty."

"As charged."

"But what are 'they'?"

"Huh?"

"The things that make you feel guilty?"

"Weddings," Tristan says. "Weddings make me feel guilty. What is this, the first act of *Rosencrantz and Guildenstern*?"

"Perhaps," Griffin says. "Either that or the second act of *Godot*. But really, since they're practically the same thing, it hardly signifies."

"But what would Westerleigh have to say about that, do you think?"

"I don't know," Griffin says. "Why don't you ask him?"

"Because…"

"Now, T.," Griffin says, "supposing for a moment that this were more than just schoolboy tomfoolery…"

"Yes."

"And that all this twaddle wasn't mere verbal pyrotechnics but actually had some objective significance. Ontologically speaking, as it were."

"Yes, yes."

"Why in the world would weddings, of all things, make you feel guilty?"

"Because," Tristan says, lowering his voice, "they remind me that I've never gotten over my first husband."

"Eek," Griffin says, eyes wide. "I spy an eavesdropper. No, make that two."

"Oh, shit."

"Can the act, you two," Nick says, walking toward them with Nicky on his shoulders.

"At the double, Colonel, sir," Griffin says, giving a fey little salute.

"It's no secret," Nick says. "I've known about it for years. And the only thing Tristan is guilty of is being human."

"Perhaps I should leave you two alone," Griffin suggests, "or, um, you three. To sort this out."

"Don't go," Nick says. "I think we'd both like to have a witness present."

"We would?"

"Sweetheart, I know you've never gotten over Big Steve. You're the world's worst poker player."

"I am?"

"Well, second worst," Nick says, nodding at Griffin. "How could you have gotten over him? Big Steve was a force of nature and I'm just a man."

"That's not fair."

"It's got nothing to do with fair. It's fact. It's not just you, you know. That's how we all felt about him. He was just this…well, you see, there isn't even a word for what he was. Is there?"

"You're right."

"And maybe I'm just a man but I'm not a fool. I'd have to be crazy to be jealous of a legend. Particularly a dead one."

"Wow," Griffin says without a scintilla of irony.

"The overwhelming majority of men in this city are in the exact same position you are, my darling."

"Meaning what?"

"Meaning very few of us are lucky enough to get, much less hold onto, the great love of our lives. Even this one here, married to the guest formerly known as the handsomest man in the world."

"I'd be careful how you bandy about that phrase 'formerly known as'," Griffin grins. "I might have to defend his honor. Even against a lady with a baby."

"No bullshit, Griffin," Nick says. "There was somebody else. I know there was. And no matter how fabulous Cooper was when you met him and continues to be right up to this minute, you've never forgotten that other guy, have you?"

"He was straight," Griffin blurts, looking stricken. "I would have walked barefoot across the Gobi Desert for him. I never saw him again."

"There," Nick smiles. "You see?"

"Just where are you going with this?" Tristan asks.

"Well, home with the great love of my life, for one thing," Nick says. "because it turns out I, of all people, am one of the lucky ones. In all your preoccupation with your imaginary guilt…"

"It's hardly imaginary," Tristan protests.

"Sorry. I misspoke. In all your guilty preoccupation with your imagined offense, you forgot one of Big Steve's most important lessons."

"What's that?"

"Didn't he always say that it wasn't love that made a match for life but destiny?"

"Yes."

"Well, you're my destiny, that's all. Lucky, lucky me. And anyway, it isn't being loved that matters most in life, it's loving someone. You're a priest: wouldn't you agree that if the scriptures tell us anything, they tell us that?"

"I suppose," Tristan says.

"So the fact that you've never gotten over Big Steve and that sometimes you're afraid you'll never love me as much as you loved him; well, from my perspective, none of that matters. It's not being loved. It's loving. That's the secret. And I get to love the one true love of my life up close and personal every single day. That makes me the luckiest man in the world."

"One of, perhaps," Griffin says.

"Oh?"

"When Cooper dragged me off to his castle to live happily ever after," Griffin explains, "the neighborhood had guys like the two of you living in it."

* * *

The Aston Martin was a gift from Kirk to Will on their tenth anniversary eleven years ago. It doesn't get driven much. It's too nice to take to work, even if Will didn't prefer commuting by public transportation. It has spent most of its life in the far corner of their garage under a dust cover. It transports them to the opera and symphony, to parties, on weekend outings. And for the last several Junes Will has perched on its tonneau cover waving at the throngs gathered along Market Street for the gay pride parade as if he's someone important.

Tonight, because Will is a drink over his limit, Kirk is behind the wheel. It would be irresponsible in the extreme to try and drive home in his state, and even if it weren't, it wouldn't do for a judge to get pulled over for DUI. You can't argue with logic like that. There's always some iron clad excuse for Kirk to be behind the wheel: shifting gears makes Will nervous and clumsy, driving on the narrow streets of the city makes Will nervous and testy, parking makes Will nervous and accident prone. The list goes on and on. Will knows that Kirk believes all the excuses he makes are motivated by his understanding of and appreciation for the pleasure Kirk experiences from driving the car. This is how powerful a force the myth of Will's altruism is in their relationship. The unfortunate result is that Kirk invariably gives Will the benefit of the doubt whether circumstances warrant it or not, a pattern Will tries his best not to take unfair advantage of. It's all an elaborate tango Will is quite certain Kirk is completely bamboozled by. The real reason Will almost always insists that Kirk drive couldn't be simpler or less altruistic: Kirk is just so damned sexy behind the wheel, whether it's his Porsche he's driving or that fiasco of a Land Rover he uses as a work vehicle at the shelter. Sitting in the passenger seat beside him sends chills up Will's spine like few other things are capable of doing. And if that's not a good enough reason to let his husband drive, Will doesn't know what is.

"You know, darling, you are the most wonderful man in the world," Kirk says, shifting into fourth.

"I know you're delusional," Will chuckles.

"Seriously," Kirk insists. "The older I get, the more the things I did in the past bother me. Tonight I was thinking about my wedding to Yvette, and that always leads to thinking about how horrible Evan and I were to you."

"It was a million years ago," Will mutters, annoyed at the prospect of revisiting this chapter of their history. "We were different people then. I never think about it except when you bring it up."

"I think that kind of proves my point."

"Does it?"

"You didn't have to do what you did," Kirk says. "You could have gone into the other room and lit a cigarette and just waited it out. Do you ever think how different things would have been if you had?"

"Never," Will says too quickly.

"Right."

"Well, even back then I didn't smoke."

"Whatever. You've never been willing to take credit for it."

"Credit for what? Anybody would have done what I did."

"But you weren't anyone. You were the wronged party. Between the two of us, Evan and I had done a pretty fair job of ruining your life. You wouldn't have had to be a psycho to let me bleed out in that bathtub. Lots of people would have been happy to take advantage of the situation. I bet it's a nearly universal revenge fantasy: nemesis kills himself. You know that."

"I guess I just wasn't raised that way."

"Come on. You can do better than that."

"Why do I have to explain it at all?" Will asks. "The past is the past."

"I know," Kirk says. "'Let the dead bury the dead.'"

"Why can't we?"

"Because I haven't made my peace with it yet," Kirk says. "My fault, I know, but there it is."

"What you haven't made is amends," Will says. "That's what bugs you. Your twelve steps say you have to make amends, but you take it too literally. I've moved on, and Yvette and the boys have moved on. Even Evan's family—I'm sure they'd be willing to let bygones be bygones if you could ever get them to listen to the story. But you; you still think there's something you're supposed to do. Beyond living your life the best way you can, I mean. Some grand gesture seems called for, but you can't figure out either the what or the how."

"Maybe you're right. But at least you did something. You called 911 and propped my head up and tried to stop the bleeding. You saved my life. That's the kind of guy you are: you save people."

"I needed redemption that night just as much as you did," Will says. "Maybe even more. I knew I wouldn't get it letting you die. That's what I was thinking of. It was purely selfish, I assure you."

"I can understand that," Kirk says. "What I can't understand is the rest of it. Taking me back to your place after the hospital released me. Making sure I got to my therapy sessions. Encouraging me to go to my meetings. And the dogs. My God, putting up with the dogs. For months on end. Your immaculate house overrun with those mangy critters, and never a word of complaint."

"Why is it you rescue your dogs?"

"Don't change the subject."

"I'm not. I promise."

"You know why."

"Let me hear you explain it."

"They remind me of me," Kirk says, voice cracking slightly, "every last one of them. Every single time I see one in one of those cages, I see myself in those days. They're lost and hungry and frightened. They live in a world that doesn't work the way their instincts tell them it's supposed to. They won't survive unless somebody decides to take care of them. They just want the opportunity to be grateful to someone for life."

"Well, that night you reminded me of me," Will says. "I'd thought of doing the same myself. I'd always chickened out at the last minute. At least you had the guts to go through with it."

"That's ridiculous."

"No, it only seems ridiculous because you're looking at it from your perspective."

"O.K., maybe. But you'd better have a good explanation."

"I was as fucked up as you were," Will says. "I was worse off than one of your dogs. I couldn't imagine why it would enter anybody's head to take care of me. Or how I could ever trust someone again. I believed Evan had ruined me forever in the trust department. But if all anybody ever did was wait for somebody else to do what needed doing, we would all still be living in caves. So I thought that if I could just find the right person to take care of, that might work. And then there you were in that bathtub. I know it doesn't make sense. Nothing ever does. We're all just making it up as we go along, no matter what anybody tries to tell you. Anyway, what I learned from the experience is that if there's such a thing as redemption, it's not some mystical religious thing. There's no visitation from the angels. You don't suddenly have an epiphany. It comes one day at a time, and it comes from taking care of other people. I didn't save your life that night, you saved mine."

"Oh, God," Kirk sobs steering the Aston Martin to the side of the street.

"What's wrong? Why are you crying?"

"There's this kid."

For a terrifying instant the ground seems to open up under the car. Will feels himself hurtling into the abyss.

"What kid?" he asks, forcing his voice to be steady.

"At the shelter today," Kirk says, sniffing. "One of our volunteers. God knows where Ariel gets them. One of those shelters for gay youth, I guess. Trevor wasn't available today, so I had to take somebody else with me on the run."

"Shooting another bareback spectacular," Will says. This isn't feeling like a confession after all. At least not that kind.

"Probably," Kirk agrees, "but this kid. Darrin. I mean he's a mess. He needs a dermatologist badly, and some dental work. And that's just for starters. He's an alcoholic and probably a pothead too. He didn't say that, but I know the signs. He's obviously smart, but he didn't finish high school. He's your typical street trash, but it's so unnecessary. So avoidable. Except he doesn't see that. All his life people have been teaching him to hate himself, so he thinks there's no point even trying."

"I get the picture."

"And God dammit, all I could talk to him about was the dogs. If you had been there, or Tristan, you guys would have known what to say to a kid like that. But me? No way. And you know how I get at a time like that. I just babbled. I felt so stupid and useless."

"Stop that," Will says. "You aren't stupid and you're far from useless. How do you know that anyone else could have helped him any more than you did?"

"Oh, come on, Will. It's what you guys do. I mean, even little Griffin would have done better. He deals with kids that age all the time."

"Don't call him little Griffin. He's the same size as I am."

"He just always looks like such a puppy dog. Next to a specimen like Cooper."

"How do you think I feel?" Will asks. "Next to you?"

"It isn't the same thing at all."

"Oh, yes, it is. But that's a discussion for another time. Here's the thing. Maybe what that kid needed today was not advice or a lecture. Maybe it was just to have a nice man old enough to be his father take him for a ride and talk to him about dogs. I bet he doesn't think you're stupid and useless at all. I bet he's back at the shelter right now telling his buddies what a great time he had. I bet he can't wait to go out with you on another rescue run."

"You think?"

"No doubt about it."

* * *

Dmitri,

It turns out I'm staying with the Luxemberg-MacDonalds—that's Cooper and Griffin. Cooper is the kind of guy you really want to hate. Even now in his fifties he's fantastic looking and built like, well, you are. He's also made a fortune in real estate over the years and doesn't mind showing it off. He'd be insufferable except he's got a great personality and he's ridiculously generous. But his most redeeming quality is his husband, Griffin. Griffin is soft spoken, rather shy and socially inept, but unfailingly considerate. You look at him and you think there must be something more to Cooper than meets the eye for him to partner up with someone so nondescript. Then you hear Griffin play piano and you figure out that he's got hidden depths. You would love him for the way he plays Rachmaninoff alone. Their condo is pretty much what you'd expect of a millionaire realtor. The guest room is like a suite at the Ritz-Carlton decorated by designers from the Bauhaus.

The wedding was very moving. You remember what it was like in Vancouver that year we first became legal participants in the institution—it was emotional like that. And elegant as hell. But without being pretentious.

Morgan and Buzz are well. They finally got an offer on their place and will be moving out soon. There was no sign of Nelson anywhere. Nobody mentioned him and I didn't ask. When we got back here, Griffin told me he checked himself out of a rehab center a few months ago and hasn't been heard of since.

The food was fabulous. I was a good boy and didn't overindulge. Griffin and Kirk don't drink, and Ned, Matt, and Ashby hardly do, so I was in good hands. It never turned into that kind of party anyway.

I'll be back in Vancouver Monday afternoon. I'll pick up the dogs from the kennel on my way home from the airport. Hope all is well aboard ship.

Love,

Sean
P.S. I know you're laughing about the old school "friendly letter" way I write emails.

* * *

The primary drawback to being married to the handsomest man in the world is not what most people would expect. After his second date with Cooper, Griffin sat down and made a list of the pitfalls he foresaw. First on it was the perpetual threat of outsiders trying to break them up. Griffin considered this so serious that he not only listed it first, but second, third, and fourth as well. Next came the inescapable fact that when your husband looks like that and you look like this, you're fated always to suffer by comparison. Griffin took this for granted but listed it anyway. Then there was the question of narcissism. He already knew Cooper had an arrogant streak a mile wide. But just how badly had his character been flawed by his looks? Only time would provide the answer to that.

It was an academic exercise, nothing more. Griffin understood that completely. He was as powerless against Cooper's extravagant charms as a planet being sucked into a black hole. He knew himself well enough to know that if his own character had a flaw its name had to be Susceptibility to Male Beauty to a More or Less Disastrous Extent. Even if it had been possible, escaping Cooper's gravitational pull would have been an empty victory at best: as spectacular as Cooper was, Griffin was bound to encounter someone else of similar magnitude eventually. He lived in San Francisco after all, and the whole thing was bound to repeat itself. He had already been through it several times and he was only twenty-two.

As it happened, Cooper and Griffin proved impregnable to homewreckers. This probably had more to do with Cooper's stubbornness than anything, but whatever the reason, word quickly got around that it was a lost cause and those inclined to make trouble went off in search of lower hanging fruit. Because of his earlier experiences, Griffin was impervious to negative judgements of himself as a worthy companion for a demigod. Not to mention that fairly early on Big Steve had given him what proved to be invaluable advice: you'll spend a lot more time looking at your husband than you will into a mirror. And Cooper's character flaws, conspicuous as they were, weren't especially focused on his appearance. It was all good, or at least good enough. But for the unforeseen issue of maintenance.

Griffin understands that if you drive a Ferrari, you can't expect to take it to Jiffy Lube. If you have a Bosendorfer Imperial Grand, you don't leave it sitting out on the front porch to get rained on. You position it correctly in a climate controlled room and you have it tuned every six months. Well, with a husband like Cooper it's pretty much the same thing. There's the gym, the chiropractor, the masseur, the aesthetician, the hairdresser, the dentist. There are products for hair and skin and teeth and, well, the list seems endless. Pretty early in their marriage they had to stop sharing a bathroom because there simply wasn't room even for Griffin's minimalist accoutrements. Over the years, Cooper's bathroom has become a kind of temple to the cult of the handsomest man in the world, an inner sanctum dedicated to his ever ramifying regimen. Nowadays, Griffin and the dogs hardly go in there, just Cooper and the cleaning lady. It's all wildly expensive, of course. But that's O.K., because they can afford it. And it's certainly worth it, because how can you put a price on being, or even being married to, the handsomest man in the world?

The real problem from Griffin's perspective is the time it all takes. Time in the morning before Cooper can be out the door wherever it is he needs to go. This one only affects Griffin on weekends and vacations, since on schooldays he's up and out long before Cooper even thinks about stirring. Then there are the perennial delays before they can depart for the opera, the symphony, the airport, even brunch with their friends. Finally, there's time, as now, lying in bed waiting for Cooper to finish his nightly ablutions before retiring. And woe be to him if he falls asleep on a night like this, when Cooper's had an offer accepted and is ready to open an escrow bright and early Monday afternoon.

That's what Griffin hadn't foreseen and what he lives with daily.

* * *

Knut stares at himself in the bathroom mirror. His skin is the skin of a man who doesn't smoke, rarely drinks, stays properly hydrated, moisturizes morning and evening, exfoliates weekly, and uses sunblock religiously. His hair is fine textured and full but he's not going to be able to keep describing himself as blond for much longer. There's a definite silvery tinge beginning to emerge. He would color it, but Ross despises men who color their hair. His pecs indicate that he never misses a workout and never cheats on his bench presses. His arm and shoulder muscles match that chest. His abs are nothing short of a monument.

But he is pushing forty. Nobody would mistake him for a twenty-six year old except in the most flattering light.

Most men his age would kill to look like this. But he spent the evening watching Ross stare at Dario Covarrubias, Jr., who is the quintessential blond, blue eyed, broad shouldered, fitness-cum-underwear model that is Ross's exact fetish. And who actually is twenty-six years old. Not young enough to be Knut's child, but young enough. Dario himself is no threat. Knut is clear on that. Dario is blissfully engaged to the female equivalent of himself, and besides, Ross would never shit where he eats.

But Knut knows that he wasn't the first young man of that type in Ross's life and he suspects he won't be the last.

Unless he can figure something out fast.

* * *

The plane hits a minor patch of turbulence. It is just enough to set Scott's nerves on edge but not enough to rouse Jared from sleep. On airplanes Jared always falls asleep almost before they leave the ground. Scott hardly manages to sleep at all, no matter how long or smooth the flight.

They're on a red eye to Frankfurt. They'll go on to Berlin for a couple of days to show Jared the sights and so Scott can meet with a couple of his authors. Then the real honeymoon starts. They're headed for Copenhagen, where they'll embark on a Baltic cruise. Cooper and Griffin took this same cruise last summer and are still raving about it.

An all gay cruise. God help him. Scott is bracing himself to feel like a dinosaur of a particularly unappealing variety.

So they're finally married. Over their thirty years together they have fashioned something barely distinguishable from what any number of their straight counterparts have been involved in, particularly if you take parenthood out of the equation. But marriage itself? The legal kind? Scott had considered it such a complete impossibility for so long that even when it seemed to become a little less impossible he could hardly take it seriously. What did they need it for? What would it prove?

He's still not sure of the answers to those questions. He knows what he's supposed to think but not at all what to feel. He understands the importance of what he and Jared did this afternoon in both practical and political terms. And he's prepared to fight like hell to keep from having it taken away. But he just can't sort out his affect.

There's a better than even chance that the election in November will go badly. He knows he's not supposed to think that but he does. He's supposed to be positive and upbeat. To encourage his friends to vote and discuss it with the straight people he knows so they'll understand and not feel threatened and vote the right way, too. He's supposed to write checks and make phone calls and put a sign in his front yard and a bumper sticker on his car. It's all crucial. He knows that. But somehow it feels like begging, and that hurts. He's a middle aged, upper middle class white male, and it hurts like hell feeling like he has to beg for something as personal, as fundamental, as this. It's a pain he can't escape and doesn't know how to forgive.

He's supposed to believe that justice will triumph at the polls, but that's the one thing he can't do. Maybe the younger ones, the ones with less history of disappointment and less experience of oppression can believe, but he can't. He fully expects to wake up the morning after the election no longer married.

Wulf says it doesn't matter what happens in November because even then it won't be over. If they win, there are all those other states, not to mention the rest of the world, to bring on board. If they lose, well, it's not forever because no defeat ever is. That's what Wulf says, and Scott knows his uncle is always right about things like that.

* * *

Ariel sits on the marble bench at the bottom of the garden. The terriers root in the darkness. The shrubbery is a source of infinite fascination for them. They would explore forever if Ariel would let them. They would dig all the way to China. And he's in no mood, really, to go inside and spoil their fun. Sooner or later, however, Trey and Chad will get back from the wedding. If they see him out here with Dominic's urn sitting next to him, there will be the usual recriminations. They mean well, but they don't get it. It's not their job to mind his business. It's his job to mind theirs. That's how this family works, period. Where would the two of them be if he'd left everything up to them? Still divorced. Still miserable. Ariel knows best, God dammit.

He couldn't go. That's all. He couldn't go without Dominic. If God was in Her heaven and all was right with the world, Dominic would have lived to see this day. They would have danced at this and all the other weddings. They would have danced at their own wedding, and Ariel wouldn't have to listen to Trey and Chad encouraging him to move on. Trey and Chad mean well, but they don't get it. Before you can move on, you have to have a place to move on to.

And besides, it's not so bad. It's really much better than they think. They're so in love with their own bliss that they can't imagine anyone being happily single. He's far from miserable. He has Trey and Chad to look after: they'd never manage on their own. He has his terriers, Patti (Miss LuPone) and Elaine (Miss Page). He has his gym buddies and his meetings and the guys he sponsors. He has the divine Kirk for a partner at the shelter. His life is full and satisfying. There is no shortage of incident. There is no possibility of boredom. And all around him there is the beauty of this city—a true heaven on earth.

And he has his dead husband's ashes in an urn sitting next to him in the dark. So, O.K., he is a little bit miserable some of the time. But just a little bit. Oh, Dominic. It's the memories that do it. As long as he doesn't focus on the memories too much, he's fine.

His phone rings. He almost doesn't pick up, but the number is an unfamiliar one so it should be safe enough.

"This is Ariel."

"Hi, this is Doctor Landau. Um, that is, Brent. Brent Landau. We met at your shelter this afternoon."

Yes. Brent Landau. Thirty-eight, Ariel thinks, but could easily pass for twenty-six. Smooth bronze complexion, smooth textured hair just a shade or two darker than the skin, eyes a startling light blue. The tiniest hint of a stereotypical nose. Just enough to indicate that he'd never bothered to have it fixed. And the finely toned build of a gymnast, which he certainly must have been once upon a time. Think of dessert rather than meat and potatoes and you've got the picture. In the old days Ariel turned up his nose at guys like this because of their boyishness, preferring instead something more elemental. Widowhood has made his tastes more eclectic now that it's too late to matter.

"Of course, Doctor Landau."

"Brent, please."

"Brent."

"I'm sorry to disturb you at home. After hours, so to speak."

"It's perfectly all right."

"I've just been thinking about those little guys ever since I left the shelter this afternoon. I know I told you I needed some time to think it over, but now I'm afraid somebody will show up tomorrow morning and want to adopt them before I can get there."

"You're talking about Isis and Zoe."

"Yes. What was that you called them when we spoke?"

"Corkies," Ariel says. "Cocker Spaniel and Yorkshire Terrier mixes."

"They really got to me," Brent says. "I didn't realize how much. I can't get them out of my mind."

"We don't adopt dogs, Brent. Dogs adopt us."

"Yes, I remember you said that."

"It's true, you know."

"Anyway, is there any possibility of putting some kind of hold on them? Just until I can get there in the morning?"

"I'm not the right person to ask," Ariel says.

"Well could you relay a message for me? Or tell me who I should call?"

"I think the parties concerned are already aware of your interest. I'll start preparing them for adoption as soon as I get in tomorrow morning. What time do you think you'll be coming by?"

"Oh, I don't know. As early as possible."

"May I suggest something?"

"Of course."

"Why don't you do all your regular Saturday errands first? That way when you get home with the dogs you won't have to turn right around and leave them in an unfamiliar place. It'll be important for you to spend as much time with them as possible before you go back to work on Monday."

"God, I'm so glad I called you," Brent says. "That's exactly the kind of advice I'm going to need at first."

"My pleasure."

"Listen, do you ever do house calls?"

"I've been known to, if necessary. I or someone else from the staff will certainly be available if you need help getting them used to your place and their new routines."

"I'm not sure I'd call it necessary," Brent says, "but I thought maybe you could come over tomorrow evening and help me get them settled in properly. I could call for takeout, and we could hang out with the dogs."

It can't be, Ariel thinks. It really can't. But what if it is?

"Are you asking me for a date, Brent?"

"I'm sorry. Bad idea, huh?"

"I wouldn't say that," Ariel says, "but I have to know if it's the date or the dogs that you're really after."

"Fair enough. How does a package deal sound?"

"I love takeout," Ariel says.

"Great. What kind?"

"Anything someone else cooks. Home kitchens are such a nuisance, don't you find? Although they do come in handy as a place to serve from. And store leftovers. Now about the dogs."

* * *

Boone downshifts and signals for a turn.

"Were are we going?" Owen asks.

"Minor detour," Boone says.

"Did we forget something back at the palazzo?"

"No."

Boone has been in one of his terse moods tonight. Owen knows the signs: it's not anger but preoccupation. Owen has been holding his tongue and pretending to ignore it just like a passive aggressive little suburban housewife. Occupational hazard when you're a mental health professional: attempting to put your skills to use in a domestic setting. You can analyze yourself all you want to but don't dare analyze your boyfriend. At least not out loud. Owen will never do that again. What a fiasco. Not that he hadn't been warned.

"Damn bus driver riding my ass."

For some reason the bus drivers of the city have made themselves Boone's nemesis—nemeses? Owen wonders if this is a firefighter thing or specific to Boone, but he senses that it's an inopportune moment to ask.

A few more blocks and several more turns. Owen finally works out their destination and begins to relax. Actually, relax is not the right word. He's as alert as he was. But it's a pleasant anticipation now. Coit Tower is never a bad sign. As a firefighter, Boone has a deep reverence for the place, emblematic as it is of his profession and its history in the city. Their first kiss was at Coit Tower.

"Well, this is a surprise," he ventures, as they fall into line behind a taxi and in front of a city bus.

"Is it?" Boone asks.

"Certainly."

"You're not just saying that?"

"Why would I?"

"You promised not to do that any more."

"Sorry. No more answering questions with questions. I'm trying to break the habit, honest."

"It's O.K.," Boone says. "You really didn't know we were coming here?"

"I really didn't know we were coming here."

"Good," Boone says. "You've gotten a little too good at anticipating my moves. I like surprising you."

"And I like being surprised," Owen says. "I know it doesn't seem like it the way I insist on trying to solve the puzzles ahead of time, but I do. Really."

"There's a parking space just up there if that guy in the Audi doesn't take it."

"I have faith in your parking karma."

"Good," Boone mutters. "Audi guy passed it up."

Finally the Jeep is parked and they're seated on what Boone refers to as "their" bench. They don't have a song or a special restaurant or certain stretch of beach somewhere, Owen thinks; they have a bench. It's so prosaic he gets a lump in his throat thinking about it.

"There's something been bothering me," Boone says.

"Oh?"

"I think I made a stupid mistake."

He says this with that sheepish grin on his face, the one Owen can't resist. "The man of your dreams" is a dinosaur among clichés, so hoary a professional like Owen should be immune to it. But that grin and the lights of the city and those broad, rugged shoulders turn him into a lovesick teenager.

"Did you?"

"I'd like a redo, please."

"A redo of what?"

"You know."

"Oh, that," Owen says, his excitement rising. "A redo. I guess I could manage it."

"Please."

Owen slides off the bench and onto one knee. He'd love to know what made Boone change his mind, but that question will have to wait for later. He clears his throat and takes Boone's right hand.

"Boone?"

"Yes, Owen."

"Will you marry me?"

"Yes, Owen. Yes, I will."

* * *

There isn't much time. It didn't run out today and it might not run out tomorrow. Nevertheless, it will be over soon. With both of them pushing four score and ten—a whole generation beyond their ordained number of days—you have to be realistic. Their doctor, Brent Landau (*il divo* is their private nickname for him, and Dave knows Wulf won't rest until he's safely married off), is more than half a century younger than they are. He shakes his head and says they'll both probably live to be a hundred. But what do doctors know? Their last one, Jamie Altman, died suddenly a few months ago. There's a lesson in mortality for you—outliving your own doctor, even though he's thirty years your junior. It's true that they have been fanatical all these years on matters of health. Diet, exercise, rest, regular checkups—they've done it all exactly by the book. But if Brent's prediction is correct and they do make the century mark, it won't be due to clean living. It will be will power alone that's responsible for it. And it will be Wulf's will power, not Dave's. Dave never had any to speak of until Wulf took him in hand. That's God's Honest Truth. Dave has decided, though, that he has just enough will power to face one crucial moment. If Wulf goes first, he won't wait around. Once Wulf is safely buried, Dave will follow. He won't do it with pills or a traffic "accident" or something like that. He won't have to. He'll call Scott to come for the dogs and then just lie down and go. He knows he can do it.

Due to a bizarre accident of San Francisco architecture, their small apartment is located directly above the building's penthouse. Dave sits on their roof deck overlooking Ned Westerleigh's much larger one. The fogbank that blanketed the city earlier in the evening has cleared. A full moon now presides over the bay like the potentate of some nameless ancient empire. Intoxicated by its light and caressed by the breeze, he tallies everything up. Snoring at his feet, Portia and Calpurnia dream of whatever it is fox terriers dream of. Inside, the man he has shared the greater part of his life with, the man to whom he quite frankly owes everything, listens to a Brahms piano quartet and nods sleepily over the *Duino Elegies*. You can take the German out of Germany, but you can't take Germany out of the German. Somewhere up in the teeming heavens, the nephew Wulf and he by rights should never have met and the man who helped Wulf rescue that nephew from a rogue policeman are off on yet another leg of their own epic. And all around the city the other members of the family they have accumulated over their decades here go about their nightly rituals. He feels surrounded by them, upheld and defended by their strength and affection—not just for Wulf and him, but for each other.

He knows how it's supposed to be. All gay men are expected to die lonely, helpless, and pathetic. Wulf and he are supposed to be frightened and miserable. That's what the world around them says. But they're not. They wouldn't know how to be. He knows that all this is just another part of the big lie the breeders tell their children in a vain effort to scare them out of being who they are. With every breath Wulf and he take they refute that myth. Tomorrow morning the cycle will start all over again. Pretty much every hour of the day and well into the night somebody will call to check on them. It has never failed. Their tribe is ever faithful and will protect them. Their tribe is equal to any eventuality. Even now, with one call, he could summon several dozen of their guardian angels.

Still, there's no escaping it. There isn't much time. Even if they do live to be a hundred, there are far more days behind them than there are left to be anticipated. Each new one is a gift wrapped in the glorious waters of the bay, the majestic, perpetually changing skies overhead, the symphony of city life drifting up from the street. You wake up each morning and watch as the gift unwraps itself around you, and last thing before you go to bed you place it on its assigned shelf in the cupboard of your memories.

Oh, the things he has delighted in that he never expected to see. Oh, the wonders that present themselves with each new sunrise. Oh, the myriad debts he owes.

Footsteps shuffle up behind him.

"What are you doing out here?" Wulf asks.

"Communing with the dogs. Looking at the moon."

"You should get ready for bed. It's been a very long day."

"I just needed to sit here and think for a moment."

"About what?"

"Life."

"Oh, that."

"If I live to be a hundred, it won't be enough."

"You always say something like that when there's a moon like tonight."

"Do I?"

"Yes, sweetheart, you do."

"It has nothing to do with the moon, you know," Dave says.

"What is it then?"

"It's you, my darling. What other reason could there possibly be?"

O farther, farther sail...

www.ingramcontent.com/pod-product-compliance
Lightning Source LLC
Chambersburg PA
CBHW071635260626
47170CB00001B/117